FAE UNCHAINED

THE MAGE SHIFTER WAR BOOK TWO

ELLE MIDDAUGH
ANN DENTON

Le Rue Publishing
320 South Boston Avenue, Suite 1030
Tulsa, OK 74103
www.LeRuePublishing.com

ISBN: 978-1-951714-06-2

To all the men who know how to handle their weapons...

all three of them.

AUBRY

I STARED DOWN INTO EASTON'S HANDSOME FACE, mesmerized by the magic that flowed through my veins. I was falling, no parachute. I was an asteroid, drawn in by his gravity. Our eyes crashed together and obliterated all the promises and excuses I'd made before. They burned up in the fire of this new magic.

Mate bond magic...

Oh my god, this was... incredible. *Impossible*. This was... going to cause an epic fuck-ton of problems.

A potion whizzed by overhead and I had to duck. It smashed against the far wall, breaking me out of my trance.

Shit!

"Aubry..." Easton said again, with a hell of a lot more conviction this time. "Don't go."

I stumbled backward, immediately feeling the strain of our bond tugging like a rubber band. My heart didn't want to leave him—not while he was so wounded and weak—but my brain knew that if I wanted to save him and all of us, then I needed to get my ass moving and help end this fight.

Against my better judgement, I took his hand and squeezed. "Just stay down and stay safe. I'll be back for you as soon as I can."

Before he could respond, I scrambled away, rejoining the fight like I'd been portaled to another realm. The moment I'd shared with Easton was like a quiet pause in time, and now that it was over, reality had just come fast-forwarding back to a live-action cluster fuck.

Potions exploded, guns fired, fur flew through the air. Blood sprayed like water fountains and colored smoke swirled around all the fighting figures. Bullet casings rang like bells as they hit the floor, magazines snapped into place, glass bottles tinkled against each other before shattering onto the floor, and people shouted back and forth. It was a war scene; just like in all the movies I'd ever seen. I'd been in my fair share of fights and dangerous situations, but none as all-encompassing as this.

Drake and Triton were no longer fighting. In fact, Trite was nowhere to be found, which made panic rise up in my chest. Had he been struck down? Was he dying or dead? Was I going to just leave him there if he was?

A memory of the first time we'd met suddenly

popped into my head. We were in a philosophy class together, where the professor had droned on and on about some idiot named Immanuel Kant who thought that it was okay to do anything so long as you got the result you wanted. When the lecture had finally finished, a younger Trite had walked up to me, all swagger and mage confidence and said, "I Kant resist. Want to be the means to my happy ending?"

My throat tightened as the memory faded. *Fucker better not be dead.*

I scanned the room before I sprinted and slid toward a dropped handgun like a baller sliding onto home plate. Drake flew around above me, scorching pockets and taking a heavy amount of gunfire as he went. I didn't let myself think about the fact that his wings were starting to look like swiss cheese. He could heal.

I hid behind the mage's body I'd snicked the gun from and scanned the room. Bodie was stalking through the station like a freaking ghost, his eyes intent as he stared down the barrel of his rifle, stepping over bodies and debris without missing a beat.

Bullets whizzed by him, either in front or behind but never touching him, and he didn't ever flinch as they rocketed past. He just calmly reloaded and fired, hitting his target *every single* time. He was so fucking efficient it was almost scary. After my initial fear-factor calmed and I realized he was just hyper aware of his surroundings, and damn good at what he did, I felt an

3

overwhelming sense of desire. Bodie was hot as hell. My mate was a fucking badass.

Then my stomach twisted, and apprehension once more struck me. He wasn't my *only* mate. Not anymore. He was going to be fucking livid. Would he even *want* to be my mate anymore?

"Aubry, down!" Bodie shouted without glancing my way. And without a second's hesitation, I ducked into a low squat. An orange potion bottle soared over my head and smashed into the benches behind me.

Oh fuck, that better not have hit Easton...

Bodie quickly and silently sniped the bastard who'd chucked the potion. I glanced over my shoulder and the fucker—now missing an eye and the back half of his head—went down.

The mages were running out of players. And potions.

As hope rose in my chest, I realized there were a number of shifters lying motionless on the floor as well. *Shit, we were going down too.*

Wait, *we*? Guess there really was no turning back now... I was officially one of them.

I popped the mag of my borrowed gun and counted the bullets—the *silver* bullets. Those bastards had come packing heat. There were five rounds left and hopefully one in the chamber.

I stood back up and aimed at a mage camping in a dark corner, away from the fight. I fired. The shot recoiled through my arm, rattling the muscles and bones all the way up to my skull, and the man went down in a twitching heap. He probably had a stash of potions over there with him.

I bent down and grabbed a chunk of brick, hurtling it through the air in his direction. As soon as it touched down, the brick set off a domino effect of reactions—white, purple, orange, pink, and turquoise smoke filled the air. Wood chips splintered; explosions assaulted our ears—some of the nearby Mage Police passed out into deep sleep.

I felt like quoting *Die Hard* and cowboying it up, but mage fire suddenly sprang up and skated around the room like it was chasing gunpowder.

Everyone scattered to their own side of the station as the blaze spread between us.

Oh, shit, Easton! I mentally screamed his name as I rushed over to him, dragging him closer to us and away from the flames. Fucking shit, I wasn't fast enough. Easton was so damn heavy.

Sweat started pouring down my brow as the fire crept closer.

"Just go," Easton muttered, bringing a filthy hand up to cover mine.

But I shook my head and yanked again, tugging him back another few inches. My heart spasmed, panicked. No way we'd made it this far just for him to go down now. "Heal faster, Goldilocks," I seethed, yanking him again.

"Trying, Spitfire," Easton grimaced and tried to use

his legs to backpedal along the floor. But the flames crept closer, leaping to a broken bench nearby.

The smoke made me start to cough.

"Get out of here," Easton growled, his eyes shifting and turning a beautiful shade of gold. It contrasted with the red of his overheated skin. He yanked himself away from me.

"I can't," I told him.

It was the truth. My soul was tethered to his. If he died, I might as well. My heart was already weeping, even as my eyes squinted through the smoke and scanned the station for some means of escape. Everyone still alive had cleared out.

Fuck.

Suddenly, Bodie appeared at my side. He hefted the bear shifter up over his shoulder, his free arm still manning the rifle. He didn't say a single word, just looked at me.

I stood and followed him through the smoke and outside through a broken window.

Human alarms and sirens began wailing in the background, and that's when the remaining mages and Mage Police on the street started to disappear. One by one, they each smashed Portal Potions on the ground at their feet, their bodies being devoured in colored smoke before they vanished. The final mage stared at me before withdrawing her potion bottle, and I realized she wasn't a mage at all. She was a fae using glamour to hide her wings. She was... my mother.

"Murderer!" she spat at me, the word stinging my cheek like a backhand. "I will never forgive you for betraying us. Never!"

Betrayal? Excuse you, you royal fucking bitch, but I was *kidnapped*—against my will—and abandoned by you, my friends, and all the damn magic users. If anyone deserved to hold a grudge, it was fucking *me*.

I sneered at her, full of hurt and rage, as she threw her Portal Potion and disappeared. "Batwings!" I screeched at her, an insult I knew stung since she was self-conscious about how thick her wings were. The Kardashians couldn't hold a candle up to the drama within my family.

I couldn't believe her. It. This. Anything anymore.

Vehicles swerved into Union Station parking lot—police cars, ambulances, and fire trucks. *Oh, shit! Time to go!* We couldn't allow the humans to find out about us; we needed to get the fuck out of there just like the mages had.

A silver tour bus pulled in around back and hesitantly eased into park a number of yards away from the building. I glanced wearily up at the clock tower on the outside of the building, which was still ticking away as if nothing had happened. Had this entire battle only taken a half hour? It felt like an eternity.

"Everybody on the bus! Now!" Drake shouted.

Larry grabbed Tee's cat carrier—how had it even survived? —and Bodie readjusted Easton on his shoulder. We all scrambled from the edge of the building up the steps of the bus as quickly as we could. It was still dark, but we couldn't take any chances being seen.

"Where we goin'?" Bodie asked, as Easton bobbed behind him on the steps, growling in pain.

"Plan G," Drake replied, helping Larry get settled into a seat. "Get as deep into shifter territory as you can. Larry, your secret locale should work. Mages can't portal to places they've never been. Now hurry! I have to blow this thing before we're all fucked."

I swallowed hard but nodded. The station had to go. If Drake didn't destroy it now, the humans would realize that something was *not* right as soon as they saw all the fur and claw marks, the potion bottles and the remnants of colored smoke. And if humans found out about magic again, all hell would break loose. Magical enslavement... unspeakable things. But also, if Drake didn't destroy the building before the human rescue workers made it in, Mage Police might just destroy it right along with any humans inside.

The scene would be too big to contain. Too much for memory wiping spells. Protocol required containment no matter the cost. Drake's way was better.

We piled onto the bus and Larry handed Drake a yellow Blast Potion. The dragon shifter ran past me down the aisle and jumped down the steps.

"Go!" Drake shouted at our terrified driver, a shifter with a faux hawk and golden eyes that I'd never seen before.

Pedal to the metal, our bus skidded out onto the

road just as Drake shifted and took to the sky, this time his dragon was three times as large as I'd ever seen him, nearly the size of the building itself. We'd barely gotten up to speed when, behind us, Union Station exploded in a giant mushroom cloud of flame, bricks, and dust.

My heart sank as I watched the ruined sight with wide, glassy eyes. One of L.A.'s most beloved landmarks ceased to exist. The orange of the blaze lit the night sky like some ominous beacon, warning us that the worst was yet to come.

How long would the city survive if this feud kept getting worse? And it *would* keep getting worse.

Because one thing was certain.

Tonight, the mage-shifter conflict had gone from an insurgency to a full-fledged magical war.

2

AUBRY

As the bus fled the scene of the crime, a very different battle raged inside my chest as I fought my own feelings and emotions.

Bodie stood behind me and rubbed my shoulder as I bent over Easton, who he'd laid on the aisle running down the center of the bus. Only the three of us, Larry and Tee, and one shifter had climbed onboard. No one else had made it.

And Drake was still out there.

I leaned forward over the huge blonde giant. "You okay?" I breathed, careful not to touch his wound, but checking to ensure that his magic was finally working and healing him. My fingers still shook as my mind replayed everything that had just happened. Too close. That had all been too fucking close.

"Yeah." Easton gave a grunt as we went over a pothole. "I'm good. Go sit before you fall on me."

I took the seat right beside him, leaning my forehead into the back of the seat in front of me so that my wings wouldn't get crushed. I was so bone tired. I closed my eyes and felt, rather than saw, Bodie slide in beside me, between me and Easton.

What a fucking metaphor for my life that was.

The wolf shifter ripped off what was left of his shirt, took a water bottle someone handed him, and started to clean my hands, which were covered in soot and Easton's blood. "Are you hurt anywhere, love?"

Love? He's calling me love? We're already to that stage?

I blinked and shook my head, still coming out of the daze I was in. It felt like my mind was full of smoke.

Hadn't Bodie seen what had happened with Easton? Did he not care? Had Easton's near-death experience jolted Bodie enough that he didn't feel possessive?

Bodie helped me take a drink from the bottle, the water soothing my parched and scratchy throat. I wished it could have soothed the rest of me—namely, my ripped-in-half heart.

My thoughts rattled around, bouncing as much as the damn bus. My mother's furious face kept popping up in my head, along with images of the fight. But no matter what, they kept coming back to Easton and Bodie.

I had a very bad feeling that Bodie was clueless. That he *hadn't* seen the mate bond take hold of Easton and me. That he wouldn't accept what had happened when he found out. That he wouldn't accept... me. Or worse. What if they made me choose?

"Where's Drake?" I mumbled. I turned to stare out the back window as Bodie continued to wipe me down.

It was easier to think about *him* than the other two. Worrying about Drake was more concrete. It was a life and death thing, not some jumbled and tangled *'what do you feel, Aubry?'* type of bullshit that would take multiple hours and countless bottles of tequila to unravel.

"He'll be fine," Bodie tried to soothe me.

But my foot wouldn't stop wiggling. My heart wouldn't stop its hurried pacing back and forth as it chewed its nails and glanced out the window eight million times. I wasn't even worried about Drake, not really. I was worried about *us*. Me, Bodie, and Easton. What would happen when the truth finally emerged?

"Where are we going?" I turned to look at Bodie.

But he didn't answer me; Larry did.

"We're going to a place I set up," he said, as he opened the cat carrier and gently pulled Tee out to check on her. He set her carefully in his lap and put his index finger on her small neck to check her pulse. "Emergency quarters, if you will. Drake didn't want to use it except as a last resort..."

"Should we drop Tee off at a hospital?" I asked, worry stacking up when I couldn't see her chest move.

"No!" Bodie and Larry barked at me at the same moment.

"She's seen too much, babe," Bodie explained.

Larry sighed. "Plus, I think she's in a coma. And I don't trust that damn underground hospital to do what's right for her. *I don't.* I did this. And I need to fix it."

His eyes blazed with a very un-Larry-like determination.

"Okay," I agreed. Larry might not be the best mage, but if he said he was going to make things right, I believed him.

The old mage gently placed Tee back inside the plastic carrier and latched it shut as the bus bounced us all around like third graders on a field trip. Somehow, Larry managed to keep her head from smacking the top of the cage each time.

"Why?" I asked.

But just then, the driver called Larry up front. The old mage set Tee's carrier aside and ambled over Easton in order to go give directions. The bus took a sharp left, forcing me to hold on tight as dawn broke.

The sky grew streaked with pink and orange; it was far too pretty for the day I was sure I'd have. My anxiety took hold again, refusing to settle even when Bodie started gently stroking my wings.

Easton was healing, but he was still in bad fucking shape. If we were attacked again, he was as good as dead. And I only had one gun with four shots left. That was just enough to hold out hope long enough to watch it be ripped away like a kite stolen by a breeze.

My eyes scanned from side to side as we bumped along, staring down every street, expecting to see people materialize and attack. Drake was who-knew-where. And the entire fucking Mage Council was gonna be after us like hunting dogs sniffing out a fox. No, something worse. Like serial killers stalking their marks. Shit. That made me want to vomit. *No more fucking watching True Detective, Aubry,* I scolded myself. I wouldn't put it past the mages to set our bodies out in a field with deer antlers... if murdered bones weren't so valuable, I had a feeling the whole damn council would have a ton of creative ways to display the bodies of their enemies. Like the old medieval lords who put heads on pikes. Maybe they'd create a council museum. Los Angeles had a shit ton of ridiculous ones. Trite had once dragged me to the Museum of Jurassic Technology to see a pair of decaying dice.

It was as if my thoughts had summoned a museum.

We arrived at the putrid La Brea Tar Pits.

The driver pulled into a parking garage down the street. We were all hustled off the bus, bags thrown into our laps as we smooshed into two cars—Bodie, and I in one and Larry (with Tee), Easton and the bus driver in the other—that separated and converged minutes later. The cars parked at the Page Museum near the pits.

Bodie reached into the bag on my lap and said, "Here, put this on."

He grabbed a ballcap and shoved it onto my head

then slid a cheap camera around my neck. "Think you're able to use your glamour?" he asked, petting my shoulder.

I focused hard and was surprised to find that Larry's spells had faded enough to let me access my magic. It usually took much longer than that. Maybe he'd been having a seriously off-night? I mean, messing up my spell *and* Tee's potion? Poor guy.

I was able to use enough glamour to hide my wings so that Bodie could slide off my torn London Fog jacket and slide on a tacky Hawaiian print shirt.

I scratched my arm and watched dully as he donned his own disguise. He tossed on a Halloween store mustache that looked horrid, some thick plastic eyeglasses, and shoved his thick torso into a bowling shirt that was at least two sizes too small. I heard a rip as he buttoned it. I decided that I needed to be in charge of future disguises.

We slid out of our ride and joined Larry and Easton, who leaned on the strange shifter I hadn't bothered to look at before now. He only drew my eyes this second because he wore a curly haired wig that made him look like he was auditioning for a disco dance competition.

Ugh. Just as disgusting as the wig was the smell of methane, which permeated the air. I had to try not to gag. I glanced at Bodie, and then over at Easton. How were the shifters not puking over this smell? Weren't their noses twice as sensitive as mine?

Their faces twisted in disgust, but everyone followed Larry as he calmly led us around the tar pits.

"This place smells awful," I muttered to Bodie, who threw one arm around my shoulders while using the other hand to carry Tee in her cat carrier. "Why are we here?"

"Because what mage would ever expect shifters to be able to stand this spot?" Bodie responded.

I rolled my eyes. He had a good point. That had been my first thought.

Two humans jogged by, eyeing us and probably wondering what the hell we were doing at that early hour.

Larry held a red flag and a bull horn and spoke way too loudly. "Alright everyone, welcome to the tour. Glad you could make it..." he trailed off after the runners left.

"World's smallest tour," I snarked. "No need for a bull horn."

"I'd rather have the world's smallest tour than the world's smallest..." Larry trailed off.

I was left to follow him, half shocked and half impressed that he could joke at a time like this. My eyes scanned the sky as we walked down the street to the George C. Page Museum. It was a huge modern construction of cement and steel, exactly the kind of architecture I loathed. It definitely had an ostentatious bomb shelter feel to it.

Larry led us to a back door and used a key card on

some nondescript employee entrance. He quickly hustled us inside so that no one would see.

I took one last look at the sky for Drake, but he wasn't back yet.

"Come on, hurry," Larry mumbled when Easton and the guy he leaned on weren't fast enough. Bodie gently nudged me inside and then closed the door behind him.

I turned to find myself in a wide atrium, filled with exotic plants and a space frame—a black aluminum web that looked like toppled tower cranes laid sideways across the ceiling. Critiques shot through my mind rapid-fire. How could anyone think this was a good idea? How was this a hiding spot?

Really, Drake? Plan G? There must be a million visitors a day through here.

We're dead.

We were walking skeletons. *The Walking Dead.* We were about to get canceled—just like the show should have been three seasons ago.

Larry pushed us through a door that showed stripped down and polished skeletons of mammoths and saber tooth tigers.

Bodie leaned over and whispered to me, "Did you know that scientists have it all wrong? Saber tooth tigers aren't animals, they're shifters."

I glared at him in the dim room. "Of course, every supe knows that."

He raised a brow. "But did you know... they're not extinct?"

That little tidbit did catch my attention. The Mage Council only worried about shifters as a whole due to their tendency to draw human attention or those clans that got aggressive. I hadn't heard that saber tooths were still roaming the streets. Interesting.

But then Easton stumbled in front of us and I hurried forward to help prop him up. "Hey!" I looked up at him. "Almost there, Papa Bear. You got this."

Easton gave me a small smile.

He was pale. Too pale. He needed to eat. And he needed time to heal. I looked forward toward Larry. "How long can we stay here?" I was thinking we had an hour tops, before the museum staff arrived and then maybe one more before the general public flooded the place.

Larry glanced back at me with a grin. He waved his little red plastic flag. "The whole back section is under construction for a new exhibit. We've got four luxurious rooms to ourselves for two weeks before construction starts. And, since this is my day job, nobody will question me roaming in and out to get you all whatever you need."

He had a day job? I blinked, surprised.

The frazzle-haired mage pushed aside some plastic sheeting like a ringmaster welcoming us inside a circus tent. And I realized that's what my life had become. A circus full of car-driving monkeys and flaming bananas where nothing that used to make sense applied anymore.

Behind the circus tent was an unlocked door. The doorway wasn't wide enough for me to go through with Easton and #thestranger, as I decided to dub the nameless guy, so I stepped back and let them enter first.

I took a deep breath before I walked through the plastic looking glass into this new messed up reality where I was a fucking criminal instead of John Wayne. In the eyes of Mage Law, I was now a black hat. And some mage somewhere was gonna try to collect on my life and cash in on my bones.

Damn. I got why cowboys went to saloons. I needed a drink. I wanted nothing more than to go to Syn right now and get the worry whipped out of me. But that wasn't going to happen.

Bodie's arm slipped back around me, but I couldn't stand to have him touch me now that I was thinking clearly. His touch felt like an ice burn because I hadn't just betrayed the mages, the fae, my fucking kingdom. I'd betrayed him. I had brushed my lips over Easton's forehead in what I'd thought was an innocent kiss for a dying man... and somehow, fate had twisted that one kindness into the worst cruelty imaginable.

Bodie had been very clear. He did *not* want to share. I had to tell him...

But Easton was so hurt, so vulnerable. I needed to wait until he could at least stand on his own two feet to have this conversation, right? Right. That's what I told myself.

My fingernails dug into my palms and that pain felt better than the fire raging inside. I needed something else to think about, something else to do. We needed something to focus on. Something outside of us.

If we were going to survive what I was sure was now going to be the full-fledged wrath of the MP and the Mage Council, we needed help. I turned to Bodie. "Can I use your phone? I want to call someone who might be able to help."

Bodie's eyes immediately narrowed. "It's not that I don't trust you, Butterfly. But who would you know that would want to help a shifter?"

I grimaced. "The fae princess in Russia. My cousin, Kira Fallton."

Kira and I had never seen eye to eye before. She had always been a rebel. Cast out by her parents at eighteen because she refused to enforce Mage Law, she was the dark fae of the family. But if anyone had ideas about how to subvert the Mage Council and live to tell the tale, Kira would.

Bodie chewed his lip. "We might want to wait until we talk to Drake—"

"She's on our side," Easton cut in from across the room, grimacing from the makeshift pallet Larry and Stranger Danger had set him on.

Apparently, scolding did the trick, because Bodie

handed over his phone. I dialed and tapped my foot as I waited for someone to pick up.

"Privet," A deep male voice answered the phone by saying hello in Russian. I heard bar noises in the background—clinking glasses, voices. I'd called a bar in Russia, one run by my cousin's only friend, a mobster who gave zero fucks about anything or anyone.

I cut to the chase. "Adrian, I need you to get a message to Kira. Tell her that her cousin Aubry needs her help. Tell her... I'm being hunted by the MP out here. I ended up mated to—"

"Shifter!" Adrian's booming voice and Russian accent cut me off. He gave a brutal laugh. "You are mated to shifter! I can tell by your tone. Oh, this news will make Kira so happy. She will find so much humor. Aubry the 'Gandon' —the little sheathe for mage dick."

Bodie must have been able to hear that mage dick part because he grabbed the phone out of my hand and hung up. "That asshole is who you expect to help us?"

"No. My cousin's the asshole I expect to help. He's just the gateway asshole. She's hard to get ahold of."

From across the room, Easton called out. "What the fuck did that guy call you?"

I sighed and pinched the bridge of my nose. "Gandon means condom in Russian. He called me a mage condom. Per my cousin, I helped the mages fuck the world."

Both my shifter assholes cracked up at that. In fact,

Larry and Stranger Things over there started laughing too.

"That's the best, most true fucking thing I ever heard," Easton crowed before his wounds made him wince.

"What is?" A low growl came from behind us.

I whirled around to find Drake walking into the room. He looked soot-stained and sweaty, but it was all I could do to keep myself from jumping on him and wrapping him up in a huge hug. My chest lightened at the sight of him. I'd been worried but I hadn't realized just how much that fear had weighed me down.

"Where the fuck were you?" I snarled.

"Saving your ass," he sniped back. But I saw the flash of gold in his eyes as he took me in, ensuring I was okay before striding over to check on Easton.

"You dead yet?" he asked Easton.

"Not today," the blond bear replied.

"Good. Heal up. Because I had to shake off at least fifteen wasps in order to get here. The hive is pissed."

Larry grumbled, running a hand through his wild Einstein hair. "We need back up, Drake. I'm only one mage. And that battle just now took out a ton of my stores."

"Already called in a favor," Drake responded smoothly, his husky voice wrapping around my ears as he walked behind me. The hairs on the back of my neck stood at attention as he passed. But that was just because his predatory animal was so close to the surface.

Drake grabbed Larry's cat carrier, opened it, and pulled a tablet out of the bottom, from underneath Tee, jostling her.

"Watch it!" I hissed at him, not wanting him to hurt her up.

She'd slept through the battle and the bus ride and everything. Maybe she really was in a coma? I stepped closer and put a hand on her shoulder. Tee was breathing—thank god—tiny snorts coming from her upturned nose as a piece of rose-pink hair drifted across her cheek. I brushed it back and turned to Larry.

"What do you think you can do to help her?" I asked.

He grimaced and ran a hand over the back of his neck uncomfortably. "I'm not sure. I don't normally do Memory Wipes. Most humans who see me doing magic just think I'm on dope."

My stomach fell a little. "But some sleeping is normal, right? That does happen? It doesn't *necessarily* mean it's a coma. And you have books to tell you how to fix her, right?" I'd skipped that division in Mage Police. Everyone was supposed to do a stint working memory modification, but Trite and Dad had pulled some strings. So I'd never really seen the spell up close.

Larry gave me a very unconvincing nod. But my worry for Tee was shoved aside when Drake pulled up the magical news on the tablet and the sight of all of us destroying Union Station played across the screen in slow motion.

"That lighting is no good for me," Easton joked.

Bodie came to stand next to me. He went pale when he saw his face on the screen. My fingers automatically wrapped around his wrist. He'd just gone from an unknown to one of the Mage Police's most wanted. Even though I knew to expect it, my own throat went as dry as sawdust when my face flashed across the screen and the newscaster called me a rogue fae.

I guessed that was true. I'd chosen a side the second I'd chosen to save Easton. But I didn't regret my decision. Even though it meant turning my back on everything and everyone I knew... and trying to figure out how the fuck I was going to fit in here.

Yeah, Aubry, how the hell are you going to do that? my mind snarked. I wanted to punch myself in the head and shut my brain up.

But the newscaster did that for me when she switched tactics and started interviewing my cousin, the one they'd given my job.

Candace came on screen wearing both her police uniform and a tiara nestled in her brown curls. She was perfection incarnate, down to the lipstick and gloss combo my mother was so often pressing on me. Guess she'd found a surrogate daughter, one who'd kowtow to her every wish. Resentment churned my stomach to butter.

"What happened last night," Candace began, "is an

utter tragedy. It just showcases how unhinged the shifter population, and unfortunately, my cousin, the former Chief—"

Drake flicked the tablet shut.

My fingers clenched in fury. "That bitch."

Nobody responded to me. Drake just gestured at Larry and Stranger in a Strange Land. "Let's go talk logistics."

My nostrils flared. First my mother. Now fucking Candace. It was one thing for me to choose a side. It was another to know that I could never turn back. There was a finality to that broadcast that threw an iron curtain down between me and the world I'd known. I wanted to punch something. Even though I was bone tired, fury coursed through me. These assholes were publicly shaming me, condemning me, and they didn't even know.

I yanked on my hair, my wings fluttering behind me. They actually gave me a tiny bit of lift. Larry's spells must have been wearing off. Just in time to do no damn good.

I started to march off to one of the other open doors, the one that Drake and Larry hadn't used. I wanted to be fucking alone to stew. And maybe throw things.

But Easton's voice made me freeze. It was soft and plaintive, each word more desperately sad than the last. "Don't. Aubry... please. Come back, *mate*."

3

BODIE

WHAT THE MOTHER FUCK HAD EASTON JUST SAID?

I turned toward Aubry where she stood frozen in the doorway, her back muscles tense.

My brain hadn't really made it past that initial question, so I repeated it, this time out loud. "What the fuck did Easton just say?"

Aubry's fingers tightened on the door frame, her knuckles going white. I turned toward the bear shifter in question, who propped himself into a sitting position. My stomach curdled at his pure and determined look.

"I said, Aubry is my mate, too." His eyes were clear. He wasn't speaking out of some kind of pain-induced hallucination.

His clarity and Aubry's stiff posture...

My heart popped like a balloon. It shattered like a potion bottle. It splattered against the wall like the

27

brain matter of any one of the fuckers I'd killed in my life. *No fucking way.* My mind frazzled like static electricity, jumping from thought to thought and instinct to instinct.

Punch him in the face? He obviously kissed her. He's hurt, though, what kind of a fucking tool bag am I? Maybe she kissed him?

"Did you kiss her?" I asked, taking a couple steps in Easton's direction, even though I knew I shouldn't. If it was anyone else, even Drake, I probably would have shot him, point blank. But Easton? Easton had always had my back, even when I went toe-to-toe with the dragon. He was the asshole that always showed up with a Tupperware meal when I was on a stake out. Could he really betray me like this?

He sat up fully and dangled his legs over the edge of the makeshift bed. "No."

I'd been stabbed once when I was fourteen. Some mage fuck saw an easy target and sank a ten-inch blade through my back. That hurt less than this. Every nerve ending screamed in pain and rage. My eyes drifted closed and I took a deep fucking breath.

Channel your rage. This woman is your mate, not your next fucking target. I had to shove down years of cold-hearted fury and dig deep to find the tendril of tenderness Aubry sparked in me.

I turned toward my Butterfly and intentionally softened my voice. "Did you kiss Easton?"

Her body stayed eerily still, but her head turned

until her big brown eyes locked with mine. And I knew. I fucking knew it was true. *God damn it...*

"Can I explain myself before you freak out?" she asked.

No, princess, I'm already freaking the fuck out. "Sure."

My eyes slid back to the bear. Could I kill Easton? He was my friend and I considered him part of my pack, but he'd been kissed by my mate. I needed to make sure that never happened again, and I damn sure wasn't killing her.

Aubry took a deep breath and spun around, fingers nervously twiddling in front of her. "When we were fighting at the station, I saw a mage shoot Easton. I tried to push him out of the way, but... he's a big guy. I couldn't move him far enough. When he went down, he didn't start healing right away. I was afraid he was going to die."

Right, which he still very well may. I haven't decided yet.

I was pissed as fuck that she thought a near-death experience was cause enough for a make out session with my pack mate.

"I..." She shook her head and her eyes misted over. "When I realized he was okay, that he was going to live, I told him the truth: that I'd committed to you. And that there couldn't be anything else between us."

I glared at Easton as he gazed at Aubry who stared down at the floor. The love in his eyes was so raw and pure, it cut me to fucking pieces.

"Are you finished explaining yourself?" I asked Aubry, my voice cold and emotionless.

She bit her bottom lip and glanced up at me, tears filling her eyes.

I'm going to take that as a yes.

"Good."

Time to freak out.

Red tinted my vision. I strode over to Easton and punched him right in his stupid, mate-stealing face. "You son of a bitch!" I growled as I punched him again. "You couldn't just let me have this one thing, this one woman, all to myself?"

In my mind, I ripped off his arm and threw it across the room. In reality, I simply threw another punch.

Easton stood and shook his head, brushing off my punches without so much as a wince. The huge fucker didn't even have the damn decency to pretend to be hurt. Instead, his animal turned his eyes gold. Good. That meant it was fucking on.

Easton's hands came down on my shoulders and he headbutted my face. Our foreheads collided, but he also nicked my nose, and instantly blood ran down my face.

I swiped my upper lip and launched into him again, but he was ready for me. He blocked and countered, our forearms clashing, our fists deflecting toward each other's shoulders.

Larry poked his head in for a moment, his eyes

going wide with shock. "You can't do that! Easton needs to rest!"

But the bear just hauled off and slugged me in the ribs.

"Fuck off, Larry," I growled, rubbing my muscles where Easton's punch had landed.

"Seriously, you guys," Larry tried again, frizzy hair bobbing. "Easton can't afford to get hurt worse right now."

"Hurt? He'll be lucky if I don't kill him," I snarled. My wolf wanted blood. He wanted to sink his teeth into Easton's neck and shake the bastard.

Goldilocks's eyes flashed gold and he said, "I'm fine, Larry. We're gonna settle this shit once and for all."

"Bodie." Aubry's tone pleaded with me. My mate bond twinged. But if she could fucking ignore it, so could I.

I spun around and smirked at her, my teeth sharpening into wolf-fangs. "What's wrong, Buttercup? Don't think your new 'mate' is strong enough to take me?"

Easton roared and charged at me, slamming us both across the room. Wood and bone snapped beneath us as we crashed through old exhibits, decimating some mastodon that had been salvaged from the tar pits.

Finally, Larry gave up. "We're leaving." He, Drake, and Russ, one of my pack members, filed out through the door.

Drake merely rolled his eyes when he saw us. He knew better than to interfere. "Fucking primates." That was his only comment before he walked out after Larry.

When they left, they shut and locked the door behind them, trapping us inside as we brawled.

Aubry just shook her head, at us or them, I wasn't sure. But then she said, "Fine, fight it out like toddlers, you pea-brained, dipshit, fucktard alphas. We can talk it out after you've both given each other concussions."

"That's the plan. If Easton makes it. But the baby bear here has never loved the fight, have you, Goldilocks?" I taunted from the floor.

Easton landed a blow to my cheek bone and my eyes flashed with heat as I used his body weight to flip him over my head then roll backward so that I straddled the fucker.

Mate thieving fucking punk!

Rage tumbled through my veins like river rapids. My wolf wanted to come out and play, but I kept him at bay. This was a man's fight. And I wanted to fuck Easton up the old-fashioned way.

I slammed forward and headbutted his gunshot wound. He gasped and winced, shoving me off and clutching his chest as he scrambled once more to his feet.

Pride and satisfaction rollicked around inside underneath my fury.

"Fucking pussy," he spat at me.

I merely shrugged. "Some might call that a cheap shot. I call it using my resources to my advantage."

Easton suddenly turned toward Aubry, a look of shock and fear in his eyes.

I immediately turned her way, freaked out, adrenaline changing from anger to fear in an instant. But Aubry seemed fine. Just a little pissed. She stood in the corner of the room, arms crossed, toes tapping in annoyance.

"This gonna take much longer?" she asked.

That's when Easton sucker punched me in the mouth. Pain exploded across my jaw until everything from ear to ear ached.

"Some might call that cheap shot," he taunted with a grin. "But I call it using my resources to my advantage."

I spit on the floor and wiped my face, the blood from my busted bottom lip now mixing with the dried-up blood of my nose. Easton's face was bruised and swollen, but not bleeding yet. I figured I'd better fix that in a hurry.

Rearing back, I pretended to jab at his face. As soon as he reached up to block, I slugged him in the gut, and when he bent down to clutch at his abdomen, I kneed that fucker in the nose. Blood instantly ran like a river, awakening my predatory instincts. *Yes.* My wolf wanted more blood, more destruction.

I picked him up—the heavy fuck—and threw him into an old saber tooth skeleton, the bones scattering all over the room. I stalked over to him, prepared to hit him while he was down, but he clubbed me in the face with a fucking femur bone, sending me straight down to the floor.

"Are you morons done yet?" Aubry shrieked. Her wings fluttered as her annoyance flared.

I grinned at her, slightly dazed. "I'm just getting started, baby."

Easton stood and clubbed me again, this time in the stomach. I curled up into a ball and groaned as he smiled over at Aubry.

"Almost done, babe." Then he fucking winked at her. "Give me a few more minutes to toy with my prey."

Oh, hell fucking no.

My vision shifted to my wolf's and everything turned shades of furious blue because he couldn't see red. I kicked out with my leg, knocking Easton onto his ass. He hit the ground hard enough to rattle the bones of the sole skeleton still standing in the far corner of the room. "Don't *ever* wink at my mate again!"

We both clamored to our feet and circled one another. "She's not just your mate, Fuzzball. She's mine now, too."

His attempt to claim her made my wolf snarl. I growled as we sidestepped and stared, never taking our eyes off one another. "I don't give a fuck what you think you feel. You're wrong. You've lost too much fucking blood and you aren't thinking straight. I'm gonna give you one chance... because you've been a friend to me, Easton. One chance. Say it. Aubry is mine."

He chuckled, near-madness dancing in his eyes. "Aubry is mine."

My beast howled in my chest, clawing to be set free. "I'm gonna fuck you up."

"I thought that's what you were already trying to do, puppy dog?"

Bastard! I roared, charging him with a shoulder to the gut, pushing until I slammed him into a glass-encased shelf full of fossilized teeth and claws. The framework gave way, crashing on top of us as shards of glass and tiny artifacts tinkled like jewels when they hit the concrete floor.

"Oh my god, are you guys okay?" Aubry asked, peering across the debris to where we both emerged covered in dust.

I grinned at her. "You like that?"

"Never been better," Easton replied almost at the exact same time.

As I turned to glare at him, I heard Aubry huff in the background. I was pretty sure she'd just gone from genuinely worried to annoyed. I imagined her crossing those amazing legs and checking her watch, wondering when the alpha showdown would finally be over.

Part of me was calmer than before. Getting a few swings in let the testosterone vent out like steam. But the hurt and adrenaline raging in my blood were like the gurgling of a violent volcano. The eruption had already occurred, but the hot pit of hurt still festered.

I snapped my teeth at Easton. "You ready for another round, you over-sized Honey Graham?"

He chuckled, lowering himself into a defensive stance. "Ready when you are, squeaky toy."

"Squeaky toy?" I sniffed out a laugh against my will. Easton had always sucked at smack talk. "That's the best you got?"

Before I could blink, his fist connected with the side of my head, making me stumble but thankfully not fall. Fuck, he was quicker than he looked.

"I wouldn't give you my best *anything*," Easton taunted. "You're just a bratty little pup too used to getting his way to play fair or share."

"Share?" I was astonished. "You're fucking kidding me, right?" I moved in, assaulting him with blow after blow as I drove each syllable home. "I. Have. Shared. Everything. My. Entire. Life!"

Easton blocked as best he could, keeping low to guard his face and abdomen. So, I started hammering his back instead. "But. I. Will. Not. Share. My. Mate!"

Suddenly, he lurched upright, and jabbed me with an uppercut to the jaw. My teeth snapped together, and, for a moment, the room spun.

"Too late," was his smart-assed reply.

That comeback fucking sucked. I was about to verbally rip apart his asshole when his gaze drifted over to Aubry once more. His eyes widened in disbelief as his jaw dropped open.

I fucking cackled. "Not gonna fool me twice, dumb-ass. Better learn some new tricks."

He reached out and swatted my shoulder, never taking his eyes off where they were locked behind me. He didn't stop looking even when I wrapped a hand around his neck.

Alright, fine. I'm intrigued.

I sighed, but kept my grip as I turned around, fully expecting a blow to the back of the head. I had a back kick for his nuts at the ready.

But instead, my eyes bugged, and my swollen lips parted.

There in the corner of the room, was Aubry. She'd removed her pants and underwear, and the Hawaiian shirt Larry had given her was unbuttoned down the middle, barely covering each of her breasts. Her pink lips curved into a sensual "O" shape as she watched us with a hooded gaze.

She leaned up against the wall... touching herself.

Jesus fucking Christ.

My mate was fucking fingering herself as she watched us, and the room was filling with the heady scent of her arousal.

Stronger men had caved for less.

My animal howled, and so did my cock, neither of us able to resist.

4

AUBRY

I WAS NOT GOING TO LET MY MATES POUND EACH OTHER to a pulp. They could do that to my pussy instead. My fingers circled my clit as I leaned back against the wall. I was desperate for this to work, but I was also slightly worried that it wouldn't. I wasn't nearly wet enough yet. So I paused touching myself and brought my fingers to my mouth. I sucked on them to wet them down, giving the guys an oral show as I did.

"Ungh," Easton groaned. I couldn't tell if he was turned on or not because I didn't allow myself to look at him for two reasons. First, I didn't want to lose my nerve if it wasn't working. Secondly, no dom would ever let me look at him without permission. And even though neither guy had given me that order, I pretended they had. It helped me slip more into sub space.

My mates needed a show. They needed me to take

care of them, to serve them in ways they couldn't even articulate yet. They needed me to end this fight for them so that neither of them would lose face. Because... at the end of the day, they needed to be *equals*. They needed to be *partners*.

As my mates, neither one of them could dominate the other or there would be continual resentment. I'd seen what continual resentment did growing up with my parents. I didn't want to experience it ever again.

So, instead, I was going to appeal to their baser instincts and make them give in to a need even more primal than dominance. Sex.

That thought got me hotter. I widened my legs and leaned further against the wall, pushing out my pelvis to give them a better view as I returned my hand to my clit.

I let my fingers tease me for a minute, before pulling my lower lips apart and letting my mates peek inside.

Bodie's possessive growl was familiar. It was the same kind he'd used during sex. I felt victory flare inside me as I snuck a hand up to grab my left breast.

"I need to come," I whispered. "But I can only do it if you both take me at once." I slid my hand off my breast and into my mouth. I lubed it up heavily before bringing it down to circle my ass.

I sunk a single finger in front and back at the exact same time and my breath hitched.

"Fucking hell," Easton groaned.

"Don't you look at her," Bodie snarled. I heard a fist hit flesh again.

God damn it! If this wasn't enough to stop them, what the hell would be? I closed my eyes as the idiots grappled, still throwing punches. I tried to imagine each smack of flesh was part of a scene where two doms fought for the right to fuck me. Which was kind of true.

Alpha shifters and doms weren't that different.

I spread my knees farther apart, moaning and adding a second finger to each of my holes as the vision took over and my need increased. I grew so wet that my scent filled the air like caramelized sugar.

The sounds of hitting stopped and I called out, "Don't. Keep fighting over me. You're gonna make me come."

Instead of complying, rough hands grabbed my hips and yanked me up. I opened my eyes to see Bodie in front of me. He pulled my fingers from my pussy and lifted them up to his mouth, sucking them clean while I watched. Then his lips popped off my digits.

"Fucking hell, Buttercup, look at how wet you are," he moaned. "That scent drives me insane."

"I love my mates fighting for me," I said.

His hand smacked my ass. "Don't say mates. That's a fucking lie." Bodie moved behind me and started to help me slide my fingers in and out of my ass.

Easton roared from in front of me. "Don't lay a

hand on her! She's not a fucking liar." I heard him huff as he started to shift.

"No! I like spankings, East," I confessed. "Take off your belt and spank me."

Easton knelt in front of me, human again. He reached out to cup my cheek, and I peered into his bright blue orbs. "I'm not gonna belt you, Spitfire."

"I sure as fuck will," Bodie responded. A leather strap smacked me across the top curve of my ass. "You promised!" His voice was laced with fury, but underneath, I knew the anger hid deep-seated pain.

"I know," I said. Part of me wanted to justify myself. But the other part of me knew he needed me to submit. The alpha in him had been wronged, he'd been undermined. He needed to put me in my place. "Punish me, Bodie."

Another whack heated my right ass cheek and I paused my fingers. This moment wasn't about my pleasure. It was about Bodie's pain.

Whack.

"Stop!" Easton cried.

"East, I'm okay." I soothed softly, staring down at him.

Bodie smacked me again before I heard him unzip. I slid my fingers out of my ass and said, "Mate."

Bodie growled and yanked my hair as he teased my asshole. He spit on it and lubed it up. "This is gonna hurt."

I just grinned at Easton but kept my tone soft and submissive. "I know."

Bodie rammed into me hard, his hip bones smashing into mine and I screamed. It hurt so good. It was like getting in that knockout punch in a fight, the kind that reverberated up your entire arm but felt amazing because it was pain and victory all in one. It was the best sensation ever.

Easton automatically leaned forward and grabbed my face. Without thinking, I kissed him.

When our lips touched, magic seemed to fill up my body. Not just the magic of violent sex. A new, unnatural warmth seemed to flow through me from head to toe, the luxurious heat of desire multiplied a thousand-fold.

"What the hell is that?" Bodie asked in wonder, his strokes slowing, his fingers brushing over my wings, caressing that spot I loved.

I shivered in delight, every single nerve ending in my body pulsing with this new sensation.

Easton shivered against my mouth and then pulled back. "Did you feel that too?" he asked me.

As soon as he pulled away, that delicious, heady, cusp-of-orgasm tingle ended. The warmth receded and the fullness of Bodie filling my ass returned. "I think it's when the three of us are connected," I gasped.

"Not. Fucking. Possible," Bodie countered, grunting with each stroke.

"Easton?" I reached down and propped up one of my breasts, asking him to touch it without words.

East's blond head sunk down and his lips closed over my nipple. *Yes.* Immediately, the hot, pulsing desire washed over us all like the surf over the sand.

"Damn it, Easton!" Bodie moaned. "Stop for a second or you're gonna make me come."

Easton released my nipple, making me want to sob in frustration. I'd been so close.

But then I reminded myself that this whole thing was for my mates. Not me. Them. I needed to be whatever they needed.

I smiled softly at Easton. He needed reassurance. His entire face lit up when he saw me looking at him that way.

Bodie smacked my ass again. "Don't look at him! You. Belong. To. Me."

I gave Easton one last smile before I reached down to the floor, lowered my head, and let my breasts dangle beneath me.

"She belongs to both of us," Easton growled, one of his hands fisting in my hair and yanking me back up.

Oh god, yes.

I didn't want them fist-fighting. But yanking me around? About to double team me? That was hot as fuck. I licked my lips as I stared up at him, hoping he'd take out his thick cock and force it down my throat.

"She does not. She's *mine*," Bodie yelled. But it was the yell of a man who knew he was already defeated.

"Bodie," I interjected, feeling his heartache resonate in my chest. The mate bond was precious to him. It had been from the very first moment we'd found it.

From that second forward, he'd been so careful to cherish me. And I hadn't done the same. My heart cracked as I thought that. Just when I'd promised I believed in us, the mate magic ripped me away. There wasn't anything I could do to reverse that. But there was one thing I could give him that I hadn't yet. "Bodie, I love you."

Bodie yanked me up by the hair and his hand went around my neck. "Don't."

A tear slid down my face.

He was right. I shouldn't have said that. I did love him. But I should never have confessed it that way.

Easton immediately pressed against my front and pried Bodie's hands off. "Stop punishing her for something she can't control!"

"She said she'd stay away from you."

"She thought I was fucking dying!"

"Bullshit!"

"I took a silver bullet, Bodie."

Bodie froze. "You wouldn't be healed now if that was true."

"She dug it out of my chest. Kissed my forehead. Then tried to hold off the stick-wielding fuckers so they couldn't get to me."

Silence met Easton's confession.

Easton's hand came up once more to my face. "She

is mated to both of us. You know it. You feel it." Easton's fingers traveled down my neck over my pulse, traced my collar bones and then tweaked a nipple. Immediately, pleasure shot through all of us.

"She wouldn't betray you. I wouldn't betray you. We both need you." Easton confessed.

Bodie howled, and the fingers gripping my hips turned into werewolf claws. I had no idea if the rest of him had shifted, I was too near the edge.

"Please, Bodie," I begged. "Please... I need *both* my mates."

Easton tweaked again and Bodie clamped down on my hips. I felt him push his shaft deep inside me, before slowly drawing back out. He pulled out all the way. For a moment, I was terrified he was going to walk out on us. To leave and never look back.

But then Bodie said, "Ride him. And then I'm gonna ream your ass so hard that you won't be able to walk straight for three days."

My lusting mind reeled from his words, but I didn't let him see it. "Promises promises."

He smacked my ass hard. "Easton, get undressed. And fuck our mate."

Easton was naked faster than I could blink. And once he was nude, I didn't want to blink. My new mate was Atlas. He was so big he could carry the world. He was all massive muscles and incredible planes. And his dick. I'd been right. His dick was a mountain, a huge red peak. I couldn't wait to climb it.

I leaned forward to take that monster cock in my mouth, but Easton stopped me. He scooped me up and held me tight in a hug, before giving me a tender kiss. Where Bodie was darkness, Easton was light.

"Aubry, you're so beautiful," he said softly. And instead of those sweet, saccharine words turning my stomach sour like they normally did coming from any other man, they lit me up inside like a little girl who'd just discovered a rainbow.

Easton set me back on my feet and continued to rain gentle kisses down on me as his massive fingers traced the edges of my body, down the sides of my breasts and stomach and hips.

He was slow and gentle until Bodie threatened, "I'm gonna fuck her twice before your cock touches her once if you keep taking your sweet ass time."

That spurred Easton on. And the hot, aggressive side of him came barreling out. He hitched one of my legs up and held it under the knee, then pressed closer to me. The heat of his massive member made my entire cunt throb with need. Easton rubbed himself over my opening. And that alone felt so good that I had to resist throwing my head back and pretend he'd ordered me to stay still.

"Can you hover so I can kiss you?" he asked softly.

I fluttered my wings and rose into the air about four inches, so that my mouth could reach Easton's. His massive hands came to my ass and he kneaded it for a couple seconds before he slid slowly into me.

I nearly fell out of the air, nearly forgot to fly.

Bodie caught me. He came up behind and held me still, biting my earlobe and whispering, "Take it, Butterfly. Take it."

I moaned and panted and moaned again as Easton pumped gently with only the first half of his cock inside me. Even with the bear shifter's hand on my clit, slowly circling, it was almost too much. Easton was so fucking big that every single movement of his cock shot sensation through my pussy lips.

The bear shifter's fingers started to move faster when half his huge shaft was finally inside me. He pulled back from our kiss. "Spitfire, I wanna fuck you so bad but I don't wanna hurt you—"

Bodie's hands grabbed my shoulders and shoved me all the way down on Easton's dick before the bear shifter could finish his sentence.

"No!" Easton cried in fear.

"Yes!" Bodie and I both shouted.

The bear in Easton took over and he yanked me away from Bodie. At first, I thought it was because he was going to be gentle and pull out and apologize. To my delight, Easton just spun and rammed me up against the wall. Then he started to fuck me so hard it felt like the building was shaking.

"Mate," he grunted. "Mate." His claws came out, like they would during a fight, and they were so strong that when he raked down the wall behind me, concrete crumbs rained down. That show of force just made me hotter.

"Easton," I panted. "Can I come?" My hand started to reach for my clit.

But my sweet mate reached down and smacked it away. "You can only come if Bodie says you can."

Fucking hell.

This was the hottest sex I'd ever had. I looked over Easton's shoulder, watching Bodie stroke himself at the sight of us, me with my wings and legs splayed, pinned to the wall like a damned butterfly by Easton's cock.

"No," Bodie shook his head.

I lowered my hand, halfway disappointed, halfway excited by his dominance.

"You only get to come when both our cocks are inside you at the same time." Bodie gave an evil grin.

"But..." the protest died on my lips. Easton was so fucking huge. It wouldn't be possible. No way—

Easton yanked his claws out of the wall, shifted them back to hands, and then carefully walked backward a few steps. Keeping us connected, he slowly lowered himself to the ground and pulled me forward on top of him.

"I want those tits, Spitfire," Easton growled.

I had to stretch so he could take my nipple in his mouth. But the second he latched, Bodie slammed into me again. The pain and pleasure and that new, magical heat all swept over me at once.

I came with a scream that made Easton reach up and clamp a hand over my mouth.

"Museum isn't open just yet," he smirked. "But I don't think the world is ready to have you as an exhibit."

I laughed. But then my mates fucked the humor right out of me. They moved in tandem and gave me three more orgasms in a row. We collapsed in an exhausted sweaty heap among the rubble. I wanted to lay there with my mates in a contented cuddle for hours.

But we only got two minutes before Drake busted into the room and said, "That psychopath has attacked a shifter school."

5

AUBRY

MY MATES AND I STUMBLED OUT OF OUR NAKED TANGLE in a panic. I'd never felt more exposed or vulnerable—not because of my body, but because my mind kept flashing me images of those little shifter kids Easton had introduced me to a few days ago.

Someone had attacked a *school*? Full of *kids*?

"What the fuck happened?" I asked, as I struggled back into my panties. "What psychopath?"

Drake leveled me with a flat stare, completely unfazed by my nakedness. "Triton."

His words blasted through my chest. *What?* My lips immediately pursed. "What makes you think it's him?"

"Oh, for fuck's sake, Aubry," Drake cried, throwing his arm in my general direction. "Use that gnat-sized brain of yours! Your BFF is hunting me down for what I did to his parents, and he's not going to stop until one of us is dead."

It felt like I'd been slapped. But not so much by Drake's words; he was always an asshat-munching set of donkey balls. By Trite's actions. Who the hell was the man I'd called best friend? Yeah, I knew he had a dark side, but this? Fuck... he was Darth Sidious.

Who could attack a school of children? I thought about Trite's tension since he'd joined the council. He'd been gone more days than not—claiming he was with his mentor Citrine. And then there was his smoking habit that had really been an arsonist habit.

I realized that whoever I used to know in college wasn't Trite anymore. He'd transformed into something else. The earth had shifted and cracked and the tectonic plates had created new continents. I was on one, and he was on another, an entire ocean away.

I bit my lip and held in my sadness. Because whatever I'd lost, whatever friendship we'd had at one point, it had clearly become an illusion. Whatever these shifter parents had lost was far more real.

I shook my head and tossed the Hawaiian shirt across my shoulders, preparing to do up the buttons. I wondered what the guys' next move would be, and if I'd be included. Did I want to be? Was it hunting down Trite? Could I handle that? There were too many questions this early in the morning, without sleep or coffee or even chocolate to cope.

"Take that stupid fucking shirt off," Drake said, eyes sparking gold as he spun around and strode into the next room.

Bodie and Easton shared curious glances, like they weren't even sure what to make of their insane almighty leader. At least I wasn't the only one who didn't seem to know what came next.

Drake reentered carrying a black duffel bag over his shoulder. Dropping it on the ground, he fished around inside and tossed each of us some random clothes.

"You can't wear the same gaudy outfits we arrived in," he said, as if we were stupid. "You wanna get caught? That's how you fucking get caught. And we can't come back to the museum, either. We need a new hole to hide in."

"But we just got here," Easton said as he shrugged on a tight pair of pale blue jeans. They were clearly not his size and I had no idea how he was going to get his junk tucked into the front. But I was damn sure going to enjoy watching him try.

Bodie grunted as he tugged on a black t-shirt. "You wanna get caught?" he asked, mimicking Drake. I wasn't sure if it was sarcasm or if the phrase had just been drilled into his head. "New phones, new vehicles, new places. Those are the rules. Unpredictability is the name of the game. The minute they sense a pattern, they'll nail you down like sheetrock and paint you in red."

I stayed silent as I slipped into a new pair of black skinny jeans. He wasn't wrong. Mage Police ate, shit, and breathed psychology and criminal behaviorism. If there was a pattern to be found, they'd analyze and exploit it like a pimp did a prostitute. Hell, sometimes they could even come to the next logical conclusion *before* the suspect did, blindsiding them at the finish line. The precinct even had a term for those ops: "Soothsayers."

We needed to be random as fuck.

I dragged a silky, lavender tank top over my head that was low-cut and sexy enough to be a nightie, and pulled my silvery white hair up into a high ponytail. Drake tossed a set of knee-high black boots at me, next. Thank god they weren't hooker heels; I'd actually be able to run in them or climb or whatever else we might need to do.

"Hurry the fuck up and lace those things," Drake growled.

I thought about throwing the shoe right back at him and nailing him in his stupid face. "I'm not the one who picked knee-high boots with a hundred eyelets and three feet worth of laces!"

Bodie grinned. "No, I picked out all your outfits. And damn, do you ever look good in purple."

Easton hummed in approval. "She really does."

Figures. He was right, I looked pretty damn good, but my tits were just one dip in the road away from bouncing right out of my top. Car rides were gonna be an issue.

"And another thing," Drake roared, turning toward my golden Honey Graham—Bodie's nickname for Easton had kinda stuck with me, "Why the fuck were you naked on the floor with them? You couldn't decide whose claim had been staked the deepest? You had to fucking sink your dicks in too?"

Bodie glared over at Easton, as if he'd just remembered he was mad at him. "We're *both* her mates."

Drake fucking laughed out loud. "No. You're *both* insane. Larry!" He turned his head toward the other room. "Hurry the fuck up with that cat carrier! And Russ, if you pack up those guns any fucking slower you may as well just shoot yourself. The MPs are gonna be all over us before we're even armed!"

Larry rushed in just as soon as I was done threading my boots, the cat carrier hanging from his long, scrawny arm. Tee slept peacefully inside, looking like a porcelain doll rather than the snarky shit she was. My stomach twisted and my throat tightened up. Was she okay? Had something happened to her? Larry wasn't the best mage I'd ever met. Had he fucked her up so irreversibly that she'd *never* wake?

God, I couldn't even think of that right now. Not when I had other, even more deranged shit to deal with. Like my best friend blowing up a school full of kids... My stomach twisted further, wringing the hope right out of me like a dirty washcloth. Drake still hadn't really explained himself.

I turned and asked again. "Why the fuck would Trite attack a school?"

"Because..." Drake swallowed hard and his jaw tightened. "I used it on my escape route to get here. And after I went in, I went underground. He wouldn't have seen me come out. Can't be sure someone else didn't tail me, too. So we need to move on."

My stomach clenched and I felt like I might hurl. But I swallowed the bile back down. "And what's our next move?"

Drake's face was hard as he said, "We need to go see if we can help. That's first, before anything else."

I nodded. Drake would always rush into the fire for these shifters. Whether he knew it or not, he was predictable that way. An alpha took care of his pack, and Drake considered himself the alpha of Los Angeles. It wasn't that different from how a dom cared for his sub... I shoved that thought away. Nope. My pussy was aching from the massive pounding I'd just gotten. That was it. Nothing else.

Russ, aka Stranger Danger, arrived a moment later, with a new, longer black duffel bag strung up on his shoulder. Between Drake's black bag full of random clothing and shoes, Larry's carrier holding Tee, Russ's weapons bag, and our unwashed hair after the fight, we must've looked like a band of traveling hippies two weeks late to an outdoor music festival.

We kept our heads down, but not too far down—we didn't want to appear suspicious, after all. Nothing suspicious about a gang of criminals carting around disguises, weapons, and prisoners. Nope. My nerves jangled like keys in my pockets. Damn. I was used to being on the other side of things. This side was way more stressful.

We got a few sideways glances in the museum as we strolled through behind Larry, a few reluctant head nods, but otherwise, we made it out to the street without any hitches. A shitty Chrysler minivan met us in the alley and Drake, Larry, and Russ slid inside as casual as if they were on their way to soccer practice. Between them and the bags, there wasn't enough room for the rest of us.

"Your ride should be here in thirty seconds," Drake said, his arm propped up on the doorframe and head casually hanging out the open window in the front passenger seat.

The driver leaned forward and waved. His greasy hair definitely added to our hippie vibe. "Hey, Fuzzball! Long time no see, man! Life been treating you well?"

To my surprise, Bodie grinned rather than scowled. "'Bout as good as it can be for a man who kills people for a living."

"Yeah, man, I was gonna ask how work was but..."

"Would you just fucking drive?" Drake snapped.

"Later, Fuzzy!" The driver gave Bodie a peace sign that Drake immediately smacked down.

Bodie sniffed out a tiny laugh. "Later, Drew."

The smoke from the Chrysler's exhaust hadn't even disappeared around the corner when another car pulled up. The tinted window lowered and a big guy with black hair and a matching beard appeared. He had reflective aviators on, and his jaw worked like he was annihilating a piece of nicotine gum.

"You," Easton growled. I turned around to find his eyes flashing gold.

The new Uber driver merely chuckled. "Your boy called me, not the other way around, I can assure you."

Bodie glared from Easton over the driver. "Just keep your mouth shut, Trey, and we won't have any problems."

The driver—Trey— chuckled. "Easy pup, I'm not expecting a tip from you. Just get in the damn car so we can get moving."

Bodie's hand flinched toward the handgun in his hidden hip holster and I was immediately intrigued with what their history with this guy was. Neither Bodie nor Easton seemed to like him much. So why would Drake have called him?

We piled into the backseat and Trey peeled out into the street, narrowly missing the front end of a sports car that was probably worth more than this guy's annual salary—tips included. Since I didn't have an 'oh-shit' handle, my hands went to the cheap fabric seats and clutched on for dear life as Trey drove.

None of the guys said anything for a while as we weaved in and out of traffic. Then the hairy ape glanced into the rear-view mirror, with a shit-eating smirk on his cocky face.

"So, Goldilocks, how's life as an outsider? I kinda

thought you'd be dead by now, living out on your own, and—"

The telltale sound of a safety clicking was my only warning before Bodie's gun was pressed tightly to Trey's temple. My wolf shifter leaned forward and growled, "He's not on his own. He's in *The Shadow's* pack now. And unless you want to find out for yourself what it's like to be dead, I suggest you shut the fuck up."

Trey swallowed, gagging momentarily before he nodded. The fucker had probably choked on his gum. Too bad he hadn't suffocated. I realized our driver must have been part of Easton's old pack. That would explain the instant animosity.

I looked at Easton, concerned. He stared out the window, but I could see from his face he was upset. Of the three, he was the easiest to read. *Poor guy.* I leaned over against him, threading my fingers through his. He sat stiffly, but when I reached up and turned his face to mine, then leaned up to kiss him, he responded. I let my tongue gently stroke his until I felt him relax a little. Then I pulled back and smiled at him. His eyes softened as he looked down at me, but his smile was still tight. I squeezed his fingers with mine and he squeezed back.

When I turned back to the front, Bodie still held his gun to the driver's temple. I had no doubt that the world—and especially Easton—would be better off without the fucker behind the wheel. What kind of person said shit like that to someone they hadn't seen in years? *Oh, hey, thought you'd be dead, haha. Asshole. Someone had clearly dropped him on his head as a baby, off the side of a cliff.* I had no doubt that Bodie—being the badass he was—would be able to take control of a moving car speeding down the highway without a living driver.

My morbid fantasy came to a screeching halt as Trey swerved onto an off ramp and barreled down the street. Ahead, a colorful uber-modern building stood smoking, pieces of its orange, purple, and silver metallic walls had been blown across the street and were now wedged like shrapnel into the buildings nearby. My heart shot up my throat like a puck in one of those strong man carnival games. We wouldn't have much time before the Mage Police arrived. We had to hurry if we wanted to help the poor kids trapped inside.

A couple of rabbits darted out the building, ears twitching as they let out terrified screeches before bolting past. A snake slithered out a first-floor window and dropped onto the grass, causing some of the humans nearby to scream. The poor children must have shifted in their panic.

The sight of people running… the sound of the screams… the smell of smoke in the air… It all somehow triggered a long-forgotten memory…

My mind flashed to my grandparents' mansion, a place I rarely got to visit as a little girl, but one that I always remembered thanks to the beautiful gardens that surrounded it. It wasn't beautiful in this memory, though. It was burning. Long orange flames licked the night like vicious whips, and the harsh sting of smoke filling my lungs.

I clutched my grandmother's trembling hand, scared and unsure of what was going on. *Where was grandpa? Why weren't the Mage Police coming to put out the fire?*

"He shouldn't have done it," grandma had said, her voice quavering. "Defiance isn't worth the price."

"Who shouldn't?" I'd asked. "What price?"

But she didn't answer. She'd simply tugged on my hand, fluttered her wings, and we'd flown away.

I never saw my grandpa again. The poor autumn fae never stood a chance against the flames that ate away his home and his bones until they drifted on the wind like the dead leaves of fall.

Years later, I learned it was his punishment for betraying the Mage Council's trust. He'd met with the siren king without the council's approval, which was as bad as doing it behind their backs.

At first, that explanation had been enough for a teen-me determined to join the MP. But now that I was no longer blinded by the council's bullshit, I could see how incredibly fucked up it was.

My internal thoughts didn't matter, though.

The memory quickly faded when I shoved my reminiscing aside.

All at once, the shattered glass front doors of the

ANN DENTON & ELLE MIDDAUGH

school in front of me flew open and several adults ran out of the building carrying burnt and bleeding children as they screamed.

Motherfucker had attacked an elementary *school?*

Jesus fucking Christ...

I saw red just before my mind went numb. My hands unbuckled my seat belt and I opened my car door before I even realized what I was doing. Easton and I were both out of the backseat before the car had even stopped moving. He landed on his feet. I hit the ground and inertia kicked in, forcing me to tuck and roll a few times before scrambling back onto my feet and sprinting for the smoldering building.

The Mage Council might have stripped my badge, but that training was still definitely a part of who I was. More than being a princess ever had been. That was a title I was born into. But a police officer... that was who I was born to be. Helping others, saving them, was a driving force that flooded my veins. I was mixed up in all kinds of shit now, and while I knew there was no turning back from that, nothing else mattered in the moment. Right now, I needed to get in there and do something for those children.

I passed a teacher as he ran up the stairs and I paused just long enough to grab some directions. "Where are the kids?"

"Cafeteria," he puffed. "The attack came before school officially started. The kids who can't afford food were eating free breakfast."

Oh my god.

"Where's the cafeteria?" I asked as quickly as I could.

The man pointed as he coughed. He must've inhaled some smoke during his trips in and out. "Top of the stairs," he replied. "Near the center."

Don't think, Aubry, just move.

As soon as I made it to the top, an arm reached out and grabbed me, pulling me into a storage closet that was big enough to be a small classroom.

"What the fuck?" I tried to shout, but Drake merely rolled his eyes as the rest of the guys filed in and he shut the door behind me.

"You sure you're a trained officer?" he asked skeptically. "You act like a fucking noob straight out of your mama's snatch. You gonna rush in there without a plan?"

That fire-breathing dildo! My eyes grew wide and incredulous. "There are injured children dying! They're burned and bleeding! We need to help them!"

Drake nodded. "Yeah, and there's a fucking psychopath on the loose. There might even be Mage Council members and Mage Police lurking around, so we need to be *cautious*. We aren't the damn police, Aubry. We don't just get to rush in there."

I took a deep breath and shoved down the urge to break his nose. He was right. I was acting like I was still MP.

Russ dropped his giant black bag and began

63

handing out guns as Bodie and Easton finally caught up to us.

"Partner up," Drake ordered us. "One person gets a kid, the other watches their six."

"I'm with Aubry," Bodie and Easton both said at the same time.

Drake sighed and pinched the bridge of his nose. "We don't have time for this shit. Bodie, you're with Larry. Easton, cover Russ. I'll keep the fly with me since *clearly* neither of you can be trusted to keep your cocks out of the henhouse when she's around."

Drake? I had to partner up with Drake? My eyes narrowed as I ground my teeth together. I tried to tell myself I'd had worse partners at the MP Academy. And I had—in terms of competence. None of them could handle four weapons-two on each hip and two in underarm holsters. But nobody beat Drake in the asshole department. He was the bossiest, rudest alpha I'd ever met.

Bodie glared and shook his head as he loaded a magazine into his rifle and gave it a firm strike. "Were you raised on a fucking farm or what? Your analogies suck today."

"Not as much as that sub did last night," Drake retorted darkly.

I was pretty sure he said it to close down any more conversation on the subject, but naturally it piqued my interest... and my nipples.

Bodie shook his head as he followed Russ out the door.

Larry and Easton were next. Our old, far-less-competent Einstein-lookalike hopped around shaking out his limbs and taking deep breaths. He looked like he was gearing up for a marathon.

Easton grinned and let Larry do his thing as he turned to me. "If you don't mind, I'd love to make you your own weapon sometime. One as sleek, lethal, and beautiful as you are."

My heart put a metaphorical hand to her chest in adoration. Violent gifts? My entire body heated at how well Easton knew me. He was so fucking sweet. "I would love that, thank you."

He grinned before leaning in and kissing my neck just below my jaw. "Be careful out there."

My eyelashes fluttered as heat swirled around beneath my skin. "I will. You too."

"Go, lover-boy," Drake growled.

Easton shot me a wink before lifting his rifle and following an antsy Larry out the door.

Then, only Drake and I were left.

"You grab a kid," the moody fucker told me, "and I'll cover your ass."

I scoffed, peering out the crack of the door as Drake clicked the safeties off on his handguns. "I don't trust you anywhere near my ass, dragon."

Suddenly, his chest was flush against my back, heating

my skin through my flimsy top, and his groin was right up against my ass just like I told him not to be. His breath was hot on my neck as he replied in barely a whisper. "I don't think that's true, Dollface. See, I watched you for weeks before we nailed down your kidnapping. I know all about your submissive tendencies, and I know exactly how close you like your doms to be to your ass when they fuck you."

My nostrils flared at the thought of them stalking me, planning my kidnapping behind my back while I had no fucking clue. But then the fucked-up side of me reared her horny head and thought: He watched me get fucked at the club? Did he like what he saw? Had I turned him on?

Why the fuck was I so turned on right now?

Stupid fucking hormones. I quickly pushed those thoughts away and concentrated on the present. I was definitely messed up if I could think about anything else right now. That, or my mind just really didn't want to accept what I knew I was about to see. Pushing the door open, I strode out into the hallway, putting as much space between Drake and I as I could. I rushed toward the cafeteria while simultaneously keeping a keen eye on my surroundings. Drake was right about one thing: if Triton was there, then there might be other council members lurking, too. We had to be careful.

It became apparent to me rather quickly though, that no one was there anymore. No one other than injured children and teachers, anyway. I entered the cafeteria, and my eyes instantly found Bodie, standing guard behind Larry as the mage poured what I assumed to be Healing Potions over several crying kids. Next, my gaze landed on Easton, he had the barrel of his gun up and was scanning the area just waiting for someone to creep out of the woodwork and attack. Russ had a little girl slung over his shoulder and was lifting another one up on the other side. As soon as he was ready, he and Bodie headed outside to deliver the children to their terrified parents.

Were they alive? Dead? My eyes scanned over the table shards to better study the kids. Some of them moved, moaned, and cried. Others... didn't. It made my eyes burn and sting with the need to cry, but I pushed the emotion down as I spotted a little girl clutching her arm and sprinted over to her. Drake stayed close behind me, never saying a word as I knelt down and studied the precious little face before me. Her golden locks were woven into an off-the-shoulder French braid and an Olaf toy lay a few feet away from her. It was the little Elsa girl I'd met during Easton's babysitting stint. The one who wanted him to be her marshmallow. Her chest was still, while it should have been gently rising and falling. Her skin was pale, and her lips were almost blue. She was gone.

I couldn't help the monsoon of emotion that overcame me in that moment. Tears flowed like waterfalls down my cheeks and I sobbed as the ache in my throat became too much to bear.

These poor, helpless children. They were innocent. They'd done nothing wrong. These kids in particular had only met this fate because they were poor, eating the school's free breakfast because their parents couldn't afford to feed them at home. Parents who busted their asses just to stay off the streets because *mages* made it hard for them to work in human industries.

Mages required shifters to be monitored if they worked in close proximity to humans, making things awkward, making it appear like shifters were on fucking parole or some shit in the eyes of the humans. I'd never given it a second thought before, because I'd been so removed. But mages fucked shifters over at every turn.

I'd been a part of that. I was partially responsible for all that had transpired. Because I'd seen them as the *problem* instead of as *people*, just trying to get by, like anyone else.

My tears dripped down and soaked the little girl's dress which was already dirtied with dust, soot, and specks of dried up blood. I couldn't even see through the blur as I gently scooped her up and cradled her in my arms.

I turned around and Drake's usually hard eyes were soft with emotion. He stared at me almost like he cared, or maybe it was the child he cared about, but either way, his demeanor softened. Thank god, I couldn't handle asshole Drake right now.

"Aubry, Doll, she's..." Drake's words cut off and he cleared his throat and looked away.

I nodded, more tears slinking down my cheeks. "I know, but she deserves to be returned to her family. They deserve the right to a proper funeral and burial."

When Drake turned back to me his eyes were lined in a gentle pink. "They can't afford those things. They'll mourn her death. But they'll be forced to relinquish her body to the crematorium. Her ashes will fill another community grave."

"No." My response was harsh and adamant. "I don't give a shit if I have to fund these burials myself, the kids who died here are going to be remembered."

Drake swallowed hard and nodded, cocking his head toward the exit to remind me we needed to keep moving. Any minute now the human police and rescue workers would arrive. Maybe even the Mage Police, though I doubted any shifters had called them. The residents of Skid Row rarely called any kind of police. And we couldn't risk being caught. Not when we had so much work to do.

I handed the limp little girl over to her wailing mother outside.

"Suzie!" the woman's sobs dropped her to her knees.

I waited for a second, frozen as I saw her grief, before Drake gently touched my shoulder and we made our way back inside. We continued our rescue while I suppressed the ache in my chest and tried to keep a calm face for the kids I carried out. Many of the kids were going to make it, especially thanks to Larry's potions, but there were a handful that were already gone. I couldn't stand it. It was... the worst thing I'd ever seen; and I'd seen some pretty graphic shit. This was just too much. Too fucking much...

A few minutes later, I escorted the last child down the stairs by hand—another kid I'd met from babysitting, the boy with the bowl cut hair—as Drake tagged along behind us, vigilantly scanning our surroundings for any hints of movement or foul play.

My heart was heavy. Broken. Thick chunks of it lay crumbled in the pit of my stomach. Some of the boy's friends had died today. This event would be burned into his memory for... eternity. Just like the apartment fires would have been burned into Suzie's memory had she lived long enough...

My chin quivered. Goddamn it, I was ready to kill someone over this. I'd certainly killed people over less.

As I handed the little boy over to his parents and they showered him in hugs and kisses, I caught sight of a magical reporter setting up in front of the building.

Reporters but no Mage Police, huh? I had always responded to every fucking call. What the hell was Candace doing? And was the council encouraging them not to respond? Leaning on the police force? Covering for Trite? What the fuck?

Drake tapped my shoulder, but I didn't turn around, I just watched Miss Dimbat primp her hair and push up her cleavage as she prepared to go live. My teeth clenched. Children had fucking died ten feet behind her and all she cared about were her tits looking good on TV? If I had a knife, I might have thrown it. Not to kill, but maybe to give her a nice dead leg limp to go with her dead-as-a-doornail ethics.

"And... go!" her cameraman said.

She smiled obnoxiously wide and began her pre-prepared speech. "Thanks, Tina. We're here at the scene of yet another violent shifter attack in Los Angeles's Skid Row. The area is notorious for poverty and crime, but it's safe to say the shifters have hit an all-time low by attacking—not only *children*—but children of their own kind. How much longer can we allow this violence and brutality to continue unchecked?"

Rage and fury filled me as I listened to the mage-fueled propaganda spilling from that bitch's lips. She expected people to believe *shifters* did this? To their own *children*? What's worse, people *would* believe it. Just as I had, for all those years.

Without giving any fucks, I marched over there, yanked out the plug from the camera so she was no longer live, and punched that bitch in the face.

"That is a lie!" I shouted at her, through clenched teeth. "*Mages* did this, not shifters!"

She didn't seem to hear me though. She was too busy falling on her ass and shrieking over her split lip.

Suddenly, broad hands were on my shoulders pulling me away. "Are you fucking crazy? Do you *want* to get caught?"

Drake led me back into the school, through a maze of hallways and corridors, and into the secret tunnel below.

I eventually yanked free of his iron hold on my arms. "We need to stop this shit."

"I agree," he growled. "It needs to end."

"Then what are we gonna do?" The question left my mouth as sarcasm, but that was only because of the frustration and helplessness that were as thick and toxic as smog in my lungs. I crossed my arms in disgust.

Drake smirked, his eyes darkening as they drank me in. "Remember what our line of business is?"

I rolled my eyes. "Unlawful shipments of illegal weapons and materials. Yes, I've read your file."

"Good." His smile spread wider. "We're going to one of our storehouses, and we're going to arm the shifters. It's time we *all* started fighting back—not just the worst of us. These mage fucks need a taste of their own medicine."

6

DRAKE

Normally, I would have walked this path alone, but this afternoon, Aubry was beside me and I could feel the fury radiating off her, nearly as hot as my dragon fire. What had happened at the school this morning had both of us clenching our fists. I slowed my steps when I realized she was half-running in order to keep up with me.

When she realized what I was doing, she grabbed my elbow and shoved. "Faster," she said roughly, her voice just a scratch after all the smoke—first at the station, then at the school.

I sped up as we hurried through the tunnel I'd used earlier on my escape route. I held a tiny ball of fire I'd created in one hand to light our way. It might have been midday outside, full of car fumes and tourists and business as usual for the humans, but this dark tunnel reflected my reality better than anything on the surface ever could. Life was a narrow fucking hole in the ground and you just had to claw your way through it, hoping every second that there wasn't a cave in, until one day you ended up buried in it.

"The Mage Police didn't even show," Aubry seethed.

I looked over at her pissed off face. "They never do in this part of town. They didn't come for the Skid Row fire either—"

"Yeah, but the fire brigade would have been better, the winter fae have all the water—"

"I just said, they don't show. *Ever*." I shook my head. For the damned former Chief Enforcer, she was still so naive. She'd definitely drunk all their Kool-Aid.

"But those are *children*!" Aubry's strides lengthened and matched mine. I glanced down to see her fists clenched as she marched, black boots stomping over the uneven ground.

Her fury on our behalf made me stop short and stare at her. "Don't tell me you care, Princess," I scoffed.

I knew she did, though. I could see it radiating out of every pore in her body. But it was too late for her to care, wasn't it? Too fucking late for any damn good to come out of this.

"Fuck you, Drake. *Anyone* would care," she pushed me, and I stumbled backward into the dirt-packed wall, dust flying around me.

She'd clearly caught me off guard, which frustrated the hell out of me, but her raw emotion was what almost made me lose my cool. I didn't hit women, but I was so fucking furious I was almost blind. Black danced around the edges of my vision.

Three kids in Bodie's pack were dead. Because of *me*. I didn't need any more guilt piled on, and least of all by a former Mage Police murderer. I was already too close to suffocating in all this sin and secrecy...

I dragged my thoughts away from the pain of emotion and onto my surroundings. I'd used this very same fucking tunnel as part of my escape route after I'd left Union Station. I kept clothes and a couple guns stashed in the tunnel here, just like I did in a hundred different drop points throughout the city.

Some dragons were obsessed with hoarding gold. I had a share of that too, but escape routes, disguises, extra weapons... hoarding those was what had kept me alive this long. *Vigilance* was the one thing that had kept me out of the mages' hands.

But I'd lost it this morning. I hadn't been careful enough. I hadn't been thinking straight. After the fight, too much rage had still been rushing through my system. I'd put so many people at risk...

Easton had gotten seriously injured, Bodie got made by the Mage Police, all of it because of me... because the mages wanted *me*. I'd been so busy thinking about how it was all falling apart, I hadn't been paying attention.

I was a fucking fool. I'd thought that since it was early in the morning, since no one was around and school wasn't in session, it was safe to go to Ninth

Street and change, emerging from the other side of this tunnel three blocks down and walking away to meet the crew.

I hadn't noticed the mage tracking me.

Just the thought of that evil fucker...

My hands shifted to claws, the fire ball reflecting off my scales as they traveled up my arm.

Slam!

Aubry smacked me into the wall again, harder this time. "You can't fucking shift in here!"

I dropped my fireball to the ground and grabbed her upper arms, my beast doing his best to take over. "Do *not* fucking tell me what to do!"

She twisted in my grasp and tried to knee me in the junk, but my claws caught her knee and shoved her back against the far wall.

I leaned in close, smoke rings coming from my still-human mouth. "Don't even *think* about it, Princess."

"If you shift, you'll collapse this tunnel on us, you stupid naked chicken," she spat at me.

She tried to hit my face too, but I grabbed her hand and pinned it to the wall. Then I pressed my body into hers so that she couldn't keep attacking me. "I have control of my beast."

"Bullshit," she snapped. "You're losing it."

A roar erupted from my mouth. My dragon batted my reason away.

Aubry hurled a fireball at my face. It didn't burn me, but it did make me pause. I wrestled with my beast internally. But finally, I got him under control enough to collect myself and loosen my hold. I took a step back. Her flames danced in front of my eyes, and with them, danced memories.

My mother laughing one second, dead on the floor the next, that bitch fuck from the council, Citrine, standing right behind her. My younger self looking out across the lawn, and seeing every single one of my family members littering the ground like rubbish...

My chest cracked and my dragon roared back up, the tenuous hold I'd had on him breaking. The shift started to take over.

Whack.

A roundhouse kick to my face stopped it. Pain burst through my eyelids and sent fireworks through my brain. I whirled, scales retreating down my neck and arms as my eyes narrowed to slits. Aubry stood in the middle of the tunnel, arms held up in sparring position.

"Where the fuck did you just go?" she asked.

I didn't answer, I just rushed her and tackled her to the ground.

She walloped me across the face. "Answer the question, lizard brain. Or is it too cold in here? Is your mind shutting down? How about I warm it up for you?"

More flames flashed across my face. Fury rose in my chest like an inferno eating a building from the inside out.

"STOP!" I raised a hand to smack her, and just barely stopped myself at the last second.

I dropped my hand and then pushed myself up. I stood stiffly, turning away before continuing down the tunnel, taking deep breaths to restore my self-control. Using a blast of flame from my lips, I created a new fireball so we could see. But... Aubry wasn't following. When I looked back, I saw she was still on the ground, shaking. I checked my dragon, ensuring that his rage was indeed leashed before sighing and walking back to her.

"You should have just fought me," she muttered.

"No."

"Why the fuck not? We'd both feel better right now," she grumbled. She kicked out and tried to sweep my legs out from under me, but I hopped over her leg easily and rolled my eyes.

"We have shit to do. Let's go."

She glared up at me with a pout, and I had the sudden urge to flip her over right there in the tunnel, yank down her pants, and spank that sweet ass.

I had to close my eyes and blow out a breath. *This is the damned wasp,* I reminded myself. She'd already stung both my boys; no way I was letting that shit happen to me. Not even when my dragon whispered that she was fireproof.

I glanced away down the tunnel, jaw twitching as I forced myself to think of all the Mage Council fucks who'd done me wrong over the years. That British dick, Daggler, had forced my dad's legit shipping business to fold. Delia Ferndoll had started a series of foreclosures on shifter property—

Those thoughts cleared my head enough to shove away the ridiculous, unwarranted lust I'd felt.

Aubry still didn't move. I was forced to reach down and take her small, soft hand in mine and yank her up. "Let's go."

"Not until you tell me what the fuck just happened."

"Flashback, okay?" I growled. "But my problems are nothing compared to these people. Let's go."

She walked reluctantly beside me and I dropped her hand like it was a hot potato.

"My parents live in fear of the Mage Council," she said, from out of nowhere.

I didn't respond.

So does fucking everyone. Welcome to the party.

"I thought if I did a good enough job, they'd ease up," she continued. "I thought if I was their golden girl, the mages would reward me. I was the best fucking Chief Enforcer they ever had. You know what happened?"

"You got fired," I growled, stomping up the steps that led to the fabric store which hid my stash of weapons.

"This is the part where *you* share," she said drily.

"Why?" I scoffed, as I turned around and used my back to open a swinging door in the basement of the store. "You wanna hear that mages killed my entire extended

79

family but stopped when they got to me? Wanna hear that Citrine *fucking* Pierce stared at me as I sobbed—I was eight—and said, 'Oh darn. The council only let me get enough tags for seven dragons this hunting season. Don't worry, pet. I'll be back next year for you.'"

I didn't look at Aubry after she gasped. I was too busy shoving down the shadows, battling to control me. I took a deep breath and willed my mind to go blank. Focus. Discipline. I needed to stay calm right now. The person who stayed calm in a crisis could weather the storm. Could win in the end. I had to be that person right now. The shifters needed that person.

I took a moment to close my eyes and meditate, gathering that calm I so desperately needed. Aubry's hand slipped into mine and my eyes shot open. I glanced down at her. She didn't look up at me. She just squeezed my hand and let go, moving forward up the steps to the store.

Had that faerie just tried to comfort me? Confusion mixed with guilt like creamer and coffee, blending together until I couldn't separate one from the other, and all I was left with was a nasty aftertaste in my mouth.

What the fuck? Aubry hates me. I mean, she should hate me.

She *needed* to hate me. I still had to tell her… about her dad.

I scrubbed a hand down my face, then watched her ass as she climbed the stairs, clad in the black skinny jeans Bodie had given her. *Fuck him.* She should be dressed in a damn sack cloth that was as abrasive as her personality. *Fucking hand-holding bullshit.* I watched her wings disappear as she applied her glamour, and an annoying twinge of disappointment ran through me after they were gone.

Goddamn it. I was going insane.

I marched up the stairs and joined her on the first floor of the fabric store, where an old Hispanic woman had a gun pointed right at Aubry's heart.

I eased around Aubry and stood between her and the gun-toting grandma who sometimes cleaned our hideout.

"It's okay, Lorena," I told the sweet shifter, trying not to smile at her improper grip on the gun. I jerked my head in Aubry's direction. "She's with me. Can you go lock the front door please? Put the closed sign out?"

Lorena lowered her gun, eyeing Aubry suspiciously. "What do you mean *with* you?"

My face heated. Aubry's cheeks flamed.

"Not *that*," the fae snapped.

Thank god she said it and I didn't have to—I couldn't even imagine why anyone would assume we were together. Ignoring my discomfort, I turned to the bolts of cloth lining the back of the room.

"You need more clothes?" Lorena asked as she hobbled to the front of the store and turned the deadbolt, then put the "Out for Lunch" sign up in her window.

I shook my head. "Nope. Need the stash. You need to take the rest of the day off. Get your family and go on a weekend trip." I didn't explain further, but I didn't need to because if Lorena hadn't already heard about the attack on the school, she would soon. Shifter news made the rounds faster than a tick on a werewolf's ass.

I reached up and grabbed a red bolt of cloth from high on the shelf. The pattern was one of the ugliest Lorena sold; it looked like a seventies hand-me-down robe, all scratchy and rough, and *way* overpriced to ensure no one ever decided to buy it. In the center of the bolt *wasn't* a thin cardboard box as usual. Instead, there was a metallic case, full of weapons Easton had custom made for us. I slid the case out and handed it to Aubry.

"Carry this," I ordered.

Of course, the nosy fae couldn't just follow my command. As I pulled down another bolt of cloth, I heard her gasp behind me.

"What is this?" she asked.

I didn't bother to look back. "Close it. We have to get the shit here, and then I've got another stash we need to hit." I grabbed three more cases before giving Lorena a nod. "Be safe. Keep your weapon on you at all times."

As Lorena nodded, I turned and went back into the tunnel, Aubry trailing behind me.

"What's the plan?" she asked, as we walked through

the dark. Both of our hands were full, so neither of us could spark up a light.

"We're done taking it up the ass," I growled, letting my nose and my familiarity guide me through the tunnels. When we came to a fork in the road, I headed right. "We're gonna give every shifter the means to protect themselves from this shit."

"Just protect themselves?" Aubry sounded uncertain.

I paused. *Do I tell her the truth?*

If she really had a mate bond with both my friends, then she couldn't really betray us. And based on the fucking orgy that I'd walked in on this morning, she at least *thought* the bond was real... or maybe she was just that kinky. She did go to Syn.

The thought of the depraved things she'd done at the sex club filled my mind in a seductive haze. Those images, coupled with the hot sight of her naked body this morning, temporarily derailed my thoughts. I had to park, reverse, and backtrack my mind to get on the right road again.

"You're going to attack them." Aubry took my silence as my answer. "But... you don't have enough magic."

She didn't need to tell me what I already fucking knew.

Irritation grumbled in my chest, muttering all kinds of useless things. Until my guilt swung back in and sawed me in half like a magician so that my stomach dropped out.

We didn't have enough magic because Larry had used a shit ton of potions defending us last night at the station. We didn't have enough magic because I'd failed to get the damn mage jewels the last two times we'd tried. We didn't have enough magic because the fucking Mage Police had been after me. *Me*. For killing... I couldn't even finish that thought.

I'd killed a lot of people and I'd never regretted it.

I definitely didn't regret shredding that wasp's wing. But the thought of telling Aubry—of seeing her face twist up in grief and pain like I'd just backhanded her...

That made me regret everything.

And it made me pissed that I'd even feel that way. I mean, what the fuck? I was trying to protect the innocent. Trying to stop those mage fucks from treating us like nothing more than a damn spice, just a little sprinkle of murdered magic to toss in their potions to strengthen the flavor.

So I'd killed a man. So what? A Mage Councilor? Even better.

Then why did I feel as nauseous as if I was back at the La Brea tar pits?

I should just tell Aubry and get it over with, I thought. *Do it while we're in the dark so I don't have to worry about looking her in the eye. And by the time we're out of this damn tunnel, she'll have her mask back on. Just like I would.*

Because, deep down, I knew she and I were the same. We both used shells like they were shields.

Sarcasm like swords. We breathed in anger like it was air. Because it fueled us to do better and fight harder. Not for ourselves. But for others.

My heart cringed a little, but I shut it down. I didn't allow *it* to make any decisions for me; my *mind* was the one in charge. And I'd own the consequences of breaking her heart like the fucked-up man I was.

"Aubry, I—" I opened my mouth to say the words, *to confess*.

But just then, Easton burst down a set of stairs in front of us, carrying a flashlight. "Drake, you've got to hurry! It's a madhouse up here."

My fast walk turned into a sprint. "What's going on?"

"The parents and the betas are riled up. I left Larry behind so I could find you because so many of them are ready to riot. They're pissed, Drake. We're lucky they peeled off and came to the warehouse, because Corey has half of them ready to attack the Mage Council."

I took the stairs two at a time, vaguely aware of Easton removing the cases from Aubry's hands and escorting her up like a gentleman behind me. As if she needed any help. She could fucking walk on her own. I mentally rolled my eyes before I took a deep breath and pulled down my alpha mask.

When I burst through the door of the warehouse— this spot held an even bigger stockpile of weapons than the fabric store; this location was one that most shifters knew they could buy black market weapons from—my face was calm and collected. There wasn't a hint of anxiety on it, despite the concern raging through my system. I made my face as cold as ice.

I scanned the interior of the industrial metal building. Afternoon light streamed from the windows on the left and cut across people's torsos. The room was packed with shifters; some of them had half shifted in their anger, and some of them were sobbing. I was somewhat shocked to see over fifty shifters spread throughout the crates in the room. I'd expected word to travel fast, but not quite this fast. My blue gaze grazed over every angry face in the room. I scented their fury, their desperation, their fear. It was a sour thing.

They'd been yelling, but I waited until their shouts turned to murmurs, then calmed into silence. Like ripples in a pond, all the sound in the room faded away as they stared at me.

I looked at Corey, a middle-aged shifter sporting a crooked nose and a bleach-white smile. He was Bodie's beta and handled most of the day-to-day shit that Bodie couldn't be bothered with. He jabbed a finger at Aubry. "What the fuck is that wasp doing here?"

Easton took a predatory step toward him. "Watch it. That's my mate. And Bodie's."

Every eye in the room widened in shock. Then the head-shaking and whispering started.

"If you're all finished texting TMZ the fucking news, I'd like to talk," I said irritably.

That shut the gossips right the fuck up. I waited until all of them had submitted, even Corey, my gaze pinning him until his eyes touched the floor at my feet, bowing to me.

Then, I spoke.

"The Mage Council attacked us directly. We will attack them, make no mistake. We will go for the throat." A cheer started to go up around the expansive room, but I held up a hand to stop it. My eyes settled on Corey again, ensuring that the freckle-faced fuck was watching me. "But anyone who makes a move before I say *go* will have hell to pay."

"You can't do that!" Corey hissed. "Drake, we can't sit on our hands!"

"They killed my son!" Ernesto, a hedgehog shifter in the back of the room yelled. His face was raw, broken like an egg, and tears oozed from his eyes like yolk.

Grumbles started up again, but I spoke over them, letting my dragon wings sprout from my back as I did. "I have no intention of sitting on our damn hands."

My wings spread out wide on either side of me, forcing the nearest shifters to take a step back, directing the momentum of the crowd to move as I saw fit.

"I've been after these mage shits for *years*," I continued. "But I will not let you walk up to their doors and get shot down like vermin. Don't think they won't. The fuckers wouldn't even bat an eyelash. We can't attack them straight on—that's suicide. We *will* attack. I'm working on a plan as we speak. And I've called in back up from New York."

That shut everyone up.

New York was a hot spot for mage-shifter skirmishes. And the shifter community there was as deep-rooted and well-connected as any human mafia. With them coming to our aid, we were already in a much better position than we had been, and this shifter mob damn well knew it.

"For now, you take these weapons. You protect you and yours. You move your families to secure locations. And I'll be in contact with every alpha in L.A. to coordinate our battle plan."

Every head in the room nodded, as the sour smell of fear receded, and determination took its place.

"Rest assured," I said in conclusion. "Today's attack was just the beginning, but ours will be the end. *We* will be *their* end."

A roar of approval met my ears and washed over me. I sent out a wave of alpha power and everyone bowed their heads, even Easton, who should have been alpha of his own fucking clan. But the weirdo had always deferred to me. Only one person in the warehouse didn't bow.

Aubry.

Her chocolate eyes stayed glued to mine in a way that made my stomach tighten and my throat grow hot.

Even though she wasn't a shifter, I was surprised that she could hold my gaze when I released the alpha magic. It was so potent, most other magical creatures—even sirens and pixies—couldn't look at me. The only ones capable of standing up to alphas were their...

No.

Horror washed through me like acid. I broke eye contact first, the only time I'd done so since I was twelve. My heart hammered frantically in my chest, but I did my best to appear calm on the outside.

Ignoring Aubry's confused look, I turned to smile at Easton. "Want to break open the boxes, Goldilocks? We've got presents for everyone."

"Sure thing, Santa." Easton walked over and ripped open a crate with his bare hands.

"Two lines," I shouted. "One for those who know how to fire a gun, and one for those who don't."

Betas kept the shifters under control as they came up one by one to get weapons for every adult in their household. Easton opened crate after crate of the guns he'd made specifically for shifter use, ones that could be magically fired even in animal form.

Corey stepped in and started explaining how to shoot a gun to the line of people who didn't understand. Even the wasp—yeah, I was back to calling her that—joined in on the tutorial. She did a half decent job of it, though the whole "proper stance" shit was bullshit. In a battle, there was no such thing. Still, she was better at it than Corey.

We handed out several hundred weapons over the next few hours, as a near constant stream of shifters seemed to come inside. We didn't stop until Easton turned around and said, "We're out," and I was forced to tell a disappointed line of shifters to come back the next day.

The shifters trudged outside, with the exception of Easton and the wasp, and I sagged against the side of an open crate.

I hadn't slept the night before—none of us had. The shit show had just gone from Union Station to the museum to Ninth Street School to the warehouse in the blink of an eye. The adrenaline I'd been running on finally gave out and I felt like I was about to crash.

But I couldn't. I needed to slam an energy drink and keep on keeping on.

I looked at Easton. "I need you to go to location fifteen and grab the weapons there. Bring them here for tomorrow's distribution."

"Fifteen? How many locations do you have?" the wasp asked.

I didn't answer, just waited until Easton nodded his acceptance of my order. But then he said, "Larry told me to tell you he's nearly out."

I sighed and nodded in return, staring at the floor.

I knew that. Larry was our only full mage and he had a very limited number of potions. That was part of why I had to keep going. I had to figure this out. I had to come up with a way to attack the mages, and I had to do it without his help.

It was gonna be a bloodbath.

"What's wrong?" The wasp glanced between Easton and me, batting those long, dark eyelashes.

"Larry's out of potions." Easton answered, walking over to her.

I turned away. I couldn't handle looking at her. At *them*. Not with the way my stomach was churning… I could just picture Goldilocks putting his arm around her. The two of them snuggled in close.

My dragon gave a little whine inside my chest, and I covered it with a cough. I pulled my wings in swiftly and shifted to full human, letting him know exactly what I thought of his opinion. *Fuck off, firebreather,* I told him.

I was so shocked to feel a small hand on my arm that I physically jumped at the contact. I turned to see Aubry, her tiny fingers digging into my skin as my whole body lit up with her touch. Desire coursed through me, burning a path all the way down to my half-hard dick.

I immediately used guilt to knock out my unwarranted attraction. I was a bad guy; I didn't deserve to feel light and warmth. And anyway, Aubry was taken—by *both* of my pack mates. And if that somehow wasn't enough, then as soon as I told her what I'd done to her father, she was going to hate me.

Forever.

Her soft brown eyes flickered under the cheap warehouse fluorescents as she stared up at me, completely oblivious to my internal turmoil. "I know where we can get more potions to replenish Larry's stores."

My eyebrow shot up. So did my heart rate. "Yeah, where?"

Then she uttered a sentence I never thought would spill from her plush lips. "We can break into the precinct."

7

AUBRY

I STARED IMPASSIVELY AT THE BUILDING BEFORE ME—THE place I'd considered my true home until just a few weeks ago—as I prepared to rob it.

My, how times had changed.

The downtown Mage Police precinct gleamed in the dull evening light. The glass windows were tinted, so we couldn't see the bustling chaos inside, but I knew it was just about time for a shift change. And in those precious minutes of case handoffs and small talk, final bathroom breaks and putting lunches into the fridge... we'd have a shot.

I licked my lips, feeling better and more myself than I had in weeks. Because I finally felt like I knew what I was doing. I was finally in charge of a mission. The fact that it was the opposite of everything I'd ever done before didn't matter—the high, the familiar rush of blood through my ears, *did*.

"Move out to the left," I directed the Easton and Drake quietly. "We need to go in through the back door."

We circled the edge of the parking lot, eyes casually on the brick building next to the station, as if that's where we were headed. Palm trees swayed overhead, and the smell of a taco cart drifted down the street, making my stomach growl. We'd eaten before coming here, but that had been our first meal of the day and my body was feeling it.

I heard Easton moan next to me. "Tacos," he said dreamily.

Drake, of course, was all business. "Don't you need a keycard to get in?"

"Yup." I moved forward without giving him further explanation.

The dragon growled behind me. "You didn't say that *before*, Aubry."

I loved the way he said my name when he was angry. Maybe it was because he was usually so damn stoic and controlled. Getting him riled up was quickly becoming a favorite pastime of mine.

"You want me to spell out every damn step for you, Guerra?" I taunted. "What is this, preschool? Do I need to pull your pants down so you can piss too?"

Easton chuckled and I flashed him a saucy grin, saying, "Guess the gecko doesn't like having a taste of his own medicine."

"Guess not." My blond bear winked at me.

"That is not what I—" Drake started to protest.

"That is *exactly* what you do," Easton interjected. "Bark orders without explanations."

"*Shh*," I hushed the pair, delighted to cut Drake off before he could respond. He'd have to just sit there and stew on his retorts. We were too close to the building to keep bantering.

I raised a brow at Drake. "I need you to shift your hand and use your claws to pop some tires."

I pointed at a car that was parked near the edge of the lot. It was a private car... Aaron's car. And if there was anything that siren loved as much as Tee, it was his car. I didn't know how he'd afforded it. Police salary definitely wasn't enough to cover the sleek Audi, but he'd gotten it anyway. And he'd gotten all the stupid bells and whistles on it. Including some dumb app that alerted him of everything. Including tire pressure. I'd been bored to tears the day he'd tried to show me how it all worked. But now, his tech addiction was going to come in handy.

Drake's brows lowered as if I'd given him the shittiest assignment ever. "Really?"

"Yup," I said with a grin. "Do it quick, because then we have to bust ass."

He grumbled and walked over to the car I'd indicated. His hand turned into a black scaled claw and he shoved a long nail into the tire. When he pulled it out, a slow hiss leaked into the air.

"Now move," I directed, dodging behind cars and hurrying toward the back door.

The three of us scurried through the lot before posting up behind a dumpster near the back door. I held my breath, not even wanting to think about how bad the smell was for the guys. Like rotten sewage. I glanced at my watch.

Drake leaned forward and started to whisper, "What the fuck—"

I cut him off by simply holding up a hand.

Less than a minute later, Aaron burst through the door, eyes searching for his precious ride. He looked like shit, and suddenly, my guilt amped up. I knew he was probably there day and night using every department resource to search for Tee, but she'd been moved so often I doubted he'd be able to track her. And if she really was in a coma... well, I had no idea how that might affect their mate bond magic.

Aaron strode forward to check on his car and as soon as he was far enough away, I spread my wings and flew, grabbing onto the door a millisecond before it latched. I landed and waved the guys over just as Aaron's "Fucking shit!" traveled through the parking lot.

We soundlessly slipped inside.

The back hallway was dark, because the cops really only used it to come in and out. It had a service closet for the janitors, and a door to the weapons room full of Sleep grenade Potions, guns, Lethal Protection

Potions, and all kinds of delicious goodies. But walking through that doorway wouldn't be as easy as the first.

"If Aaron comes back in, knock him out. Do *not* kill him," I glanced back and forth between both the guys as I led my crew to the storage closet.

Easton immediately nodded. Drake just stared.

"Drake?" I waited mid-hallway and put a hand on my hip. I was not gonna fucking back down on this.

The dragon glared at me and released some strange scent into the air. It smelled like a damned air-freshener. Sweet apple cider or some shit. He'd done it in the warehouse too, which was weird as fuck. I had no idea what that meant but my damn nipples puckered every time he did it.

"Stop fucking distracting me with sex hormones," I growled.

Drake's eyes widened.

Easton's jaw dropped and he glanced between us. "*Sex hormones?*"

"Agree," I demanded, focusing on the dragon's angry blue eyes and furrowed black brows. "Now. Or I'm not fucking doing it."

Drake's teeth sharpened and ground together as he held my gaze. "Fine."

"Good," I said in the syrupy sweet tone of victory. "Wait here. I'll be right back."

I turned on my heel, then let glamour wash over my body as I transformed into Tee's husband, uniform and all. I shot up in height and my arms hung down like thick logs—I felt like an ape.

Immediately, I had to fight the urge to scratch—it was maddening, right from the start. I loosened my walk and threw back my shoulders the way Aaron normally did. Then I pushed through the hallway door into the precinct lobby and walked through the busy room straight toward Shelly's desk.

Shelly was the world's dumbest administrator. She'd had her job since before Jesus was born, so nobody had the heart to fire her. But the old pixie puttered around the office, making delicious-as-dishwater coffee and misfiling paperwork because, even with her glasses, she couldn't tell the difference between an 'E' and an 'F' anymore.

"Shelly, I lost my keys," I groaned, in typical Aaron fashion. "I locked them in my car."

"Oh, dear!" Shelly blinked up at me sympathetically from where she sat, six inches tall, in the middle of her desk. A Post It note the size of her torso sat on her lap and she was in the middle of painstakingly writing a note.

I waited. But she didn't say anything else. My smile grew a little strained. "Can I borrow your keys for a sec?"

Her brow furrowed. "But, how will that help you get your keys?"

I swallowed a sigh. "You have a skeleton key, don't you?"

For some unknown reason, back in the day, someone, somewhere had entrusted a mage-spelled key to
Shelly. It could unlock just about anything.

"Oh, yes! I forgot." She set aside her note and fluttered to the edge of her desk. Then she bent over to
yank at the top drawer. Unlike Tee, Shelly rarely used
Growth Potion to get larger. She claimed it gave her
hoo-ha a rash, a fact that HR had to come talk to her
about. Shelly was from an era before 'work-appropri-
ate' conversations were a thing. I didn't know what
Tee's excuse was.

She dug through the drawer, pulling out pens
nearly as tall as she was, chewing gum, and other office
detritus. I had to work hard not to tap my foot and just
yank the drawer out of her desk, walking off with the
whole damn thing. I did glance at the overhead clock.
Aaron would be back inside any minute.

Finally, she held up the gleaming silver key.

I had to force myself not to snatch it right out of
her tiny hand and accidentally end up flinging her
petite body across the office. "Thanks! I'll be right
back!"

My heart swelled as big as a bullfrog with each beat
as I made my way back across the office. An itch traveled up my spine like a shiver and I had to think of
something else to keep my mind off of the annoying
sensation.

Drake's face popped into my head.

No.

I shoved it away and pulled up Bodie's face instead. I hoped my shifter assassin was safe.

The last time he'd gone on a mission, he'd been hunting down Trite, too. He hadn't found him then. Should I be hopeful Bodie wouldn't find his target this time either? Or should I secretly hope Trite got taken out? Because, I wasn't gonna lie, after the day I'd had with those kids and their grieving parents... I was kinda pulling for the latter.

Yes, a huge piece of my heart broke to even think the words in my head, but an even bigger chunk of my heart broke for those innocent children, robbed of their lives and their futures all because of a crazed mage with a grudge. Drake killing Trite's parents was an accident—I wasn't sure why, but I truly believed that. Maybe it was the haunted look on Drake's face when he'd first admitted it. Or the fact that Trite had never told me his parents were murdered. The fact that my best friend kept the murder a secret, when typically, mages were all about blaming shifters for everything, spoke volumes. Triton had never talked to me about it, never gotten it off his chest. Instead, he'd allowed it to fester deep inside until it corrupted him right to his core.

I strode through the lobby door and back into the hallway where Easton and Drake stood over a motionless Aaron. I lurched into a sprint as panic filled my lungs. Had they killed him? Even after I made them swear they wouldn't?

"Relax, Sweetheart," Easton cooed with a grin as he hefted the male siren up. "He's just knocked out."

One deep breath later, I nodded and led them over to the storage room door, which had been painted again and again, the same shitty shade of battleship gray. There were two locks on the old metal rectangle. One was a high-tech laser scanner for special Mage Police ID cards. And one for the old-fashioned skeleton key I'd just thrust into the lock. With a slow twist, the lock popped. And because it was Shelly's key, and the pixie couldn't carry both a keycard and her skeleton key in her small form, the light on the laser scanner automatically turned green. The heavy door creaked open like a piece of rusty playground equipment, and we scuttled inside, locking it behind us.

As soon as I had the opportunity to drop the glamour, I damn well did, but it didn't stop the itch. I immediately started scratching, raking layers of skin off as I dug and dug to soothe the annoying burn.

"What's wrong, Dollface?" Drake mocked as he removed the expandable pouch from his belt. "Catch some fleas from your animal lovers?"

"Fuck you, you over-sized dragon dildo."

I struggled with my lavender top before throwing it over my head and onto the floor. Drake and Easton's jaws both dropped as they stared at my bare breasts like two teenage boys who'd never seen a rack in real life. I dug my nails into the meat of my flesh, dragging the tips all over my exposed skin.

"What are you staring at?" I snapped. I then fumbled with my black skinny jeans, struggling to drag them down my curvaceous hips. Fuck that rumor about fae being shapeless. "Get the supplies you need and do it fast. We have no idea when Aaron's going to wake up."

I pointed at the unconscious man in question as he lay haphazardly on the concrete floor before getting back to scratching. I hit a spot that made my leg want to twitch like a dog's. *Yes.*

Easton's pale blue gaze drug up and down my body with painstaking slowness as he bit his bottom lip. "Fucker better not wake up with you looking like this."

I clawed at my thighs as I chuckled. "Is my mate feeling jealous of my best friend's hubby?"

"You mate is feeling like fucking the itch right out of you on the storeroom floor," Easton muttered, taking a few healthy steps my way before Drake whacked him in the back of the head with the pouch.

"Goldilocks, focus! Let's get the supplies and get the fuck out of here. I don't wanna creep around the lion's den any longer than we have to."

Easton rolled his eyes before he turned around and followed Drake to a shelf full of potion bottles, muttering about mates and sex and bullshit. They made quick work of snatching every single item in sight, moving from shelf to shelf with unnerving efficiency. No vial, tablet, booklet, bottle, pouch, or jar was left behind. All the while, they each stole hasty glances my way.

I didn't quite get how they managed to pocket every item without any glass shattering on the floor due to their distraction. From Easton, the sideways glances didn't really surprise me. He'd made it blatantly obvious how he felt about me recently. But Drake... I was intrigued at the number of times I caught him staring. For someone who supposedly hated me, he didn't seem too upset by the sight of my naked body.

By the time they were finished, I was almost itch-free, so I put my clothes back on.

"Oh, come on," Easton grumbled, clearly miffed that he'd lost his chance to do me on the dirty floor. Not that my scratching would have allowed for much pleasure or touching.

Aaron groaned from his spot on the floor, his legs barely dragging across the floor as he slowly came to. In one swift motion, Drake bent down, reared his arm back, and punched the siren right in the side of the head. He was back out like a light.

Instead of being appalled at the scaly Neanderthal for knocking out one of my friends—again—I was fucking stunned to find I admired his competence and efficiency. I bit my bottom lip as I worked that thought over in my mind. Why in the name of god would I ever admire a damn thing about Drake 'The Shadow' Guerra? He was an asshole and we hated one another. Plus, I was literally mated to his pack brothers, so what the fuck was that?

His fingers as he shook out his punch should have

been the last thing on my mind. His lips as they curled into a smug grin shouldn't have enticed me. And his cock, as it jumped in his pants under my steely gaze, definitely shouldn't have gotten me hot and bothered.

Easton cleared his throat, jolting me from my embarrassing thoughts like a night terror. I rushed to the door and fumbled with the lock once more, rattling the stupid thing in my quavering grasp.

"I have a theory," Easton said as he bent down to pick up Aaron once more.

"I don't want to hear it." Drake smiled sarcastically as he re-buckled the magical expansion-spelled pouch at his waist. It jangled and clanked with all the potions now inside it.

Easton sighed. "Well, you're going to anyway. You know how Bodie and I both have a mate bond with Aubry, even though that shouldn't be possible for a bear and a wolf?"

Drake scratched at the dark stubble on his chin and shot Easton a mocking smile. "Why no, Goldilocks, do tell me more." Then his gaze shot over to me. "And for fuck's sake, Dollface, just get the key in the lock. It's not that hard, I can assure you."

Thoughts of Drake putting his ginormous dragon-sized key in my lock filled me with lust and caused my hands to shake even more.

Get it together, Aubry! You're acting like a witless preteen, preening over every ounce of pathetic attention you get. You're a badass independent woman, mated to two sexy-

*as-sin shifters, and you are not in any way shape or form
attracted to the Night Fury over there.*

Images of the kid's movie danced around in my
head and I remembered the Light Fury and the cute
little dragon babies they'd had. Drake was dark; I was
light...

Oh, fuck no. No way in hell was I about to imagine
that.

I thrust the key into the hole and twisted, doing my
damnedest not to think dirty thoughts as I did so. As
soon as we shut and locked the storage room behind
us, Easton lowered Aaron onto the floor of the back
entrance of the precinct, in the rarely used hall, and I
tucked the skeleton key into his pocket. He looked all
sorts of conspicuous, but as long as we got out of there
before he woke up or someone found him, then I didn't
really give a shit.

We slipped from the building and clung to the
shadows created by the foliage nearby, sidestepping
around the edge of the parking lot once more. When
we were in the clear, we speed walked down the
cracked sidewalk and all but jumped into the old
mustang Drake had procured for our outing. He fired
up the engine, threw the stick shift into drive, and
peeled out onto the street like it was nothing more
than a greased-up slip-n-slide.

Easton, who was sitting shotgun while I peered
between their headrests from the back, hadn't
forgotten what he'd been saying back at the precinct.

"You know the one race I know of that can have multiple mates?" he asked us.

Drake remained silent, while I wished I'd paid just a bit more attention during shifter biology and sociology.

"Dragons," Easton finished with a smug grin. "It's not uncommon for a valor to share a female amongst themselves."

Drake glanced at him before returning his eyes to the road. "That's cute and all, Goldilocks, but I'm the one who had a valor, not you or Bodie. And I don't have a valor to speak of anymore, anyway. So, your point is... well, pointless."

Easton lightly smacked his friend's bicep to get his attention. "Yeah, but there's where you're wrong. I think you do have a valor. I think Bodie and I are a part of your clan. I think we filled that void in your life, and you became our alpha."

Dead silence reigned until Drake shifted and gunned it. The roar of the engine filled my ears. Street-lights started to flick on as night set in, and they were as blurry outside the window as my thoughts were inside my head.

Holy shit. Is that even possible? Psychologically, it didn't seem too far-fetched, but as the implications of what Easton suggested hit home in my mind, my jaw dropped to the floor.

Drake's eyes met mine in the rear-view mirror.

"Shut your face, Doll, before I give you something to fill it. "

"See?" Easton said, as if Drake's raunchy threat was somehow proof of them having a valor. "You have all this sexual tension." Then he turned back to look at me. "You said he was emitting sex hormones or something?"

Drake scoffed. "As if that's actually a thing."

"Right," Easton agreed with a grin. "I think it was your alpha power. Don't think I didn't notice that she didn't bow back at the warehouse. Who can resist that? Only an alpha's ma—"

"Easton!" Drake shouted, gripping the wheel tightly. "Fucking drop it! She didn't bow because she's a stubborn asshole hellbent on defying me. She's not my mate because it's magically fucking impossible. And you two are not a part of my valor because I don't have a fucking valor, and even if I did, you two are not dragons."

Oh my god, oh my god, oh my god...

No matter what bullshit spewed from Drake's angry lips, I couldn't un-see the logic in Easton's words. Drake had lost his valor as a boy—when Citrine had murdered his entire family. Easton had left his pack. Bodie technically still had his though. But... even he mostly deferred to Drake. And the way all the different shifter kids had come to the guys' hideout... it seemed like Drake was treated like the alpha no matter the type of shifter.

And it was obvious to any outsider that the three guys had bonded and basically formed their own three-man-pack. But what if it wasn't actually a pack? What if it was a valor? *Could I be Bodie's mate... Easton's mate... and... my heart beat fast... Drake's mate?*

My head spun at such an unfathomable idea, and yet... it made so much sense. Too much sense to just ignore it.

Maybe I should force him to kiss me? Just once. Just so we know for sure?

"It makes sense," Easton continued. He was hesitant but pushing through his discomfort in order to try and make Drake see. "How else would Bodie and I—"

"You know what?" Drake asked sarcastically as he jabbed the mustang's radio dial. "Let's just listen to some music and shut the hell up. It's been a long few days, we just had an incredibly successful afternoon after an absolutely horrific morning, and your nerves are shot. I think we need to just... chill."

Country music began blaring through the speakers. Whoever used this car before us definitely did not share my taste in genre. Drake's either, apparently, because he jabbed the little button on the right and the channels started scanning. We bypassed some heavy metal, reggae, and pop and eventually landed on some bass-pumping rap.

I'd never really pegged Drake as the rap-listening type, but he was such a gangster that it totally fit.

We rolled up to Pacific City Bank in Skid Row a

few minutes later, making sure to drive past and park a few blocks down in a public parking lot. Drake would probably make sure the car was gone at first light, anyway. He was so damned efficient. I found myself staring at his broad shoulders as he walked ahead of us, the muscles of his back rolling beneath his shirt, and Easton's words once more flitted about my head like sparrows on the verge of spring.

Could he seriously be my mate? What the hell was Bodie going to think when he came back and heard the news? Would he be pissed? Surprised? Jealous? Or would he help us prove the theory wrong, making me feel stupid for ever believing it could be real? My stomach curled into knots at all the possibilities.

We entered the bank from the back, because it had closed a few hours before. The shifter manager was a friend of Drake's, and he let us in. We followed him down a set of granite stairs to the sub-level, "the underground," where there were meeting rooms, a singular teller station for magicals, but most of all where there was a huge vault sprawled out like a beached whale. Inside, shifters of all shapes and sizes were unrolling sleeping bags and fluffing children's pillows. They passed around red solo cups and shared containers of microwavable mac and cheese. It was like a hidden shifter refugee camp. And as sad as it was, it was also uplifting to see them coming together like that.

We stepped inside and wandered through the

groups of people, checking on them before we left to deposit our new weapons.

"Drake." An elderly woman with cropped hair hugged Drake around the waist. He stiffened at first, but eventually gave in and patted her back.

She repeated her hug with Easton, and then, to my surprise, with me. "Aubry, thank you. You brought my granddaughter back to us, so she can be laid to rest."

She latched onto my hand and pulled me over to her family, where I recognized the mother of the little girl who'd loved Elsa. I gave a thin, awkward smile, feeling like an intruder. But each and every one of them hugged me, until my right shoulder was soaked with tears.

"Please, sit," the older woman, clearly the matriarch, gestured toward a closed cooler. I sat down on the lid. "I'm Naissa. This is my family."

Two men in the corner squatted over a portable camping stove. The butane burner flickered under-neath as one of the men chopped toppings and the other handed out omelets around the circle.

"What do you like in your omelets?" Naissa asked, her leathery face crinkling in a smile.

"Oh, um... " My eyes scanned the room for the guys. But Easton and Drake were busy answering questions from shifters who were sprouting all kinds of fur in their agitation and anger. They were going to be occu-pied for a while.

"Um, just plain ham and cheese," I responded, opting to keep it simple.

Naissa patted my hand and then settled on top of a moving box next to my cooler. "I'm glad to see that someone besides Larry is finally seeing the way of things."

I didn't bother to tell her that I'd needed to be kidnapped in order to start changing my mind. Because, ultimately, what really mattered was that she was right.

"What do you do for a living?" I asked, trying to change the subject.

Naissa laughed. "I make custom pinatas for birthday parties for the rich and famous."

My eyebrows shot up. I tried to imagine that job. After being MP, running on adrenaline 24/7, that sounded like a vacation.

"It's a family business, Nana. Don't act like you do it alone," one of the men manning the stove piped up. He grinned over at Naissa and wiggled his thick, bushy brows.

"Didn't say I did, now did I?" Naissa teased back.

The guy turned to me. "I'm Zane, the tyrant lady's son, and I—"

"*Oh*, next time we shift, I'm gonna tug your tail, boy!" Naissa exclaimed. "Tyrant. *Psshh*. If I had a dollar for every time I coddled your furry ass, I'd have—"

"A million bucks!" everyone around the circle chorused and burst into laughter.

They all exchanged light-hearted smiles, and a sense of relaxed camaraderie washed over me. Conversation had *never* been anything like this in *my* house. Was this what family was like for shifters?

I glanced around the room. Tears were met with hugs. Jokes were met with laughter. No one stood alone. Not even Drake-the-Dick. It was the exact opposite of every experience I'd had with fae royalty, where I'd felt like a lone swimmer surrounded by sharks.

I ate my omelet in contented silence and listened to the shifters share stories with a wistful smile on my face. When I was finished, I turned and clasped Naissa's hands. "Thank you."

"No, thank *you*," she replied.

I gave her a genuine smile. "Of course."

Then I stood and started to make my way toward Drake and Easton, who were still talking with shifters on the far side of the vault. I had nearly reached them, when I paused near a group of about eight squirrel shifters—in squirrel form—sitting in a single lawn chair in front of a tablet propped up against a sneaker to achieve the proper viewing angle.

I glanced down to see what they were watching. On the screen, was a reporter—the same fucking bitch I'd popped in the mouth earlier that day. Guess I hadn't hit her hard enough if she could cover the mark up with makeup. I glared as I watched her and found myself shuffling closer despite myself.

The newscaster said, in a faux serious voice, "The murder of Indigo Summerset still remains an open investigation for the Mage Police..."

My brain hollowed out and her voice slowed into near silence.

Did she just say... Indigo Summerset... the King of the Los Angeles Fae... *my father*... was dead? Murdered?

I was numb. Instantly and completely. The only thing I could feel was the racing of my heart, like a hummingbird on crack. Is that what a heart attack felt like? Was I going to fucking keel over at any moment?

The woman continued to speak in her snooty, news anchor voice, but for me, everything slowed down... her voice dropped and deepened, and my vision flickered, her face losing color, like I was watching a slow-motion scene in a black and white film.

"The dragon shifter known as 'The Shadow' is the main suspect."

My lips parted and my eyes burst open wide, my petrified gaze traveling over to Drake on autopilot. Our eyes locked like a set of handcuffs, my furious glare pinning his remorseful stare down like the criminal it was. The criminal *he* was.

And suddenly... I knew the truth.

Drake had killed my father.

8

AUBRY

I WASN'T A SHIFTER, BUT IT FELT LIKE MY HEART WAS howling brokenly at the moon.

My father is dead.

The words didn't feel real. Until, suddenly, they did.

My world stopped. No. It spun. Like a tornado. Like I'd been lifted into the air and pummeled with debris; slammed in the heart by a fucking two-by-four or something.

As I stared up at Drake, I watched his eyes morph from dark blue to pure gold as he looked right back at me. Smoke drifted out of his mouth; black scales erupted on his arms. He took a step backward, away from me, like he was worried I was going to attack.

"I was just trying to get a mage jewel," he admitted, as if that somehow explained it all. As if that simple fact made this whole thing okay.

It felt like I was listening through cotton, because

his words didn't penetrate. I had to repeat them inside my head before I understood.

He'd gone to my parents' house... to take the mage jewel my father guarded for the council... and then he'd killed my father.

"Is that why you said we had to leave the cabin?" Easton asked. There was a hardness to his tone that my cracked heart appreciated.

But I didn't hear a response. I was too busy with my own thoughts. *Drake... the dragon shifter that I almost thought was my—*

The tornado in my mind suddenly stopped spinning, dropping me right out of the air. Every bone in my body shattered as I hit the ground. It was like I ceased to exist.

The blonde woman on the screen leaned forward to showcase her plastic cleavage as she said, "The manhunt for the shifter responsible continues. Mage Police are offering a ten-thousand-dollar reward for any information—"

A couple of the squirrel shifters spit at the screen.

I just sank slowly onto the cheap industrial carpet. I stared at a gum stain, which was fitting. Something bright and delicious had been smashed flat, stepped on, and turned black. Just like me.

My mother's anger suddenly made so much more sense. No wonder she was flinging wild accusations at me. Turned out, she wasn't quite as delusional as I'd thought.

I hardly noticed when Drake shut off the tablet, because I had already stood. I was already running. Out of the vault, through the hallway, and into a tiny office space at the end. Once I hit that dead end, I just stared at the wall.

Easton had apparently followed me; he slipped into the room behind me before shutting the door.

"Oh, Aubry." He sat down on the edge of a desk and reached for me, scooping me up with one giant hand and plopping me sideways onto his lap. Careful not to crush my wings, my mate wrapped me up in a hug.

It was the hug that broke me. The dam I had erected years ago that separated mind and emotions, that carefully meted out appropriate amounts of smiles and laughter, seriousness and sadness, broke. Everything came bursting forth at once. I sobbed into Easton's shoulder, clutching him close.

"I hate him. I hate him!" I screamed into Easton's neck.

"*Shh*, sweetheart. I know. I know."

I cried and I ranted into his neck, feeling sick, feeling evil. Because deep down, I knew it wasn't my father's death that made me sad—the man and I had barely been on speaking terms. But Drake's betrayal... That's what gutted me.

I clutched Easton closer. I wanted to climb into his body and escape mine. I didn't want to feel... this.

"I want to leave."

Easton hugged me tighter, but he didn't say a word.

My sobs eventually slowed, and I swiped at the wet mess my face had become. I took a few deep breaths before turning to Easton with a composed face. "I want to leave."

He stared at me, conflicted, eyes wide and unsure. "I know you're upset…"

I pushed off from his lap and stood, glancing around the meeting room for an exit. "I want to leave *now*."

"Aubry, there's nowhere safe we can go."

I shook my head. "I don't care."

"Well, *I* do. *Bodie* does. You want to leave, but we can't guarantee your safety out there."

"I'm not a fucking child, East."

"I know," he growled, standing and shoving his hands into his pockets. "I'm not trying to tell you what to do. I'm trying to tell you—"

"What I already know? That it's *never* gonna be safe." I gave a raw, bitter laugh as I strode toward the door.

Easton's hand on my wrist stopped me. "Wait, Aubs. Where do you wanna go?" His voice cracked. "This… damn it, this is the worst fucking time."

"Yeah, sorry it's so *inconvenient* for you that Drake murdered my father!" I yelled.

"That's not what I meant," Easton sighed, sounding way too fucking reasonable. I didn't want reasonable. I wanted to fight.

"Where the fuck is Bodie?" I growled.

He'd fight me. Or maybe he'd fight Drake on my behalf.

Easton looked crushed by my question. "Aubry…"

My stomach clenched at the thought that I'd hurt him. I didn't want him to think I was rejecting him. But I needed more aggression than he was giving me.

Drake shoved open the door and shut it carefully behind him. Then he walked up to me.

"I'm sorry."

My fist flew out and smashed his chin. *Fucking hell!* Was his chin made of iron? My entire arm hurt— fingers, wrist, and forearm. But I didn't stop. I gave him an uppercut, and then a kick to the stomach.

He didn't even flinch.

"Fight back," I sneered.

"No."

"Fight the fuck back!" I roundhoused that mother-fucker in the gut. It was satisfying to finally hear him groan and watch him double over in pain. But not as satisfying as it would have been if he'd tried to punch me and I got the upper hand.

I shook my head and dropped my stance, like I was too disgusted with him to continue. I walked toward Easton, who stood off to Drake's side. But as soon as I passed the dragon, my hand lashed out like a snake. I fluttered my wings and jumped as I landed a karate chop straight on his Adam's apple.

Drake's eyes flared gold and scales crawled over his skin.

"Come on, dragon, don't you wanna wipe out my entire family just like that bitch did yours?" I cut him deep, not caring what it took, just needing the fight.

Drake came at me with a roar.

Brutal victory coursed through me as he slammed me into the wall.

Yes.

But a second later, Easton ripped him off me and shoved his body between us.

"Get the fuck out, Drake!" he yelled. His eyes were golden, and his teeth had elongated. Soft, caramel-colored bear ears poked out of his hair, looking so fucking ridiculous that I couldn't help but give a snort.

He turned to me with a question in his eyes. Pretty sure he was questioning my sanity, actually.

"It looks like you're wearing a little girl's headband." I gestured toward his ears as a laugh bubbled out of me, one that quickly dissolved into tears. With it, my desire to fight dissolved too.

Easton's ears returned to normal as he scooped me up again, cuddling me close and planting soft kisses on my forehead. He made his way to a small meeting table in the corner, pulled out a chair, and sat down with me on his lap. He caressed my back and murmured sweet nonsense into my hair. I reclined against him, just soaking up his gentle strength.

I heard the door open and shut, knowing Drake had left us.

I didn't have the energy to call out after him. I

wasn't even sure what I wanted to say. Did I want to insult him? Hurt him? Apologize? Or cry and ask him to hold me? I closed my eyes and decided not to decide. I wouldn't think about Drake.

"I still want to leave."

"Let's wait 'til Bodie gets back, sweetheart." Easton tilted my head up and kissed my cheek. "We don't want to worry him."

I nodded vaguely, staring off into the distance, which wasn't far. We were underground, so I couldn't even stare out a window. Instead, I played with Easton's hair and tried not to think about real life. I focused hard and was finally able to point my thoughts in a different direction.

"Easton?"

"Yeah?"

"If you'd actually been trying to pick me up at the bar that night, I would have gone home with you," I said, wishing things were different.

It was like the sun had risen on his face; his smile was so bright. "If I could change things, I would totally have gone home with you that night. And every night after."

I giggled. "I don't think I'd be able to walk straight if it was *every* night."

"Who needs to walk straight when you've got wings, right?" He grinned and pulled me close, snuggling his face into my neck.

"Definitely not me."

"That's the spirit." Easton pulled back and planted a chaste kiss on my lips, studying my eyes intently.

"Don't do that," I scolded. "We're playing make-believe. We are not dealing with reality right now."

He sighed before a mischievous grin slid onto his slips and his eyes darkened. "Okay. I'm making believe there's nobody else in this building and I can just lay you back on this table, spread your thighs apart, and—"

The door swung open, cutting off the naughty things Easton was about to say. I swiveled in his lap, surprised to see a little girl come striding in like she owned the place. She had wild black ringlets that sprang when she walked, and I immediately recognized her from babysitting. El Fuego's little cousin, Mariana.

"I wanna cheese stick!" the shifter girl whined. "Where's the kitchen?"

Her mother hurried in after her, scooping her up. She glanced over at us and bowed her head toward Easton. "Sorry. Sorry. She just… ran." She scolded the little girl in her arms. "I already told you, Mija, there are no cheese sticks here."

"But I want one."

"Well, we don't have any," her mother replied with the patience of a fucking saint.

"Then let's go get some."

"It's not safe to leave," her mother's voice cracked. "Remember how I told you Lucien got… *hurt?*" Her chest heaved and her eyes closed.

She didn't mean hurt. She meant gone. She just didn't know how to say it yet.

The make-believe that Easton and I had started up quickly swept away, and reality came crashing down on me like a violent, twenty-foot wave. I'd lost my dad, sure. But this woman had lost her *son*. I could see the agony ripple across her expression like lightning, though she tried to hide it from her daughter.

Had she even gotten a chance to cry?

I stood, swooped forward, and held out my hand to the little girl, shoving aside my own pain. "You're Mariana, right?"

"You remembered," the little girl said, smiling at me. "And you're Aubry."

"I am," I replied with a warm smile. "Can I help you on your cheese stick quest? Your mama looks a little tired. Like she could use a rest in here."

I gestured toward the door, and Easton was at my back a second later. "I'll help too. Bears are great at sniffing out cheese."

"No, they aren't!" Mariana giggled, scrunching her nose and pointing at him. "*Mice* are good at sniffing cheese!"

"Nuh-uh," Easton shook his head. "Bet I can sniff out some cheese faster than you can!" He partially shifted again so his bear ears popped out.

Mariana and I both giggled. She squirmed out of her mom's grasp and mine and then darted down the hall, laughing.

Easton stomped after, playfully sticking his arms out like Frankenstein's monster and yelling, "Cheese! Cheese!"

Seeing how good he was with her made my heart crack a little. Easton deserved so much better than this. All the shifters did.

I turned to Mariana's mother. "Take a minute for yourself."

The woman grasped my hand, tears already slipping from her eyes. "Thank you."

I nodded as I closed the door behind me and went after Easton. He slid his arm around my shoulder as soon as I joined him, making me feel all warm and fuzzy inside.

I'd stay for a little bit longer… to help with Mariana, and maybe a couple other kids. But as soon as Bodie came back, we were leaving. *If* Bodie came back.

My stomach clenched at that thought.

No, Aubry, don't be stupid. He's the best assassin the shifters have. Just because the mages know his face now doesn't mean they'll miraculously catch him…

So *when* Bodie came back, I wondered if he'd return empty-handed or if he'd have Trite's head on a stick. Last time, he'd returned with Tee in tow… my sassy pixie friend who *still* hadn't woken up.

God, the world was so fucked up right now.

We went upstairs to where more offices littered the back half of the main floor, which was lit for evening, like most businesses in Skid Row, in an attempt to deter thieves. Mariana opened a door and walked into some random room. We followed behind, watching as she dove under the desk, sniffing and announcing, "No cheese here!"

Easton strolled over to casually stand beside a mini-fridge, hoping Mariana would take the oh-so-subtle hint.

"I dunno," he scrunched his face and stared around the room. "If I were cheese, and I was hiding in this room, where would I be?" He looked behind a painting on the wall. "Not here!"

Mariana giggled and headed straight for the mini-fridge, yanking it open. "Here!"

Against all odds, she was in luck. Whoever worked in this office had apples and cheese sticks in their mini-fridge. A health nut.

Mariana tried to take four, but Easton told her she could only have one. After a brief bout of pouting, she happily munched on her cheese as we made our way back to the vault in the basement.

Shifter families were settling down for the night beneath the gleam of flashlights that glinted off safe deposit boxes. Mariana found her dad and waved at us before skipping off.

I turned to Easton, asking softly, "Is there any way we can check on Bodie?"

East stared at me for a minute. Then he sighed. "Sure. I'll be right back."

Not a minute later, he returned and led me to the stairs, handing me a burner phone.

"You can text him. I'm sure he's gonna want to know you're ok, too. But there are rules. One text per burner, so even if he replies, you can't text him again. Also, you have to make it sound like a business transaction. Nothing obvious. I'll give you some space."

I wanted to roll my eyes. Fucking Drake and his stupid fucking rules.

But, at the same time, that fork-tongued lizard had kept my guys alive thus far. Hidden and safe thus far. And I didn't want to ruin that.

So I sat on the steps, thinking long and hard before I typed my message.

I wrote: *Your pie is hot and ready for pickup.*

I waited. And waited. But Bodie didn't text back.

Nervously, I wandered up the stairs and into the office where Larry had deposited Tee's cat carrier. The room was empty, aside from the sleeping pixie. God, why hadn't she woken up?

And why hadn't Bodie texted me back?

I glanced from the cage down to the burner phone in my hand, squeezing the hard plastic case in worry and fear until my knuckles were white. My stomach twisted itself into knots, and my heart pounded out an irregular rhythm, as I stared at the blank screen before me.

I leaned into the wall behind me and slowly sank to the floor.

My mate bond twinged. It felt stretched tight. The shifters might know what a mate bond stretch felt like because they and all their family members had mates, but I didn't. The other magical beings who'd had mate bonds for years might feel secure, but I didn't. Fae rarely got mates. And I'd only just learned to treasure mine. I didn't know what these feelings meant. Any little twinge set me on edge.

Bodie was out there trying to find a psychopath. And he wasn't answering his phone.

Please be okay, Bodie, I thought in desperation. *Please…*

9

EASTON

TWO DAYS HAD PASSED. *TWO* BURNER PHONES MELTED into a puddle in Aubry's fiery palm because Bodie didn't respond. She and Drake didn't acknowledge one another unless absolutely necessary—being in a room with the pair of them felt like walking on a tightrope over Niagara Falls—*too* much stress.

I knew I had no chance of making Drake ease up. I could see the guilt and the fury that hit his eyes whenever he thought about someone he'd killed. On the surface, he acted like it didn't affect him. But inside, I knew he wasn't like Bodie. He couldn't shrug it off. Life meant something to him. All life. Maybe having his family ripped away when he was young did that. I didn't know. All I knew was that he would focus on the shifters even more and avoid Aubry whenever possible.

Drake stayed busy. On the flip side of things, Aubry had become nearly a statue. I didn't know if it was because she was worried about Bodie, worried about her friend Tee—the pink-haired pixie still hadn't woken up and Larry had no idea why—or if she was still reeling from her father's death.

No matter what the cause, I needed to do something about it. As her mate, it was my job to make sure she was taken care of and happy. And I felt like I was failing. It was a horrible feeling.

So I spent every spare moment I had—which wasn't much considering how worried and freaked out all the other shifters were—working on a surprise.

When it was ready, I went and found her in the bank manager's office. That's where Tee's cat carrier lived. Aubry had made a habit of sitting on the floor beside Tee and just staring at the beige wall blankly.

My heart gave a painful squeeze. I hated seeing that empty look on my Spitfire. From the moment we'd met, Aubry had been full of sass and attitude. Now... I was gonna help her get it back.

"Come on," I said, taking her hand in mine. I loved how small and delicate her fingers were. "I have a surprise for you." I helped her stand, then I brushed back her soft, pale hair and kissed her gently.

"A surprise?" Aubry questioned with a raised brow as I led her up the bank stairs.

She gave me a shy smile, one of those sweet grins that melted my heart, the grins she saved only for me.

"You looked like you could use a pick-me-up." I shouldn't have used that phrase because instantly, I imagined the last time we'd fucked, how I'd picked sweet Aubry up, shoved her against the wall and slid inside that hot wet pussy. I scolded my dick like it was a dog; we weren't here to just give Aubry sex, she could get that from Bodie, but what she couldn't get from anyone else... was romance. Adoration. I started to sweat.

What if she didn't like it? I mean, we'd researched her. I wasn't an idiot. I knew she was into kink and stuff. But part of me wondered if that was because she had never formed a real connection with anyone before.

I wanted to be that for her.

I wanted it so badly that my stomach was tying itself in knots.

I tried not to let my hands or voice shake as I pushed open the door to the bank's lobby. The lights were off and the windows were covered in plastic. We'd set up a "Closed for Refurbishment" sign outside.

"Are we leaving the bank?" Aubry asked, hopefully.

I scrunched my nose. *Damn it!* Should I have tried harder to get this date somewhere else? Was she going to start off disappointed? My stomach dropped. "Sorry, it's not safe. Plus, you know Drake..." If he thought we'd compromised this location, he'd fucking nail me to the wall. Maybe even literally. Drake hated murder and torture after the fact, but in the moment...

"Fuck Drake," Aubry spat with a glower.

Great. I'd said the D-word. I'd promised myself I

wouldn't say the goddamned D-word and ruin her mood. *Good start, East. Just great.*

I led Aubry across the shiny tiles of the bank's lobby and into a corridor behind the teller desk. There were a few closed doors on each side of the hall, but near the end, on the left, a single door stood ajar. The delicious aroma of Vietnamese cuisine filled the air. I glanced back at Aubry. Could she smell it? I could never tell with non-shifter noses.

It was a sucker punch to my heart when her face lost that dull look and lit up. "Oh my god, you ordered my favorite takeout. I might love you forever."

Those words. Did she even realize she'd said them? My heart rate doubled, and my neck got hot. Those words were everything. My bear wanted to come out and wrap her in a hug. But I knew she hadn't really meant love. Not yet. Because I hadn't earned it.

But I would.

I grabbed both her hands just outside the big door. "It's not takeout. Homemade by yours truly. And I wasn't sure if you were ready to heave the big L word around already—"

She groaned and her cheeks turned an adorable shade of pink. "Damn it, I knew you'd pick up on that."

I lifted her hand and kissed the back of her knuckles. "I'm just going to say that, as my mate, you're kinda stuck with me forever. But I want to make sure you mean that L-word next time you say it."

She giggled nervously. "*You* know how to make Vietnamese?"

"Spitfire, I know how to make anything. Bears love to *eat*." I winked, making sure she caught my innuendo as I pushed open the door and led her into a big meeting room equipped with at least a dozen chairs, a big smart board on the left hand side of the wall, a flat screen TV on the right hand wall, and large floor to ceiling windows in between—all of which were drawn shut.

On one side of the grandiose meeting table sat an array of steaming dishes and a portable stove top typically used by recreational campers, which I'd borrowed. And on the right, was a makeshift dinner for two. A tablecloth had been draped across the end, with two plates and silverware and fancy crystal glasses. A vase of assorted summer roses stood tall in the middle, their red, pink, coral, yellow, and white buds practically bursting with beauty and sweetness. And beside the vase, also in the center of the two plates, sat a tiny flickering candle.

The meeting room screamed romance. I glanced down to see if it was too over the top.

Aubry's eyes were wide. She took a step backward. *Oh fuck. She hates it.*

"I can get rid of the flowers," I said in a rush.

Damn it, were summer fae opposed to cut flowers? Why the fuck didn't I know the answer to that?

"No. I just..." Her eyes welled up. "Thank you."

Her gratitude was soft and genuine, and she actually seemed quite touched. Exactly what I'd been going for. I gave a sigh of relief before I led her inside and shut and locked the door behind us. "I'm not gonna let any cheese hunters interrupt our date," I explained.

Aubry's eyes flickered with desire. "Oh, is this date gonna be rated something worse than PG?"

Damn. I loved that naughty look on her face. But instead of answering, I flicked on the smart board. An online radio station pulled up and started playing. Of course, the song was "Let's Get It On."

"This is a station. I didn't pick that," I told her.

She laughed. "Sure, Goldilocks." But the skip in her step as she made her way to our seats told me that her mood had picked up. She was having a good time.

The tension in my chest started to unravel.

I grinned and bit my bottom lip as I followed her and tried not to ogle her ass. I pulled out the chair for her and she sat.

"I feel like I should have changed clothes," she said, glancing down at the off-shoulder t-shirt she wore and the distressed skinny jeans with rips all up the thighs. Rips that showed delicious hints of her creamy skin. Rips that I wanted to make wider.

I smiled as I strode to the other side of the table and began serving her. "You crazy? You look gorgeous no matter what you're wearing. Besides, I don't plan on you wearing anything for very long."

Her intake of breath and the way she squeezed her

thighs together let me know she liked the dirty talk. Good. I'd keep it up.

I scooped us some pho into two wide bowls and then arranged the sides between the two of us so we could share. Aubry leaned forward and inhaled deeply. "You know, this reminds me of childhood."

"Yeah?" I asked as I took my seat opposite of her.

She gave a little smile. "We had a Vietnamese maid. She'd make me stuff when my parents were out of town."

"They travel a lot?"

She nodded. And I could see the ghosts creeping back into her eyes. I had to banish them. So I said, "Hope you don't mind double dipping," as I placed a napkin on my lap. "I'm totally a double dipper."

The line did the trick. Aubry's eyes cleared and she raised a seductive brow. "You can *double dip* whatever you want when it comes to me, Papa Bear."

Oh fuck. That nickname went straight to my dick. The sounds swirled around and surrounded it like a cock ring. I was instantly hard as a rock.

My eyes became hooded. She wanted to play like that? Okay. I was game. "I plan on dipping all sorts of things, Spitfire. My fingers... My tongue... My cock... But first... I'm going to dip my meat in this sauce." I plucked a strip of beef off a plate and dunked it in the bowl of broth. I let my tongue come out, lapping the juice off before drawing the bite into my mouth.

Holy fucking hell, it was hot in here.

"I'll give you something juicy to dip your meat into..." Aubry smiled and leaned back in her seat, tracing a finger down her cleavage.

I nearly fucking choked. Damn. We needed to slow down or I was gonna blow my wad just listening to her. We ate for a while in companionable silence before I had calmed down enough to introduce a new topic.

"Tell me something about you I probably don't already know."

Aubry studied me for a minute before she said, "You know I used to be engaged right?"

My throat tightened at that. I vaguely remembered something about a high profile break up, maybe. But hearing her say it made my bear tremble with both fear and possessiveness. Damn it. Did I want to spend my date talking about her damn ex? Why would she bring that up? "I don't know any details."

"He wasn't my mate. It was gonna be an arranged marriage. Fae like to do that shit with their royals for some reason. I liked his mom though, so at least there was that."

I nodded, unsure where this was going, unsure if I wanted to hear or to stop this. But listening... that wasn't something Bodie was good at. It was something I could give her to take care of her. And maybe my mate needed to get something off her chest. I could do that. I could listen. Even if it was painful.

Aubry licked her lips and swirled her spoon around in her soup for a minute before she said, "He cheated."

She gave a harsh laugh. "I should have expected it, given the arrangement. But you know what he told me about why? It wasn't 'marriage of convenience' or 'we should both get some on the side.'" Her hands turned to fists as she set them on the tabletop and tried to rein in her hurt.

I wanted to reach out and pluck her from her seat and pull her onto my lap. But I could sense she needed to finish this and get it out.

"Gerrard told me that he cheated because I was a robotic workaholic without a scrap of love to give." She shook her head then stared down at the soup. "Fuck. I've always wondered if he was right. Suspected it even. But look, this is proof. You did this huge, sweet, romantic thing and I ruined it." Tears filled her soft brown eyes.

I stood and went over to kneel next to her chair. Even kneeling, she was so small and petite that we were almost face to face. I cupped her cheek in my hand. "Not ruined. Never ruined."

I had to shove down the rage I felt at some asshole fae who could just discard my precious mate. The animal side of me wanted to gut him with my claws and lift him in the air with my hand still inside his stomach. I suddenly knew how Bodie could kill without remorse. But the mate bond told me that I needed to suppress my rage and comfort Aubry. She was more important. "He's wrong, you know. What you did for Bodie a couple days ago? That… that was love. Staying here even after you found out about your dad, so you could help us... that's love, Aubry. It's not all flowers and poetry and pretty words. Love is sacrifice. And if he couldn't see that, he was an idiot. Can I also add that I think his head would look great stuffed and mounted on my wall?'

Aubry let out a peal of laughter. Then I started to laugh too. Any time either of us stopped, we'd make eye contact and start all over again. It gave me the best feeling ever, like I was walking on air and shooting sunbeams out of my fingertips. I'd made her feel better.

My sweet mate laughed until tears came to her eyes and she swiped at them.

I wanted to cheer her up even more. I didn't want this giddy feeling to end. I rubbed her knee for a second as I said, "I have a surprise." Then I stood and strolled over to a side table. I blew out a breath, stupidly nervous all over again.

"I thought the dinner *was* the surprise?" she asked curiously.

"Nope."

There was a coffee maker on the table, some plastic cups, a jug of sparkling water, and... a tiny gift box wrapped with a bow. It was small enough to be a diamond ring. I hoped she didn't freak out about that. On the flip side, I hoped she wasn't disappointed that it wasn't that.

"Don't tell me you can wrap gifts and cook." Her tone was wry.

"You can't?" I asked with a grin. "Just kidding. I had one of the shifter grannies help me wrap this."

Her grin looked tight as I handed her the box. "What is it?"

"Open it and see."

I sat down across from her once more and folded my hands in front of my face, sinking my chin down onto my hands, both elbows resting gently on the table.

She cocked her head and exhaled a shaky breath. "Okay..."

I held my breath as she peeled the paper, slowly at first, hesitantly, but eventually she got impatient and just ripped it off like a Band-Aid—kind of like the way I'd prefer to rip off her clothing.

She didn't breathe at all as she flipped the lid and opened the black velvet box.

I was terrified and at the same time so excited to see her response.

She plucked out a pair of earrings from the box and this glorious rainbow of a smile crossed her face. "They're beautiful, Easton. I love them!"

The earrings looked like miniature daggers, but the detail on the blades and hilts were all hand-engraved. It had taken several tries to get them right. She didn't even want to see the pile of mistakes I had hidden in one of the offices.

Now that I knew she loved the gift, I was capable of joking. "Spitfire, you look a little pale. What did you think it was gonna be?"

She leveled me with an unenthused stare. "I think you know damn well what I thought it was going to be. And just for future reference, if you ever do get any crazy ideas about that, you damn well better clear it with me first. I'm not usually a fan of surprises."

I chuckled and leaned back in my chair. "You seemed to enjoy your candle-lit dinner surprise just fine."

She gave me a grudging nod but couldn't help the soft little smile that cropped up.

Goddamn. Her smiles were gonna give me a heart attack. I swear, the fucker in my chest leapt every time she grinned.

"I have enjoyed dinner." She licked her lips and the naughty vixen came out to play. "I'm going to enjoy my dessert just fine, too. But, like… proposals and shit... I don't want that sprung on me. I want it to be a joint effort."

I gave her a knowing smile. "You want every party involved to agree." It made complete sense, after she'd been forced into one engagement that she didn't want to rush into another. And there were three, maybe four of us, if Drake ever pulled his head out of his ass. So… it was a little more complicated. Honestly, I was not in any rush for that part of my life to begin.

I held out my hand. "May I?" She placed the box in my palm and watched as I pulled the earrings out.

"They're special," I told her with a wink. "The backs contain just a pinch of Growth Potion, so you have to be very careful putting them on. But when you remove the earring stem, it's like pulling a plug. And if you drizzle that potion onto the knives... *Voila!* Insta-weapon. That way, you'll always have protection."

Her lips parted in awe and her hand came up to touch my arm over the table. "Easton, did you...?" She shook her head then tried again. "Did you *make* these?"

I smiled wide, staring down, enraptured by how her eyes sparkled in the candlelight. "I *am* a weapons specialist, Princess. Violent gifts are the best kind, aren't they?"

Aubry suddenly stood and grabbed my neck, pulling me across the table. I had to swoop sideways to avoid roses to the face. But it was worth it because she gave me a kiss that left me breathless. When she released me and settled herself back in her seat, she asked, "Is there extra potion? Like, can you show me how it works?"

I nodded. "It only takes a drop, and there are three drops in each earring back. But yeah, Larry has more."

I carefully removed one of the earring backs, which had a dual compartment so that the potion could only be intentionally accessed and wouldn't accidentally drip onto the earrings while my mate was wearing them.

I tilted the earring back ever so slightly until a drop of potion escaped and landed on the blade. Instantly, it stretched in my palm, moving from pea-size to dick-sized—at least, my dick's size, which was a little large. I had to admit, I'd wanted Aubry to think about my dick whenever she held one of my blades in her hand.

The dagger glimmered, reflecting the candlelight off its pristine blade. It gleamed like undisturbed water. The hilt was metallic, but the blade itself appeared to be black as night, a subtle pink glow surrounding it where it lay on my hand.

"East... why is it glowing?"

I pursed my lips before I said, "I may or may not have asked Larry to spell the metal as I was making it. It's imbued with a special Limiting Spell."

Her eyes went wide. "No offense, Honey Bear,"—I smiled at the new term of endearment—Aubry continued, "but I don't really trust Larry's magic as far as I can throw it right now. Tee is still unconscious from his freaking memory wipe. I'm afraid he made her brain-dead or something."

I shook my head. I'd worked side by side with Larry for years. I knew the care he put into his magic. I knew how he fretted over Tee's coma too, and how he worried he might have overdone things on the little pixie. But Aubry didn't need to hear that. There was nothing she or I could do about it right now anyway. So, I said what I could to comfort her. "I'm sure Tee will be fine. Larry tries not to use murder bones in his spells, which makes everything a bit different. Plus, Power Limiting Spells, like the ones on your blades, are Larry's specialty. They're, like, the one thing he's really, exceptionally good at."

My mate pursed her lips and stared at the knife in my hand with distrust. "I suppose..."

I flipped the blade in the air, catching it between my thumb and forefinger before holding the hilt out to Aubry. I couldn't wait to see it in her hands. "Take it. See how it feels."

Hesitantly, she set her napkin on the table then reached out and gripped my knife.

"You like the weight?" I asked. I felt like a kid at Christmas, only, instead of unwrapping presents, her expressions were my gifts.

Aubry bounced her hand up and down, testing the weapon with an experienced hand. The corner of her lip quirked up. "Yeah. It's not too heavy but not so light that I can't bash a fucker's head in. It's perfect."

Yes. Hearing her compliment my weapons was nearly as good as hearing her compliment my cock. But I tried to stay low key. "Sweet. How about the texture?"

She ran her hand along the hilt. I couldn't help but imagine her gripping my dick the same way. Her fingers tightened. "It's smooth, but the vine-like pattern you carved into it gives it grip. Like, I don't think it'll slip in my grasp even if my hands are sweaty."

"How do you like the rosy glow?"

She glanced down at the knife and sighed. "Okay, fine. Tell me about this special Limiting Spell that Larry did."

I reached out and traced my finger up and down the

blade's shaft. Aubry immediately responded, her eyes lighting, lips parting. The air between us grew charged. "With every second it's in contact with the victim's skin," I said in a low whisper, "the blade removes a bit of the victim's magic. Hold it up to someone's throat long enough, and they'll be completely powerless, even if you never cut them." The blade's pull on my magic was just as intense as Aubry's pull on me. I couldn't help but focus on those lips, those soft kissable lips.

She pulled the knife away from my fingers and raised an intrigued brow. "And what if the person has no inherent power?"

I smirked. "Then it's still a sharp as shit blade, and you can slit their fucking throat."

"Perfect," she said breathlessly. Her breasts heaved in her tight little shirt. I could see her nipples start to pebble.

I knew I was fucked up. Talking weapons and violence with Aubry had gotten me so hot. My dick was throbbing and my bear was growling. There was just something so incredibly sexy about a woman with murder in her eyes...

Like I said. *Fucked. Up.*

Aubry set the knife aside and rose from her chair. Then, in a move I didn't expect, she came quickly around the table and dropped down into my lap so that she was straddling my thighs.

Neither of us had to say a word. Our mouths simply

met in perfect harmony, our tongues teasing and stroking one another, just as our hands teased and stroked each other's bodies. There was this delicious push and pull of aggression and sweetness that we somehow tossed back and forth as we kissed. No matter how hard or how softly we kissed, it was still in sync, because the other naturally responded in exactly the right way.

My mate is perfect.

Eventually my cock grew so hard that it was uncomfortable in my pants. I growled and pulled away from her, lifting us both from the chair. I squeezed her ass then turned, walked a bit, and set Aubry down on the meeting table, to the side of our romantic dinner. "Get undressed. I want you naked and spread out on this table in twenty seconds."

She rushed to obey this gentle command while I pulled the tablecloth I'd put on part of the meeting table—including all the serving dishes on it—over to the far end of the table next to the rest of the meal items and the portable stove. That left the entire left-hand side of the table empty and ready for us. We were gonna need it. If my cock had his way, I'd jackhammer Aubry across the entire fucking room.

She unhooked her bra and let it fall to the floor, eyeing me seductively. "You know, I had a fantasy about you doing this very thing back at the cabin."

My dick twitched and my eyebrows peaked with interest. She'd been fantasizing about me? *God, yes!*

That was like a fucking touchdown and a churro mixed together. Fucking epic. "Oh yeah?"

She nodded, climbing onto the table as I took a seat and patted the shiny wood in front of me.

"And what happened in this fantasy of yours?" I asked.

She leaned back, taking off her pants and sliding silky panties down her endless legs. Her wings flared out behind her and she looked better than any centerfold I'd ever jerked off to. Especially when she sat back up in front of me, knees together, tiny feet resting on the chair between my legs. Her nipples were hard and pointed up, just begging for me to lick them. But I watched her eyes and didn't let my hands do anything more than trail over her hips. I wanted to hear all her dirty thoughts first.

Aubry lowered her eyes and said, "You were cooking that Italian dinner and I imagined you doing it while wearing nothing but an apron."

I chuckled darkly. "Oh, so you want me to be the feminine one? Not gonna happen, Princess."

She grinned and shook her head. "No, I just wanted to imagine you naked, I think. You were so... I dunno. Hot in that moment. In your element."

My bear liked hearing that—our mate calling us hot. I squeezed her hips. Time to reward her for sharing.

I moved my hands down her legs until I gently

cupped her knees and spread them apart. Her skin was so soft.

"What else happened?" I asked as my gaze dropped from her beautiful face down to *my pussy*. I could hardly breathe. Heat flooded my body—even my lungs —making me feel like I was sitting in a sauna.

"You told me to climb up on the table, just like this," she muttered quietly.

Fuck yes. This was her fantasy? Come to life? My dick and heart were in a race and I wasn't sure who was pulling ahead. All I knew was that I'd never heard anything better in my entire life.

My grip moved from her knees to her thighs. My fingers dug in hard, knowing she liked a little pain with her pleasure, as I forced her thighs to open further.

"Then what, baby?"

Her breathing grew shallow as I lazily drew a pattern with my finger over her inner thigh. I could already smell her arousal, and I hadn't touched her yet.

"You told me you wanted to devour me," she panted.

I growled. I did want to devour her. I stared down at those pink pussy lips, which hid a little bit of heaven on earth. I reached my pinkie forward and gently teased her as I asked, "And did I get to? Devour you?"

She bit her lip and shook her head. "The fantasy ended there."

"Well, let's pick up where you left off, shall we?"

I leaned in and put my mouth on her lower lips, kissing them and sucking them, tongue lapping and swirling with the precision of a seasoned pro. She tasted so good.

"You've eaten a lot of dessert in your life, huh?" she panted.

I pulled back and chuckled. "All that matters is that this is the last dessert I'm ever going to taste. And you are so sweet, sugar, I could eat this pussy for hours."

To emphasize my point, I licked her slowly, gliding through her folds and circling my mate's sweet little clit as I hummed in delicious approval. She started to shudder beneath me. My hands slid up her thighs, over her hips, up her stomach, and onto her breasts. God, her body was hot. I rolled her nipples as I continued to eat her out.

She started to shake, and I glanced up as I sucked her in hard. That brought her close to the edge. Her head tilted back and her eyes started to roll. Pride filled me. But at the same time, I remained aware that I needed to maintain control—because she liked it that way.

I dropped her clit. "Eyes on me, sweetheart."

Her lashes fluttered open and she gazed down at me, our eyes locking intensely as I returned to stroking her over and over with the flat of my tongue. The longer we stared, the more aroused I became. Her pupils became this vortex of desire that sucked me in deeper. Just like her cunt would.

She started to moan, her breaths increasing in tempo and her hips slowly rocked up to meet my face.

I paused and murmured against her sex, "That's right, baby, watch me while I make you come."

She fought her submissive tendency to look away in order to give me what I wanted. And it was so amazing to watch her eyes as she became more and more vulnerable to me.

I watched her closely as the pressure built, loving every time she squirmed, every fucking moan as her pleasure and pressure built. Her muscles tensed and I tweaked her nipples hard, setting her off like a bomb, her orgasm shaking the table as she bucked.

It was just like one of those scenes in classical paintings where a demon sucked the virgin's soul out through her clit. God, I wanted her soul. Every piece of her. She was magnificent when she came, wild and thrashing—my Spitfire. I sucked on her clit gently and tried to draw the sensation out as long as I could. Eventually, she collapsed backward onto her elbows.

That was when I stripped my clothes and Aubry's eyes traveled over me hungrily.

I took a deep breath to calm myself but that didn't work at all. Because the scent of her arousal was so inebriating. "Fuck, you smell so good. Addicting." I brought my fingers to her sweet pussy then rubbed her cream all over my hardened shaft.

"How do you want me?" she asked, voice soft.

I just shook my head and kept stroking. Watching her get off had pushed me too far. "I need to relieve some of this pressure," I groaned. "After I get off once, I'll be good to fuck the hell out of you."

"Let me help you," she begged.

I loved how she tilted her face to look up at me and asked from her knees. It made the alpha bear inside me roar. I nodded.

She slid from the table and slowly dropped to her knees, looking up at me like I was the master of her entire existence. I had never felt more fucking powerful or more turned on. Holy shit. I needed her mouth on my cock.

"Please," she begged, "Let me suck you til you come."

Damn it, she was gonna make me explode all over her face. I exhaled sharply and fisted her icy white hair in both hands before sliding my dick between her lips. I groaned as she swallowed me up, the thick mush-roomed tip of my shaft pushing desperately into the back of her throat.

So warm. So wet. So good.

She pulled off to look back up at me. "Fuck my face as hard as you want."

"Oh, shit, Aubry." A growl rolled up my throat and I yanked her head closer, I pumped, trying to stay shal-low, but as mindless pleasure started to take over, I pressed harder and harder. When I heard her gag, I pulled back. She slid her tongue along the bottom of my shaft. And that was all it took. Seconds later I shot hot cum into the back of her mouth.

I stared down, watching her try to swallow it all like

a good little mate. But part of me loved that she couldn't. I loved that it was seeping out of the corners of her mouth.

When I pulled out, I was still hard as a fucking rock.

"Oh my god, you're so fucking hot," I told her, brushing her mouth clean with my thumb and feeding the drips back to her. Then I lifted her up and impaled her where I stood.

"Unnnnhhh," she moaned. "It hurts so fucking good."

She rolled her hips, riding me with shallow strokes as I walked her backward until her back pressed into the feathery blinds of the window. I reached out and yanked the rope, lifting the blinds so that the evening streetlights filtered in with a pinkish purple glow.

"Easton, we're supposed to be hiding, remember?"

I grinned and pulled out of her before spinning her around and pressing her breasts up to the glass.

"It's dark out," I murmured as I kissed up her spine between her gorgeous wings. "And the windows are tinted." I moved her hair and kissed up her neck. "And I kinda like the idea of some random stranger watching as I fuck you raw."

She whimpered, and I could feel her body react to my words, shuddering in anticipation. My fingers gently grazed the edges of her silken wings and she started to buck.

I paused. "You like this?"

She pressed her palms into the window for support. "Yes," she whispered.

Well, that was gonna be a fun thing to play with in the future. But I was done playing. I needed to be inside my mate. I needed to fuck her, to connect with her, to make love to her—all of it, all at once. I bent my knees and entered her from behind, thrusting deep as I continued to caress her gossamer wings with one hand.

So. Good.

"East," she panted, my name nearly coming out as a whine. "I'm gonna come soon."

"Good," I praised in a gravelly whisper. "Come for me. Give that stranger a show."

She peeked open an eye and caught sight of a man walking his dog across the narrow street. He'd completely stopped and just stood there, mouth gaping and crotch bulging, as he stared at Aubry's tits as I rammed into her. I could tell he was a shifter because of the gold tint to his eyes. No human would have spotted us. The sight of some random stranger's arousal, the excitement of our exhibitionism, and the undeniable pleasure of my cock in my mate's cunt... it was all too much for her.

She came, the show for a stranger exciting her just as much as it did me. The feel of her pussy clenching nearly did me in. I groaned as I pulled back. Then I jerked Aubry away from the window and lowered the blinds.

I turned her so we were facing again. Then I pushed

back in, filling her to the brim. I loved how stretched that little pussy looked around my cock.

"One more time, baby," I coaxed as I lowered us into a leather executive chair. I gripped the armrests tightly and I tipped my head back to look up at her. "Come for your Papa Bear one more time. Fuck me so hard you can't sit for a week."

At my command, her hips started to move. They rocked back and forth, harder and harder, as she lifted herself up and dropped back down, impaling herself on my dick. I loved every fucking second of it. Her parted lips and ecstatic expression. Her bouncing breasts. The soft slide of her most delicate parts against mine. Her nails dug into my shoulders as she struggled to take me all the way. I could tell when she swiveled her hips that the head of my dick was rubbing tantalizingly against her G-spot.

My vision narrowed as she fucked me. Sensation started to eclipse my other senses until the only thing I could see was the nipple right in front of my face. I leaned forward and sucked it into my mouth.

Her pants became desperate once more and my whole body tensed in preparation for orgasmic bliss. But I wasn't going without her. I reached down and rolled my thumb around her clit, pushing her over the edge like a derailed steam engine.

I erupted when I felt her clamp down on my cock. I grabbed her hips and pumped up hard, tapping that cervix as I spilled my seed.

We clung to each other for a little while after, simply smiling and chasing our breath, gently grazing our fingers across one another's glistening skin.

Once we recovered a bit, Aubry leaned onto my chest and said wryly. "Yeah, I'll definitely have to fly or hover for the rest of the week because it's gonna hurt like a bitch to walk."

I liked that. I liked it a lot. So much that I started to swell again.

"Cocky bastard with your utility-sized pole." She laughed against my chest.

"That's right, my pole's electric. It just lit you up."

She sat back and laughed, sunshine and relaxation pouring off her. "God, I feel like some terrible Electric Slide pun is coming—"

"That could be *our* song," I teased.

"No. Never. That would be torture."

I grinned and kissed her nose. She fluttered her wings and rose into the air, but my hands found her hips and I pulled her back down again. I wanted a post-sex snuggle.

"Don't tell me you're ready for another round again?" Aubry asked, incredulous.

I chuckled and stood, setting my mate down on her feet. "Baby, I could go like this for hours. But we should probably get dressed and finish eating. Drake could only guarantee me an hour of uninterrupted time with you, and I have a feeling someone is going to come knocking sooner rather than later. We'll table the song discussion 'til our next date."

Her lips pursed as I went around gathering our clothes. We both dressed quickly, though the sight of her half-dressed nearly made me lunge for her and bend her over the table so I could fuck her caveman style.

When we were both dressed once more, I pulled her into a tender embrace, my big arms wrapping around her tiny body as the warmth of her scent swirled around me. I took a moment to close my eyes and inhale deep, flooding my system with the heady citrusy smell of Aubry and sex—a potent combination.

Then I showed her how to shrink her earrings and put them on. We'd hardly gotten to that when the lock on the door clicked open and a gentle breeze rushed in.

Fuck Drake. I told him to stay the fuck away. I started to growl.

But then our guest spoke. "Hey, Butterfly."

Her eyes burst open and she scrambled out of my arms.

My chest ached at that, it stung like rejection or pixie magic, until I saw her tears as she clutched Bodie.

My mate had been scared she'd lost him. Just like she'd been scared she'd lost me in Union Station.

"Bodie!" she whisper-shouted.

Aubry's other mate held her close. "I'm back," he soothed her. But figures showed up in the hall behind him. He wasn't the only one who had arrived…

AUBRY

MY COUSIN, KIRA, STEPPED OUT FROM BEHIND BODIE,
pale golden wings flickering in greeting when she saw
me—and she smirked to see me hug a shifter. Behind
her was another huge guy, covered in tattoos—back up
had arrived—and with it, I hoped, some damn ideas to
help us kick mage ass once and for all.

I let go of Bodie reluctantly as he said, "Found these
shady characters hanging around outside."

I moved forward, holding out my hand toward Kira.
She tossed her curled black hair over her shoulder and
walked in, taking my hand but pulling me in so she
could kiss each of my cheeks instead of shaking. After
the kiss, she touched the tip of her wing to mine, in a
familial fae love-tap, a move my parents and I had
never bothered to do. She looked good, tall and slen-
der, with a dark red shirt that set off her brunette hair.
Of course, unlike most fae, Kira embraced human

oddities like nose rings, and who knew how many other secret body piercings she had.

Behind her, the huge beast of a man shook Easton's hand and I reveled to see someone who actually rivaled my bear shifter in size. "Beretta, long time no see, man." His voice had a gruff, no-nonsense, New York accent.

Easton gave the guy an easy grin. "Rocco, good to see you too." With a quick sideways glance at me, one that made me smile and become very conscious of the delicious ache he'd left between my thighs, Easton cleared his throat. "Go ahead and take a seat. I'll go tell Drake you're here."

Rocco laughed. "You still his pool boy? Pretty boy running around at his beck and call?"

Bodie turned to Rocco and used his death glare on the huge shifter. His light green eyes became ringed in gold as his wolf rose to the surface. It gave me a little thrill to see him step up and defend Easton. His voice was dark when he said, "Excuse me, I don't think we've met."

Rocco, oblivious to how pissed he'd just made Bodie, stepped forward and offered his hand. "Rocco De Brun. Saber tooth shifter. You... smell like wolf, yeah? Hard to tell over that one's sexy time aroma," Rocco winked at me. "Smells like it was delicious, sweetheart." He gave me an appraising look.

I turned redder than a fire hydrant. Easton stepped in front of me, blocking me from view, just as chivalrous as always. Me? I wondered if I could kick hard enough to find New York's apples. They were obviously smaller than an amoeba if he was making uncouth comments like that. The part of me that wasn't pissed was processing this info. I knew shifters had good noses, but really? This dickwad could smell *that* over all the Vietnamese food that still was scattered around the room?

"Way to score," Saber tooth said. "Always wanted to give a wasp a ride."

I clenched my fists so I wouldn't punch him in the face. *This dude was invited because he's useful,* I lectured myself. Useful how, I didn't know, so it was really fucking hard to resist smacking him.

Bodie didn't shake Rocco's hand. Instead, my mate moved over to where I stood and slid a possessive arm across my back and over my hip, tugging me closer as Easton left the room. That made Tony the Tiger's eyebrows shoot up as he glanced between Bodie, Easton's retreating back, and myself.

"Kink—" he started to say, but Kira put a hand on his arm.

"Even I know you should shut up right now," she said. "And I typically love to say inappropriate things in front of family."

Since Bodie was Orange-Threat Level pissed, I spoke. "Why don't you have a seat, Tigger? Unless you want to insult any of Drake's other people before he gets here."

"Whoa, look I was just jok—"

But I stepped forward out of Bodie's hold and stared Shere Khan in the face. I realized he had some acne pockmarks under one eye that kept him from being a complete knockout, for a middle-aged dude. My tone was dry when I said, "You're friends with Drake? Explains why you're such an asshole. Please do sit down. Take two chairs if your over-sized cinnamon hole needs it."

Bodie snickered as Rocco narrowed his eyes. "I didn't fucking come across the country to—"

"We didn't invite you across the country to insult our pack," Bodie retorted coolly.

"This is so much fun," Kira clapped and laughed as she pulled out a chair and sat down in the meeting room. She kicked her heels up on the meeting table. Four-inch-long stilettos wrapped around her ankles before her skintight leather pants took over. She looked utterly at ease. And way too fucking hot when I was a hot mess.

Rocco and Bodie temporarily stopped arguing to stare at her.

I smacked Bodie's ass and he turned toward me, nuzzling my ear. "I got your texts."

"Why didn't you text back?" I huffed.

"Drake told me I couldn't."

Another reason to kill the overgrown lizard. Reasons kept stacking up like Jenga blocks. Pretty soon I was gonna knock that fucker down.

"So, tell me," Kira said from her seat, where she

laced her hands behind her head, "what are the problems you're having with these mages?"

Rocco strode across the room, and while I thought he might settle next to Kira, instead he sniffed, and then sat down right in the spot where Easton had eaten me out.

My cheeks flamed and he grinned as he pulled over a bowl of unfinished food and took a bite. "Mmmm, yeah, tell us all the gritty details."

He didn't mean about the mages.

Bodie growled and stepped in front of me toward Rocco. I let him. I didn't want to deal with this fucking shit anymore.

Just then Drake entered, with Easton and Larry on his heels. His eyes flared with heat when he felt the tension in the room. "Everyone sit the fuck down. I don't care what beef you've got going. We've got real problems. And we need a solution. Fast."

Everyone sat. I made sure to place myself between Easton and Bodie so that I couldn't see the stupid dragon or the nasty saber tooth. Instead, I smiled over at Larry, who smiled exhaustedly back at me. The poor mage had been working day and night with those injured kiddos.

Drake gave the rundown to the new people, not even batting an eye at the fact that I'd called in a fae to help us. Either he'd heard of my rebellious cousin and her quest to fuck up the status quo in Moscow or... he was starting to trust me.

I didn't want to think about the latter. Because I sure as fuck didn't trust him. And I didn't want there to be any soft feelings between us. There never had been. Only animosity. That's what I told myself as I clutched Bodie's hand under the table, reluctant to let him go after I hadn't been able to talk to him for days. The angst I felt was all for him. Only for him.

When Drake finished, Kira spoke up. "In Russia, we have a saying: what will win, the television or the fridge? The media or the empty bellies?" She shoved her legs off the table and leaned forward, steepling her fingers as her golden wings flared out behind her. "It sounds like... in America, no one starves. So, the television wins."

"Shifters go hungry every day," Easton protested.

Kira pursed her lips. "No, not just shifters. You have to look at all the magical community as a whole. In order to beat the television, you must empty the fridge."

"Impossible," Rocco said.

"That's immoral," Larry argued.

The guys all started speaking over one another. But I could see her point. The media always skewed things against shifters.

"We could do our own social media campaigns," I tossed out.

Only Easton liked that idea.

"Too slow," Rocco shot me down.

"Doesn't solve the issue at hand," Drake agreed.

"Which is: the thousands of homeless shifters from the fire, and now with the shooting... there's nowhere safe for them to go. Plus, shifters are out for blood."

I resisted shooting a fireball at him. But only because it would burn down the building and the sweet kids sleeping in the vault below. Not because he didn't deserve a flame in the face.

"In New York," Rocco said, "we solve our problems in the streets." It figured that Crouching Tiger was only clever enough to think of street fighting.

"Yeah, but your gangs have been fighting for thirty-odd years," Easton countered. "Our civilians can't handle that. They aren't prepared. Half of them don't know how to hold the guns we gave them."

"Violence rarely begets anything but more violence," Larry said.

Nobody listened to him. Not even me. With kids' funerals set for tomorrow thanks to my now-empty bank account, and a little memorial full of candles and photographs set up in the vault below, it was hard to think of anything but violence as an answer.

"Well, they attacked a school. Why don't you attack one of their schools?" Kira asked, as if that were the most natural solution in the world.

"More children?" Larry thundered. "No!"

"Calm your jets," Kira responded, getting the saying wrong. She waved her hand. "I don't mean children. They have a mage university, right?" Her accent became prominent on the word 'university.'

Silence was the only answer.

Until Bodie nodded.

Larry exploded. "NO! Just no! They might be legal adults, but they still are *just* students."

"They're a puppy mill, churning out potions for the Mage Council," Drake countered.

"They are eighteen-year-olds who've never attacked anyone!"

"Yet," Bodie said.

My eyes swept around the room. Kira and Rocco looked triumphant. Easton was hesitant. Bodie's face was dark, shut down, wearing the mask I assumed he used when he had to go out and kill someone he'd never met in order to protect his pack.

I leaned over and looked at Drake, who looked calm as a fucking cucumber. But, somehow, I knew he wasn't. That expression was as fake as most women's eyelashes, only taken off when he went to sleep. When he really felt things.

If he felt things.

Murderer.

I sat back, hiding myself from him once more.

Across from me, Larry's eyes bulged. His entire face was red as he slammed a fist on the table. "I will not stand for this 'eye for an eye' shit! No! I'm out."

He shoved back from the table and stood his hair standing on end. He looked just as frantic as Doc in *Back to the Future*. But not nearly as funny. Larry was dead serious.

Next to me, Easton's jaw dropped. Bodie's expression didn't change, but his hand tightened around mine.

I didn't know how integral Larry was to their plans and inner workings. But he'd been there every day since I'd arrived. He was the only thing that stood between life and death for some of these poor shifter kids.

He couldn't just walk away.

We couldn't let him.

But the assholes in the room didn't say a damn thing as Larry stomped off.

Panic jittered my heart and I dropped Bodie's hand, standing, my wings flaring out. "Larry, wait."

He turned and looked at me.

Everyone looked at me.

Fucking shit.

"Did you have a plan you wanted to share, Doll-face?" Drake used that damned nickname just to piss me off further.

No, I didn't have a plan. Other than to keep Larry from walking out the door. "We have other options. We just need to talk them through."

"What other options?" Rocco gave a harsh laugh. "If your people can't fight—"

I stared at Larry, ignoring the others. "Larry... "
What the fuck can we do? I ran through Mage Police scenarios in my head. The guys had already tried to take a political prisoner and negotiate.

That hadn't turned out well, if you discounted the mate bond.

The Mage Council wouldn't negotiate.

But... on the other hand, one prisoner was easy to ignore. An entire school... how could we take an entire school prisoner?

My eyes scanned the room and kept coming back, annoyingly to Drake. Why the hell was my subconscious mind stuck on him? Fuck him. His hands went to his pockets and he shoved back from the table. He appeared to enjoy my discomfort as he crossed his legs and moved the pouch on his hip to the side.

The pouch.

We had raided every damned potion that my station had. His pouch held a magical arsenal courtesy of the MP.

I turned back to Larry and said, "What if we use sleep grenades? What if we take the entire school hostage instead of killing them? We'll cut off the Mage Council's supply of potions, get ourselves a safe place to hole up. We can take all the shifters there. They can't attack us without killing hundreds of mages. We could draw a movement restriction circle, the way the Mage Council does for their hearings, to ensure nobody can move if they step into the circle without authorization from the spell caster. So even if the MP try to attack, they get stuck."

Behind me, I heard a single clap. Then another. I turned to see Drake applauding.

I glared at him. "Not funny, Dragon Ball Z. I'm serious."

"Not laughing, shoo fly," Drake shot back. "It's a good, non-violent solution. They might have ignored it when we took *you*—"

I cringed when he brought up that sore point.

He continued, "But how can they ignore all those kids? How can they cover that up?"

Kira leaned forward. "You'd also starve them of magic. The stupid councilors don't make their own potions anymore. Most of them treat the college students like indentured servants, free labor. They use words like internship and job training and crap. But they are no better than dictators who take without earning."

Bodie's hand came up and slid over my ass. "I like it, Butterfly."

On my other side, Easton smiled. "That's my Spitfire."

Across the table, Rocco rolled his eyes. "So, we have a damned idea. But now, we need a solid plan."

That was true. Ideas were one thing. Execution was another. We needed a *damn good* plan.

AUBRY

"AFTER SITTING HERE, BREATHING IN ALL THIS SULTRY and savory air," Kira commented dryly, "my only *plan* is to eat some food and get laid. Any takers?"

I leveled her with a scorching glare that only a summer fae could master.

She might have been here on business, but she was clearly single and ready to mingle. She'd just better keep her magical faerie cunt away from my guys' over-sized shifter cocks.

Rocco turned and gave her an appreciative eye, skimming up and down her lithe body like she was a strip of lean white meat. But Kira didn't seem to notice. Because she had her eyes set on Drake.

Heat shot like a flare gun up my spine. I growled internally... and maybe externally, too.

Bitch! Moving in on my shifters!

My eyes went wide as soon as that thought crossed

my mind. Technically, Drake was not off limits. Because, technically, Drake wasn't mine.

My pussy disagreed.

What kind of fucked up world was I living in right now? I had two damn mates. I didn't need more.

Bodie and Easton each shot me a glance. Easton's was a knowing smirk. Bodie's look was full of angered confusion. Shit. I forgot he had no idea about the would-be additional mate bond bullshit. Ugh. He had no clue about my possible connection to Drake thanks to these two idiots joining his clan or valor or what-ever-the-hell it was called.

The bastard dragon had the nerve to glance my way before pinning my cousin with a sultry stare. "I think we need to keep the conversation on the topic at hand. But, maybe after, we could discuss our options? I have very specific sexual preferences."

Those words made my nipples turn to diamonds. I wanted to know... had to know... what did Drake like? My lips parted a little and I had to squeeze my thighs together.

Rocco chuckled and put an arm around the chair-back next to him as he leaned toward my cousin. His fingertip brushed the edge of her wing suggestively. "Not I, baby. I'll fuck anything with a cunt. And yours smells delightful."

She turned to him and smirked, as if just now real-izing he was still sitting there, and that she actually had options beyond the sexy dragon shifter.

Not sexy. Stubborn. The stubborn dragon shifter... who may or may not have just agreed to a one-night stand with my cousin.

My blood boiled for the second time in a minute, and I was almost positive I let another fucking growl escape my clenched teeth. That dickhead.

"What is your problem, babe?" Bodie asked me, trying to piece their words and my actions together into something that made any fucking sense whatsoever.

Kira threw her head back and laughed. Then she propped her head on her hand, her elbow leaning on the armrest of her chair, and with a smirk she said, "Spending too much time with your new shifter lovers, I see. You're even picking up on their animalistic tendencies and instincts."

Goddamn it, she was right. I had never growled to show possession over something, let alone *someone*, back when my life was... normal? I didn't even know what to call it anymore.

My eyes met the dragon's for a second. But his curious blue gaze was too intense and we both quickly glanced away. I ignored how my stomach dropped out like a gumball from a vending machine.

"Anyway," Drake said, steering the conversation in a different direction, "we need a plan for securing the school. Any suggestions?"

"I am an autumn fae," Kira said haughtily, "Wind is my specialty."

I crossed my arms and scoffed. "What are you going to do? Pick the university up in a tornado and drop it off here?"

She pursed her perfect Russian lips and smiled, allowing her perfect cheekbones to shine like apples. Poison apples. Shifter stealer.

She tilted her head and asked, "Aubry, my dear cousin, have I done something wrong? I am sensing hostility in you."

Drake glanced my way but addressed Kira. "You haven't seen each other for a while, I take it. Aubry, here, always has a shitty attitude and disposition, don't you, Dollface?"

My eyes snapped back to his. If I could have slapped him, I would have. *Stupid skink.* But I had no doubt Bodie or Easton would stop me.

Bodie slid a warm hand across my knee. He glanced between Drake and I, trying to understand our stupid staring contest and obviously failing. "I don't know what sort of fight the two of you got into while I was gone, but Drake, you need to lay the fuck off my mate. She's clearly upset with you, and I don't want you making it worse."

Shit. That was yet another thing Bodie hadn't found out—the fact that Drake had killed my father. We had so much to catch up on.

Drake dragged his glare away from me and let it land on Bodie, pausing there for just a moment before moving on to Rocco. "What about you, saber tooth?"

Rocco chuckled and held up both hands. "What you see is what you get. I'm packing brains, brawn, firearms, and fighters. My boys are downstairs as we speak getting acquainted with your shifters. Even brought my mage along because, why the fuck not?"

Drake nodded and turned to Larry, who looked uncertain. "What's wrong, Lar?"

Larry shook his frizzy-haired head. "I don't like the brawn, firearms, and fighters part. I thought we agreed this would be peaceful? And as for the brains part..." He trailed off and shook his head once more.

I nearly chuckled. Apparently, Larry was as impressed with Rocco as I was.

"Let's approach this from a different angle," Drake said with a sigh. "How are we going to get on campus without being seen?"

"There will be spells surrounding the area," I said flippantly. "It's in Bel Air near UCLA so there are a lot of spells to ensure only the right crowd gets in."

"What sort of spells?" Drake asked, staring straight at me.

"Compulsion Spells, if I recall correctly," I said, staring at my nails so I didn't accidentally look into his eyes. "They surround the campus grounds so that unsuspecting humans get the urge to just turn around and walk away."

Drake nodded, taking my word without argument, which made me irrationally smug. I needed to get the fuck off this stupid high horse I was riding where he was

173

concerned. Who cared if he fucked Kira? I shouldn't. Who cared if he thought my ideas were good or not? I shouldn't.

"So how do we get around the spells?" Easton asked, glancing at Larry. "Can you and Rocco's mage friend take care of that?"

"Tony," Rocco supplied with a jutted-out chin.

Easton shrugged because the dude's name was pretty damn inconsequential at the moment.

Larry shook his head. "I mean, we *could*, if we had to. But this Tony fellow and I probably need to be working on Movement Restriction Spells so we can surround the school and make sure no one gets in or out after we secure it."

"What about flying in?" Kira suggested. "At night when no one can see?"

Drake smirked. "Not everyone has wings like us."

Us. He was grouping the two of them together? My fucking lip curled. Even if I sincerely *hated* Drake, instead of... whatever I felt... I still didn't want to see him cozying up to my cousin. And I did *not* want to address the reasoning behind that or acknowledge the supposed 'feelings' in question. I stared at the table and started to scratch the crappy veneer.

"So we carry them," she said, as if it were simple. "Aubry and I have wings." Then she eyed Drake suggestively. "And I'd love to see *your* wings. I bet they're simply *massive*."

She bit her lower lip and I got the distinct impression that she was not talking about his wings at all. Thirsty fucking bitch.

Stop it, Aubry! She's not doing anything wrong. You're mated to Bodie and Easton, not Drake. Easton's theory is wrong. And Drake's technically fair game. He's also attractive as hell and so is she. They'd make... a gorgeous couple.

Ew. My stomach curdled and my head spun. For a moment, I was afraid all that Vietnamese food was going to come back up. I stood, unsure of what I was even going to say or do.

"I..." I swallowed hard and blinked. "I need some fresh air."

Rocco chuckled, a big belly-laughing thing. "Can't stand your own scent anymore, pretty little fly?"

Bodie stood behind me and pointed a finger at the saber tooth. "One more vile or perverted word to or about my mate and it'll be the last fucking thing you say."

I turned and touched his chest to calm him. "It's okay, Bodie. It's not him. I just... need a minute."

I strode toward the door, and to my immense surprise, Drake spoke.

"Aubry," he pleaded softly as I passed. His hand lifted ever so slightly, like he wanted to reach out for me, but he squeezed his fist and lowered it to the table before him. Clearing his throat, he addressed the rest of the group. "Never mind. We'll just... carry on without her. We need to hammer this plan out. Okay, if we can get in via the sky, they'll be able to do so as well. *Unless* we protect it."

My teeth gritted together, and I grabbed the door handle with a little more force than necessary. Behind me, I heard Bodie mutter, "You better fill me in on what the fuck is going on *real* soon."

I assumed he was talking to Easton, but I didn't get the chance to find out. I just shut the door behind me and wandered aimlessly down the hall.

I do not care about Drake. I don't. He cut me too deeply when he kept my father's murder a secret from me. I can't just forgive and forget that. No matter what my stupid heart might feel.

Kick the bitch while she's down, my brain rioted. *Forget her and listen to logic. He's evil. Awful. He's the mastermind who trapped you in the first place... stole you away from everything you loved!*

But my heart glared up from the puddle of tears she was sitting in. *No, kick your* cousin *before she takes what's ours.*

I ignored my heart's feeble request. She could deal with this shit on her own. I was done. Fuck the internal drama.

My feet carried me down the stairs and into Tee's room on autopilot.

It was almost a habit at this point—just going in there for some solitude and staring at the walls so I didn't have to acknowledge the irritating shit my heart and head were arguing about all the damn time.

I stepped in and shut the door behind me, slowly sinking to the floor as I usually did, but to my immense surprise, my eyes were drawn to movement in the cage. I blinked and scrambled back onto my feet, rushing over to the cat carrier to peer inside.

"Tee?"

She groaned like she was seasick or something, but it was the first sign of life she'd shown since the cabin, and I was clinging to it like a flotation device.

I opened the cage and very carefully pulled her out. I sank down to the carpet and leaned my back against the wall as I cradled her in my hands.

"Tee?" She didn't respond.

Fuck. I leaned my head back against the wall, sadness and bullshit feelings churning back to life thanks to my disappointment and guilt over her condition. Why the hell wasn't she okay yet? Larry had tried at least three restorative spells.

A single tear dripped down my face as I muttered, "Tee, I miss you. I need you to come back and tell me what an asshole I'm being. Tell me that I should hate Drake. Like completely and utterly. Okay?" I coughed and wiped away the treacherous tear. I shouldn't have been crying. I really shouldn't.

I tried to pull up a happy memory with my father. He'd let me buy whatever I wanted, and he'd always given me a gift when he returned from a trip. I'd never gone without.

But did those things actually equate to *happiness*?

I stared at the office desk, trying to think.

There'd been no bedtime stories from my parents. Travel, yes. But usually with a nanny to watch me so they could go off to their dinner parties. My dad had tried, I supposed. He'd taken a hands-on approach with my physical training, teaching me how to fight and also how to control my fire. That thought *did* drag up a happy memory.

I glanced down at Tee. "Did you know my dad could make his fire into the shape of a unicorn? He did it for me when I was seven. I told everyone about it for days." Saying it out loud made another tear drip down my cheek.

That was a pretty old memory, though, so I tried to pull up a newer one.

Dad had hugged me—might even have had tears in his eyes—when I'd become Chief Enforcer. But it was hard to remember the good times. Part of me wondered if it was my fault, because ever since my failed engagement, I'd purposefully stayed away, hardly seeing or speaking to either of them.

Not that it mattered, now that he was gone. There would be no mending fences. I'd get no more chances to make happy memories with him.

And that was because of Drake. The dragon's shifter's face drifted into my mind.

"I wish he would have told me, Tee. I wish..."

But I didn't know what I wished. Instead of fury like before, everything about the situation filled me with sadness this time. At least with Drake, there was still a chance for me to mend all those metaphorical fences. There was a chance to repair all the shit that stood between us.

I just didn't know how to do it. I'd never done it before. I hadn't forgiven my parents. How the hell was I supposed to forgive him?

I was so fucked—

Suddenly, Tee stirred in my hands and I leaned down, looking her over from head to toe. She groaned and her eyes flickered open.

"Tee, oh my god, are you okay? How are you feeling?" Relief soared through my chest when I saw her blink and scrunch her nose.

"Like shit," she muttered, pushing up on shaking arms to try and get into a sitting position. She blinked hazily, her gaze unfocused as she asked, "You got any Health Potions lying around?"

I sniffed out a laugh. "Probably. The guys and I..." I almost told her about raiding the precinct, but then I thought better of it. "We've collected a variety of potions over these past few days. But for now, how about I grab you a nice cup of coffee?" A cup for her would be more like a thimble, but I didn't have those laying around. Hopefully, she could make do with a regular mug.

Tee sat up in my hand and stared around the office, dazed. "What the fuck kinda hut is this? What did you do to that tree?" She fluttered out of my hand and ran her fingers over the desk. "Poor thing," she muttered to it.

Alarm bells and sirens started going off in my head. "Tee… are you feeling okay?"

"Already told you I'm not. Where the fuck is Aaron? Is he off hunting things?" She flitted around the office frantically, landing on a keyboard. When the computer screen lit up in front of her, she leapt into the air with a scream and fell into the office chair.

I rushed toward her. "Tee?"

"Mage magic. We are in a mage house. Shit, Aubry. Mages don't invite people to their homes! We're going to get killed!" She flew at my face and ended up tangled in my hair. I reached up, trying to untangle her as her wings whipped my cheek and her tiny fingers scratched at me.

"We have to leave, Aubs. The only place worse than this would be a shifter's den!"

I extracted Tee the rest of the way and held her gently but firmly in my hand. Trepidation filled me up. She'd woken up and seemed to know me, but she definitely wasn't acting normal.

"Tee, this isn't a mage's home. This is a bank."

"A what?" She scrunched her nose.

"You know, a bank, where humans bring their money."

"What the hell are you talking about? What's a human?"

Oh fuck.

My stomach sank. Her utterly confused expression told me she wasn't joking. Not even a little bit. She had no idea what humans were. Or computers. *Fuck*. Larry hadn't just wiped the memory of a day, of her kidnapping. He'd wiped out an entire species. The fucking species that ruled the planet. And with it, I suspected Tee had lost her knowledge of every human thing.

Shit. Shit! I had no idea if there was any coming back from this. I had no idea if there was a spell we could do to reverse the damage.

"Does this thing make Healing Potions?" Tee asked, fluttering off my hand and over to a side table that held a coffee maker that might've looked like a potion brewing stand. "I'd really like one before Aaron gets here."

"Oh, Aaron. Um..." I didn't know how to tell her that she couldn't see him. Based on the way she spoke, it didn't seem like she remembered her kidnapping at all. I chewed my lip.

"Yeah, he's gonna be here soon. My mate bond is going berserk. And I really need one of those potions to help freshen up, you know?"

I froze as horror poured like burning coffee down my throat. "What about your bond?" I spun back toward her.

Tee squinted and said, "It's going nuts. My heart's hammering like a pixie playing the sticks. You think he's okay? He feels really distressed..."

My teeth almost broke when I ground them

together. *Shit!* Did that mean her mate had finally found her now that she'd woken up? Was he literally on his way here right now? Tense music started playing in my mind, the kind that played during action flick chase scenes.

"Tee," I asked hesitantly, "what's the last thing you remember?"

She groaned, moving her palm from her head down to her heart. "I remember getting kidnapped by your shifter mates and falling asleep in a strange place. But that's about it. Why? What's going on?"

Great. Larry's stupid fucking memory wipe spell hadn't even worked. She still remembered the kidnapping. She probably still remembered Easton's and Bodie's faces. All this was a total fucking waste. And now Aaron might be on our trail.

I had to find out if she could feel him getting closer, the way Bodie could feel me leaving. But I needed to be subtle.

I wandered over next to her and pushed start on the brewer. "Yes, this thing makes magical potions that perk you up and make you feel more alert as soon as you drink them."

"Oh perfect!" she said, eyes lighting up as the coffee began streaming into a mug.

I kept my tone casual and crossed my legs, leaning back against the table as I asked, "Do you remember anything about your assignment? Or any broadcasts you might have seen on TV?"

Her brows knit and her nose scrunched. "What the fuck is a TV? Seriously, Aubry. I feel like you're fucking with me."

I laughed, but it was just as hesitant as the rest of my actions. She honestly didn't seem to remember TV. "Alright, Tee, truth time. You were given a memory wipe, but it was clearly a dud. You're just now waking up after days of being asleep. I'm trying to figure out if you're still good."

She winced and wiped a bead of sweat off her little brow. "Seriously, my heart is racing like a mage who lost his wand. What the fuck was in that Memory Potion? And why the fuck did you give me one?"

"Well... they guys said it was either that or kill you, and obviously I wasn't going with the latter option, so..."

"You got some interesting mates, huh?" she commented dryly. "Whatever. Mine's pretty hardcore, too. I can't wait to see what happens when they finally meet face-to-face. Aaron's probably gonna kill them for kidnapping me."

Shit. So she did remember that. I put a little stirring straw in the cup of coffee and set it down in front of her. "He hasn't been able to find you, Tee. We've been moving around a lot and being extra vigilant with precautionary methods."

"Not vigilant enough for my Aaron—he found me once when I hid in the forest in a knot in this huge old Redwood—he can find me anywhere," she said, rolling her eyes before taking a sip of the steaming black liquid before her. "Oh my god, what is this shit? It's awful."

Okay, she was seriously starting to worry me. "It's coffee, Tee. You love coffee. And what do you mean, not vigilant enough for Aaron?"

"Well, it's nasty, and there's no way I ever loved it." She tried to push the mug away, but either the bars interfered, or she was still too weak. "How could something that tastes so awful possibly help perk you up? I mean, honestly."

I grabbed the cup and decided to drink it myself. "Tee, focus. What did you mean about Aaron?"

"Oh," she said with a shrug. "Just that he's getting closer. I can feel my mate bond relaxing—finally."

Shit! I spat my coffee and hurriedly set it on the desk before running out into the hallway. That action music inside me turned to horror music.

"I told you that shit was awful!" Tee called out after me as I took the stairs two at a time. Adrenaline rushed through me, river rapids churning through my veins.

If Aaron was getting closer, then he had finally found Tee. And if Aaron had found Tee, he was most likely about to attempt a rescue, and if he was smart—which he was—he wouldn't be doing it alone. In other words, we were about to get hit.

Motherfucking shit!

I ran across the lobby floor and burst back into the

meeting room. God, it really did smell like sex and pho in there. Not a bad combination, actually.

"We're about to be attacked!" I shouted breathlessly. It wasn't the stairs that had winded me, or all the running, but the fucking stress. The near-constant stress of death.

Drake, Bodie, and Easton immediately shot up from their chairs and asked questions at the exact same time.

"Who?" Bodie asked, believing me immediately; he just needed to know who to kill.

"When?" Easton added, hopping on the belief train, too, but required just a bit more info.

"How do you know?" Drake asked, irritating the hell out of me with his lack of faith.

"Aaron and the Mage Police," I said, answering Bodie's question first.

Bodie's eyes narrowed. "Who's Aaron?"

Ah, sweet jealousy. It looked so fucking good on him as his green eyes flashed gold.

"Tee's mate," I explained. "The little pixie downstairs? She finally woke up. I think it triggered their mate bond. She said he feels close."

"Fuck!" Drake cursed, slamming a fist on the table. He then directed his attention at our guests. "Alright, grab some weapons and assemble your best fighters. We meet them head-on and we keep the fight upstairs and away from the shifters below. No mage gets through our defenses, got it?"

Everyone nodded before moving into go-mode,

determinedly pulling out and checking the weapons they had on them, then stalking from the room like grim reapers about to sow death and destruction.

"Thanks for the heads up," Drake muttered as he passed.

A thank you? What!?! My heart pattered hopefully but my eyes rolled in response. "Oh, now you're being nice to me? I thought I always had a shitty attitude and disposition?"

Drake shrugged. "Never said you didn't. Only said thank you."

"Yeah well fuck you, Mushu!" I retaliated because, apparently, my comebacks were lacking lately.

"Back at ya, Mulan," he retorted before disappearing around the corner.

Huh. He'd gotten the reference. Actually, I was pretty sure he'd gotten all my ridiculous pop culture references. Not that it mattered. It didn't make him a better person or anything. He was actually the worst person. Ugh.

I trailed after him, sure to leave some distance between us as we crossed through the lobby.

A moment later, the bone chilling sound of shattered glass filled the lobby along with the sound of hissing potions and gunfire. Bodie, Easton, and I sprinted into action as quickly as we could. Rocco disappeared downstairs.

Cowardly fuck.

"Do not breathe!" Kira commanded everyone, and

suddenly her wings flared out. She stood still as she moved them faster and faster, activating her wind power. She blew huge gusts of air toward the broken front doors, expelling whatever potions Aaron and the mages had thrown in. Probably sleep grenades. Possibly Weakness Potions. Maybe even Pixie Dust Potions. Her winds were so strong that the front walls started to bow out a little near the windows.

Rage roared through me and my battle hungry inner lion sprang to life. I hoped that Kira's blowback hit those fuckers right in the face. We had innocent kids below.

As the air cleared of smoke and dust, it suddenly filled with the alluring sound of music. Siren music.

Oh, fuck.

"Cover your ears!" I shouted.

Bodie did as ordered but spun around and shouted at me, "How are we supposed to fire our weapons with both hands on our fucking heads?"

He had a damn good point.

For people like Rocco—who had guns so large they took both arms to wield—it was nearly impossible to cover their ears in time. Aaron's compulsion magic immediately dropped him to his knees.

I knew siren magic pretty well, considering Aaron used to be on my team. It had the power to force anyone to do anything physically, but not *mentally*. Rocco and the few others who'd been affected were just going to have to wait long enough for Aaron to get distracted…

Speaking of… I watched as a big chunk of bricks fell down from the top edge of one of the shattered windows, and finally Aaron's song petered out.

As soon as the sound was gone, an idea came to me. It'd be super ironic to fight Aaron using the same power as the mate he was trying to rescue, but it was the best I could come up with off the top of my head.

"Drake!" I shouted, taking a hand off my ear so I could point to the pouch on his belt. "Pixie potion!"

As he fumbled around for the little black potion bottle, Aaron's song started back up again, the tune filtering into the dragon shifter's exposed ears. His motions slowed until he stopped completely. Then he took a mechanical step toward the door, like he was going to just welcome the siren in with open arms.

Shit! I knew exactly how that felt. I raced over to Drake with my hands still clamped over my ears and my elbows flapping like I was some mutated chicken. I hopped onto his back and quickly plugged his ears with my elbows while still cupping my own with my palms. A couple steps later and he paused once more.

Out of the corner of my eye I saw Aaron step through a broken window, looking like vengeance personified. His pearlescent skin glowed and his eyes were wide and angry. His mouth was open and even through my hands I could hear a little of his enchanting melody.

Drake tried to shake his head, but I just squeezed down on him tighter.

"Don't even think about it, Drogon. Just reach into the bag and pelt that fucking siren with pixie dust!" I ordered. Then I started to yell tonelessly, trying to block the siren song.

The dragon shifter did as asked, which was a little difficult considering he couldn't really move his head. But he launched a bottle skyward and it busted at Aaron's feet. The siren was surrounded in a swirling vortex of buzzing black pixie magic. It was like thousands of miniature flies biting at his skin, scraping it raw, as they flew around in a flurry.

Needless to say, his song ended as he focused all his attention on battling the magic around him. I quickly climbed down from Drake's back, annoyed at the heat swirling around my lady bits because of their close proximity to his body. Just because he was hot—his skin, like his temperature, not his body or his face—didn't mean *we* had to be.

I'm looking at you, vag.

My vag opened her lips to retort but another round of potions crashed in, only one from the left, one from the right—so either Aaron had brought less backup than I feared and only had two people with him, or they were simply trying to fake us out. I peered through the windows, trying to see.

Just then Rocco appeared at the top of the stairs, toting a machine gun with a string of bullets tossed over his shoulder like a deadly scarf. He was followed by a couple of rough-looking guys with guns. The New York tiger put on a burst of speed to get in front of us before planting his feet wide and letting the mother-fucking gun spit. He sprayed bullets left and right, their metallic points pinging off of shit outside, the gun blasts echoing all around us in the lobby of the bank.

"Come on, you pussy-ass bastards!" he shouted as he fired. But no one outside made any moves. Eventually, he ceased fire and waited.

The only sound was that of Aaron's grunts and groans as he fought the buzzing mass around him. Then the siren shouted, "Just go! Get in there and get Tee out!"

A purple potion bottle rolled inside across the floor, unsmashed, not leaking. It looked like someone outside had accidentally dropped it.

Rocco raised a brow and cupped his mouth. "Missed me!"

Suddenly, there was a blast at the far side of the lobby and a giant hole appeared in the bank's brick exterior wall.

"That's what I'm talking about," Rocco muttered as he directed his fire into the new hole until the idiot had wasted every bullet he had.

Rocco's guys shouted back and forth, moving to ensure as much ground was covered as possible, when suddenly a new potion flew in. It landed directly on top of the unbroken one, shattering them both at once.

Talk about a trick play. The first one was a Mage Fire Potion, the other, a Blast Potion, so when they went off, chunks of magical fire flew everywhere like a volcanic eruption.

My mind reeled as the fire quickly spread. Those bastards! Did they know we had children downstairs? Did they even fucking care? My fingernails dug into my palms.

The bank's sprinkler system kicked on, but it did nothing to soothe the magical flames.

Kira tried to blow on it, but that only fed the flames.

"Drake!" I shouted once more.

"Yeah, I'm on it, Dollface," he replied, rifling through the bag at his waist once more. He pulled out a few Mage Fire Counterpotions and began throwing them at the patches of fire. Some of them hissed and sizzled before petering out, while others continued raging, the potion fluid not quite reaching the flames where they danced.

Two MPs leapt through the empty glass of the bank's front doors, wearing black SWAT gear. They were two enforcers I recognized but had never really spoken to—John Marrow and Tammy Day, both of which were from another unit. John was a gnome, barely two feet tall with a permanently grumpy expression and a tank-like disposition despite his minuscule size. And Tammy was an elf, tall and lithe and extremely well-versed in marksmanship, especially archery.

John let out a battle cry and charged through the room. Our guys shot magic and bullets at him, but it was no use. A gnome's skin was tough as nails—just like their personalities. Bullets weren't going to take John down, at least, not as quickly as we needed. We were going to have to trap him, instead.

Damn it.

As thoughts of nets and metal boxes passed through my mind, Tammy attacked. She fired a spray of bullets from a handgun before ripping an arrow from the quiver on her back and sending it flying with a small bow I hadn't even noticed her carrying.

Our side took cover, ducking behind the bank's teller counter and slipping into nearby offices. Drake made sure to cover the stairs that led to the vault, and it was a good thing, because that's exactly where John and Tammy headed.

The dragon partially shifted, allowing a massive plume of billowing fire to erupt from his jowls and burst into the lobby. John stood his ground, bracing his tiny body against the flames as if he were pushing back against a gust of wind or something. Tammy, however, was forced to run for cover or risk severe burns. As she retreated, Easton grabbed her from behind, wrapping his huge arms around her.

Bodie went over and quickly disarmed every weapon she was carrying.

Tammy growled in frustration. "Let me go, shifter scum!"

But Easton merely smirked and rolled his baby blue eyes. "Call me something I haven't heard, elf."

"Milksopping cockalorum!" she spat.

Easton raised his brows and nodded appreciatively. "Yeah, I've definitely never heard that one before. One point for creativity, but negative points for the weird Shakespearean vibe."

She hissed as he wrapped her wrists in a set of iron cuffs. As an elf, the iron wouldn't burn her skin like it did a fae, but it still pissed her off that she'd been caught.

As soon as Drake's fire stopped, John charged at him.

On instinct, I shouted, "Use the bag!"

Somehow, Drake knew exactly what I meant. It was like our brains functioned on the same wavelength, something that made my heart flutter in a totally annoying way. He grabbed the bag and held it open then turned it to face the gnome.

John dug his heels into the floor but couldn't stop his full-body run in time to keep from sliding right into the bag with the magical expansion spell. It swallowed him whole like a black mamba swallowing a rat.

I realized our error a millisecond too late, when the potion bottles inside suddenly smashed on John's impact. Drake quickly squeezed the top of the bag shut as muffled explosions went off and tiny plumes of dust leaked from the cracks at the top.

Oh my god, had we just lost the entire stash of potions we'd stolen from the precinct?

Upon seeing the horror on my face, Drake shook his head. "Relax, princess, I put most of the bottles in a secure location. All I had in here was a couple of each type, just in case."

I exhaled loudly, my whole body sagging with relief. Then I realized that Drake had been able to read my look and know exactly what I meant. I stared up at him. He stared back at me. My lips parted...

That's when Aaron attacked.

Apparently, the Pixie Dust Potion had finally worn off. His skin was bright pink, like it'd been rubbed raw, and the look on his face was pure madness and determination.

"Tee!" he screamed, his voice harsh and scraping. "I'm coming, baby! Hold on!"

Rocco's goon fired a new round of bullets while Drake produced another jet-stream of fire, but Aaron dropped to the floor and dodged them both. Before I even realized what was going on, a tune filled the air. My limbs went numb. All around me, people were lowering their weapons and simply standing with furious expressions. We knew what was happening, but we couldn't do a damn thing about it.

Somewhere in the back of my head, I knew I needed to *do* something, to cover my ears, to fight back, but my limbs were sluggish and refused to heed my thoughts. I watched in mild curiosity as Aaron stood, walked through our frozen forms, and disappeared down the stairs. As soon as his song filtered out of my ears, I shook my head and launched into action, flying through the air since it was faster than running.

I found the siren marching down the hallway, poking his head into random rooms as he went.

"Aaron!" Tee called from the room just ahead of him.

He let down his guard when he heard her voice; I saw his entire body visibly relax. That's when I kicked my flight into high gear and tackled his ass straight to the ground in the doorway of Tee's room, wrapping my hand around his mouth to keep him from singing.

"Aubry!" Tee cried from her carrier. "What the hell are you doing? Let him go!"

"Sorry, Tee, no can do," I grunted as he thrashed around beneath me, damn near getting free. I blasted him with a quick burst of fire, enough to singe and sting, but not enough to melt his skin or catch his clothes on fire. He cried out in pain, just as Tee cried out in horror.

"Aubry motherfucking Summerset! You stop this bullshit right now! What the hell has gotten into you?" Tee shot magic at me, but the buzzing black cloud flew over my head and hit the wall behind me, scuffing the paint until it rained in little flakes onto the floor.

Bodie was behind me seconds later, covering Aaron's mouth with industrial-grade duct tape and wrapping him up in iron chains, careful not to let the chains near me.

I nodded in thanks to my mate. Then I stood and put a hand on my hip as I caught my breath. "Sorry, Tee. But he, John, and Tammy just attacked us. It's self-defense at this point."

She clung to the bars of her cat carrier and shook her head. "And what's your excuse for kidnapping me? That wasn't 'self-defense.'"

Bodie glanced at me before turning to Tee. "Your kidnapping was a mercy, rodent. You're lucky you're not dead."

Drake and Easton came downstairs with the other two prisoners in tow, and the rest of our motley crew on their heels. After securing the three of them in Tee's office-slash-cell-room, Larry entered and began spelling them to stem their magic.

Drake strode out into the hallway, joining the rest of us with a dark look in his eyes. "Get ready."

Easton's brow furrowed as he glanced between me and Drake. "For what?"

"We were just attacked *on our turf* by three MPs," Drake spat gruffly. "There are innocent shifters and children in here that need our protection, and I won't risk exposing them to another attack."

He scanned the group with a heavy determination in his gaze.

"We're taking over Mag-Sorgin University. And we're doing it *tonight*."

BODIE

IT WAS MIDNIGHT AND WE WERE HUNTING PEOPLE, BUT unlike the hundreds of other nights I'd hunted alone, tonight I had my pack.

"Don't kill anyone, don't kill anyone," I whispered to myself.

Fucking hell, Larry. Him and his damn bleeding heart. That was gonna go against every instinct I had.

Drake and I stared at the school dorms of Mag-Sorgin from the roof of the restaurant across the street. The haze of the surrounding streetlights annoyed my golden, shifted eyes. My ears twitched. Unlike other shifters, I had gradually developed enough control over myself to shift my senses without shifting my entire body. So I stood on the roof next to Drake in human form, but I used my wolf senses to listen for trouble. I used my nose to scent the human couple at the nearest dormitory door. I held up a hand, signaling for Drake to wait until they were inside.

He listened.

We couldn't afford for one of these stick wavers to find us. So, it was up to me to make sure the coast was clear.

Drake and Easton were the only people I'd ever told about my ability to sense shift. It was a secret I kept close to the chest because it was how I'd managed to make so many damn kills.

I pulled off the pair of glasses I'd worn here, part of my 'just a student, nothing to see here' vibe for the university area, though I did sometimes use the things. My human eyes were annoying that way. They had trouble with focus if I'd been using my shifter eyes for too long.

I peered down over the roof at the glass doorway to the dorm. The brick building was lit by a couple lampposts, but otherwise, the campus tried to emulate that UCLA, brick and stone vibe.

The young guy below gave the girl a kiss before sauntering back to his dorm building. She disappeared inside and my senses tracked him.

My heart tapped impatiently in my chest, the way other people's feet tapped in the line at the grocery store. I wanted to get a move on. But at the same time, I knew better. Tonight, we had to move perfectly.

All in all, we were going about this fast. I typically hunted for days before I went for a kill.

But after the attack at the bank, we had to take action. If one of Aubry's little patrol shits could find us, then the Mage Council... and that twisted Triton fuck could too.

I couldn't let them find Aubry.

He'd almost taken her before.

She'd almost gone with him.

That memory still felt like a jagged piece of glass in my chest, even though she'd apologized for it.

I pulled her face up in my mind. The soft trusting look she'd given me, peering up through her eyelashes just before we separated tonight. Just that look made my dick hard. Everything about her made me hard.

She'd gone with Easton as part of the plan to surround the campus. While part of me was still rankled over Easton being her mate too, at least I knew for certain that I had someone to watch her back. It was better than her getting paired up with that Rocco fucker. I felt bad that her cousin was paired off with him, but Aubry had been insistent. She'd sworn up and down that she knew that Drake would watch my back better than either of those two would.

Maybe that was true.

But would I watch his?

I wondered as my eyes trailed the male student heading up the stairs to his brick dormitory.

Easton had told me all about his little theory. That Drake had somehow adopted us as part of his valor.

But that would make him my alpha.

And fuck that.

I didn't have an alpha.

I *was* one.

The wolf in me snarled at the thought that the dragon would try to trap us that way. It wanted to challenge him. I leashed the beast, because I knew better than to do that. But still. Even Drake's proximity rankled.

The kid went in and I lifted my hand to my earpiece, ready to give the go signal—when another teenage fucker came striding out. Damn it! Didn't these idiots sleep?

Another three minutes went by, during which Aubry activated our earpieces and whistled, using the signal Drake had made everyone learn for check in. That meant she and Easton had finished scanning the parking lots. Good.

I touched my earpiece and gave the 'negative, not time to move,' owl hoot as a response. It made me feel like an idiot. My wolf fucking hated making a bird sound. It was beneath us.

Of course, Drake just assigned the noises. Fucker didn't make them. It made my jaw tic how we had to live by every one of his stupid rules, though a part of me knew they were important.

"Next fucking animal noise is yours," I growled.

"Nope."

He didn't even glance over, didn't even negotiate. That arrogant fuck.

"You aren't my alpha," I told him.

"Never said I was," he responded, still staring out at the night air, calm and still as a tide pool.

"Then stop acting like it," I clenched my fist. One punch. It would feel so good and it wouldn't really hurt either of us. But I knew Drake and I would never stop at just one punch. And Easton wasn't here to play the peacemaker.

"You came up with this bullshit system—"

"You can come up with the next one," he said, completely missing the fucking point.

"Your system, you talk."

"No." Drake's hands clenched on the rooftop and it was the first sign of humanity I'd seen from him all night.

"Why the fuck not?"

"You know why."

"Because it's a stupid system?"

"Because she doesn't want to talk to *me*."

She. Aubry.

I glared over at Drake, ignoring the bumbling college student I was supposed to be watching. I could hear the drunken fool well enough.

"What the hell do you mean?"

"What I said."

"I heard what you said, but why the fuck do you care what she wants?" My stomach churned as Easton's new theory passed through my head. No. I hated that theory. Goldilocks was dead wrong. I was not sharing my mate with yet another fucking dude. Especially not Drake.

Even though Aubry had approached me and told me about it, trying to get it off her chest, trying to be honest. Even though I'd seen the longing in her eyes when she mentioned him. Even though I'd told her—as I shot myself in the fucking heart—that I would love and support her no matter what.

Aubry making a move was one thing. Drake making one was another.

His mouth twisted in a rare grimace.

Aw, fuck no.

I looked away, staring out over the campus, trying to spot Aubry and Easton where they were supposed to be holed up in the parking lot, after popping tires to ensure no one could make a quick getaway. "She's not yours to care about."

The silence after my statement might as well have been a damn sonic boom—it pounded in my ears.

"I know." Drake's response was way too quiet to be truthful.

I turned back to him and grabbed his shirt, unable to curb my wolf, who wanted to chase this mother-fucker off and pee a ring around Aubry so that no one else ever came within five feet of her again. "She's mine."

Drake didn't fight. He just gazed down at me dully. "I know." He didn't take his eyes off mine, didn't submit. But he didn't pull my hand off his shirt either. From Drake, that was practically a bow.

I let him go and turned back to the idiot who'd crossed through campus and finally entered another building.

Then I activated the earpiece and gave a tiny, ridiculous mouse squeak. Drake's code for 'go.'

It was time to move out.

The campus grounds were surrounded by a compulsion spell that convinced any random person walking, without the proper supernatural ID, to turn around and walk in the other direction. But that spell didn't extend into the air. And we had three winged vigilantes on our side.

Drake partially shifted, letting his black wings sprout from his back, the clawed tips soaring high above our heads. Though his dragon could take on different sizes, this was the biggest I'd ever seen him make his wings.

"Compensating for something?" I jested.

"Yeah. Your fat ass."

I rolled my eyes. That wasn't even a good retort. But then I moved into position on the edge of the roof, climbing up onto the ledge like a jumper.

Seconds later, I felt Drake's hands wrap around my waist.

"Sorry, I don't like you that way," I told him as he jumped with me tight in his grip as we took to the sky.

"Keep joking. Go ahead."

"Alright. What do dragons call Jon Snow? Wait for it. *Mother*fucker."

Drake loosened his hands on me, letting me slide down a little, showing me what he thought of that joke. But I wasn't worried, his earlier acquiescence even had me feeling a bit cocky as we passed over Larry and Rocco's mage—whose name I'd already forgotten.

They glanced up as our shadow covered them, but quickly bent back to their work. They were crouched in the hedges that surrounded the campus, creating a Movement Restriction Spell. If any magical being was able to get past the campus' compulsion spell, this spell would trap them. Any person who stepped inside the glowing turquoise circle would be stuck, feet unable to move until Larry or Rocco's mage lifted the spell or verbally released the person. Our mages created a few feet of the spell at a time, then covered their work with leaves and grass clippings from a shifter lawn care company so that the glow wasn't visible.

I hoped they were working fast enough. The campus was pretty big.

Drake and I landed on the roof of the nearest dorm.

I felt slightly smug about getting a couple swipes at Drake, but an even bigger chunk of me was worried about Aubry. My mate bond tugged at me, letting me know she was slightly to the right. I turned, just in time to see her and Easton emerge from around a rooftop HVAC unit hand in hand. My heart relaxed. So, she'd made the flight from the parking lot into campus alright. Easton swung her in a circle and picked her up to nuzzle her nose.

My jealous mind and dick both responded to the sight. Part of me still didn't like him touching her at all. The other part of me didn't like that he was touching her alone. I wanted to walk up behind her and sandwich her between us again. God, I could still hear her moans replaying in my mind.

The sight of Kira touching down with Rocco on the building to our left knocked sexy thoughts out of my head, though. It was time for business.

"Everyone have their powder?" Drake asked through our earpieces.

Everyone confirmed.

We'd emptied out at least eighty sleep grenades, pouring the powder into plastic baggies that we'd duct taped inside our shirts. If some human cop were to bust us, we'd look like coke runners.

Drake barked out, "Alright. Let's get this done quickly."

He and I walked to the unit on our rooftop. We bent and made quick work of the AC unit's cover, pulling it off. Then I yanked out a plastic baggy full of sleep powder and set it beside the unit so Kira could fly over and use her golden wings to push it through the vents quickly and put the whole building to sleep in under two minutes.

Once our cover was off, Drake grabbed me. We flew off the roof and landed in the grass. We posted up at the exits, ensuring no one could get out while Kira worked her magic above us.

Then Drake and I flew to another building on campus. Then a third. The plan was to hit every single building with sleep grenade powder, just in case someone was inside. It would make a hell of a mess, but Kira assured us she could blow the sleep dust out of there quickly after all was said and done.

When we reached our fourth building, the Student Union Building—by peering into the windows, it looked like this was where all the campus fast-food was —we happened to touch down on the roof at the exact same time as Aubry and Easton.

That's when Drake pulled the most pussy-assed move I'd ever seen from him.

He fucking took a step back, said, "I'm gonna check... over there." And he flew off.

What the hell? I'd never seen him act like that. He'd killed dozens of people, maybe not as many as I had. And, while I adored my mate, her parents had been dead to me from the moment they hadn't fought to take her back. That was shit right there. A pack didn't leave a man behind. I leaned over the roof and watched Drake stride over to guard an exit, shaking my head. "He was my goddamn ride."

"Thought I was your ride," Aubry teased.

I scooped her up and squeezed her ass. "Don't start shit right here, Butterfly. Not yet." But I loved her sass. I smacked her butt and Easton and I got to work pulling the two AC units on this building's roof off.

Aubry wandered over to the edge of the building. I could have asked why, but I liked the view of her ass in the moonlight while I worked, so I didn't.

She turned around and said, "I'm gonna go let Kira know to get this building next." Then she fluttered those gorgeous wings of hers and rose into the air, giving me an even less restricted view of her body as her shirt was tugged down by the wind and the top of her cleavage peeked out.

She turned and pressed her feet together, her lush, biteable, peach-shaped ass dangling just above us before she flew off with a soft whoosh. Even though the sight of her entranced me, I still heard the scuff of someone's shoe.

And it wasn't mine or Easton's.

I turned and gave Easton my wide eyes. He knew that meant to freeze. He did, his eyes glancing side to side, trying to tell what it was I sensed.

I sniffed the air, but nothing came to me on the breeze. So, no one was on the roof. But I turned my head and spotted an access door.

There.

I pointed.

Easton and I made our way toward the door silently. We'd worked together often enough that he knew to let me take point and he covered my six. I pulled out a gun with a silencer already attached.

Easton's eyes widened and he shook his head. But I was too busy listening to the person on the other side of the door. Whatever mage fuck was on the other side was busy chanting. I could hear him.

I yanked open the door and said, "Like to spell? I got one for you. D-E-A-D." I shot him through the forehead before I finished the line... but still, I thought he got the gist.

The body tumbled down the stairs and I peered inside, looking and listening for any of crusty-old mage fuck's friends.

Easton immediately grabbed my arm. "Dude! We aren't supposed to kill anybody!"

I curled my lip. "Oh. Yeah. I forgot."

Easton rubbed his forehead in frustration. Then he laughed up at the stars. "Damn it. We better hide the body, so Larry doesn't see it." Then he glanced at me. "You've got a little something..." Easton gestured across his face.

I reached up and touched my own face then glanced at my fingers. Blood splatter. "Fine," I sighed. "We can hide him." Part of me was annoyed, another part slightly pissed. The mage I'd killed was definitely trying to attack us. It was absolutely self-defense. Not that I cared about that. But Larry would.

Easton was right though; it would be better if Larry didn't know.

If we called Aubry, she could ash the body and then the three of us could repeat the other night... I went to call out the new plan, but Easton was back at my side way too fast.

"Aubry already flew off to help Kira," he stated, like he was some damn mind-reader at the fair.

"We could have brought her with us," I grunted. My wolf felt sulky. I'd barely gotten back and now I hardly got to see my mate.

"What if there are more down there?" Easton shook his head. "I don't want her getting hurt. It's better if she's gone."

I wanted to make a face at him for being so fucking considerate. Fuckwad. Aubry was tough. "She can fight her way out." I said as I yanked a little too hard on the access door and started down the steps. The mage idiot hadn't bothered with a light, so we got to descend in darkness. Awesome. And the stairs were slippery from mage fuck's blood. Double awesome.

"Aubry could fight. Yeah. But she shouldn't have to." Easton said.

"Stop being the thoughtful mate," I growled. "Don't make me the asshole."

"Dude, it's not a competition."

"Everything's a competition."

"If I thought that, I'd always be losing." Easton replied as we neared the body, which had tumbled down the stairs.

"What the hell does that mean?"

"You're a fucking assassin and Drake's 'The Shadow.'

The police gave him a nickname and you are just...
you."

I furrowed my eyebrows and stared at him. "You do
realize we don't enjoy killing people, right? Not
completely anyway. Ok, only sometimes."

Easton laughed. "Yeah, well, next to you, machining
a couple guns doesn't feel like much."

"You're the nice one," I told him as we reached the
mage's body, which was sprawled across several steps;
he hadn't fallen conveniently all the way down. He'd
have to be carried. And we'd have to try not to get
blood all over ourselves so that Larry wouldn't spot it.
And clean the stairs at some point. Or just never *ever*
let the mage up here.

I sighed.

"You know what they say about nice guys," Easton
told me.

"Please, I saw how she looked after that dinner you
made her." My eyes flashed gold despite my efforts to
tamp my wolf down. "I smelled the room. How many
orgasms did you give her?" I tried to make it sound
casual, but next chance I got, I was totally gonna beat
his number.

"That doesn't matter," Easton said. "She was worried
sick about you for days. You should have seen it."

"Well, you should have seen her sappy-ass lovesick
face when I walked in. And it wasn't for me." That had
hurt. Yeah, she'd rushed to me after. But the idea that
she was okay while I was gone, though I spent every

fucking waking minute tracking that Triton fuck—who was a goddamned ghost—thinking of her... I wouldn't have been surprised if someone walked up and told me I had died and gone to hell.

Easton grabbed my shoulder and turned me to face him, even though it was black as hell. "I only gave her that dinner because she was pining for you. She wouldn't eat. Wouldn't give Drake back the burner phones so he could destroy them even though she ended up burning them up herself on accident. She just sat on the floor half the day, staring at the wall. She needs you too, Bodie."

I wouldn't have thought that hearing another person was miserable would cheer me up. But it did. It fucking did. "You telling the truth?" I asked gruffly, trying not to let vulnerability seep into my voice.

"Yeah. You can ask anyone. She helped with the kids in the vault a little. Met with us to talk when she had to. But whenever she was alone... it was bad."

My mate bond sang a little. "Well... thanks for taking care of her, I guess."

"Always," Easton replied. "We're pack."

I had to swallow the lump in my throat when he said that. Anyone else who was pack wanted to know what I could do for them, how I could help them, protect them. It's why Easton and Drake had been my refuge. They didn't ever ask me for things I didn't want to give. They tried not to ask for anything at all.

Fuck.

I was not gonna have some 'bro' moment with a dead body at my feet.

I blew out a breath and studied the body before bending and grabbing his arms. "You got legs?" I asked Easton.

"Yup."

Together we wrangled the body down the rest of the stairs and into a hallway that at least had a couple of lights. There were quite a few doors.

I grinned at Easton as he dropped the legs and I started to drag the body toward the closest door. "Alright, Deadly Dursley... let's go find you a cupboard to hide in."

"Dude, that was a total Aubry line." I could hear Easton's grin in his voice. "Our mate's rubbing off on you."

"No. I'm the one who rubs off on her," I bantered back. "Speaking of, let's get this guy hidden and lock down the school so I can go do that."

"Roger Dodger."

We stuffed the body in a janitor's closet. Then hurried back up to the roof, so that Kira could activate the sleep powder and shove it through the vents.

But when we made it to the roof, the night sky was lit up with mage spells that crackled like fireworks.

AUBRY

"MAGE ATTACK!"

I heard the words echo across the night sky, but I had no idea who'd uttered them. It didn't even matter; I immediately took flight in the direction of the voice, no matter whose it was. I spread my wings out and tucked them back with blistering speed, shooting through the dark air. We had to head off those mages before they somehow ruined what we'd *almost* achieved —the unprecedented act of taking over a mage school.

My pulse thrummed, ready to fight. But we had to stop them *peacefully* thanks to Larry and his bleeding heart—and my plan to keep that bleeding heart on our side. That meant the other side got to fight full out while we had to show restraint.

This was gonna be so hard…

I spotted Rocco pulling out a gun as a potion arced through the air and splashed onto the grass beside him.

Diving, I touched down a few feet away and forcefully lowered his firearm.

"Peaceful takeover, remember?" I reminded him sternly.

The saber tooth sneered. "We didn't get powerful in New York by being pussies. You can't be afraid to shed a little blood."

"I'm not afraid of bloodshed, pussy cat," I said, stepping up into his personal space. "But you made a deal with us. You said you'd do this clean, and you damn well better hold up your end of the bargain."

Rocco glared at me, and I glared right back. Another potion bottle splashed at our feet, and a couple drops of damaging potion kissed my ankle like poison. By the looks of the grimace on Rocco's face, I assumed he'd been hit by it too.

Great. Because we'd been arguing, we'd each lost a little bit of our magical ability. My fire wouldn't be as hot. I had no idea what the potion would do to the tiger —shorten his fangs? But he needed to give in so we could fucking move out of range.

He stuffed the handgun into his belt and grunted. "Fine."

I cocked my head. "*Fine*. Now go tell Kira to hurry her ass up. We need sleep grenades in—" I peered through the shadowed windows of the building as best I could. I thought I saw rows of little vials and faucets on the tables, and maybe a shadow ducking down. "— the science lab. ASAP."

Rocco nodded once and took off across the lawn. I was surprised he'd listened, but I didn't have much chance to mull that over because my eyes were busy scanning the area for our attackers.

Drake touched down near me a moment later, his heavy muscular body landing on the yard with a solid thump. "What's going on? I heard someone yell '*mage attack*.'"

I nodded, tilting my head so I could better listen for those mage idiots. "That was Rocco. I sent him to get Kira over here *stat*."

"Where'd the attack come from?" Drake asked, eyes watching my six.

I tipped my head in the direction of the science center. "In there. Apparently, some mages in the science building haven't been hit with the sleep grenades yet. No idea how many little shitstains there are, but they've only thrown a couple potions, so I assume we can spank them all soundly and put them to bed."

To my surprise Drake smirked and handed me a black piece of cloth. I unfurled it, holding it up to see the boney mouth of a skeleton printed in white. Drake tugged his own piece of cloth over his head—black with sharp white teeth—and covered his mouth and nose.

Then he lifted a challenging brow at me. "You feel like wrecking a few mages?"

"*Peacefully*," I mocked with an eye roll.

But I wasn't one to back down from a challenge. In fact, part of me was skipping around like a little girl on a playdate. I pulled my own mask over the bottom half of my face and readjusted my ponytail, allowing the cascading waterfall of silvery white hair to fall over the front of my shoulder.

"Right," Drake agreed just as scathingly. "*Peacefully*. On Larry's honor."

I snorted. "Pretty sure you're supposed to swear on your own honor."

Drake's eyes crinkled in the corners, a sure sign he was grinning, even though I couldn't see it. "I have no honor to swear on, Dollface. Better to use his, since it actually means something."

Wasn't that the truth, I thought wryly.

"Come on," he said, ducking down and slinking over to the shadows surrounding the building.

I followed him, half tiptoeing half fluttering.

"We're out of sleep grenades," Drake whispered. "Kira has the last of them. So, we'll have to do this the old-fashioned way."

I grinned. "Sounds perfect." My blood started to rush, and my fingers tingled with anticipation.

His eyes searched mine for just a moment before he swallowed and turned back toward the door. "On my signal, we bust in. You take left, I'll take right. Got it?"

I nodded. "Got it."

Drake held up three fingers, silently ticking them down until there were none left standing. We burst through the door and immediately took action. He rushed right, while I tucked and rolled to the left. A potion bottle sailed over my head and crashed onto the tile floor behind me.

It had come from the classroom on my side of the hall, where a door and a window were both propped open. Drake and I walked in just as the mage who'd chucked it ducked behind a back table with a sink and a Bunsen burner on top. Little vials and potion bottles littered the surface, along with a thick spell book open to a page in the middle.

I followed the mage's lead and found a chemistry table of my own to hide behind. Peeking up so that only my eyes showed, I scanned the potions before me, looking for one that was a powdery white—a sleep grenade—but I found none.

I peered across the room to where Drake was hunkered down behind a different table. There must have been at least a dozen of the damn things—three rows and four deep: my row, Drake's row, and the middle row between us, stretching back with four tables between us and the back of the class. Surely *one* would have the potion we needed. But then again, we didn't actually know how many mages were back there. We might've needed quite a few.

Drake caught my eye and signaled with his hand for us to move forward. I nodded before glancing around the corner and scurrying up to the next table in line.

Clear. No mage fucks squatting in the shadows. I

glanced over at Drake. His side was clear too. Six tables down, six to go. Two more rows.

He signaled again, but I shook my head, pausing to check my new table for Sleep Grenade Potions. I grabbed one that I thought might be right, sniffing it ever so slightly to see if I could detect the sugary smell of a properly completed potion. But I couldn't exactly tell. It might've been ready, but it might not have been. Either way, I grabbed it just in case. A half-assed weapon was better than none.

Actually, a half-assed weapon was *better* than a good one—especially when we weren't supposed to harm our targets. So, if this wasn't a Sleep Grenade Potion, but some kind of Damage Potion, hopefully it would only half work.

Drake followed my lead and palmed a white-colored bottle, then signaled once more to move forward. This time, I nodded.

We moved up to the third row of tables and we both glanced across the aisle. Clear again. Which meant, the mage—or small group of mages—was hiding somewhere in row four, just a few feet away.

My blood sang at the prospect of hand-to-hand combat, even though I knew I should try to avoid that if at all possible.

Use the potion first, I told myself, gripping the bottle firmly. *If it fails—and it very well may—then I can whip out Jill and her lesser known counterpart, Vil.* I just barely resisted the urge to hold up my clenched fists and glamour the letters up, so they were tattooed on my knuckles. The point was, if the sleep grenade failed, I was going to bibbity-bobbity-throat punch that mage bitch.

Drake caught my attention once more and held up three fingers, counting us down. Three, two... one. On his signal, I ducked low and raced around the corner of my table.

The squeak of sneakers on shiny tiles filled the air around us as Drake and I converged from each side. We found two mages holed up near the middle of the back wall.

Young bucks, the fuckers still had acne and skinny arms. But their expressions were scornful. A small stash of potions was scattered on the ground between them where they crouched.

All four of us reacted at once, chucking our potion bottles as fast as we could. Drake and I bombed the mage students with whatever we'd picked up, while they'd hammered our torsos with Mage Fire Potions. What they weren't expecting, though, was that Drake and I were both fire-proof.

I gave a cocky grin as the fire burned away my shirt. I didn't have a bra thanks to Bodie.

Drake chuckled.

The mages' eyes widened, and I wasn't quite sure if their slack-jawed expressions were due to my rack or the fact that I simply walked forward covered in fire. I didn't get a chance to ask, because apparently, our potions *had* been sleep grenades. Maybe not fully brewed, because thing one and thing two weren't instantly knocked out. But their expressions dulled after a second and they slumped onto the floor, fast asleep, while Drake and I casually put out our flames.

Suddenly, his head jerked up and he stared at me with wide eyes, stepping closer.

I inhaled sharply and every piece of me tightened in anticipation. Half a step more and his naked chest would brush against mine.

But then Drake whispered, "The squeaky sneakers. I can still hear them but they're getting quieter."

My eyes went wide too, because that could only mean one thing—one of the mages had eluded us. There was another out there.

Damn it.

We both jolted into parallel sprints, racing down a long hallway where trophies perched behind glass encasements. I kept one arm over my chest, the other ready with flame, just in case I needed to use it. Finally, our target came into view up ahead.

It was a girl, if the round ass and swaying brown ponytail were anything to go by.

She must have snuck through the middle aisle at the same time as Drake and I moved around the outer aisles. Sneaky little bitch. I was gonna abracadabra her ass.

"Oh fuck," Drake growled, pushing his legs even faster.

I flapped my wings in order to keep up. "What?"

He nodded slightly. "She's headed for an emergency alarm. It's that red thing in the wall. If she pulls that lever..."

Then we were going to be flooded with mages and MPs before we'd even secured the damn campus.

Shit!

Drake touched his earpiece and radioed our teammates. "Two mages down in the science center. Lab five. Get there and chain them up now! Another mage on the run, in pursuit of an emergency lever. Be prepared for a heavy attack if she reaches it..."

We were gaining on her, but there was no way in hell we'd reach her before she got to the lever.

Damn it! Do something, Aubry! My mind bitch-slapped me into clarity.

I yanked one of Easton's earrings from my earlobe, careful not to lose either of the pieces. In my haste, I was pretty sure I used every last drop of Growth Potion, but regardless, the glowing pink blade grew and came to life in my palm. I knew I wasn't supposed to kill anyone—and I was going to try damned hard not to—but if I had to choose between one girl and a bloodbath, then...

The girl stretched her arm out as she ran, almost to the lever. Just a few more feet and it'd all be game over. Hell no. I couldn't let that happen.

I took a deep breath, aimed my knife at my target just as I always did with darts, and let the blade fly. It tumbled through the air faster than the girl's feet could carry her. And with a slushy *thwack*, it nailed her fucking hand right to the brick wall behind it.

She screamed bloody murder, her eyes widening in terror as the blood spilled from her hand and onto the floor at her feet. She completely forgot about the lever, too focused on her injury as she tried to yank the knife out and only succeeded in cutting her own hand more.

Yes!

"Fucking nice!" Drake shouted enthusiastically.

When I glanced over, I saw he'd pulled his mask down and there was a massive, genuine smile plastered onto his handsome face.

Jesus fuck me with a dragon dildo... Thank god he almost never smiled. I'd never be able to resist.

As soon as we reached the girl, Drake pulled out a set of cuffs from the expandable bag, and I wrenched my knife from her hand and the wall as she shrieked. I shook my head, eyeing her without mercy. What a whiny little bitch. It was just a little stab wound. Nothing to cry about compared to what could have happened to her. I wiped her blood on my pant leg and stuffed Easton's knife into my waistband, since I had no idea how to re-shrink it after use.

Then I yanked on her shirt. "Take it off."

I stripped her shirt off—because she did have a bra and would at least be covered—and then I shoved the thing over my head. Bodie would be disappointed by it. It was black and had some nerdy science saying on it and there was absolutely zero chance of the girls popping out of it.

I turned around to see Drake staring. But he just cleared his throat and busied himself by cuffing the sobbing girl as Rocco and Kira came down the hallway. They each had a chained up, sleeping mage slung over their shoulders and a gun held in their free hands. They looked like badass heroes from an action flick—all that was missing was the slow-motion victory walk with the burning building in the frame behind them.

Drake hefted up our own prisoner like she was light as a feather, and she kicked and screamed in his grasp. My eyes narrowed at the sight of his hand on the back of her thighs, her ass and pussy so close to his face. A growl reverberated up my throat, and I coughed to hide the evidence of my jealousy.

What the fuck, Aubry? Get it together!

"Anybody got an extra sleep grenade?" Drake asked the two newcomers.

Rocco smirked and pocketed his handgun, pulling a baggie from his vest. "*One.*"

"Perfect." Drake lifted his mask over his nose and sprinkled powder into the flailing girl's mouth.

Her body quickly slackened. Drake held her out in front of him like a doll and shook off any excess powder, before tossing her back over his shoulder like a sack of potatoes.

His disinterest in her had my ego stroking herself like a cat, or a wanton slut.

"Let's get these assholes to a classroom, shall we?" Drake asked cockily. "Shifter school is now in session."

Rocco and Kira chuckled as they followed Drake down the hall, carting the three mages' sleeping bodies away. I took a deep breath and followed just a few feet behind them. I definitely did not let my eyes slide to Drake's ass. Not more than once, anyway.

We'd done it. We'd successfully taken over a mother fucking *mage school*—a feat that had never even been attempted before. I was flying high inside, riding a wave of adrenaline and dopamine as the hormones cascaded through my bloodstream. Disbelief and awe and just pure punch-the-air-victory ran through my system.

A small skirmish had just been won, but it was a massive triumph for the shifters. I had no idea how many other fights lay ahead of us, one thing was for sure...

Here in L.A.? The ultimate battle in this nasty mage shifter war was *About. To. Go. Down.*

I just hoped *we* didn't go down, too.

14

AUBRY

WE'D BEEN ARGUING ALL DAY, SO MUCH THAT IT FELT like I'd been throat-punched. My voice was all raw and rusty-sounding, like an old nail had been hammered into my vocal cords.

After taking the school over, locking the students up in the bursar's office, cleaning up the sleep powder, and getting the shifters settled in, we'd all basically slept through the entire day yesterday—other than our guard shifts, of course.

So today had been our first attempt at discussing what we should do now. And holy fuck was it ever backfiring.

Everyone disagreed about the next steps we should take. After hours of quarrelling around a circular dining table, we *still* hadn't come to a decision. Go after another mage jewel? Destroy all the known caches of potions? Pile all the mages on a pyre and burn them like witches?

To say our disagreements had been fierce would have been an understatement.

Later that evening, I was back to squabbling with Rocco as we stood on a rooftop watching over the starry night sky. Dude just wanted to go all *Gangs of New York* on everything. Wasn't gonna happen, though. Not on my watch.

"There are some good fucking cops out there," I said, shooting his argument down for the third time.

We were posted next to a mounted sleep grenade launcher that Easton had designed and built, because even though we'd protected the *grounds* themselves from infiltration, pixies and fae could still come at us from the *air*. So, we'd set up a number of these gun outposts on the roofs in order to ensure the safety of the countless shifters who'd been filtering onto the campus all day and night looking for shelter.

Larry waited at the gates, verifying identities and giving the incoming shifters permission to move once they were inside the circle, while Kira escorted them all to the first level of the Student Union Building—where Rocco and I were currently on watch.

"Good fucking cop," Rocco snorted. "That's an oxymoron."

"You're an oxymoron," I retorted.

"Careful," he warned. "Kittens like to chase butterflies."

Pfft. Kitten? He was a forty-something-year-old saber tooth with a bad attitude. *Kitten* wasn't even close.

"Try it." I winked at him, trying to push him just a bit more. "Bodie and Easton would love to have an excuse to fuck with you."

After all the arguing we'd done, a nice bruising fight sounded fantastic.

But he didn't take the bait.

"I still think we ought to just hunt down the Mage Council fucks," Rocco said before he hocked a loogie onto the rooftop.

I stepped away, my lip curling in disgust. "Great plan, Meow Mix. Only, our best assassin can't find my psychotic former best friend—and he's only a minor player on the Mage Council. So how do you propose we find the rest?"

"Your assassin must not be the best then," Rocco snorted haughtily.

How fucking dare he insult Bodie! I clenched my fists and told myself that pushing him off the building would be a very bad idea. Instead, I allowed a pretty visual to run on replay through my head: one of him falling and exploding in a cartoon-like cloud of dust, Wylie Coyote style.

"*And*," Rocco continued as he pulled a pack of cigarettes from his pocket, "your idea to move out of the city is even worse than you think mine is. That's fucking rolling over and taking it."

"*No smoking*," I threatened through gritted teeth. "And fuck you anyway, Calvin and Hobbes. I actually care about the safety and wellbeing of these innocent people. You don't give a shit about casualties."

"The world's not all daisy chains and sing-alongs, Princess," Rocco stated, lighting up despite my death glare. The glowing cherry at the end of his cig brightened as he took a long drag.

Yeah, because that's what my childhood was: *daisy chains and sing-alongs*. More like training at the gym everyday with private Krav Maga fighting lessons, an endless stream of tutors teaching me the weaknesses of various shifters, a Mage Council member visiting my house and zapping me with Pixie-Dust Potions every time I got a question wrong in magical Political Science. Stupid cat had no clue.

Whatever. I rolled my eyes and went back to ignoring him.

A minute later, Easton opened the door to the roof, carrying some packaged crackers and a Gatorade. "Broke into a vending machine. Thought I'd see if you wanted a snack."

"Yeah, somebody get this bitch a Snickers bar. She's getting mouthy." Rocco smirked as he walked over to the edge of the roof and peered down.

"I fucking hate that guy," I told my mate as he opened up the bottle and handed it to me. I grabbed it and took a swig.

"Yeah, but he's got one of the few other mages that

have swapped sides right now," Easton said. "And Larry and Tony are going through the potion stores here… they're pretty extensive. It will be way faster if Larry has help."

I sighed. "Beggars can't be choosers."

Easton ran a hand through my hair, which felt so good. I leaned into his palm as he said, "I dunno… if you *beg* me, you can pretty much *choose* anything you want." He winked.

Damn. How could he be sweet and hot in the same moment? With any other guy, I'd roll my eyes at that, but the blush that crept over Easton's cheeks at that admission, and the thrum of my mate bond let me know he was being completely genuine.

I bit my lip and batted my eyes, trying to appear innocent. Then I clasped my hands in front of me and pressed my breasts together as I gazed up at him. "Please, pretty please can you finish off my shift, Papa Bear?"

"Fuck," Easton groaned. "Not fair."

He pulled me in for a hug and I could feel he was already hard.

I decided to press my advantage, *literally*, pressing my hands down over the head of his cock in his jeans. "I promise I'll be a good girl for you later."

"Damn it. Get out of here. But leave the snacks. I'm starving." Easton released me and took a step back.

I watched intently as he reached his broad hand into his pocket and then adjusted his ginormous erection. The sight of it made me lick my lips. Now *both* sets of my lips were wet.

Easton pointed to the door. "Go. Before I send Rocco away and we end up fucking on this rooftop and getting killed because a legion of pixies fly down and maul us when our eyes are closed."

I giggled and blew him a kiss. God, he was the sweetest mate. "I'm gonna go for a swim to cool off. Meet you back at our room."

"If you fuck Bodie before I get back, there'll be hell to pay." Easton warned.

"Got it."

"Stop talking about fucking, you godawful saps. *Fated mates*. Shit. This is why you don't fucking let women into the inner circle."

And that was my cue to leave. Otherwise I was gonna pull out the dagger earrings that Easton had given me and remove Rocco's balls from his body. He could eunuch his way through life just fine. He definitely didn't need any progeny.

I'd taken one step toward the door when I heard Easton yell, "Fuck!"

I swung around and immediately saw Rocco barreling through the shadows, straight toward the big mounted gun. My first thought was that the twisted asshole was attacking my mate. I lit a fire in both my palms, jumping into protective mode faster than I could blink.

But then Easton grabbed a Sleep Grenade and

loaded it into the cannon. Rocco manned the dual handles and swiveled the heavy beast upward so that the barrel pointed at the dark sky.

I squinted into the night, cursing the fact that I didn't have their shifter senses. Finally, I spotted movement. It looked like a bird. No... a pixie. *Shit.*

BOOM.

The guys fired off a shot and the sleep grenade flew through the sky. I watched in a bit of a daze as it exploded in midair. The powder surrounded the pixie in a cloud of white dust.

The council had *already* found us? That didn't seem right...

I watched the pixie start to plummet and immediately my training kicked in. I extinguished my flames and took a running leap toward the snoozing creature. She fell ten times as fast as the dust that drifted on the breeze. I swooped in and used my shirt as a hammock to snag her without letting the powder touch my skin. Then I immediately propelled my wings forward so I'd get out from under the cloud of magic.

When I did that, I ended up hovering above one of the rooftops on the edge of campus, searching for anyone else who might have come with the pixie. When I didn't see anyone suspicious on the streets, just clueless humans going about their evening—walking dogs and heading into a coffee shop across from campus, I glanced back down at our new captive.

She wore an MP uniform, street patrol style, and

she looked young as she snored peacefully in my shirt. Unlike Tee, her hair wasn't bright pink, but rather a natural green. I didn't recognize her, although these days that wasn't uncommon with the new recruits.

Maybe she was just on patrol. Maybe the college was part of her beat. God, I hoped so. That would at least buy us a few hours if she didn't check in. Otherwise, if someone had sent her on purpose... but just then the radio on her shoulder buzzed with normal check ins. Relief washed over me that she likely wasn't wave one of some attack. At least, she didn't appear to be anyway.

I flew above the trees that dotted the campus, enjoying the night breeze as I made my way back to the guys and gently set the cop on the rooftop with them. "She's probably gonna be out for a while. Looks like a beat cop to me."

"Yeah, well, when she wakes up, she'll definitely be a beat cop," Rocco growled.

I clenched my teeth and turned to Easton. "Maybe *you* should question her when she wakes up." The fucking cat couldn't retract his claws for even a second. *Ugh.*

Easton nodded. "I'll take care of it. Good thinking to save her so we can see what the word on the street is right now."

I nodded. But inside I cringed. Was that why I'd saved her? For information? Was that who I'd become? At first, I'd thought saving her was an instinct. But as I trudged down the stairs to go change—and figure out something that would get this damn antsy feeling out of my chest—I couldn't help but wonder.

I decided to push off the thinking. Philosophy could happen when I was old. But I had to get out this nervous, frightened, furious energy that kept swirling around like shoes in a dryer, kicking my ribs from the inside.

I changed and headed to the gymnasium, which was dark. But the pool lights were still on under the water, reminding me a little of the late-night swims I used to take at home. That had been one of my few moments of reprieve, after the tutors were gone and my parents were off at some function or another. I'd loved going down to the pool and doing laps, faerie style, wings propelling me from above and skimming my body along the surface.

I shoved down the nostalgia as I climbed slowly into the cold water. Instantly, goosebumps rose on my skin and I started to shiver. *Perfect*. The cold and the exercise would exorcise my thoughts, compel them to leave.

I was finishing my twentieth lap when I heard the squeak of a door opening. I stopped swimming and touched down in the three feet of water at the shallow end to see who it was.

Fucking Drake stood there in black swim trunks. And no shirt. The blue ripples of the water lights danced across his abs.

My swim was officially ruined. The calm I'd found from sliding through the water was gone.

I waded over to the steps and climbed out of the pool. I didn't bother to reach for a towel from the stack by the wall since I was just going to shower off anyway. Instead, I fluttered my wings to get most of the water off of them, incidentally splashing Drake with a few drops. I put a hand on my hip as I stood there, the rest of my body still dripping wet and clad in nothing more than a purple bikini courtesy of my go-bag, which included bikinis for some reason—thank you, *Bodie*.

Irritation flooded me as I stared at Drake, the stupid, peace-killing interloper. Why had he picked the pool? Why had he picked this very moment? He was a damned dragon, for fuck's sake! Shouldn't he go swim in a volcano or something?

Drake's eyes scanned down my body slowly and I didn't miss the fact that his cock twitched beneath his swim trunks. His eyes narrowed before flashing back up to mine; his face stiff and angry, like he didn't enjoy the fact he'd been turned on and then caught.

Well, I don't like it either, Buddy. I hated the incessant tension that filled the air between us. Like he constantly expected me to sneak up and stab him in the back. Unlike *him*, I didn't do shit like that. If I was gonna kill him, I'd watch his face while I did it.

But the errant thought made my throat tighten. I wasn't quite sure how deeply mired I'd become in this new criminal underworld, but I was *not* going to allow myself to kill for hatred. Survival? Yes. Hatred? No. That made a person into a beast of a totally different color.

Drake's jaw twitched as if he'd sensed my thoughts about murder and then deliberately misinterpreted them, just like the fucker often did my words.

The reality was, I didn't hate him for what he'd done. I hated him for who he was. That damn, smirking, arrogant, know-it-all quality about him just chafed me raw. I liked to be dominated in bed, not out of it. I gave him a fake ass smile. "Pool's all yours."

He just grunted in response.

Caveman. Ugh.

I hurried toward the locker room, ready to be away from Drake. I was so fucking *done* with the arguing and the stress. The MP was nothing compared to all this. That was the entire reason I'd wanted to hit up the pool —to chill the hell out. Well, *that*, and I was also hoping the sight of me in my bikini would tempt Easton and Bodie into another three-way. A devious grin crept onto my face.

But Drake called out just before I could escape through the orange locker room door.

Damn it all. Why couldn't he just ignore me like he used to? Like when I asked questions and he didn't even bother to answer? My heart began thumping out an answer to that question, but I didn't want to hear it.

I turned slowly, highly aware of my long, glistening legs and how cold the air was on my nipples. I wanted to be someplace else, anywhere else. And yet... I didn't.

"Aubry. There's something I want to bring up with the team later." He scratched his side, which made me hyper aware of his six-pack and that tiny line of black hair that had haunted more than one of my dreams.

He strode toward me casually, or as casually as Drake could manage with that giant tree branch shoved up his pompous ass. He was still quite a few feet away when he stopped and shoved his hands into his trunk pockets.

Fuck. I think he paused to adjust himself. So his hard-on wouldn't be so obvious. I tried not to let my eyes flicker south to confirm my thoughts.

I narrowed my gaze, waiting for him to speak, but he just cleared his throat and flicked his gaze away from me, like he couldn't stand the sight of me in the bikini. Was he pissed he was turned on? Or maybe it was guilt?

Nah. That fucking lizard is too cold-hearted to feel anything. He probably just realized that my nipples could cut glass. It's probably making him uncomfortable.

For some childish reason, that thought made me smirk.

"There are a lot of Portal Potions nearly finished here," Drake finally said. "I can get Larry and Tony to finish them up and then I can portal to different Mage Council houses around the globe. I can try to find another jewel."

His words bashed my heart in like a set of brass knuckles.

He wanted to repeat exactly what he'd already done? No, not even what he'd done—what he'd *tried* and *failed* to do? What the fuck had happened to being unpredictable? What was wrong with him? Did he have a death wish?

The dark look in his eyes made me worried that he might. But even with that, I couldn't tamp down on the rage he'd invoked in me.

"What? No!" I immediately stormed over to him, glaring up at the tall, muscular fuck. "Do you even hear yourself? Do you know how idiotic that plan is? I thought you were the thinker, but what the hell? It's like the wheel's spinning but the hamster's dead in there. That is the stupidest fucking thing—"

"We need a jewel so we can hide permanently. This?" he gestured at the college in general, "is just temporary. We can't man guns on the rooftops forever. And going to a Mage Councilor's stash seems to be the only way to get one. They've clamped down on transporting the damn things and—"

"There's no way in fuck the guys will agree to this!" I wouldn't let them.

"They will if you back me," Drake said quietly.

A whole new round of emotions set off like fireworks inside of me. Whizzing shock. Sparking fury. Shrieking despair. He wanted me to manipulate my mate bond? Use it so he could get his idiotic, masochistic way?

"Fuck no!"

Drake shoved a hand through his black hair, yanking on the ends. He was frustrated as fuck. *Good.* That made two of us.

"Why do you even give a shit, as long as I get it done?" he growled.

I stayed silent, anger seething in my veins as I tried to sort out the answer to his question.

Why do I give a shit?

"What's your fucking problem with everything I do?" He took a step closer, but I held my ground, clenching my fists at my side.

"Everything you do is reckless and stupid!" I spat.

"Who the fuck cares?" he shouted, throwing his arms out wide. "My pack is dead! There's no one left to worry about me!"

"Yeah, well, *I* worry about you, you stupid Horntail!"

I swallowed hard. Fuck me. I hadn't meant to say that out loud. He'd made me so mad that my filter had burnt to a crisp.

"No. *You* don't get to worry about me," he growled as he stared down into my eyes. "Not after what I did."

"You don't get to tell me what to do." I stepped up into Drake's face, enjoying how his eyes flashed gold. Pissing him off and defying him gave me this twisted sense of satisfaction and I clung to it, embraced it, fanned the flames. "You aren't my alpha. Or my mate."

Those last words cracked open a gash in me that was as long and deep as the Grand Canyon. I almost couldn't breathe.

"Thank god for that," Drake's tone was sarcastic, but his body told me he didn't believe his own words. His chest heaved and a smoke ring escaped his lips.

Clearly, I'd cracked him open, too, just as I had myself. Why were we always doing this to each other? Why did we love to hate and hurt one another so much?

My heart thudded wildly, and my nipples tightened further under my swimsuit, sending a zinging electric feeling all the way down between my thighs. I could feel the anger radiating off of him, the need to dominate me pouring through his veins like liquid fire, and that instantly made me wet... and pissed off. I should *not* be getting wet for this asshole.

I jabbed a finger into his rock-hard chest. "You couldn't handle me as a mate, anyway, *Maleficent*."

"I wouldn't *want* to, you praying mantis—you've already bitten off the heads of both my friends." He stepped closer and my finger slid up his pec. His body was so hot that the sweat rose off him like steam.

Every nerve ending I had was screaming for me to kneel—not because Drake was my alpha or my mate— he wasn't—but because his fury turned me right the fuck on, and my submissive side wanted to come out to play. To take his anger and watch it transform into control and orgasms. So, so many orgasms.

That sweet apple cider smell invaded my senses once more. And now that I knew what it was—his alpha pheromones trying to subdue me—I couldn't help but slip just the tiniest bit into sub space. He needed me—needed to control me—because everything else in his life was out of control.

My eyelashes fluttered and I lowered my gaze, pressing my breasts forward like a good little sub presenting herself for her master.

Wait.

My eyes snapped back up.

My master? Drake? *Fuck no.*

The rational side of me was pissed that I'd looked down. To make up for it, to take back some of that control, I reached out and grabbed his dick—which was hard as a fucking rock.

Big mistake. *Huge* mistake. It was massive... the mistake.

Drake gripped my shoulders and spun me around. He shoved me against the locker door, smashing my cheek into the painted orange wood. "You don't touch me without permission."

"Yes, sir."

I couldn't help it. It just... slipped out.

He growled, but it quickly turned into a groan of barely contained desire.

And that's when I knew...

Neither of us could resist any longer.

15

DRAKE

THE MOMENT THE WORDS 'YES, SIR' SLIPPED OUT OF
Aubry's luscious mouth, I knew I was a fucking goner.
I'd held back my sexually aggressive and dominating
nature for so long that I thought it might *kill* me. The
tension between us had built until it was as thick as my
cock.

But not anymore.

I reached around her hip and threw open the locker
room door, shoving us both inside. I pushed her across
the cement floor and toward the opposite wall. My legs
moved like they were demon possessed, never stopping
until I pressed Aubry's chest and right cheek up against
the cold metal of a long row of silver lockers.

I pulled her arms up behind her back and made her
clasp them like a good little submissive. She did it will-
ingly, which was just as much of a fucking turn on as
her 'yes, sir' had been.

Mine, my beast growled. The sight of a helpless princess roused my dragon. Damsels were his favorite.

Aubry gasped, whether it was from the chill of the metal or from my actions, I wasn't sure, but I reveled in it just the same. My dragon reared his horny head as the room filled with the scent of her arousal, and I felt my eyes burn as they flashed gold and horns sprouted from my hair.

Down boy, I warned him darkly. A puff of smoke shot from my nostrils, but I felt my eyes cool off.

My gaze traced over her figure from behind. I loved her hair. It was so long, perfect to wrap around my hand and pull. And her legs were willowy but had enough curve that when I ran my fingers over her ass, I could dig in.

I did just that, playing with the hem of her bikini bottoms, teasing her as I studied her. Her skin was pale. And those wings. I couldn't even say why they turned me on so damn much. My dragon loved them. He practically fucking purred at the sight.

Part of me wanted to order her to strip, but there were two big problems with that. One, she was already mostly naked, the buildup of anticipation would be lost. And two, I was so fucking aroused I was nearing the point of madness, and I didn't have the patience for that fucking shit.

My fingers raked up her sides, leaving long pink lines in their wake. The hiss that escaped her parted lips and the involuntary roll of her hips, told me all I needed to know. She was into this. She wanted this as badly as I did. *Needed* it... as badly as I did.

I yanked on the strings of her top and ripped it away, replacing the purple triangles with my greedy hands. She moaned as I found her nipples and squeezed, rolling them out into deliciously hardened peaks. Just touching her after I'd been thinking about it for so long, *denying myself* for so long, sent my mind into a golden haze.

Jesus. Fuck. This was... everything.

I swallowed hard and shoved that thought as far away from my conscious mind as I could. Now was not the time to read too far into things. It would never be time for that. Ever.

I smacked her ass hard, using it to clear my head and enjoying her yelp before I asked, "Sensation play?"

She nodded.

Yesss.

"Pain?"

She nodded again and my cock jumped. I pushed it roughly against her as I shifted one nail on my right hand into a sharp claw. I raked it down her side, not hard enough to break the skin, but hard enough to leave a beautiful pink trail showing where I'd been.

She gave a whimper and I could smell how wet it made her, so I repeated the process on the other side. Then I used my claws to slowly slice the back half of her bikini bottoms to ribbons, striping her ass before I shifted my hands back to human and untied the swimsuit and dropped it to the floor.

"Please," she begged. "Please."

I returned to kneading her breast with my left hand, and with my right, I grazed down the lean plain of her stomach, past her hip bone, and into the hot, creamy folds of her mouthwatering cunt.

Fuck me, the scent of her arousal was inebriating. Like catnip. No, crack. No, catnip on crack. It had been driving me wild since the night I'd spent on Bodie's couch, tossing and turning because that damned red rug in his room had been laced with her cum. I felt my eyes flash with heat once more as my fingers slipped in and out of her. A growl rattled up my throat and another puff of smoke escaped my lips.

I wanted so badly to force her onto her knees and fuck her mouth as she gazed up at me with wide doe-eyes, like a lost, wounded animal. But I couldn't risk it. I wouldn't let her lips anywhere near my body for fear of inducing the...

Again, I swallowed hard and buried my thoughts like I'd buried the bodies of my victims. The worthless criminals who couldn't follow through on their promises to me. Or mages who'd taken sadistic pleasure in hurting others.

No, I was just going to have to fuck her from behind. Spread her ass cheeks and sink my dick into that tight pussy over and over again until I broke her, and maybe keep going even after that.

I fingered her for a few seconds more, rubbing her clit with my dripping wet fingers, relishing the desperate sounds coming out of her throat and mouth. Even though she tried to suppress them like a good little sub, I hadn't ordered her to keep silent yet because those sounds alone edged me.

Her whole body quivered beneath me. Aubry's soft wings pressed against my chest and teased my nipples, and those desperate sounds she made started turning into dangerous moans. She was gonna come soon. The air was damp with her desire and need. But I didn't want to give it to her. Not yet.

So I slipped my hand back out of her and stepped back to stare at the breathtaking view of the most fantastic ass I'd ever seen. Small, but plump and so fucking round, I just wanted to bite the hell out of it.

But I couldn't. I wouldn't allow *my* lips anywhere near *her* body, either.

Goddamn it, this was frustrating.

My fingers gripped her hips with enough force to leave bruises as I prepared to lift her up and lower her down on me, like my own personal blowup doll, an object I would use again and again for my sadistic plea-sure. But before I could get her feet off the ground, she spun around and glared up at me.

Oh shit. Was she pissed? Had I gone too far? Fuck, we hadn't even discussed safe words, and that was one of the most important rules in a dom-sub relationship. Not that that's what this was... a relationship. Not at all.

Shit.

My heart hammered in my chest where sweat beads slowly rolled down my skin and evaporated into steam. My flames flared up internally, ratcheting up the heat so it matched my discomfort.

But Aubry's glare—the one I'd come to love and hate all at once—morphed as she moved her hands. Her soft fingers replaced those droplets of sweat, gliding up my abs and pecs with a gentle determination. I glanced down at her, relieved to find the glare had morphed into a devious little smirk. Her fingers kept trailing higher, over my shoulders, and around the back of my neck. Our faces way too fucking close for comfort, but I couldn't seem to move. She had me paralyzed, completely entranced by her touch.

Damn it all.

Was she part fucking siren? I didn't do this shit. I didn't get entranced. I fucked. *Hard.* But I couldn't move because she had me so damn tangled up in feelings.

"I want to watch your eyes turn gold when you come," Aubry said.

She leaned in, about to bring her lips to mine, when *finally*, my wits came crashing back. A kiss could be an irreversible curse for us both.

I grabbed Aubry's throat and smashed her back into the lockers, making sure I didn't actually choke her hard enough to scare her. I knew I hadn't scared her at all when her tongue came out and wet her lips. Those goddamned plush lips...

"Don't you dare top from the bottom," I hissed. Was she one of those subs who got off on being naughty and then punished? I smacked her ass hard three times.

Based on her moans, I took that as a yes. No wonder she always smelled wet and ready when we argued.

"Rules," I growled. "Absolutely no touching me. I am going to use you and you are going to come more times than you can count, but only if I allow you to. Got it?"

She nodded beneath my grasp, her chest heaving, pushing her hardened nipples into my forearm. "Yes, sir."

She lowered those brown eyes, the way she never would in real life. In real life, she'd fight me tooth and nail. But now, watching her completely give in and submit made my dick harder than a rocket. I was gonna blast off so hard I'd shoot cum into space.

A shiver of delight raced up my spine and I fought the urge to smile. There were so many ways I wanted to torture her...

"When you're submitting to me," I said, snarling slightly, "I want you to call me Alpha. I know all those douchebags at Syn have stage names and shit, but that's not what this is. I *am* an alpha. This shit is *real*. Okay?"

"Yes, Alpha," she replied, and fuck if I didn't love hearing that word on her tongue.

I growled at my own ridiculous thoughts. "What's your safe word?"

She rolled her eyes. "How about dino?"

My brow lifted. "Like, dino *dildo*?"

"How'd you know about that?"

This time, it was my turn to roll my eyes. "Please. I've heard you talking about the damn things. Besides, you were my target. I watched you meticulously for weeks. I've seen what those dinos can do."

My cock swelled as I watched her eyes widen. I grinned as I recalled peeking through her windows, hovering just outside the Intrusion Spell on her sill and watching her arch those hips up on the bed and deny herself an orgasm over and over until finally she grabbed that toy from her nightstand and went to town. I'd nearly sprayed her window with cum jerking off to the sight.

"That's right, Dollface. I watched you get yourself off every single night. But you wanna know a secret?"

She bit her bottom lip and her breaths came in shallow waves as she nodded.

"I can make you come harder."

I spun her back around, so she faced the lockers then lifted her ass up, sliding the head of my dick through her hot, creamy, wetness. God, she was so tiny in my grasp. I was afraid for a second that I might tear her in half if I tried to enter, but then I reminded myself that she'd fucked, not just Bodie, not just

Easton, but Easton and Bodie *together*, and all those reservations faded away.

I thrust forward and pulled her hips down to meet me, jabbing all the way to the end of her tunnel before I'd even gone balls-deep. Her pussy clamped down around my cock and my beast tugged at my control. Mmmmmm.

Deeper, my dragon urged.

Shit. She really was small. I was nearly hitting her cervix already. But my dragon and my fucking cock decided to make it their ultimate mission to weasel in as far as they could.

My fingers clenched down on her hip bones. Her body tensed as I drilled in deeper, shoving her roughly against the lockers with each thrust. My dick pushed against her cervix. *Fucking yes.* Her pussy squeezed in response to the sensation, surrounding me tightly, and it was fire and bliss and heat and everything.

Perfection.

Aubry hissed through clenched teeth. That made me pause.

I wanted to dominate her, to use and humiliate her, make her beg and submit to me, but at the other end of that spectrum, I also wanted to please her and pleasure her. Being a dom was a delicate push and pull, a tango of pain and decadence, of power and freedom, of giving and taking.

So I eased out a bit and fucked her slowly, shifting her hips back so she wasn't quite as smashed against the lockers, changing the tempo, rubbing her sexy ass that fit in my palm like a perfect little peach. A peach I very much wanted to eat... but couldn't.

I pulled my hand away and slapped her right butt cheek. God, I loved the sight of a freshly smacked ass. That jiggle and the warm pink color.

Aubry gasped and her body loosened slightly. She bit down on a moan, but I heard it anyway.

"You like that, Dollface?" I murmured into her hair before quickly pulling away, just in case my lips got too close.

"Yes, sir."

I smacked her ass again, pissed this time. She was too smart to have done that on accident. "What's my name?"

"Alpha," she all but shouted, trying to amend her mistake quickly.

But I wasn't done punishing her. "Tuck your wings in tight."

I pulled out and she tucked them away, but I guided them ever so slightly apart and toward each ass cheek, so I had room to slip back inside. I thrusted into her a few times, then lit a ball of fire in my hand. Leaning over her shoulder, I reached around her tucked wing and encased her right nipple in my flames.

God. Fuck. The sight of the fire and her breasts bouncing in the flames… I had to stop thrusting or I was gonna blow my load.

Aubry gave a wanton moan.

"Tell me you love the fire," I demanded in a rasp.

God, my hand was shaking. I'd dreamt of doing this to a woman for so long. Mixing fire and sex until they exploded like TNT. But no woman could have handled it—other than a dragon shifter, and L.A. was apparently fresh outta those—no other woman was fireproof.

Except for my little Aubry here, writhing and moaning in my heat.

She pushed her breasts further into the fire and breathed, "I love it. The heat feels so damn good, Alpha!"

The shocked pleasure in her voice made me hotter than before. I'd shown her something new. That thought made my cock swell inside her tight passage. I grinned to myself since I knew she couldn't see it. "You want more?"

Again, she said, "Yes, Alpha."

"Too bad." I dropped the flame, reveling in her pouty sounds as I smacked her ass a few more times before rubbing out the sting with gentle, kneading hands. Then I thrust again, pressing my dick deep inside until her body gave a bit more, relinquished some space it didn't seem to know it had. But not quite enough. I repeated the process of stinging shock and then followed it up with another round of gentle caresses.

By the time I was done turning her ass red, she was nothing more than a whimpering puddle of heat and need in my hands. She was dripping. And her tucked wings were caressing my balls.

Fucking hell.

I took a deep breath, savoring the smell of her desire as it rode the air and swirled through my lungs.

"You have my permission to come," I told her. "*Once.* If you start getting close after that, you tell me."

She nodded, keeping her forehead pressed to the smooth metal locker before her.

I went back to fucking her slow and deep, rotating my hips so that the head of my dick rubbed her g-spot almost constantly.

"Who's your Alpha, baby?" I asked her quietly as I corkscrewed into her.

"You are," she replied on a moan.

That admission forced me to wrestle with my self-control. Like an alligator, lust reared up and I had to tackle it and strangle it in order to subdue it. *God, I loved this.* The struggle to wait for the delayed gratification. The hot feel of my woman around my cock.

A *woman,* I corrected myself. *Not* mine.

I took a breath and leaned forward to bat at her breasts where they hung down, trying to focus on her instead of my own stupid head, which was getting just as out of control as my cock. It was being stupidly possessive. "What's my name?" I asked again.

"Alpha." Her voice quivered and I felt her clench around my shaft tightly.

I didn't know what the fuck got into me, but

suddenly, knowing she was about to come on my cock for the first time ever, Alpha just wasn't what I wanted to hear.

"What's my real name?" I coaxed her quietly, feeling conflicted even as I did so. This was crossing a line. A line between dom-sub sex and reality. I could feel it. She could feel it.

But I didn't take the words back. My dick and heart both swelled with fear.

Then Aubry muttered, "Drake."

Oh hell. Fucking Superbowl confetti cannons went off inside me. My name on her lips drove me wild. More than wild. My beast wanted to spit flame and burn the building around us and fuck the first and only fireproof woman I'd ever taken in the beautiful yellow-orange cocoon of our magic.

I fucked her a bit faster, reaching around to circle her clit while I focused on hitting her pleasure center inside.

"Say it again."

"Drake," she moaned louder.

"Louder, Dollface."

"Drake!"

Oh, fuck yes. The ripe scent of her arousal permeated the room like a fog, getting me high. She was so close to coming even *I* could barely see straight. One more thrust of my hips, and one more circle of my finger, and she was shattering apart in my hands. Her pussy strangled my cock like the bastard it was.

I was close, but I held back, instead gazing down at Aubry, watching her shudder in delight.

She rode my cock like a wave, gliding on a weightless high until crashing to the shore and gently receding back to the sea. As soon as I saw it start to ebb, I let my fingers change tempo, slowly building her up again. And just like a wave, her pleasure mounted and started gaining speed. She moaned and I prepared to rake her across the sandy beach yet again and wring every last drop of ecstasy from her body before retreating.

"Alpha..." she panted, chasing after her breath like she couldn't quite catch it. "I mean, Drake. I... I'm going to come again soon."

"I know, baby, I can smell it."

"But I... I don't have your... permission."

Mmm. Every muscle and nerve in my body thrummed in harmony to the same invisible tune. Sweet servitude. Sweet submission.

Sweet soulma-

Whoa! No fucking way!

My eyes burst open and I immediately stopped moving. Sweat trickled down the side of my face and meandered over the highs and lows of my abs. I was breathless, and terrified of my own mind and thoughts.

Contemplating murder? Fine. But contemplating *that*? *Twice*? The first time, I thought it was just a possessive slip. But soul—I couldn't even think the word. I'd never thought that word before. Ever.

Don't think, Drake, I told myself. But I was shaken, like I'd just woken from a nightmare to the exhausting relief and realization that it wasn't real.

"Drake?" Aubry questioned again. She was still slick with need and shaking with an unfulfilled orgasm.

I took a deep breath and regained my composure. *Alright, fine. You can think. Just as long as it's with your* other *head...*

I reached out and threaded my fingers through her long snowy hair before squeezing tightly and pulling her head back until she arched enough that I could see that beautiful face. As her big, doe eyes gazed up at me with longing and need, I completely lost myself. Those chocolaty brown irises captivated me, drawing me deeper in every way until I no longer knew my way out.

My dragon wings flared out as I unintentionally went into a partial shift.

"Drake," she whispered—*pleaded*—as a tear streaked down her face.

I knew some sub-dom relationships got intense like this, but I'd never been a part of one. It froze my mind, heart, and soul, but apparently not my cock or my mouth.

"You can come now, Dollface," I whispered, pulling her hair with one hand and lifting the other to wipe her tears away. All the while, I slowly stroked in and out of her, angling to hit her g-spot as I gently pushed her over the edge.

'I want to watch your eyes turn gold when you come.'

Her words suddenly echoed in my mind, and as her body jerked and convulsed from the inside out, and my pleasure built to incredible heights, I couldn't help but give her what she wanted. Staring deep into the watery depths of her gaze, I felt the heat of my eyes flashing just before I exploded, rooting in extra deep as I blew my fucking load inside of her with a roar.

My wings stretched wider, shivering like leaves in a breeze as I came.

There were several moments where I felt suspended above the ground, just like I felt when I was flying, right before I went into a dive. It was perfect. Pure. Addicting. Slowly, I returned to reality, stroking a few more times to draw every sensation out for the both of us.

Coming inside a woman. That was new for me.

I knew she was clean and protected. I'd heard Bodie talking to Easton about the spell that fae royalty placed on their children at birth in order to protect against mothering or fathering any bastards. But if I was being completely honest, I didn't really give a fuck. Not in that moment. The stakes were too high, the emotions too raw. There would have been no backing down no matter what. Hell, even the thought of *soulmates* and shit hadn't stopped me. It had scared me, but not enough to stop me.

But now...

Now that she'd climbed off my dick and slowly

spun around in my arms... Now that she smiled softly as she stared adoringly into my eyes... Now that my throat had clogged up 'cause I was starting to fucking catch feelings... *Now*, I needed to get the hell out of there.

"Drake..." she whispered, taking a step closer before I could move. Her breasts pressed into my stomach, and I took a moment to simply breathe her in—like an orange orchard and a drizzle of honey.

She searched my eyes for something—I had no idea what, nor did I *want* to know—as her palms glided ever so softly up my pecs. I swallowed hard, caught between the irrational yearning to wrap her in my arms and never let her go, and the urge to flee, to run as fast and as far as I could and never look back.

My dragon snorted, annoyed at me for thinking about fleeing anything. Ever.

I knew it was my duty as a dom to take care of my sub afterward, but... she had Easton and Bodie for that. They'd take care of her after I crushed her... After I crushed us *both*. But who would take care of me?

Her warm breath fanned across my throat as she fluttered her wings and her lips rose up to meet me. She was completely unaware of the battle inside me when she murmured, "Kiss me, Drake."

16

AUBRY

OH FUCKING GOD. I FELT LIKE A CHEESY HIGH SCHOOL love poem, all angst and bad metaphors: *I'd thrown my heart up into the air like a volleyball and smacked it over into Drake's court. Now, it was his turn to make a move. To bump, set, and spike his heart right back to me.*

I tensed, holding my breath as I awaited his response.

The longer he took to answer as he stared down at me, the more nervous I became. The more the butterflies in my stomach churned things up until it was frothy and unsettled like the ocean before a storm.

Drake's eyes suddenly darkened and shuttered, his jaw twitching before he clamped it tight. He turned away from me. "No."

That word stung like a whip. But no pleasure accompanied it. Only this discombobulated pain that made me wince and made my chest curl inward.

No? After what we'd just shared? *No*?

He'd tossed my hope into the junkyard and crushed it like a beat-up car.

No.

It hurt. Oh, it hurt. The locker room around me started to dim as the pain took over and eclipsed my other senses.

I'd been so vain, so sure. I leaned back against the wall, unable to hold up my own weight as I processed the fact that Drake had said... *no*.

I must have misinterpreted every glance he gave me, every touch, every word. *Stupid*. It had all been wishful thinking on my part.

Drake strode away, his careful movements as graceful as a dancer, his chiseled body as beautiful as a sculpture. He shifted so that his wings and black horns retreated before he grabbed his swim trunks from the tiled floor and slid them on. He was just as fucking heartless as a man carved from stone.

He'd used me and tossed me aside.

No. *Worse*. I'd begged him to use me. I'd dug my own hole and then let him push me in.

And now I was dead. He'd killed me, just like he'd killed my father.

That thought sparked rage, and I clung to that tiny flicker of light like a cavewoman, breathing life into it until the flame grew bigger.

Fuck him!

"You don't get to tell me no!" I marched after him as

he yanked open the door and exited the locker room. I threw the door open even wider so that it smacked the wall, and I followed him out.

He didn't respond. He didn't even pause. Just kept striding down the hall like he couldn't hear me.

Stupid cold-blooded reptile.

If he thought that being naked would stop me, he had another thing coming. I'd had doms parade me through parties before, completely nude except for a collar and leash. I hadn't given two shits when we'd run down the hall after that mage during our takeover of the college.

I flew after him and yanked on his shoulder. "Fucking look at me."

"No!" he roared, refusing to stop and shoving my hand away.

Every rejection I'd ever had in my life hurt less than his literal brush off.

"Drake."

He kept walking.

"Drake!" I yelled.

He was nearly to the double doors that led outside.

"I could just fucking force a kiss on you," I snarled. "Bodie and Easton would hold you down if I told them to. And I could fucking force you."

That was when he whirled, and his wings came back out. The rest of him stayed human, but those big, gorgeous dragon wings flared in fury. Their black, leathery texture blocked the arc light shining through the windows of the double doors behind him. It made him truly look the part of *The Shadow*. The tiny claws on the tips of his wings scraped against the walls. That apple cider scent of his hit my nostrils, even from down the hall. Drake's eyes glowed gold.

"You. Will. Not." I could hear the alpha command flowing through his voice, his tone getting deeper and more resonant.

"Your bullshit doesn't work on me." I planted my feet on the tiles and crossed my arms defiantly, glad that I'd finally evoked some kind of reaction out of him. Some kind of fight. Because after how he'd made me feel, I wanted a brutal fucking massacre.

I wanted to wreck him. I wanted to make him bleed.

Drake dropped his wings and strode forward, eyes locked on mine, his face hard. He stopped about three feet away. "You will *never* kiss me."

His words swung down like a guillotine and sliced through my ire… and my heart. The despair that my anger had been suppressing welled up and filled my eyes. Drake's face grew blurry.

"Why the fuck not?" I asked, struggling to keep my tone even.

"Because I won't have a mate who hates me. And I won't…" he swallowed and clenched his fist before he continued, "let you have a mate you loathe."

Tears burned my eyes and the traitorous fuckers streamed down my cheeks. My throat grew so tight I couldn't have spoken if I wanted to.

Drake just stared at me for a moment before he closed his eyes, took a deep breath, and walked away. When the outside door of the gym opened and then closed behind him, leaving me well and truly alone, I crumpled to my knees.

I sobbed, staring at the floor, the walls, and the glass-cased sports trophies until I couldn't cry anymore. The yellowy-gold awards lined the hallways on each side, other people's triumphs turned into nothing more than cheap plastic.

My eyes roamed the dull, dark hall and counted seven doors. I memorized every detail, just like I did at the scene of a crime. Because this was a crime. What he'd just done was a crime.

He knew it.

I knew it.

Mate bonds were sacred.

And he'd denied ours.

He didn't even want to *try*. I was pretty sure it was because we both *knew* it was there, and that was possibly the most frustrating part.

I curled my fist and beat it against the floor until it felt bruised. But by then, my feet were prickling, about to fall asleep. So, I picked myself up and wandered back to get my swimsuit.

I tied the purple strings in a daze, hardly noticing that the bottom portion was nearly shredded to ribbons along my ass. I vacantly tugged my swimsuit cover over my head. Bodie had bought it for me, a sheer black veil that looked more like lingerie than anything else. I didn't bother to find my sandals.

I tried not to think as I strode through the campus, avoiding the paths and weaving through the grass, letting the blades brush against my toes. Shifters wandered around me. A bat family screeched by as they snacked on insects. Some others played soccer on the opposite side of the quad, using the building lights and a glow-in-the-dark ball. Russ, aka Stranger Danger from the museum, waved at me as he and his wife walked over to the library.

I lifted my hand briefly; glad they were far enough away that I didn't have to pretend to be normal as I trudged toward the Student Union Building in the moonlight. Tears leaked out at random until my eyes ached.

I just wanted it to stop. I wanted everything to stop.

I entered the building, avoiding eye contact with a couple shifters who looked at me curiously, and made my way to the second-floor office where my mates and I were staying. Bodie and Easton were already there waiting for me.

Jon Bon Jovi's "Shot Through the Heart" blazed from a tiny speaker that one of them had linked to their phone.

Fucking right, Jon. Fucking right. Drake gives everything *a bad name.*

When my gaze landed on both my mates, my chest

gave an aching pulse. It hurt so fucking bad that I had to grip onto the door frame.

"Aubry?" Easton immediately ran forward and scooped me up. "What happened? Where are your shoes?" As soon as he touched me, he sniffed, and his face scrunched in sympathy. I knew he could smell Drake on me.

"Who the fuck made my Butterfly cry?" Bodie asked, coming over and brushing back my hair.

Easton carried me over to the futon couch we'd all been sleeping on. It was way too cramped. We barely fit, even with me on Easton's lap. But the guys insisted I stay with them, so I had been sleeping piled on top of them at night in a hot tangle of limbs. It was very... shifter.

But it was also nice. I didn't have any siblings and I'd never been that close to my cousins, so I had never done the sleepover thing before. But hearing them murmur sweet things or tell jokes before we drifted off, having them play with my hair or just comfort me with their touch had made bedtime the best part of my day.

They did the same thing now. The two of them sat together, legs touching, and spread me out over both of them. Easton cuddled my torso and Bodie rubbed comforting circles onto my calves as he simultaneously used his phone to stop the music.

"What happened, babe?" Bodie asked, once it was quiet. He looked scared, his green eyes wide, brow furrowed. He never looked scared.

"Drake..."

I'd hardly gotten the word out when both of them inhaled.

Bodie grew stiff and the circles stopped. "You fucked him?!" His tone was accusatory. He shoved my legs off his lap, and he stood, running a hand through his hair.

Easton, as always, came to my defense. "He's her fucking mate, Bodie. I know you don't want to share, but fuck."

"Fuck you, East. Aubry and I already talked about this." He rubbed at his chest like it ached. "But another fucking mate? Damn it."

I shook my head, and said brokenly, "He's not. He doesn't want to be. He wouldn't kiss me."

"So, he fucked you for shits and giggles?" Bodie punched the wall, his hand going straight through the wallboard.

I felt like I might throw up.

"Dude! You are not helping. Aubry's hurt right now," Easton chided, tucking me even deeper into his arms and leaning his chin on my head so that I felt cocooned by him.

"I just—I just—" Bodie couldn't finish his thought.

I murmured into Easton's chest, "I thought he was my mate." I tried to soak up his goodness. His strength. But I felt like a sieve, all that goodness running right through me.

My honey bear rubbed my back gently. "I know, sweetheart. I know."

For a minute, there wasn't a lot of sound, just the soft scuff of Easton rocking me back and forth, his shirt sliding over the couch.

But then a new set of hands wrapped around my waist and pulled me out of Easton's grasp. Bodie lifted me up and then sat down next to his friend, plopping me down on his lap and shoving back my hair, which had started to cling to my wet face.

"Buttercup," he sounded broken.

"I'm sorry. I thought he was—" I couldn't finish my sentence. I cringed thinking I'd made Bodie angry. Thinking I'd betrayed our bond. That just made me hurt all over again. Drake hadn't just betrayed me. He'd betrayed the two of them.

Bodie shook his head and his expression grew soft as he stared at me. "Drake is stubborn. Just like someone else I know." He ran a gentle hand over my cheek and cupped it. "I remember a certain fae who was pretty damn adamant she wasn't my mate. Denied it to high heaven. And look how that turned out?"

I laughed but my throat was so raw it turned into a cough.

Bodie hugged me to him then, hard and tight and possessive. I clung to him, needing his forgiveness, his acceptance, and most of all, the reassurance that I was right. That Drake was a stubborn idiot and he would come around.

"Bodie," I clutched him tighter.

"I'm gonna go talk to Drake," Easton rose next to us.

I immediately reached out and grabbed his hand, which was so huge, I could only wrap around a few of his fingers. "No! Please." I'd threatened Drake with the guys but the thought of them arguing about me... it would be worse than Easton and Bodie's fight. And there was no way I could end that fight the way I'd ended theirs. There was no way I could ever look Drake in the eyes again.

Easton's blue eyes softened at the panic on my face. But my sweet mate gently pried my hand off his fingers. "He can't do this, Aubry. We can't be divided like this."

He pulled open the door to leave.

But panic surged through me. I didn't want to be separated from Easton right now. And I really didn't want him to talk to Drake. But the look in his eyes was stubborn. I didn't think I'd be able to keep him in our room. I'd have a better chance of convincing him if I had more time. I needed more time.

"Wait. I'm coming, too." I stood up, pulling out of Bodie's hold but grabbing his hand and yanking him up.

"You aren't going around dressed like that, soaking wet," Bodie scolded.

"This isn't a field trip, the whole class is not invited," Easton shook his head and grabbed the doorknob.

I rushed over and blocked him from leaving.

"If you're going to talk about me to Smaug the asshole, then I want to know what you're saying. Though I don't think a damn bit of it will get through unless you have a black arrow to pierce the pony-eater's heart." I crossed my arms.

Easton gave me a half-grin. "Glad to see he hasn't hurt your tongue, Spitfire."

"Didn't get that reference," Bodie said.

Easton and I turned to him, aghast. It was Easton who spoke. "Lord of the Rings! The Hobbit! Dude, we've watched that together like three times!"

Bodie shrugged as he tossed a dress and some leggings my way. "Oh. Must have fallen asleep."

I kept my spot in the doorway as I did a quick change. Both my mates' eyes flashed gold at the sight of my naked body. But now wasn't the time. Bodie gave me some flats and I slid them on without socks. Then we left to go confront the asshole together.

As we walked together through the grassy quad and the stars crawled through the sky, I tried to convince the guys that now wasn't the right time to do this. It was way too soon.

Bodie shook his head. "Nah, babe. Drake needs a good dick punch."

Easton pinched the bridge of his nose. "Aubry, you have to understand… we're outlaws. We've spent years suppressing our 'feelings.' Drake more than most."

I stopped short as Easton's words soaked into my mind and their meaning became clear. What he'd said was true. The criminal life shot up emotions and left a trail of broken, bleeding hearts in its wake. Gangsters didn't have time for happiness, hope, or love. Because an enemy was always there, waiting just around the corner, armed and ready to plug you full of holes.

Suddenly, I froze.

Speaking of guns around the corner...

We'd no more than rounded the next bend when Triton appeared in a puff of red and orange smoke in the courtyard before us—gun at the ready—with four mean-eyed fae hovering in the air behind him.

17

AUBRY

"WELL, WELL, WELL. FACE TO FACE WITH MY ARCH nemesis at last."

Triton's sarcastic voice echoed across the courtyard, ricocheting between buildings and fading into the darkness. My best friend stood in the middle of the courtyard, next to a fountain we had left running as a water source for shifters who wanted to bathe in animal form. His normally cropped beard was longer, his sandy hair wilder than ever. His clothes were wrinkled and unkempt and he looked incredibly haggard.

Memories suddenly flashed to the last time I'd seen Trite standing at that very fountain—the day we'd graduated. He'd been waiting for me so we could line up together. He'd been smiling and was so full of joy.

What a contrast that was to today. Today, Triton's look was manic.

The four autumn fae that floated a few feet behind him were tall and lean. Three men and one woman hovered on golden wings and had absolutely zero smiles for us. They didn't wear MP uniforms and I didn't recognize them. So I wasn't sure where they'd come from. Magical beings for hire, that was certain, because I knew—or thought I knew—every single one of Trite's friends because the fucker had never been that friendly to begin with—possibly because he was a psychopath and I'd never noticed.

I couldn't speak; I couldn't swallow; I could barely breathe. So many strange and outrageous emotions poured through me that it was difficult to fully comprehend.

Shock. Fear. Happiness? No. Anger. Hesitation. Nostalgia?

It was... complicated. Triton had been my best friend for so long, it was difficult to paint him in a new light without also seeing the colors I used to know so well shining through. Still. I needed to remember what he'd done and focus on that.

I cleared my throat and crossed my arms. "Drake's not here."

Unless he meant... *me?* The thought kinda made me sick to my stomach. I pushed through it and found my inner bitch, the one who wanted to break Triton's nose for lying to me about his parents and knee him in the nards for setting fires, and roundhouse him and knock his teeth out for attacking a school. "Heard Drake killed your parents. I think that's a thing for him—killing parents. I assume you heard he offed my dad."

Triton's cold smile melted a little as he turned toward me. But to my surprise, he didn't even bother to respond, just held up a single finger and pointed skyward.

A roar rent the air. All around the quad, shifters who'd been out walking suddenly ran for cover. That roar was the signal that we were under attack. I glanced up, horrified to see at least twenty more fae and pixies fluttering overhead like black shadows.

But then I heard a yell. "Not on my watch, mother-fuckers!" And Rocco and a couple of his guys started pelting the fliers with bullets and potions from East-on's cannons.

A second later, Drake landed in the grass beside us with a rumbling thud, one knee in the grass, the other leg bent. Drake was only half shifted. He was a man wearing all black with huge leathery black wings, just like he'd been when we'd—

God, if I thought my stomach was upset a moment ago, it was a writhing pit of snakes now. I had to look away, which set my gaze back on Trite.

"*Now*, I'm face to face with my arch nemesis," Triton corrected with a broad fake grin. "Good of you to show up, Shadow."

Drake rose from the knee he'd landed on and

squared his big broad shoulders. "Wish I could say the same, you limp-dick wand wanker."

The grin fell right off Triton's face at Drake's insult. "I shall rather enjoy *killing* you, while my friends *become* you and kill the rest of them."

His words made no sense to me at first... but then the faces of the four fae beside him began to change... they glamoured and suddenly I was looking across the quad at a floating mirror image of myself with wings that had changed from golden to shadows, just as mine did when I tried to disguise them from humans. I turned left, Easton stood across from a hovering Easton, and Bodie stood across from a winged Bodie with a demonic expression. I turned right, and sure enough, two Drakes were glaring at one another on my right.

What the hell? Was this *Face/Off*? Was Nick Cage gonna pop up around a corner and do his creepy laugh? Fuck.

The fae raised their guns and everything seemed to decelerate into slow motion. Behind them, at least three bodies fell to the ground as Rocco's men shot down Triton's aerial force.

I barely even noticed the bodies falling, though. I was kind of still stuck on the image of me staring back at me. Trite was gonna kill me? And have a fae pose as me in order to kill other shifters? Who did that? Who, other than an insane lunatic or cartoon fucking villain, did that shit? Any sliver of doubt I'd had about Trite being guilty disappeared faster than a mage with a Portal Potion.

Sick bastard.

Trite's arms moved, like he was about to march over to us, but then they wavered in the air, almost like he'd lost his balance. He jerked, a deepening frown on his face.

What the hell?

The snarky side of me wondered if he was having a seizure. He damn well fucking deserved to have one. Even his henchmen froze where they hovered, guns at their hips, and looked at him with alarm. But he reached down and clutched his thigh with both hands and pulled until his shoe came off and remained stuck on the ground.

That clarified it. *Looks like he just discovered our immobility spell.* I raised an eyebrow and smirked at him. He glared back.

Trite pursed his lips in an angry scowl and said to his companions, "Don't touch the ground. There's a Movement Restriction Spe—"

BAM!

A shot interrupted Trite's warning. Fae-Easton fell from the air. He slammed into the fountain, and tumbled limp onto the sidewalk. Easton's handsome face dissolved and the fae's real face reappeared as a red puddle formed beneath him. Next to me, real-Bodie grinned proudly as a bullet casing fell at his feet.

Try to catch me now, Frank Abagnale! Fucking con man!

Seconds later, we were all blown backward by hurricane-strength winds. My elbows smacked into the sidewalk, sending pain shooting up and down my arms.

Round one went to Bodie. Round two went to those stupid fae. But as soon as I realized we were about to have another showdown, my pulse bounced on its toes and took a couple of practice jabs, determined to win round three against these identity thieves. I shoved up from the ground.

Triton smashed a Portal Potion into his chest and disappeared in a puff of yellow, blue, and orange smoke before I'd made it to my feet. Only his shoes remained behind. Just like the damned Wicked Witch. Of course, he didn't take his lackeys with him. Witches didn't give a damn about their flying monkeys and mages didn't give a damn about the fae.

I shot a bolt of fire at the autumn fae glamoured to look like myself only to watch her blow that very flame toward my Easton. I leapt in front of him to block the flames.

Damn it. That fucking backfired. Literally.

Then everyone moved at once. Easton's bear claws came out and he lumbered toward whichever fae was closest. Drake shifted into a dragon and beat his vast, leathery wings, rising a few feet off the ground before letting out a blazing burst of fire.

The remaining imposter fae scattered like flies.

No wonder shifters always called us that.

Bodie lifted his gun again and fired three more shots off after the fliers. But the autumn fae pumped their wings and shot out jet streams as they flew, and the bullets zoomed harmlessly off-course.

"Fuck!" Bodie cursed. "Stupid wasps."

Oh, yeah. There was that lovely nickname too.

The fae flew away, pulling their guns out as they soared toward the more used buildings on campus. *Shit!* I burst into a sprint before launching into the air, chasing down those posers like a bolt of greased lightning.

My gaze flickered when colored smoke appeared in the corner of my vision. Triton reappeared on the roof of the science center, very cleverly avoiding his bare feet touching the *ground*. Motherfucker had found a workaround.

Son of a bitch.

"I've got the mage! You get the wasps!" I heard Drake yell from behind me, but I didn't turn to look.

"My fae's dead!" I heard Easton shout. "I'm staying to help with Dickless!"

Dickless? I wondered in the back of my mind. When the hell had they given Trite *that* nickname? And why? Not that it actually fucking mattered. He deserved to be dickless after all the evil he'd done.

From the corner of my eye, I saw Bodie tracking left, so I focused on the fae on the right. I kept my eyes trained on the fantastic butt in front of me and pumped my wings hard so that I shot forward. I had a great fucking ass if I did say so myself. My hair looked pretty, billowing like liquid moonlight as the wannabe-Aubry-fae soared ahead of me. Her flying was top-fucking notch. Too bad she was a body-snatcher, otherwise I might have asked for tips.

I had to admit, chasing myself through the air of a mage university that'd been kidnapped by shifters... felt a little like I was caught in some hokey kids' movie, to say the least.

But the stakes were so much higher than any kids' movie. There were *real* kids here that I had to protect. Kids who grabbed my hand when I walked by. Kids who offered to share their toys with me. The night we'd helped the shifters move in, one little girl had insisted on crawling into my lap until she fell asleep.

I could not lose.

I put on another burst of speed, letting my adrenaline take over and fuel me to go faster. But the harder I pushed, the harder that fake-bitch-Aubry bit back. A gust of wind suddenly hit me like a brick wall and sent me spiraling. By the time I stopped tumbling, I'd nearly slammed into one of the trees that lined the quad.

Fury and determination lit me up like stadium lights and my upper lip curled into a snarl. *Bring it on, evil twin.* Except, I was all dolled up with nowhere to go, all raging and fuming with no clue how to effectively direct my anger.

"How the hell am I supposed to beat the wind?" I muttered.

A smooth, accented voice spoke up from behind me. "The wind's weakness is that it can only blow one direction at a time. To defeat it, you must come at it from two sides."

I turned to see my cousin Kira floating next to me like a goddamned motivational quote come to life. Where the fuck did she get all her little sayings?

My cousin smiled at me. Her black hair was in a ponytail and a set of binoculars were hanging from her neck. Based on those accessories alone, I kind of expected her to be wearing a pair of camo pants and a tight black tank, army-girl style. Instead, she wore an airy plum dress and heels. She was... *unique* like that.

"Were you on duty?" I asked.

She nodded curtly. "But Rocco has taken all the fun out. He's killed all the airborne. I take right, you take the left?"

I gave her a grin. "Looks like I'm about ten seconds away from watching the most embarrassing moment of my life."

Kira's brows furrowed in confusion.

"I'm about to watch you kick '*my*' ass." I used air quotes.

Kira laughed and zoomed off to the side. We watched from separate angles as fae-me struggled to open the door to the administration building. But we'd locked all the mages in the bursar's office, so that building was a big no-go.

Time to see if this bitch has eyes in the back of her head.

I shot out, flying straight towards her, hoping to draw her attention. She let go of the door handle she'd been struggling with and quickly spun around, blasting me with another wave of wind that met my face like a concrete wall.

Fuck, that hurts!

But as my evil twin focused her windstream on me, Kira snuck up behind her and literally kicked her in the ass. Poser girl lost her balance and before she could use her wings to keep herself upright, Kira battered her with a blast of her own wind, and sent the imposter flying face-first onto the ground.

As soon as Kira's windstream let up, I was back in action and in fake-me's face. I knelt on the ground and my hands squeezed each side of her head. She tried to lift her hands and claw at me or punch me, but they were glued to the floor like magnets thanks to Larry's spell.

The fae glared up at me and I shook my head. "You know, Kira, I'm like eighty percent sure this lady doesn't like me."

"You? Impossible."

"Right? But I'm one hundred percent sure I don't give a flying fuck."

With a sadistic little grin, I snapped fake-me's neck like a glow stick. Her head dropped weightlessly into the grass beneath her, and I watched her hair turn from white back to its original shade of violet.

Kira and I clasped hands before bumping fists and

letting the tips of our wings brush against one another. I'd never been close to her before, but after tackling an enemy together, I felt a camaraderie that hadn't been there earlier.

"Thanks, cuz," I said.

She smirked. "I gotchu, boo."

I sniffed out a laugh because it sounded absolutely ridiculous in her Russian accent. "Picking up on some of that L.A. slang?"

"Perhaps. You like?" She asked the question as if she wanted my opinion on her current outfit or some shit.

"Yeah. I like it. Maybe if you stick around for a bit, you'll pick up even more?"

It was a hint-slash-invitation for her to stay as long as she liked. I'd never really gotten to spend much time with any of my cousins, and after collaborating with her on a takedown, I realized just how much I'd missed out on growing up. It'd be nice to have another friend in my life—just in case Tee no longer counted. If she ever got her memory back, I was pretty sure the little pixie was gonna be more than furious with me.

"I wish that I could, dear cousin. Particularly now that you have crossed over—is that the saying? —from the dark side. But my friends say things are getting heated back in Moscow. I'll probably have to leave sooner than I had hoped."

Damn. Just when we were finally starting to hit it off…

Suddenly, she cocked her chin and her gaze darted

toward something over my shoulder. "We must go. The other two fae are no longer in the quad."

We took to the sky and scouted things out. Bodie was fast, but he had the distinct disadvantage of being grounded. His fae counterpart had already reached the library.

Damn it.

I expected explosions to go off and bricks to start flying, but they didn't. Instead, I heard the distinct sound of automatic gunfire.

Pop. Pop pop pop.

My eyes went wide as realization dawned, and I pushed my wings even faster. These imposters were trying to get inside and start shooting shifters. That was why they glamoured themselves to look like *us* before they did so. They were trying to turn our own people against us. Make it look like *we* were the ones murdering our followers.

Those lowlife mother fuckers...

I crashed through one of the library windows, tucking and rolling as I landed on the first floor. I ignored the cuts that sliced my arms and shoved myself up, my eyes immediately taking in my surroundings. I was in a reading room, one that held long tables with green lamps in the center and bookshelves lining either side.

In the main area, the shifters were already screaming and running. Parents picked up their children and bolted wildly in every direction. Books crashed to the floor as a disoriented gorilla accidentally smacked into the shelves and toppled them over. Couples sprinted hand-in-hand away from the carnage.

A terrified and confused expression crossed a young woman's face as she stared at the fake-fae and said, "Bodie?"

A second later, the horror and blankness of death overtook her.

Nearby, I saw Russ, aka Stranger Danger from the museum. He rushed out of the stacks, flinging aside a few books as he scooped up the woman's body. "No! Cheryl! *No!*"

"Bodie's attacking!" a man yelled as he ducked behind the stacks.

"It's not us!" I screamed at the top of my lungs as I sprinted toward fae-Bodie where he hovered, mowing down row after row of innocent people between the bookshelves. "It's autumn fae! They glamoured to make you think it's us! Bodie can't fly!"

I tried to appeal to their reason. But they were *way* past that.

Animal screeches and piss filled the air as I ran toward my target. So did twirling fur and feathers, caught in the vortex of fleeing shifters as they rushed away.

At the sound of my voice, fae-Bodie cocked his head and turned his gun on me. "Nice of you to join me, Princess Aubry. I love it when ladies chase me, but I already told you, I'm just not that into you."

His words stung. Which was stupid. I knew it wasn't actually Bodie speaking but it was still his voice I heard, his face I saw. And the fucker could tell he'd gotten to me. He smiled as his finger pulled the trigger.

Gritting my teeth, I jumped into the air, spiraling into a barrel roll just as his gun went off and countless bullets sprayed beneath me. He lifted his arm, aiming higher. But just before the next round could graze me, the real Bodie charged into the room and shifted to a huge, six-foot-tall black wolf in less than two seconds. He leapt into the air with a fierce growl and tackled fake Bodie to the ground.

His fangs descended and clamped around the entire head of the fae beneath him with a sickening crunch. He jerked his neck back and forth twice and then all at once the body was left on the puke-green library carpet —headless.

The wolf spit out the head, which no longer looked like Bodie. The fae's original face returned in death— some random fae fuck with black hair and pale skin and eyebrows nicer than mine.

Once the threat was gone, I turned to look at the rest of the room. I had no idea where Kira had gone, but the shifter crowd was hysterical. Half of them were still shrieking and crying over the sudden slaughter of their loved ones like Russ. Others had fled. Still other people stared at Bodie in shock and horror.

My mate turned to me, no longer in wolf form. "Did you get yours?"

I nodded in reply.

He then glanced up at the shifters with a stoic expression. "There is still one more glamoured fae and a mage on campus. The wasp looked like Drake the last time I saw him, but he can change his appearance at any moment, so be careful. And the mage is a deranged bastard popping up in random locations without shoes. Don't let anyone inside. Understand? *No one*. No matter who they look like, until you hear the all clear signal. Got it?"

Some heads nodded in response, but many others were too numb to even blink. I wasn't sure his words had even penetrated their thick walls of emotion.

I scrubbed a hand down my face, because this fight wasn't done yet. Instead of basking in relief after surviving a series of gunshots, I had to continue pushing onward. I had to find yet another burst of energy somewhere, even though I felt like a car on a dusty highway without any gas, rolling on nothing but neutral gear and hope.

I had to keep fighting.

Bodie ran back outside and I followed on foot before taking to the air once more.

From up above, I saw Drake and Triton fighting on a new rooftop, the English department, while Easton sprinted across the quad to rejoin them. They must've switched locations again not long ago. The two of them blocked and exchanged blows faster than I'd ever seen. Potions and fire lit up the sky as they attacked, neither backing down.

Don't you dare lose, Godzilla, I thought. Then I swallowed hard and forced my gaze away, concentrating on finding and eliminating the *other* Drake.

From the corner of my eye, I could see the flashing of gunfire and hear the rattling of the bullets. The *clickity clack* sounds erupted from the cafeteria inside the Student Union building—where most of the shifters had holed up.

NO! Shit!

Fear burned the back of my throat like cheap tequila, and I screamed down at Bodie. "The Union Center!"

"On it!" He shifted into his massive black wolf almost faster than I could blink and immediately charged on ahead.

As he ran, I darted through the night sky like I'd been catapulted, speeding ahead of Bodie, never once slowing down until I crashed through one of the cafeteria windows on the first floor of the Student Union. I rolled across a round table, accidentally crashing into the next table in line. Plastic chairs tumbled across the floor, some of their legs broken off and scattering, and the entire table flipped on its head.

It wasn't clean, calm, or collected. It was sloppy.

My damn heart was beating as fast as a keyboard the night before a report was due. My chest was already pulsing with impending sadness. I wasn't in the moment; I kept picturing the aftermath.

This could *not* be like the elementary school incident. It couldn't.

Snap out of it, Aubry, and help these damn shifters, my brain barked.

But I wasn't fast enough.

Fae-Drake came out of nowhere and grabbed me by the back of the neck, careful not to touch the ground before pumping his 'dragon' wings and lifting me up into the air. His lips curled into a cruel smile, one I could almost believe belonged to the *real* Drake.

Without a word, he aimed his Tommy gun right at my chest. I lashed out with the butt of my palm, changing the direction of his gun's fire just before the bullets bit into me. They shattered more of the glass windows as the shifters screamed and scrambled in the background.

How many had he already killed? I couldn't bring myself to look. Not now when I was all that stood between them and a fucked-up gang of magic users hell bent on extermination.

How could I have been one of them? How could I not see the heartless bitch I'd become? What Triton had already become...

Behind me one of the shifters tried to use a gun. But I saw the man's eyes close as he pulled the trigger and the shot went wide.

These people couldn't save themselves.

They needed me.

Fury rushed through my veins and gave me an extra burst of energy. I reached behind my head and grabbed fae-Drake's arm, then I somersaulted in midair, flipping him up over my back and dropping him onto the ground. The wind knocked out of his chest as his back hit the concrete tile, but he continued firing his gun. The bullets raced toward the ceiling, blackening some of the dim lights as glass and dust and chunks of industrial ceiling tiles fell from above.

Spinning, I roundhouse kicked the gun right out of his damn hand. He jerked like he was about to get up and chase after it, but he couldn't move.

My eyes lit up. The Movement Restriction Spell! Yes! He was officially grounded now! Unless he stripped out of his clothes, that is, but I had no intention of giving him that much time.

I grabbed his gun and aimed it at Drake's chest—no, *fae* Drake's chest. Sadness and hopelessness filled me as I gazed into Drake's dark blue eyes.

They're not his, Aubry, I told myself. But I couldn't help but imagine that they were. I'd been so pissed at him. I'd wanted to draw blood. To make him hurt like he'd hurt me. And now that the time had come where I could enact my angered vision... my heart wasn't in it.

Right before I pulled the trigger, Bodie finally caught up to me and leapt through the glass as a wolf. Where I had faltered, he had *no* reservations. He bent down, clamped his teeth into the fae's skull, and ripped fake-Drake's head off like it was a mother fucking squeaky toy.

I let out a shaky sigh of relief. But I realized, no matter how upset I was at real-Drake, I didn't really want to hurt him. In fact... we needed to go help him.

I turned and locked eyes with Bodie's wolf. "Triton is the last one left."

He nodded his massive, shaggy head. "Then, let's go take him down."

Bodie leapt out the window, and I followed closely behind, taking to the air like a bird of prey. I scanned the rooftops as if I were a hawk, searching for any signs of movement and finally finding it on top of the gymnasium.

Drake and Triton had moved *yet again*. And once more, Easton was running across the grounds to catch up. Trite must've been absolutely blowing through Portal Potions...

Without a second thought, I surged into action. My wings practically whistled as I pushed through the air, and tears leaked from my eyes due to the speed. Never slowing, I tucked my wings so I could plunge faster. At the last second, I kicked my feet in front of me and crashed into Triton's back from behind.

The contact was jarring, shooting pain up my legs and spine as my bones crunched together. His entire body lurched forward and smashed down into the pebbled rooftop, leaving a stone-free skid-mark fifteen-feet-long behind him.

I winced as I pushed onto my hands and knees, panting as I tried to catch my breath. Drake hurried over and helped me up. Sweat glistened on his face, his limbs shook, and his breath was heavy. The momentary contact of his skin against mine was... bittersweet —calming, invigorating, arousing, and heartbreaking.

As all those emotions cycled through my heart like a washing machine, a pink puff of smoke hit the air above Trite's head. A fucking Healing Potion. Of course, the bastard would cheat.

He suddenly leapt up as if nothing had happened while Drake and I stood there still trying to catch our breath. I had a feeling he'd been playing unfairly this entire time, dragging the fight out as long as he could, wearing Drake down until he had nothing left while Triton had all the energy and power in the world.

It was the mage way.

"Aren't you just so fucking lucky you stole my precious Aubry from me?" Triton sneered at the dragon shifter as he shoved his favorite necklace back into his shirt. It must've jostled out after I'd sent the fucker flying. I smiled at my tiny accomplishment as a flash of yellow-gold caught my eye then disappeared. Apparently, the metal necklace chain had caught a moonbeam as he stuffed the black gem away. "If she hadn't shown up and saved your ass, you'd be dead right now."

Drake snarled at him, but pain momentarily flashed in his eyes, making it look more like a grimace. Was he hurt? Had I seriously just kept him from dying?

The thought of Drake being gone cut like a knife, but dead? Knowing there was still so much unresolved angst between us, so many unspoken words, so many unfulfilled promises... it would have been unbearable.

Triton threw a potion out of nowhere. I hadn't even seen him reach into his pocket or rear back his arm. I'd been too engulfed in fear, worry, and sadness.

Just as quickly, Drake reacted, shoving me onto my ass a few feet away as the potion bottle smashed to the ground at his feet. Steam hissed into the air and a gaping hole ate through the roof. My eyes went wide. It hadn't been a potion after all—at least, no potion I'd ever seen. I was pretty sure it was just straight acid, which would have eaten through my body just as quickly as it ate through the concrete and stone around us. It would have... killed me.

I glanced up at Triton in utter shock as the rooftop door burst open and Bodie and Easton joined us on the roof. They were back in human form, but both armed, weapons pointed right at Trite. Unfortunately, Drake and I were right behind him, so they wouldn't be able to get off a clean shot right away. He was the sniveling monkey in the middle, but *we* were the ones with the disadvantage. *Damn it all.*

Triton smirked—or maybe it was a sneer—as his gaze rapidly darted from left to right. He reached into his robes for a potion, just as Drake and I each took a tiny step in opposite directions, trying to open up a shot for Easton or Bodie.

Trite patted his pockets almost frantically, his eyes wide as saucers until he finally pulled out a single rainbow-colored Portal Potion. Must've been his last one. Without another word, he smashed it and disappeared into the smoke.

Drake and I dove to the ground like we were sliding into home plate, and as soon as we were out of the way, Easton and Bodie fired into the hazy air. But each of their guns only had one or two shots left, and we *didn't* hear Triton grunt or groan before the magical vapor dissipated.

"Goddamn it!" Bodie cursed, growling up at the moon as he tugged on his hair like a madman.

Easton huffed as he caught his breath, looking just as pissed and disgusted as Bodie at the fact that Triton had just gotten away.

But Drake... Drake just looked devastated. Over what, I couldn't tell, couldn't understand, but it made me want to comfort him.

"Drake," I said softly, reaching out to skim his fingertips with mine.

But he pulled away from me *yet again*. Walking to the rooftop edge, he jumped and flew away into the night.

My throat and my heart both squeezed. My lungs and my eyes all burned. It was like my entire body was wrapped in an anaconda's coils and I was slowly dying a horrific death of bone-crushing agony.

He'd saved my life from that acidic potion, but

when he walked away from me... when he left me standing there brokenhearted without a single backward glance... he may as well have smashed the acid into my chest himself.

Because that had fucking killed me.

EASTON

THIS GAME OF *HOT AND COLD* THAT DRAKE WAS PLAYING with our mate had to end. And *I* was gonna be the one who ended it.

I left Aubry in Bodie's arms, ignoring his wide-eyed 'get back here and help me' look. He could drag his heart out of the vault he kept it in for a few minutes to deal with our tearful mate.

I needed to find Drake, because that was the only way to stop Aubry from crying off and on every few days from some new rebuff. It was also the only way to ensure Drake could focus on our true threat—*Triton*.

Annoyance rippled through me. I was pissed that I even had to do this shit. Drake should fucking know better because he could read people. He had to know he was fucking hurting her. But, just like Bodie, he had too much pride.

Unlike Bodie, however, Drake believed that he was

unclean. That he was soiled and stained in sin so bloody it would never wash out. I knew, because I'd felt that way once.

I didn't know if the fucker would be able to listen to reason or see any sense. I certainly hadn't been able to take in my grandma's words of wisdom all those years ago. But if logic didn't work, I had fists.

"I hope it doesn't come to that," I grumbled to myself. But I knew there wasn't much sense in hoping.

When I reached the Student Union Building, I searched from top to bottom, but Drake was nowhere to be found. I was sort of guessing that he might fly there and use the crowd to hide, but apparently, I was wrong.

Before I could leave and continue my search for the brooding iguana, I got tangled up with a couple of betas and had to reassure them that the threat was really gone.

"It's all clear," I told Corey, Bodie's second-in-command. Rocco's guys were manning the guns and Kira was doing a perimeter run, ready to use her wind power to blast away any unwelcome fliers. "You're free to go outside as needed."

Next to him, a squirrel shifter beta nervously swirled her head, like she was still looking for attacks. Corey didn't look panicked like her, just pissed off.

"Dude, we thought the bank was safe, too, and that even had a vault. This is way more fucking exposed."

Corey gestured at the floor to ceiling windows on the first floor of the Student Union.

"We should shift into our animals and hide out in the forest until you have a new location," the squirrel shifter said, throwing in her two cents.

I sucked in a sigh and glanced away. Damn it all. I didn't know how to deal with this. It was Drake's fucking forte to get people to fall in line, not mine.

I put a fake smile on my face as little Mariana and her mother passed by.

"I smell cheese," she said, scrunching her nose and pointing her little finger up at me.

This time my grin was real. "Sounds like we'll have to go on another hunt soon."

"Aubry, too," she decided. "Can we go tonight?"

"No," her mother interrupted. "Not tonight."

"Not fair," Mariana groaned, as her mother guided her down the sidewalk.

I turned back to Corey and the squirrel beta. I didn't know what the hell I was supposed to say, but I had to at least *try* because the stupid Shadow had disappeared into the night. "Look. I get what you're saying—"

"I know we've got those hostages," Corey said, cutting me off and completely ignoring the fact that Mariana and her mother were barely ten feet away.

"Man," I grabbed his shoulder and steered him away. Glancing back, I watched Mariana's black curls bounce as she looked up and asked her mom if she could go see the 'ostriches.'

"Kids don't need to hear that," I scolded him. "You're lucky she thought you said ostrich instead of hostage."

"Most of them have seen worse," he countered with a shrug. "But people are antsy here. They don't feel safe, especially after what just went down. What's the next move? When are we getting out of here?"

The squirrel beta, I thought her name was Karen, nodded. "We're leaving soon right? For somewhere safe?"

"We're working on it," I said tersely. No wonder Drake just spat orders and never gave explanations. "We handled the attack tonight just fine. My guns did their job."

I didn't even mention the fact that the Triton fuck—who was our biggest concern—had escaped. People didn't need to worry any more than they'd already begun to. They had enough on their plates.

Corey had another twenty questions for me—none of which I had the answer to—but he was a persistent bastard. Eventually, Karen couldn't handle the stress of the back and forth and she shifted into a squirrel, running off to climb a pillar. As soon as I could, I broke away, feeling just as antsy as both of those betas about our future. Because our leader was currently being a fuckwit instead of a fucking dragon.

I left the Student Union and went to the science building, following an old scent trail of Drake's. I smelled Aubry there too, and spotted the broken potion bottles in one of the classrooms. But Drake was nowhere to be found.

Mother fucking hell.

My bear growled and my stomach rumbled. It annoyed me that the stupid dragon kept going off on his own. Drake had never been a coward—never before this, anyway. But now, I was starting to doubt him. And that was fucking *bad*.

After an hour of playing hide and seek, I finally found Drake in the gymnasium, sitting by the pool where the chlorine masked most of his scent. Clever fuck.

He sat in a white plastic lounge chair and stared out across the turquoise water. The look on his face was dark. His brow was furrowed, blue eyes squinted, and he clasped his hands together in front of them, squeezing and releasing like there was so much frustration inside him that he needed to relieve the tension and get it out somehow.

I knew the feeling.

I grabbed a chair off the far wall and sat down beside him. My ass hardly fit on the scrawny thing, and the plastic bent beneath me. But I decided to start off casual. Bodie always fucked shit up with Drake because he didn't know how to attack issues *from the side*; he ran at problems head-on and shot them right between the eyes.

Machines were a little like people. Finicky. You had

to take them apart in the right order or you'd fuck things up. And while I was no people expert by any means, I'd seen Bodie and Drake go head to head enough times to know that Bodie's approach was a no-go. I was gonna have to pick Drake apart my own way.

"Good save tonight." I leaned back in the crap chair and crossed my ankles. But the give of the plastic quickly made me sit upright again.

"Don't." Drake's response was monosyllabic.

"Don't compliment you?"

"I know why you're here." He waited a beat and then unclasped his hands and ran them over the back of his head, giving a sigh. "She's crying."

"Why would you think that?" I asked.

Drake gave me a wry look.

I gave him one right back.

For the first time since I'd met him, Drake looked away first.

But I didn't feel triumphant. I felt annoyed, angry even, that he *knew* he was being a little shit and he wasn't doing anything to stop it. He was dragging all three of us through the mud, because—like it or not—when Aubry was miserable, Bodie and I were too. Whenever her beautiful face collapsed in tears, my bear wanted to smash down a tree.

"It shouldn't be like this," he muttered.

"A lot of things shouldn't be the way they are," I replied.

He shook his head. "Larry's got some half-finished Portal Potions. When they're done, I'm gonna—"

"*You're* gonna do fucking nothing," I said, my vision going white hot. He was going to change the subject on me? And not just change it, but he was going to bring up leaving? When he knew what that would do to Aubry? I leaned forward in my seat and jabbed a finger in his direction. "*We* are gonna do something. *Together*."

Drake shook his head. "It's too dangerous. Triton Vale is unhinged."

"So are most mages."

"Did you see his eyes?" Drake shook his head and stood, groaning.

That's when I realized the side of his shirt was drenched in blood.

"Shit! You got hit!" I moved forward to shove his shirt aside and check the wound, but Drake slapped my hand away.

"It's fine."

"It doesn't look fucking fine," I growled.

"I pulled the bullet out. It's nothing."

"Did you shift to heal?"

"Don't try to babysit me, Easton."

That pissed me the hell off. Concern was babysitting? That goddamn fucker had sat at my bedside for three days after one of our firefights with council member John Daggler and his lackeys. I'd taken three to the chest and healing was a bitch. Drake had been a fucking nursemaid, changing bandages and shit.

"Don't want to be babysat?" I asked mockingly. "Then don't act like a fucking child!"

"I'm not!" Drake's fingers curled into a fist and he lifted it.

For the first time since we'd met, I swore he looked ready to punch me. I didn't give a shit, though. My bear was eager to fight, ready to meet him head-on. But I held him down.

Not yet.

Drake was getting emotional. He *never* got emotional. Which meant that this situation made him feel things; Aubry made him feel things. I just needed to nudge him in the right direction.

"Look, I shouldn't have said that," I apologized.

That was a fucking lie, but whatever. I needed him to calm down in order to hear me out. If the idiot wasn't even taking care of his wound, then I doubted he was thinking all that rationally.

"Point is, you don't go it alone." I wanted to add, *'especially not after what happened last time with the goddamned mage jewel.'* But I didn't. I wasn't Bodie.

Drake shook his head and didn't respond. He just turned and strode out into the hallway, making his way toward the locker room door, before pulling it open and disappearing inside.

I followed.

Instantly, without the overwhelming stench of chlorine invading my nostrils, I smelled Aubry. Her orange scent, the scent of her arousal, *all of it*. This was where he'd taken my mate… and then rejected her.

Drake's hard eyes met mine.

The fucker knew what he'd done, coming in here. He knew it would rouse my beast. He wanted to fight. He deserved to get his ass kicked. And then some. He wanted a beat down? Fine. I'd give him one.

But not the way he wanted.

"She cried for hours," I told him. "She could hardly talk."

That might have been a stretch, but he didn't need to know that. Her throat had definitely been scratchy.

"You made her feel like a whore." I accused.

I couldn't help the way my fist curled then. That part was completely true. And saying those words aloud made my rage flare up. My indignation started to tunnel my vision and my eyes turned gold.

Drake saw. The gold in his eyes flickered too and he widened his stance. He was ready for an attack.

"You can try to fight it all you want, but you're gonna be distracted and sloppy as hell until you give in. I was," I told him. "I was a damn mess."

Drake shook his head. "You're too soft, Goldilocks."

Soft.

The word triggered years and years' worth of pain and anger from my childhood. Verbal abuse that spewed from the mouth of my supposed father, physical abuse at his hands and feet. Years of thinking I truly wasn't good enough, because of the color of my pelt, because of the gentleness of my temperament. And suddenly, I lost all control.

"Yeah? Well, at least I don't get *hard* on fucking other people's mates!"

I charged at him and grabbed him around the torso before smashing him into the silver lockers. His grunt of pain was music to my ears. I reared back and sent a right hook smashing into his perfect, smug jaw. My teeth elongated and I roared.

Drake didn't fight back. He just smiled at me and said, "Your mate would be disappointed. You hit like a girl."

On autopilot, I smashed his face again and again. It took me nearly a minute to reign myself in. By then, Drake's eye was swollen shut, his nose was bleeding, and one of his teeth looked cracked.

I dropped him. "Jesus! Fuck! Why do you gotta punish yourself like this? Why do you have to make me the bad guy?"

"You aren't the bad guy," Drake sank down onto one of the wooden benches in the middle of the locker room. "I am."

I shook my head and rolled my eyes, still breathing heavily from my onslaught. "You're the only one who thinks that, you know."

"I killed her father, East. *Her father*."

"Yeah. Ever ask her how she feels about that?" I retorted, moving to lean against a locker beside him.

"I'm sure she feels how anyone would feel." His head dropped into his hands.

He looked broken. So lost. Not like Drake at all.

I shook my head. "You need to talk to her. But know this: she knows why you did it. She knows it was for a mage jewel to protect all of us. Not some personal vendetta or some cheap shot or some bullshit. And she *still* wants to be with you."

I knelt down and peered into Drake's broken face.

"You didn't search her family out and hunt them down. You are *not* Citrine Pierce."

Suddenly, Drake pushed onto his feet and strode off.

I'd obviously struck a nerve.

Question was, was it the right one? Could he ever forgive himself? Or would he doom himself, and with him, all of us?

19

AUBRY

My mind was numb. In a daze. So many thoughts, questions, and emotions ran through my head, trampling me down until I was so overwhelmed that I couldn't even feel them anymore.

I strode across the campus quad, the sun shining brightly in the morning sky, robin's egg blue. It was like a picture in a children's coloring book. The sun smiling, the flowers dancing, all the colors vibrant, all the creatures happy, so totally fucking fabricated it couldn't possibly be real.

It was like the day hadn't gotten the memo about what had happened during the night.

But *I* hadn't forgotten.

Triton had attacked. If there was ever an ounce of doubt in my mind that he'd attacked that elementary school, then it was now gone. His lackeys had stolen our identities and killed at least sixty shifters. Innocents who'd been lulled into a false sense of calm and security, thinking they were *finally* in a place that was safe.

We *all* thought they'd be safe, that the five hundred hostages here would be security for us...

Now, the shifters were more restless than ever before. Just the sight of our faces drained the color from their lips. Their leaders, the people they looked up to and trusted, had become triggers for heartache and anxiety, fear and sadness.

Wrong didn't even begin to describe it. Terrible didn't. There weren't words for it.

It wasn't fair. It wasn't right. And I couldn't help but think... none of this would have happened if I hadn't been thrown into the picture. Their lives were bad before I'd arrived, but they'd only gotten worse ever since I'd shown up. Like, a *hundred* times worse.

I couldn't combat the guilt swirling through my chest at the thought. Not when I was already too worn down from all the other emotions boring a hole in my heart.

I entered the dull brick bursar building, scanning the long row of empty cubicle windows where magical beings would have stood in line to pay their tuition bills or handle any other financial business. Now, it was a prison cell for our captives. Not too different from the original purpose, I supposed, now that I thought about it. Student loans and iron chains were pretty fucking similar.

I pushed through a side door and walked into the office on the other side of the glass, where administrators would normally rifle through filing cabinets and click through digital forms on their computers, all while lit by unflattering fluorescent lights all day. From the main administrative room, other rooms and offices were located down a short hallway, each one holding a small group of prisoners that'd been magically locked up with a Movement Restriction Spell.

The first door on the left held Tee, Aaron, John, and Tammy. They were separated from the mage students, who were considered less of a threat. But since these four had fighter training, we had taken additional precautions. Tony and Larry often dropped by with Power Limiting Spells to try and reduce their ability to attack, particularly Aaron's ability to sing. They were also chained up and watched twenty-four-seven by a guard. We could never be too cautious.

I didn't have Larry's or Tony's permission to cross the threshold, so I simply shoved the door open and sat down in the hallway behind the glowing turquoise line, crisscrossed my legs, and stared at them through the open doorway. The bursar's offices were all interior rooms with no windows, so the four of them were huddled against the back wall while all the office equipment and furniture were shoved into a corner to give them enough space to sleep.

Tee looked annoyed as she raised a brow and fluttered her fingers at me. "If it isn't my ex-friend-slash-captor. Come to feed me poison again? What did you call it? Coughing?"

I frowned slightly. "*Coffee*. And it's not poison. You used to love it. Come on, Tee, you know I'd let you go in a heartbeat if I could."

"Right," she said in a singsong voice. "It's those fleabag mutts—I mean *mates*—of yours who won't let us go."

I sighed and rolled my eyes but didn't argue. I just looked at each one of them instead.

They were a strange crew, all lined up in chains and sitting against the wall. Tammy was the tallest, an elf who was willowy thin, and she kinda looked like a Twizzler in foil. Followed by Aaron, a siren, who was— for all intents and purposes—normal human sized, like me. Then John, the gnome, who was barely two feet tall, and finally Tee, a pixie who was a mere six inches on a good day.

"Where are you keeping us, anyway?" Tee asked, glancing warily all around. She was literally in a small white room with a desk and filing cabinet. Nothing fancy. "One cave to another."

"This isn't a cave, Tee." Pity filled me. "It's an office."

A look of panic flashed through Tee's tiny eyes. "She's doing it again, Aaron! She's fucking gaslighting me! That's not even a word."

"No, baby, no," he cooed, looking just about as frantic as she did as he gazed at her. "You're just having trouble remembering, that's all. The fucking shifter's pet mage wiped your memory, love. Do you recall that part?"

Tee nodded quickly. "Yeah, I remember that part. I just don't remember anything he wiped... obviously."

I bit my lower lip. "Actually, I have a theory."

"Do tell," Tee said, rolling her eyes. She shook her head and glanced over at Tammy, as if Tee thought *I* was the crazy one.

"You know how normal memory wipes cause humans to forget magic?"

Tee merely blinked.

"Well," I continued, "I think in your case, it caused you—a magic user—to forget human stuff."

"Undo it," Aaron demanded from his seat, chains rattling as he leaned forward to stare at me. His dark eyes gleamed and I could tell he was tempted to use his siren song on me. But he didn't. Not when Tee might get hurt if he did.

At least, those were the thoughts I imagined I saw flicker through his features as he ground his teeth together.

I gaped at him. "You know as well as I do that memory wipes are permanent..."

"Then spell me too!" Aaron cried, his eyes wide and expression determined. "If that's what it takes, fine, but you need to fix this!"

My brows furrowed. "Dude, how would that fix anything? It won't make Tee magically remember shit; it'll just make you both clueless."

Aaron nodded vigorously, his chains rattling as he moved. "Exactly. And that'll fix everything."

"No," John, the gnome, protested. He stood, his chains giving him just enough room to put a small, squat hand on Aaron's shoulder. "Don't."

But Aaron shrugged him off. "I can't stand feeling so mentally and emotionally separated from her. It's driving me insane!"

Tee gazed over at him with sympathy in her eyes. "I'm so sorry, baby. I didn't mean to get spelled." Her wings fluttered but she couldn't take flight with the Movement Restriction Spell.

"Don't you dare blame yourself, pixie pie. It's *their* fault. But they're going to fix it. Right, Aubry?"

"Yeah, Aubry," John added in his squat, grumpy gnome-tone. "Aren't you some sort of a fated mates expert, now? Surely you know how much pain Aaron's in?"

I leveled him with a flat look. "I never claimed to be an expert, John."

Tammy scoffed. "Definitely never said you were one."

I wanted to laugh and cry at the same moment. Their attitudes and demands reminded me so much of myself when the guys had first taken me. They knew I didn't want to kill them, or I would have already. But, unlike demanding pho, what Aaron wanted was so much more heartbreaking. He wanted to lose so much of himself in order to be with Tee.

"Agree, Aubry," Aaron demanded impatiently.

My mouth fell open. "You're insane."

"Yes!" he shouted, eyes going wide. "That's what I've been telling you! It's driving me mad!"

I hesitated, realizing that even if I wanted to, I couldn't ask Larry to spell the siren... not yet, anyway. "I have a few questions for you first, Aaron."

He shook his head and clamped his mouth shut. "I'm not telling you a goddamn thing until you spell me."

"If I fucking spell you, your memories will be gone before you even answer my questions!"

Aaron glared at me. I glared right back. I hadn't become chief enforcer by being a naive little shit. "You want a staring contest? Because I'll wipe the floor with your ass like those kittens-versus-thugs staring contests on Key and Peele."

"Agree to spell me immediately after," Aaron bargained, eyeing me skeptically, "and I'll answer your questions."

"Truthfully?" I asked with a scoff. Part of me wondered if I'd trust him even if he said yes. But it would at least be more information than I had before.

Tammy interrupted, "Aaron, don't."

Aaron glared even harder at me, not even bothering to look at her. "Yes. Truthfully."

Part of me was worried by his answer. His one-track mind and utter determination to lose his memory. Were mate bonds really that intense? Would

I go crazy if something happened to Bodie, Easton, or...

I cut that thought off in the middle and sighed at Aaron. "You seriously want to lose all memory of humanity? This is like, half of your life... gone. Wiped away. Vanished."

Pain lined his eyes in pink rims. "It's what happened to her. If she's expected to get through it and move on, then I want to be right there with her. We'll get through it together."

My heart ached like it did whenever I watched *The Notebook*. That movie twisted me up and left me pulsing with love and heartbreak at the exact same time. Somehow, I knew I'd feel the same way about my guys if we were in their shoes. Because, somehow, I could feel that pain already, even vicariously.

I let out one last sigh of reluctance before nodding. "Deal."

The relief that crossed his face was nearly palpable. It lightened my own heart to know that he and Tee would be good again. That, if nothing else, they'd have each other.

But... I thought of my situation with the guys and the shifters... What if we didn't just need each other? What if we needed something more? Something... else... in order to make this right?

My stomach sank, a bubbling mire of acid and desolation and sadness. I didn't even want to think about what might need to be done. Not if it was going to hurt as much as Aaron and Tee were hurting.

"Well, ask away, traitor," John goaded, tottering his head pompously and flipping me off with his stubby fingers.

"John, you're about this close to getting shot in the dome." I pinched my thumb and forefinger together until there was barely a space left in between.

He scoffed. "Wouldn't hurt. It'd just ricochet off my head and lodge into the wall or something."

"I know," I retorted with a smirk. "But it would still give me the satisfaction of shooting your dumb ass."

He rolled his eyes and glared at the pile of furniture, where Tammy had already been staring, deciding this whole thing was far too boring for her precious elf sensibilities. Bitch.

I suddenly heard a door opening, and voices filtered in from the lobby, muttering back and forth. The door shut, and the voices grew louder as they slowly approached. I remained silent, watching curiously as Bodie and Easton entered the bursar's office carrying a… body.

What the fuck?

I stood and walked toward them. "Guys…?" I asked curiously as they shuffled along. Bodie had the cadaver's arms while Easton carried his legs. The dead weight almost sagged to the floor in the middle.

"Oh, uh, hey, Aubry," Easton said, smiling sheepishly. In his nervousness, he accidentally dropped the corpse's leg to rub the back of his neck. The weight of the dead guy's leg dropping jerked his arms out of Bodie's grasp, and his whole body hit the floor like a sack of potatoes. I could see the dead guy had been ten-ringed.

"Fucking hell! What are you doing?" I hissed, stepping closer.

They knew the rules! No killing the students! And by the looks of his Mag-Sorgin hoodie, which I could see now that I'd stepped closer, he was most definitely a student. If Larry found out... and he *left*... Drake would flip his lid and rain down fire and brimstone on this entire operation. It would *not* be pretty.

The two of them scrambled to pick the dead guy up.

"It's nothing, Buttercup," Bodie insisted as they quickly shuffled around the corner. "Just an accident."

"A *what*?" I whispered harshly.

"An accident? Yeah right," John scoffed from his spot in his room. With the door open, the four prisoners could all clearly see what was going on.

I ignored the gnome. I knew as well as anyone that accidentally killing someone was totally a thing. But Bodie? He was a murder machine. It was pure instinct for him. It had probably been a knee-jerk reaction that he couldn't control.

I sighed and listened as they shuffled around the office, out of my view. "Where are you putting that thing?"

"Uh..." Bodie didn't seem sure.

"The printer room?" East didn't seem sure either, but since he'd given an actual example, Bodie freaking ran with it.

"Yeah, the printer room! Don't worry, Buttercup, we'll move him out of here as soon as we can. Larry was just getting too close to sniffing him out."

I blinked. "How old is this body? I'd rather not smell him, either."

Easton chuckled nervously, and I heard the sound of another door opening. "Just a couple days. No worries."

There was a thud, followed by a dusting of hands, and finally a door shutting.

I narrowed my eyes and turned back to the chained-up prisoners. All four of them were looking at me now. Staring. Judging.

"Oh, fuck you guys!" I snapped. "As if MPs are any better."

"*MPs?*" Tammy asked with a scoff. "You even *sound* like a gangster now."

"Well, considering my mates are shifter mafia warlords, I suppose that officially makes me the Bonnie to their Clyde, huh? May as well get used to it." It was my new reality. I moved my glare from Tammy onto Aaron. "You still want to make a deal? Tell me why Triton fucking Vale attacked us last night."

At first Aaron's lips remained sealed.

"Aaron Dirkman," I threatened darkly, "You answer my questions truthfully, or there will be no memory wipe. You and Tee will just have to remain on separate pages of the same book for the rest of your godforsaken lives. And you know I'm the only reason you all are still alive right now."

I conveniently failed to mention Larry's peaceful proclivities. These MPs attacked us, and unlike the students, they *weren't* innocent. If I couldn't get any information out of them, then I might have to reconsider just why the fuck we were keeping them.

The siren's eyes snapped back to mine, a mixture of fury and fear swirling in their darkened depths. His jaw ticked, his lips pursed, and finally, he started fucking talking. "Triton had been greenlighted to head an operation in the event that mine failed—which it did. Thanks to you and your criminal mutts."

My gaze drifted over to Tee. "I thought you were tailing Triton because the council suspected him? Why would they approve a mission for him if they knew he was the one starting the fires?" Part of me wondered if she'd remember her investigation. Then again, it had nothing to do with humans.

Tee raised a sassy little brow. "Well, ya see, Princess, I was never able to report back to them with my findings. Because—like my mate, here—you and your pets kidnapped me."

So the council had no evidence that Triton was guilty. Then, once Aaron failed to stop us, they were left with no other choice. But why Triton? He wasn't an MP, he was a councilman.

I asked Aaron as much.

"Because Triton volunteered," Aaron replied matter of factly. He might've tried to shrug, but it was difficult to tell beneath the mountain of chains.

I glanced out the window into the dazzling sunshine as I tried to collect my thoughts. Triton had volunteered because of his vendetta with Drake. He'd become hollow and bitter, consumed by it, which made me sad as much as it made me furious. And I still didn't even know exactly what had happened with his parents. But what did all this mean?

"What exactly has the council permitted him to do?" I asked. "One attack? Multiple?"

Aaron shook his head solemnly and something in his gaze shifted. He was almost... forlorn looking. "Aubry... Triton's already tried and failed, too. The next step is Doomsday."

My mouth went dry. "What the hell is that supposed to mean?"

Aaron shook his head softly. "The council won't be made a fool of. They can't afford another failure. They're going to rig the game. They're going to ensure that they win."

"How?" I asked, though I wasn't actually sure that I wanted to know.

"Picture... an atomic bomb. But magical."

A mountain collapsed on top of me and a million stones crushed my soul. *No. Fuck no.* My eyes went wide. Pretty sure my heart stopped beating. They were going to bomb the school? Kill us all? Just like that? The picture of it happening played through my mind. I could see the newsreels, imagine how they'd twist the story and say we'd done it ourselves. *Mother-fuckers.*

Tee glanced fearfully between Aaron and me. "What's a bomb? What does atomic mean? Guys! What the hell are you talking about?"

No one answered her.

I swallowed hard and stood to leave, but I heard the sound of the door opening once more in the lobby, so I paused. At first, I thought it was Bodie and Easton leaving, but then I heard Larry's telltale voice.

"Oh, hey, guys," he said, apparently to my mates.

"Uh," Easton stammered.

Yep, they were definitely still there.

"Hey, Larry, what's up?" Bodie asked, quickly covering up Easton's obvious nerves.

"Nothing much. Just printing off some ingredients for a spell Tony and I are about to try. Accidentally sent it to the wrong damn printer." Larry smiled at them, then his eyes found mine. "Morning, Aubry. Beautiful day. After such a dark night, I can't help but think this is a good sign."

My heart sank at his chipper demeanor, but I tried to put on a smile. *Oh Larry, if only you knew.* Things were about to go from bad to worse. To hell in a mother fucking hand basket.

"Uh, why didn't you just resend it to the *right* printer?" Easton asked, taking a step toward the printer room door to block it.

Larry scratched his frazzled, salt and peppered head and chuckled. "Guess I didn't even think about it. Technology and I do not usually get along. I'm a little too old-fashioned for it."

Larry made to move past Easton, but my bear shifter sidestepped and continued blocking. "Larry, I actually *really* need your help on... something. First."

Larry paused and cocked his head, intrigued rather than suspicious. The poor gullible old man. "Oh yeah? On what?"

"On..." Easton looked like he was absolutely wracking his brain to think of an idea. "A new special weapon I'm designing. See I have this idea for a special barrel with a special shaped potion bottle... Actually, how about I draw it for you?"

East put his arm around Larry's shoulders and led him over to a desk where he grabbed a pen and paper and started sketching.

Bodie shot me a wide-eyed look and whispered, "I gotta move this thing. Make sure he stays distracted."

I was still shell-shocked by Aaron's revelation and I wasn't thinking straight. I reacted to Bodie's request on autopilot. I took one step away from the prisoners' room and Aaron lost his mind. "Aubry! Don't leave! You promised!"

I shot him a look that said, 'Calm down, dude. Hold your tits.' Then, I decided on a plan that would kill two birds with one stone. "Larry, I'll grab your paper for you while Easton shows you his drawing. I actually need to head to your chemistry lab next anyway, to see about another Memory Wiping Potion."

Larry smiled brightly. "Oh wonderful, thanks for grabbing that. But... um... a Memory Wipe Spell? Are you sure they wouldn't rather have a Fireproof Spell or something? I did a really good one for El Fuego once. After the last Memory Wipe, I don't think I should..."

I jerked my head toward the prisoners' room. "No. I'm sorry. It has to be a wipe. Tee's mate wants it. Aaron wants to be on the same wavelength. Says it's driving him insane she can't remember anything from the human world."

Larry nodded solemnly and looked over at the open door of the office-turned-prison. His face filled with sympathy. "Oh yes. Mate bonds are strong and serious magic. I feel awful that the potion didn't work right. That was never my intention. Of course, I'll whip up another batch to help her poor partner cope."

"Thank you," Aaron shouted into the hall.

"You're welcome!" Larry shouted back.

What... an odd fucking exchange. But that was Larry for you. Dumbledore's less competent brother, who was good at heart, despite appearing to cater to assholes.

Bodie and I swapped another look, his green eyes thanking me, before I quickly slipped into the printer room. The body was wedged into a corner with a fucking lamp shade over its head and a printer stand pushed in front. *Oh my gold-digging god.* These guys were mobsters? One of them, a professional assassin? It was sometimes ridiculously hard to believe. But then again, they never had to worry about hiding the bodies before…

I swiped Larry's paper off the printer tray and got the hell out of there.

That's when I heard the sound of shattering glass and ear-splitting gunfire. Screams ripped through the air from the prisoner room down the hall, accompanied by shouts and crude slurs.

I almost thought it was Triton and the Mage Council attacking again, coming to finish the job they'd started the night before. But as soon as I heard the words, "murdering mage scum!" leave someone's mouth, I knew it wasn't them.

It was the *shifters* retaliating for Trite's attack.

And they were pissed as hell.

20

AUBRY

I FLEW DOWN THE HALL AS FAST AS MY WINGS COULD carry me, speeding past the guys, spurred on by the sound of fearful shrieks being abruptly cut off—muted by death.

Fear and fury wrangled inside me. *Motherfucking damn it!* I knew *exactly* what was happening and why it was happening, but at the same damn time, I was fucking pissed. The shifters should know better.

My eyes scanned every detail, and my ears turned to high alert, my MP training kicking in to try to gauge the fight I was about to fly into. How many shifters were there? How were they getting in? How many students had they killed in the five seconds it took me to get there? How many more would die if I didn't do something, and fast?

I hung a hard left at the end of the hall and barreled into one of the meeting rooms we'd used to contain the younger magical students, the first-year mages, elves, and fae that had been on campus. Each student had been placed *barefoot* inside their own three-foot circular Mage Restriction Spell, so that the carpeted floor looked like it was covered in glowing bubbles.

Unlike the office where we'd kept the MP prisoners, this meeting room had windows, which were broken, and had clearly served as the shifter's entry point.

It was a bloody fucking massacre. It looked like that scene from *Alice in Wonderland* when the cards painted the roses; the shifters were splattering blood all over the fucking place like stain or varnish. Even the students who hadn't been shot yet were covered in blood from their peers. And they couldn't fucking move other than to crouch.

Sobs wove like ribbons through the room.

"Stop!" I screamed, seeing the attacking shifters' faces only after I'd taken in all the blood.

Corey, Bodie's beta and second in command lowered his weapon when Bodie came barreling up behind me and let out a growl. Russ, the wolf shifter who'd helped us during the shootout at Union Station froze with a handgun to a mage student's forehead. He stood just outside the young autumn fae's turquoise circle, and his teeth were clenched in fury, while the girl's face was dull with shock.

Naissa and her son Zane, the shifters I'd met at the bank, the ones who'd thanked me for returning little Suzie's body to them by sharing an omelet with me, stood side by side. Their faces were wild and blood-spattered.

"This isn't the way!" I cried as I launched myself in front of Naissa's shotgun barrel, careful to avoid stepping into any of the Movement Restriction circles.

Easton and Larry darted into the room after me, immediately matching themselves up with Russ and Zane.

Naissa burst into tears almost immediately, and as soon as the broken-hearted grandmother lowered her gun, I pulled her into a hug.

I wasn't sure what had gotten into me.

She'd just killed people in cold blood, and I was hugging her. Around us, mages sobbed and pissed themselves in fear. And still, I hugged her.

I tried to hug her hurt and her hate away, knowing it was impossible, but still wishing it wasn't. I closed my eyes and stroked her spine, trying to fill her with peace, trying to fill myself with it instead of the molten horror brewing inside me.

For some reason, I just felt so deeply connected to these people, these shifters who so graciously opened up their world to me and welcomed me despite the fact that I was fae. They'd taken me in and shown me kindness, and honestly, I wanted to do that for them too. They were hurting; that's why they'd done this. They thought they could negate that hurt by hurting someone else. It became a vicious circle.

Would the mages and the shifters *always* be trapped in this never-ending loop of violence?

I opened my eyes and the sight before me wasn't promising.

Zane dropped his gun and held his hands up the moment his mother lowered hers. But Corey and Russ were still giving Bodie and Easton a fight.

"You are a beta!" Bodie growled at Corey. "You don't get to make calls like this. You're not an alpha!"

"Yeah, but I should have been!" Corey spat, his bleach-white smile stained pink with blood. "I would at least do what's right! I'd get revenge on behalf of my people!"

Suddenly, Bodie released him and brought his hands down hard on Corey's lowered gun barrel, dropping it to the floor. Then he grabbed both sides of Corey's head and snapped his neck before I could even gasp out loud. The beta dropped to the floor, where Bodie looked down and finished his speech.

"Taking revenge is *not* what's right. Disobeying your alpha is *not* what's right."

Several of the university students leaned away from Bodie and Corey, unable to move because their feet were literally stuck to the ground.

Bodie didn't seem to notice, other than a small twitch of his nose, which told me he could scent their fear. These poor students had every right to be afraid. And furious. But none of them said a single word as Bodie took control of the room.

He turned his green-eyed glare over to Russ, who had finally stopped fighting Easton. "Are you next?"

Russ held up both hands, breathing heavily as he lowered his tear-filled gaze to the floor. "No, sir." He choked back a sob.

"Good."

I couldn't help myself. I needed to comfort the shifter. "I'm sorry about your wife, Russ." I knew that the horror in the library was on repeat in Russ's head. I knew, because it was on repeat in mine. All of these atrocities played again and again in my mind each night, like infomercials that wouldn't turn off, like lyrics for a song I hated that wouldn't leave my brain, like ghosts that dogged my every step.

Tears streamed down his cheeks as he nodded, silently accepting my sympathy.

Part of me wanted to comfort the students too, but I didn't know if that was possible. Or if I'd just come off as a bitch. So, I simply stared at each of them numbly.

Bodie's eyes softened a bit after that conversation, but he still looked around the room with disgust slathered all over his face. I didn't think it had anything to do with the blood, either. I think he was just... pissed off. About what his people had done. About what his people were going through. About everything and everyone. About the injustice of it all.

It was fucking unjust.

And it needed to end. Somehow.

I stroked Naissa's hair as she continued sobbing

into my shoulder. The students who were still alive sobbed. Sobs and silence mingled as the true weight of what had just happened drug us all down. It gave me a hollow sensation in my chest, and my thoughts from earlier this morning circled back once more.

Everything had gotten a hundred times worse since I'd arrived. And it just kept getting more and more hopeless the longer I stayed.

Russ broke the silence by walking over to stand in front of Bodie. "Alpha." He bowed his head. Then he straightened and stared at Bodie. "Please."

I wasn't exactly sure what he was asking at first. But when Bodie's chin lifted and he swallowed hard before nodding, I had a feeling I could guess. Two seconds later, Russ collapsed to the floor, neck snapped.

"You," Bodie walked over to Zane and shoved the man backward. Zane stumbled and fell into one of the turquoise circles that held a dead mage student. The kid's lifeless body had fallen backward, limp, but his knees were bent because the circle still glued his feet to the floor. "You can wait here for your alpha. In fact, why don't you wrap your arms around that kid you killed while you wait."

Zane's eyes widened but when Bodie took a menacing step forward, he immediately reached out and gently grabbed the body. He pulled it upright next to him. He started to shake as he wrapped his arms around the young boy's ruined torso.

Bodie only had to look at Naissa in order to make

her do the same. It was harsh, but nothing more than they deserved. I had no idea if their alpha would execute them. In all honesty, they deserved it. But that didn't make me less sad. Justice and kindness were often worlds apart.

I exhaled and I realized my hands were shaking. I hadn't been this nervous over a fight in... years. Probably because I hadn't been emotionally attached to anyone for that amount of time. I wasn't sure how I felt about that. Part of me wanted to scold myself for getting soft. But the other part cherished the time I'd spent with the shifters and my mates, cherished the loving softness I'd acquired for the first time in my life, and wouldn't trade it for the world.

Easton walked up and placed a comforting hand on my shoulder before going to check on the injured students.

Larry bent down and handed a handkerchief to a mage student who had leaned as far outside his own circle as he could and was trying to use his hand as a tourniquet for his friend's arm.

"Here," Larry said gently, giving the kid the square of fabric.

The student, a dark-skinned boy with curly black hair, nodded as he accepted the old mage's offering. He quickly tied it around his friend's arm, as Larry rifled through potions in the inner pocket of his jacket.

Eventually, Larry pulled out a pink Healing Potion and passed it over.

"Thank you," the boy mumbled.

Larry gave him a tired smile. "You're welcome."

My gaze lifted as Larry stood back up, and I was suddenly met with the full weight of his devastated stare.

I sniffed and looked away, as if coming face to face with terrified students covered in blood was a better sight to see. As if the bodies littering the floor were easier to look at than Larry's disappointment. In a way, they were. Larry represented the better part of all of us. And his disappointment and shame were worse than any hit I'd ever taken.

I glanced over at Easton and Bodie. "You think you guys can clean up this mess while Larry and I mix up some potions?" I hadn't forgotten Aaron. I had no doubt that some of these students would also volunteer to forget anything to do with guns.

"Yeah, Sweetheart. We got it," Easton replied gently.

Bodie simply nodded.

I gestured toward the door, but as Larry shuffled toward the exit ahead of me, the same student from a moment ago stopped the old mage.

"Wait," the boy said. He seemed to be gathering his thoughts, or more likely, his courage. "You're helping them."

His eyes flicked onto me and then to Easton and Bodie for a moment before returning to Larry's weathered face.

Larry sighed. "Yes, I am."

"Why?" the boy asked.

Larry ran a hand through his frazzled salt-and-pepper hair, messing the hell out of it. "What's your name, young man?"

"Decker, sir."

"Well, Decker, I'd love to talk with you about it sometime in more detail. However, it will suffice to say: we're all born with our eyes shut, but in order to see what's *right*, we need to open them to the truth."

Decker paused for a moment, and I could see his keen mind soaking up Larry's words like a sponge. A nod was his only response, so Larry and I continued out into the hall.

At the end of the corridor, I bent down and grabbed the ingredients list that I'd picked up from the printer for the mage. I must've dropped it in my haste to reach the back room. God, it was insane how fast shit could happen. How fast everything could shift, how fast an entire life could change. Or end.

We pushed through the doors and entered the warm, yellow sunshine without speaking.

Yeah. So much for things looking up, huh, Lar?

I took in a deep breath of fresh air and let it out slowly. "What are we gonna do, Larry?"

He glanced at me, the same sadness from before filling his old brown eyes. "We're already doing all that we can."

"Are we?" I asked. "I can't help but feel like there's more we should be doing. Something we might've missed. It can't keep going on like this, and total anni-hilation is not an option." Aaron's warnings came back to haunt me and visions of the college disappearing in a mushroom cloud filled my head. "What else is there?"

Larry exhaled and shook his head thoughtfully. "I don't know, Miss Summerset. This war has been going on for a long time. I joined *years* ago, thinking I could make some sort of a difference, but even with the nonstop work I do, it still isn't enough."

I nodded my agreement. I knew that feeling. That worn-down sensation of dissatisfaction. I could never do anything right to please my parents. Eventually, I realized that I needed to stop trying; they weren't worth it.

But this? This was most definitely worth it.

"Aaron said Triton's attacks will keep coming," I muttered by means of casual conversation, not wanting to say the worst aloud. "And they're only going to get worse."

Thanks to you, my brain hissed at me. I'd never heard it sound so harsh. But it was right.

If I would have done my job as a princess and an enforcer, I never would have gotten kidnapped in the first place. If I'd done my job as a best friend, I would have comforted Triton instead of allowing him to stew and fester in his own putrid thoughts. If I could take it all back, and change everything... would I?

My heart ached at the thought of losing Bodie and Easton and... I took a deep breath, cutting the last name off in that procession. But if I could keep the shifters safe, if I could protect them somehow, or change their fate, wouldn't *that* be worth it?

"The mages hate us," Larry said. Then he chuckled humorlessly. "*Us*. As if I'm not a mage, myself." He shook his head as we walked across the quad. "But Triton Vale... He seems to hate us more than most, and I don't understand why."

Drake must not have told him. There must not have been any time. No opportune moment to bring it up.

"It's because Drake accidentally killed his parents," I explained, unsure of how he'd react.

To my surprise, it was like a light bulb went off in his dusty old head. "When he was young, Drake had a difficult time controlling his fire. Not that it was volatile, but it was... addictive. He was always playing with it, curious as to what it would do. He loved to watch things burn."

I smiled up at him, imaging a child-like Drake, one who was still sweet and innocent, one who smiled, one who was still mesmerized by beautiful things like flames dancing on his fingertips. "You knew Drake as a boy?"

Larry smiled fondly. "I did. I told you, I've been on this side of the war for a very long time now." He took another deep breath as we reached the science center and strode inside. "When he was a teenager, things were even more difficult for him. With his family passed, he had no one to guide or direct him in the ways of a dragon. I tried to be there for him as a mentor, but ultimately, I couldn't tell him who he was or what he should do. He had to decide."

We walked down the shiny tiled floors until we reached one of the special chemistry labs that only mage students were allowed to enter: a potions room. The rooms were restricted for non-mages in order to deter other students from entering. So they could keep their magical secrets.

"So, what happened?" I asked, taking a seat at a lab table as Larry immediately began collecting ingredients for the Memory Wipe Potion.

"He *learned*," Larry said sternly. "At a very steep cost, too. He learned who he was, and who he wasn't."

I was pretty sure I knew who Drake was nowadays. The dickheaded prick. Cold, heartless, and cruel. Impossible to reach out to or connect with. Even as part of me slammed the door on that asshole, another part of me cried out with longing. As Larry ground the walnuts, avocado seeds, and white powder—which I had to assume was made from murder bones— I couldn't help but ask, "So, who *wasn't* he?"

Larry glanced up; his grinding momentarily halted. "He wasn't a murderer. He wasn't a slave to his dragon." Then he got back to grinding.

But I wasn't done talking about it.

"So what does that have to do with Trite's parents?" I asked, clearly unable to help myself.

"Killing them was the cost of that knowledge."

That sliced through my heart and drained the color from my cheeks. Poor Drake. But then I narrowed my eyes. "I thought you just said he wasn't a murderer?" If he wasn't, why had he killed Triton's parents?

Larry sighed and added in bright green chunks of avocado flesh to the mixture, thickening it into a paste. "He tracked Citrine to the Vale's house one day, and the beast within him took control. He burned the entire mansion to the ground, killing Samuel and Cordelia in the process."

Larry reached into a drawer and pulled out a wooden spoon, then picked up an empty glass jar with a corked lid, and began filling it up with the paste which had somehow turned a mysterious shade of lavender.

"Citrine," he continued as he worked, "was a councilwoman, and as such, had simply portaled out, but Drake didn't know that then. Furious, his beast soared through the night sky above the burning building searching for her. All he found was a scared little boy in the living room window, choking on the smoke, desperately calling out for his mother and father."

Triton. Oh my god.

"Drake, he... He saw so much of himself in the little boy. He remembered what it was like to be a child all alone, his parents murdered before his very eyes, and he couldn't stand the thought of leaving him there. Drake swooped down and burst through the glass, then grabbed the boy and flew him to the nearest hospital—

in case he needed treatment for burns or smoke inhalation."

So, Drake had killed Triton's parents on his quest to kill Citrine, but he'd actually saved Triton's life in the process?

When Trite joined the council, he found out the shifter who had saved him was the very same one who'd killed his parents. No wonder he hated Drake so deeply. Admiration and hero worship had turned into the deepest, darkest kind of loathing there was.

Larry filled the jar half full of the Memory Wiping Potion, then re-corked it. He handed the potion bottle to me before taking a seat across the table.

"Drake vowed, that very night, to never again become that which he hated. He's killed people since. It's even been on purpose. But that purpose is something far more noble now. It's something that even the ethical side of me can respect. He won't kill for vengeance or hatred or greed. His crimes are those of *passion*, crimes of love and protection and sacrifice for his people. The beast may rage inside of him, but he has never allowed it to consume him like that since."

Fate snapped her fingers and my fury at Drake faded away. Just like *that*, I didn't hate him so much. I was pretty sure I never had, honestly. If anything, I...

No. I couldn't admit something like that. Not even to myself. Not when it would never be reciprocated. Not when it hurt me to even say his name out loud.

I mulled my thoughts, and Larry's words, and every

event that had happened over these last few weeks, around in my mind, trying to come up with a solution.

Everyone in this entire damn war was so busy chasing ghosts, avenging them, fighting for the memories of loved ones lost.

Ghosts...

Finally, something clicked. It was like the clouds opened up and sunshine radiated down on me like a halo.

"Larry," I said, unable to keep the slight tremble out of my tone. "I think I have a plan. But I'm going to need your help."

He stared at me without blinking. "I assume it doesn't involve the murder of innocents?"

I shook my head. "No, it doesn't involve the murder of innocents."

"Then count me in," he said with a smile.

My lips curled back at him even though my stomach was twisting into tightly coiled knots.

I finally knew what I needed to do...

BODIE

"I can't believe I had to kill Corey."

I closed my eyes, leaning against the office door of our temporary housing. I didn't normally feel guilt. This time wasn't an exception. I didn't feel guilty; I was disappointed by him, and my own judgement. I'd somehow let an asshole become my beta.

Easton sat on the futon across the room, cradling his blond head in his hands. "I know, man. I'm sorry."

I shook my head slowly and let out a sigh. "It was his own fault. He should have followed his fucking orders. That was his only job as beta—carry out my commands—and he couldn't even do that. I should have canned him a while ago." My fault.

Easton nodded, scrubbing a hand across his face before meeting eyes with me. "And Russ."

Sighing, I ran a hand over my own face, too. "Yeah, that fucking killed me. I know why he did it, and I feel

so bad about Cheryl, but it's just… I can't allow insub-
ordination, you know? I can't tolerate it. That's no way
to run a pack."

I'd seen it happen far too often, alphas with mutiny
on their hands. We already had enough enemies. We
didn't need any damn in-fighting.

"Yeah, man, I agree. Sometimes leaders have to
make difficult decisions. I don't think anyone blames
you for it."

I nodded. I didn't really give a fuck if anyone
blamed me or not. I was doing what was right for the
pack and for shifters as a whole. But I did hate that
annoying sensation of remorse that swirled in my gut
about killing Russ. I would miss having him around.

"Speaking of leaders making difficult decisions…"
Easton said, drawing my attention once more. "What
the hell are we going to do? Drake's not doing his job
as leader, the shifters are rebelling, the mages keep
attacking, and I honestly don't know how much longer
we can keep this up."

I stayed silent. I didn't want to admit that he was
right, even though he was. We'd taken the school
because we thought it would give us the upper hand.
So far? It had only made things worse.

And Drake… *Don't even get me started.*

As much as I hated it, I was starting to think he
should just kiss Aubry and get this mate bond shit over
with, so he could pull his head out of his ass and start
thinking straight again. I was an assassin, a faceless

ghost if I did my job right, and I couldn't run all of L.A. on the side. We needed him for that. He was the one with a backup plan for every back up plan. At least before now. *Stupid dogged fuck.*

"We're gonna have to talk to Drake," I said in response to Easton's statement. "We need him to get his shit together and do his goddamn job. No one can do it for him."

Easton sighed, tapping his toes as he sat in thoughtful silence. "Been there. Tried that. He's too stubborn. You think Aubry is okay?"

"Yeah, man, she's tough. She can handle it." I didn't doubt that shit for a second.

She was our mate. She was *ride or die* now. And I couldn't even begin to express how fucking hot that was to me. To know she had our backs no matter what. That she'd stay cool and not lose her shit over the fucked-up things we did. Even though she might beat the hell out of us after.

I grinned as I pictured her tiny frame and mile-wide attitude. She didn't give a fuck that we were hardened criminals three times her size; she'd go head-to-head with anyone.

Speaking of our sweet little fae devil...

Aubry burst into our crap-tastic room and immediately removed her shirt. It still had blood stains from the epic shit-show from earlier, and I could tell she was totally *done* with wearing it. And I was totally *down* with that.

343

She balled it up and threw it on the floor. "We need to do laundry."

It took me a second to completely register what she'd said because she was standing there topless and my eyes were admiring the girls.

"Nah," I responded with a wink. "We need to do *you*." We definitely needed to experience some positive energy after the negative shit that just went down. And she was already halfway undressed.

Aubry couldn't seem to help the smirk that crossed her face, and I fucking loved seeing that smile. Goddamn.

I glanced over at Easton, who stared at me with raised brows. "*We?*"

I shrugged and went over to scoop Aubry up, tossing her over my shoulder just like I had after the fire. God, I loved the feel of her. She was so tiny but so curvy. Those legs. That ass. My mate was fucking hot.

I turned and gave Easton an arrogant stare. "Fine. Just me, then. Your loss."

I gave Aubry's ass a good smack, enjoying her delighted squeak, showcasing just what Easton would be missing out on. Then I turned and grabbed the doorknob, pretending I was gonna walk off without him.

"Whoa! No. Wait. I'm in! I'm in!" Easton hurried to catch up.

Aubry wriggled in my arms. "Both of you, knock it off. I'm serious. I need to wash my shit." She squirmed around enough to push herself upright. But that only put her pretty boobs right near my face. I latched onto a tit and sucked.

Damn. Yes. *This.* I needed this. And I had a feeling she needed it too. A chance to destress and depressurize. A moment for us to reconnect in the midst of all this disconnect.

I used my tongue to flick her nipple. It was so fucking perfect. Soft and pink but it got nice and stiff in my mouth and I gave it a tiny bite. My dick rose to attention.

I hardly felt it when she smacked my arm. The blood was already rushing south. I was getting into the zone. Especially when I felt one of her little hands squeeze my shoulder. She might be telling me to stop out loud, but her body was giving me the green light.

Then I felt Easton's hand on my shoulder. He said, "I've heard washing machines can feel like vibrators if you fuck a girl right up against them."

Immediately, Aubry stiffened. "You *heard*?"

Oooh, our little mate was jealous. I decided to play with her. I unlatched and leaned back to look up at her, resting my chin on her chest, her soft breasts pressing against my cheeks. "He might have heard, but I *know*."

Her face turned down toward me and the cutting look in her eyes was glorious. It was vicious and brutal, and it made me want to take her right there.

I couldn't stop the laugh that burst from me. And I wasn't a laugher. I was more of a smirker. "Gotcha."

Easton chuckled as Aubry rained down punches on me. She actually got in a few solid hits. When my ears started to ring, I handed her over to Easton, draping her over his shoulder and smacking the sweet curve of that ass again. "Here, you carry her. I'll carry the clothes. And then we'll test out this washing machine theory."

I snagged our clothes from a pile in the back corner of the room, then walked back to scoop up the shirt she'd dropped by the door.

Easton had swung Aubry down into a bridal carry and was kissing her lips gently. The jealousy that had once flared like acid in my throat didn't show this time. Maybe that meant I was adjusting. I didn't analyze it, just shucked off the shirt I was wearing and tossed it at Aubry.

"Here. Cover up."

Easton wrinkled his nose. "Dude. I would have given her my shirt."

"Snooze, ya lose," I said, yanking open the door. "Now she's gonna smell like me."

So, maybe there was still a little bit of competitiveness left inside.

But Easton just chuckled as Aubry slid my shirt on. She had to fold her wings down to do it, but that just made the shirt stretch tighter across her chest. I considered that a win.

Damn. If I had to rank my favorite sights in the world, first would be Aubry naked, but a close second would be her wearing my clothes. A month ago, my answers would have been very different. A month ago, the sight of a full moon or of my gun barrel smoking after a perfect shot would have been top of the list. Now, those things were so far down they didn't even compare. I was here, fucking domesticated, carrying goddamned laundry I didn't even know how to do— and I was excited about it.

The world was a fucking crazy, awesome place.

Easton and I walked to the other end of the Student Union Building before the three of us made it outside. Without speaking to anyone, and without any real idea where to go, we wandered through the afternoon sunlight with our mate and our laundry in tow.

"Over to the right," Aubry called out and pointed toward the nearest dormitory.

The plaque outside said "Sundara Hall, est. 1928." We opened the wooden doors with a skeleton key we'd found in one of the offices and made our way inside.

The lights were still on. We hadn't bothered to turn them off in most of the buildings, just to help maintain pretenses for anyone walking by. The college looked full and operational. But some buildings hadn't gotten quite the cleaning job that others had. We'd yanked prisoners out of this dorm, but Kira clearly hadn't come around to "sweep up."

"Careful not to get the powder on you." I warned. "Anybody know where the laundry is?"

"Basement," Easton and Aubry called out simultaneously.

I glanced back to see them start giggling together.

"What the fuck? Have you done this laundry thing together already?" Had they had sex without me again? My wolf changed my vision and I lost the reds and magentas. My eyes could only see blue, but that's how I knew when I was pissed.

"No! Nothing like that. It's just... jinx!" he said.

Aubry said it at the same frickin' time. Like they were fucking twelve-year-old BFF's with braided bracelets and shit. I wanted to yank her out of his arms and carry her instead. I wanted to give her a secret handshake and teach her the different sorts of howls I did and what each one meant.

Goddamn motherfucking mate sharing bullshit.

Damn it. I thought I was past this.

Guess not completely.

I sighed and turned, trying to convince my wolf that we were soon gonna be buried so deep inside our mate's sweet snatch that it wouldn't even matter. When he brought up the mental image of wolf fucking, it gave me dark, delicious ideas.

Mmm. Yes.

There were things I could share with Aubry that Easton couldn't. That Drake couldn't—if he ever pulled his head out of his flaming ass.

Part of me hoped he didn't.

The other part was too busy picturing me riding Aubry to care about much else.

My dick was hard as a rock, tenting my shorts so that I had to adjust them to ease the pressure before I walked down the stairs.

As basements went, this one wasn't that creepy. It had a couple of hallways that seemed to go around the edges of the room. In the back corner, a walled off area and a low humming sound let me know where we were headed.

I grabbed the door to pull it open, just in time for someone to push on it from the inside. Larry's grizzled head popped out.

"Oh!" His hand flew to his heart and he seemed startled to see me. "I wasn't expecting—I'm sorry. I didn't see you there!" He gave a little nod hello toward Aubry and Easton and then made his way toward the stairs, a container of detergent in his hands.

"Mind if we use your soap?" Easton called out.

Larry turned and didn't make eye contact with us. Damn it all. "Oh, um. It's empty, I was just bringing it up to recycle it," Larry said. "But I saw some in there. On the shelves."

He scurried off.

I didn't give him a second glance, too eager to get these damn clothes out of my hands and fill them up with something else. Someone else. Aubry.

I shoved the clothes into a machine, got the soap, and started it. Then I hopped up on top of the rumbling metal box, sat down, and unzipped. My cock popped out with ease, so hard it was throbbing.

"Buttercup, come suck me," I requested.

My mate shucked my shirt and flared those gorgeous, half-translucent wings before she stepped forward and bent to take my dick between her plush lips.

Oh hell, yes. This was what people meant when they talked about heaven on earth. Sensation shot from my balls all the way up my spine as her soft lips and warm wet mouth wrapped around me. She did something with her tongue and my toes curled inside my shoes. Aubry was so damn perfect.

"Do that again," I said, reaching for the back of her head. I wasn't going to press down, just hold her in place, but then her hands came down on top of mine and she shoved.

My dick slid down the back of her throat, farther than I ever expected she could take me.

My eyes rolled in their sockets and I had to focus on something else—fast—or I was gonna come.

I glanced over at Easton, who was just staring at Aubry and stroking himself through his jeans.

"What the fuck are you waiting for, a mailed invitation?" I growled. "Strip her."

Easton lunged forward and grabbed Aubry's jeans. He undid the button and zipper but got impatient yanking the things off her legs. I heard a loud rip. Then her pants were gone. Another quick snap and her panties fell to the ground, too.

Aubry popped off my cock for a second to look, but I pushed her back on. "Don't worry about it, Butterfly. I'll buy you more clothes."

She mumbled a reply against my cock that I couldn't hear, but damn, it felt delicious the way her tongue thrashed.

"Thought you were into submissive shit, not back-talk, babe," I said with a grin. "East, she might need a little swat."

That shut her the hell up. If possible, she might have increased the suction on my dick.

Easton gave her the weakest of taps. But it still pushed her forward on my cock, her nose pressing into my torso.

She and I both groaned and I could tell our mate liked it.

"Again. Harder," I said, since she was currently too preoccupied to talk.

The second smack was harder, and Easton rubbed his hand over her ass cheek, where he'd left a print. He bent and started kissing it, which made me think about how it had felt when I was stuffed inside that dark, forbidden back hole. Damn.

I yanked Aubry off my cock and pulled her face up to look at me. I loved how swollen her lips looked from sucking on me. Even more than that, I loved that sassy mouth, her snark, her selflessness when it came to the kids in our pack. I fucking loved *her.*

And I was gonna show her. One orgasm at a time.

"Widen your legs so Easton can eat you out," I told her.

Her chest heaved while she complied. I didn't bother to look and see how Easton felt about me giving him orders. Our mate wanted it; it was clear as all hell from the fresh scent of arousal that filled the room after my command, and that was all that mattered at the end of the day.

Easton dove between her legs, and a slurping noise filled the room.

Aubry moaned. I pulled her long hair into two pigtails like handlebars and then guided her face back to my cock. "Just work the tip with your tongue," I instructed.

She did and I instantly regretted that instruction. With Easton licking her and Aubry sucking me, that fucking intense mate magic swirled through us all.

I had to yank my dick out of her mouth so that I didn't come too soon. I wanted to wait, to let the pressure build, so that when I exploded, my vision would fill with stars.

And, I wanted Aubry to be a sobbing, orgasmic mess before then.

I leaned forward and kissed her, tasting my precum on her lips, swirling our tongues together. I reached down and grabbed her breasts where they hung. I played with their full weight for a minute, squeezing them before I pinched her hard nipples, pulling down and enjoying how my mate moaned into my mouth.

After a minute, I pulled back and scooted toward the wall.

"East, you should make her come like that while I watch, then fuck her up against this machine and see if all the rumors are true."

His jaw started working twice as fast from where he knelt on the floor. Aubry ended up shuddering so hard that she reached forward to grab onto the machine. I didn't let her. I shoved my hands out and let her prop herself up on my forearms instead.

"Look at me when he makes you come, Butterfly," I instructed.

Her beautiful brown eyes couldn't turn feral like a shifter's, but I could tell when she was reduced to nothing more than instinct. Her jaw grew slack and her expression grew plaintive, her face begged for the peak the way her words never would. There was nothing more beautiful in the world than the sight of my mate on the cusp of an orgasm.

I couldn't resist. She looked so open and vulnerable in that moment that I couldn't help but lean forward and peck her lips. I just had to kiss her, even the tiniest bit.

That kiss triggered our mate magic, which ripped through the three of us like lightning. I had to grab my dick around the base and squeeze hard so I didn't come, but I felt my sweet mate shudder against my lips and heard the soft moan escape from her mouth and enter mine. I loved breathing in her pleasure.

Easton drew out her orgasm as long as he could until I heard him tear himself away from her sweet cunt with a groan. "Fuck, sweetheart, you're so perfect."

He stood behind her and rubbed his hands up over her hips, along her stomach. He squeezed her breast so tight she gasped before he walked her forward and pressed her against the washing machine.

She bent and that gorgeous mouth was near my cock again. I couldn't resist. I let my shaft slip inside her lips as Easton gently parted her folds and slowly worked himself in down below.

While he thrust gently, it was perfect. I floated on a cloud of lust and could hardly see a thing beyond Aubry's wings fluttering in front of my face. It was like seeing the world through a kaleidoscope, the view changed depending on which delicate facet of her semi-transparent wing I looked through. Gradually, Easton started to go faster. That's when I pulled out and grabbed Aubry's torso, supporting her as Easton pistoned in and out.

Her sweet breasts slapped against my chest with each thrust and I couldn't help but stare into her eyes. My soul left me in that moment—or maybe I finally just noticed it was gone. But it wasn't mine anymore. It was hers.

"Aubry, I —" I licked my lips, nervous for the first time in years.

"I love you." Her words came without hesitation.

My heart fucking exploded like a party popper or a firework or a condemned building brought to its fucking knees—decimated irreversibly.

"I love you," I whispered, pressing my forehead to hers. I'd never admit it, but goddamned tears gathered in my eyes and I had to blink hard to shove those motherfuckers back.

"Kiss me?" she asked.

My lips swept over hers, mate magic surging through us all, and she and Easton cried out in a wave of ecstasy that made me happier than I'd ever been. A happiness that had less to do with me than them, which was a first.

When they came down from their high and sagged against the vibrating washer, I petted Aubry's hair for just a moment, letting her catch her breath, before I asked, "So, was the machine all it was cracked up to be?"

She raised her head and gave me a wry smile. "Oh, yeah. It was totally the machine."

"Hey!" Easton smacked her rump.

She giggled. "All the machine."

He spanked her again.

"Only the machine!"

"Careful," I stuck a finger under her chin and raised

her eyes to mine. "You know where we fuck mates that are naughty."

Her eyes glittered with unfettered mirth. "Oh, I know."

And that was my tipping point. I didn't care if she needed more rest. I couldn't wait. I had to sink inside my mate's cunt. Now.

I surged forward, knocking her and Easton back. He stumbled a step before righting himself, but she just fluttered her wings and tried to fly away from me.

I snatched her wrist and yanked her around in the air until her front smacked against my torso. I loved the feel of her curves pressing against me. "Oh no, Butterfly. I've caught you."

I grabbed those sweet hips of hers and squeezed. She flapped those pretty wings, but I just dug in tighter and sank my lips over a nipple. Seconds later, when I bit down hard, she stopped trying to escape.

"*Yes*," she moaned.

I dropped her hips, letting her feet touch the floor. "Lay down," I ordered.

As soon as she was on her back, I climbed on top of her. Without preamble, I sheathed myself inside her. She was soaking wet and the heat and the grip of her soft flesh felt so good that my eyelids fluttered. I pushed myself up onto my hands, planting them between her neck and wings, so I could watch her. I fucked her hard, slamming our bones together, letting the blood flow to my dick. I got harder. And bigger. I watched her eyes widen beneath me.

My wolf howled and panted.

Just wait, little Butterfly, I thought. *Just wait. You haven't met the big bad wolf yet.*

"East, you might wanna stroke her wings. She's gonna need it." She thought she'd seen thick with Easton, but she hadn't seen anything yet.

The base of my cock grew even thicker and Aubry's moans became little gasps of intense pleasure. I kept fucking her hard, her shoulders slamming up against my hands with each thrust. Glancing down, and saw her breasts bouncing, those cherry red nipples still hard as rubies. I grew thicker still.

Aubry's legs spread wider and she gasped, "Holy shit! What the hell is happening?"

Easton sprang forward and asked, "What *is* going on?"

I stared down into Aubry's chocolate eyes. "Knotting."

It was as much of an answer as I could give because my wolf shifted my eyes just then and tried to shift my teeth into fangs. He desperately wanted to mark our mate.

I shoved him back. *Not yet,* I told him.

I rutted harder, swelling even more.

Aubry groaned.

Easton started stroking her wings and that mindless, golden sunlit pleasure shot through me. I gave one final thrust that sent my hip bones crashing into Aubry's. And then I came. My dick pulsed and my knot jumped inside her, searching for that perfect spot. As I throbbed again and again, my knot knocked against her g-spot.

Aubry came with a scream that made me feral.

My fangs descended and I lowered my head to bite her neck.

Easton shoved my face back, stopping me. "She's not a shifter. You don't know how she'll take it."

I growled, but backed off, instead focusing on my knot and riding out the sensations inside. I started to thrust again, letting the knot brush up and down along Aubry's sensitive interior instead of just pulsing against it.

I felt her spasm a second time.

Then she sagged against the floor. "Mercy. Please. Just give me a few minutes."

I leaned down and trailed my nose over her delicious neck, inhaling that orange citrus scent. I pulled my fangs back, so that I wouldn't be tempted to mark her. "I can't, babe. Not until it's over."

Her eyes widened. "What?"

I gave a grin. "When wolves fuck, this is what happens. We're now physically tied together until the knot goes down. I've been going easy on you."

Instead of flashing with alarm, like any other woman's might, Aubry's eyes glazed with lust. "*Fuck*," she said.

"Yes, ma'am," I started thrusting again, setting a rhythm only slightly less punishing than before.

Easton stroked her wings and then reached a hand between us to tweak her nipples.

Aubry arched her hips up and the new angle—I couldn't fucking stand it—I closed my eyes and spurted again.

"Yes!" she cried as I filled her up.

My fangs descended again and dug into my lips as I clamped them together and drew out the sensation for both of us.

My perfect mate lolled her head to the side and said, "Okay, for sure, that had to be it, right?"

I just laughed, leaning up to circle her clit as I fucked her gently. "Not quite, babe."

Her jaw dropped then, giving me a little more of the shocked panic I'd expected initially. "Don't worry, Butterfly. Easton and I are gonna make sure you O every single time."

She shook her head and started to squirm. "You're gonna rub my clit off."

"Aubry, the more you struggle, the more you're gonna turn me on. My wolf likes it." I groaned and a bit of an animalistic growl seeped through my voice.

She bit her lip and nodded complacently, relaxing in my grasp. It took two more rounds before the knot finally shrunk. And when I finally slid out of her, I turned her limp form onto her side and smacked her ass.

"See, there? Clit fully intact." I winked.

Aubry didn't glance over her shoulder to look at me, but I heard her breathless chuckle.

I watched her for a second before Easton scooped her up. He gave her post-sex cuddles while I went over and switched the laundry into the dryer. I grabbed one of my clean wet shirts and cleaned her up. I was just about to demand my turn for cuddles when Aubry leaned up and whispered something in Easton's ear that made him smile softly. He turned and nuzzled her.

Damn it to fuck. There he goes being the nice one again, I thought, annoyed, even though I'd just given her seven amazing orgasms.

My mate noticed when I sank down to the floor, my back against a washing machine, watching them with jealous stillness. Immediately, she shimmied off of Easton's lap and crawled toward me. Even though I was completely spent at the moment, I still memorized the image for the spank bank later.

She climbed onto my lap and snuggled in, resting her head just below my chin. My hands wrapped around her and I had to swallow down a pussy-sounding sigh of contentment. "Mate," I whispered.

"You're amazing," Aubry told me.

My chest grew light and airy. Aubry kissed me on my pec, just over my heart.

Then she hopped up and sauntered naked over to the dryer. I watched her ass as she pulled out a pair of stretch pants and put them on. I'd *just* put that load of laundry in; there was no way in hell it was dry yet, but she didn't seem to care. She tossed on a wet shirt, too.

I smiled, amused when she surrounded herself in a little circle of flames that dried her clothes. She was so adorable. Her magic. Her cute little nose. Her wings.

I was feeling post-knotting giddy.

I closed my eyes and savored the feeling.

Easton's question startled my eyes open. "Aubs? Where are you going?"

Aubry stood by the laundry room door. When had she walked over there? She pressed her lips together and a frown marred her beautiful face.

The light, sunny feeling in my chest was covered by a cloud.

What the hell was going on?

Aubry's eyes flickered between us and her expression settled into one I was very familiar with. It wasn't the open, vulnerable expression she'd worn minutes ago. It was one of hard, stubborn-as-fuck determination.

I stood, not caring that I was naked.

Aubry yanked open the door. "I'm leaving. I don't want either of you to follow me. I don't want you interfering in any way."

"What?" I lurched forward.

But Larry was behind Aubry. And there was a damn glowing turquoise line on the ground—the same kind of line that surrounded the campus—a Movement Restriction Spell. A sense of betrayal rolled over me like fog. Had Larry been in here setting up that spell? For *us*?

"What the fuck?" I roared. Fear, anger, fury, betrayal, all of them attacked me at once, like a pack of wolves tearing me apart.

"Aubry?" Easton's voice wasn't angry. It was hurt and pleading at once.

Fuck that shit. I wasn't gonna plead with her. I was gonna *demand*. I threw every ounce of my alpha power into my command. "Tell us what the fuck you're doing!"

My mate didn't answer. She just turned away.

Larry looked at her. "I grant you permission to leave the circle."

Without another word, my mate, my love, my everything—walked out—leaving me trapped and completely horrified. Because why the fuck would she leave and trap us here, unless she was gonna do something irreversibly awful?

22

AUBRY

I took one last deep breath, gathering my courage. I smoothed my icy white hair down over my shoulders. Then I exhaled, sprinting through the Movement Restriction Spell that protected Mag-Sorgin University from the outside world.

It only took seconds for Mage Police to surround me.

Two MP fae shot out of the sky like spears, wings tucked. All I had time to do was smash a Lethal Protection Potion onto my chest before they got to me. It wouldn't buy me a ton of time, but hopefully it would buy me enough. I needed them to take me in.

My nerves jittered like wind chimes. But not the beautiful kind, the tinny, monotone kind that grated on my nerves and made my teeth clench.

Rough hands grabbed me, and water shot at my face and into my mouth, making me choke. *Winter fae, fuck-*

ers. They didn't try to rough me up while I sputtered and coughed up the water in my throat. I was surprised they didn't waterboard me again. But maybe they'd seen the green goo on my chest and knew that murder would be a no-go for a few more minutes. Maybe they were biding their time.

Their pale blue wings, shaped like snowflakes and hard as fucking ice, scraped against my arm with bruising cold as the two guys shoved me between them. They each grabbed an arm and frog-marched me down the street to a spot where a female mage in a dark purple suit waited, arms crossed.

Citrine Pierce, Triton's mentor, stared down at me coldly. Her silver hair was slicked back into a bun. A sneer curled her lips and she raised a brow, revealing a set of forehead wrinkles she hadn't been able to spell or Botox away.

"Well, well, looks like we caught ourselves a renegade," she sneered.

"Councilwoman Pierce," I nodded toward her respectfully.

I saw her eye twitch in fury at my response. She hated the way I didn't bite back, and she wasn't able to feign nonchalance because, just like Easton, she wasn't the greatest actor. Hopefully I was better.

We're about to find out...

At least I was a big enough threat to rate a senior Council member for my 'arrest.' Or was she here to watch the campus itself? Had the shifters really struck a nerve taking out the local mage supply chain?

Citrine grabbed several Portal Potions from her purse and passed them to the fae, keeping two in her own hands. They all smashed their bottles against the ground. Shards of glass and colored smoke surrounded us, yellows, reds, and greens blending to an ugly muddy brown as the world around us faded and reshaped behind the magical fog.

When the smoke cleared, we stood in front of the precinct. The big glass building loomed over me, seven stories tall. I'd never thought of it as intimidating before but standing at the base and staring up at the tinted windows—times had changed.

MPs coming out the front doors stopped short when they saw me in custody. They stared like I was some circus side-show—a bearded lady cartwheeling through fiery hoops while riding an elephant. One elf even spat on the ground in my direction.

I clenched my fists against the urge to knock that bitch back into last week. She wanted to act like a llama? I'd shave her head and knit her a scarf, then strangle her with it. Just imagining my revenge calmed me down.

The two winter fae dragged me up the cement steps, and the building became nothing more than a black shadow, backlit by the sun. It felt like I was heading into a crypt.

Maybe I *was* stepping up to mine?

Shut up, Aubry, you got this. Be brave. Every brave act was just the outcome of a foolish lack of self-preservation, anyway. Every hero in history stamped down and beat their own survival instinct until it was a slavering, sobbing mess on the floor. Then bravado took over.

I waited for mine to come, but the fucker didn't show.

Instead, my mate bonds were tugging at me, rubbing the inside of my chest raw. I pushed them aside as hard as I could. I tried to shove *all* emotion aside.

Go numb. If I couldn't channel arrogance, then I didn't need any damn emotion. *Just focus.*

I took a deep breath and closed my eyes as I was dragged through the glass front doors. I tried to pretend this was another mission. Another fight. I had a plan and a goal and all I had to do was execute it. Inside, though, I knew that this wasn't the same. It was way more than that.

My mates would think I'd betrayed them. And I supposed I had, by trapping them and leaving them behind. But I had to stop all this bullshit. I had to end it.

And I was the only one who could.

I opened my eyes just as Citrine gave me my flattering intro, "Presenting, Her Royal Highness, Princess Aubry of the Summer Fae!"

The gasp that went through the precinct lobby sucked all the air out of it. I kept my head high and made eye contact with each and every person in the room nearest to me. Most MPs stood up at their desks, lips curling as they eyed me with distaste.

That was fine.

I wasn't here for them.

Shelly, the little pixie secretary, fluttered around the shoulders of MPs blocking her view, eager to see what the fuss was all about. When she spotted me, she seemed to forget how to fly. She tumbled down and would have smacked right onto the floor if a siren woman with purple hair hadn't been standing next to her and caught her at the last second.

"Traitor!" she yelled in my direction, from where she sat in the siren's palm. Her high-pitched voice was barely a squeak, but it broke the silence.

That's when the *roar* of sound began, as loud as an ocean wave as it crashed into a rocky coast and swallowed up everything in its path. Their fury washed over me and made it hard to breathe. I was a lone swimmer, struggling against the tide, pinned between a rock and the crushing weight of their ire.

I swallowed hard and glued my eyes back to Citrine. She was enjoying this little moment of victory. Mages tended to get off on displays of power. Several of them had been doms at Syn, but I'd always preferred humans. They were less sadistic.

"Aren't you going to ask me how I escaped *The Shadow*?" I looked at Citrine expectantly.

Her eyes narrowed. "You didn't escape. We captured you."

"No." I nearly scoffed. "No, I ran out of there right into your awaiting arms. I practically gift wrapped myself and put a shiny bow on my head. Those shifters have been dosing me with Memory Wiping Potion. At first…"

I shook my head as if ashamed of what I'd been through.

"At first, remembering *anything* human was impossible. I didn't even know what a coffee maker was." I shook my head and scrunched up my face. "They have a mage on their side, Lenny or something, but he doesn't do the spells right. I didn't even know what my shoe was for twenty-four hours!"

I heard Shelly let out a sympathetic gasp. I didn't dare glance over at her. I needed to stay in character.

"Lies!" Citrine cut me off. "Get her in the elevator."

She shoved me and went over and pressed the elevator button herself. But the light indicated that the elevator was on the top floor. I had nearly a minute before it arrived. Unless she wanted to waste more precious Portal Potions to get us out of here, and I honestly didn't think she did.

I shook my head and put on a hurt expression, which wasn't hard, since my chest felt like I'd swallowed abrasive pixie magic. "Eventually, the Lenny guy screwed up and I started to remember—"

"You idiot girl," Citrine snapped. "The Council has

been watching you." She gestured at the two fae holding me and they started to drag me to the elevator, away from her.

I looked over my shoulder, moving my wings to one side so I could see her face. "You have? Why didn't you guys rescue me? Shouldn't MP officers get a rescue?"

"You weren't kidnapped. You disobeyed orders and abandoned your post. Then you helped those rebels attack a bank and a university."

Rage filled me then and I couldn't see past it. I just couldn't act like an idiot any longer. "NOT FUCKING TRUE! You told me to get The Shadow and then when I was taken, you turned your backs like I didn't exist."

I glanced past her to the officers frozen at their desks around the room. "Who the fuck got put on a rescue team here, huh?"

No one answered.

No one raised a hand.

I shook my head and tears filled my eyes as I looked back at Citrine as the elevator dinged and the doors slid open. I was about to let my lip waver, but I pulled back, thinking that was overkill. "If their mage wasn't so incompetent, you would have left me to rot—"

Citrine shoved me inside the elevator.

I didn't even care when my face smashed into the back wall. I kept myself facing the plastic so that she couldn't see my smirk.

She shouldn't have stopped to gloat and show me off to my peers. Now they'd all wonder, if they were ever in my shoes, would anyone try to rescue *them*? They'd start to question if the job was worth it.

Good.

They should.

The doors closed with a thump and then the councilor spoke. "I'm going to enjoy torturing you." Citrine's voice was casual, as if she were discussing the weather.

"Since when do kidnapping victims rate torture? You think I didn't get enough of it there? They ripped my wing!"

That was the fucking truth. I even had the scar to prove it.

Both the fae next to me tucked their wings in tight. Just the thought of wing injuries made most fae clench. Like getting your shin bones smashed with a sledge-hammer, except times ten.

"You know why," Citrine sneered.

"Because I embarrassed you by calling out the council's failings in public?" I asked.

Next to me, one of the winter fae stiffened and glanced down at me, a little bit of awed disbelief on his face. No one talked back to a council member like that. No one.

Except me.

"Shouldn't the council question me and decide on the appropriate torture first?" I asked in faux naivety. "Isn't that normal protocol?"

"*Normal protocol* is execution for those who've been caught red-handed—"

"Red-handed?" I exclaimed in shock. "What have I done?"

"You fought against, and kidnapped, several Mage Police," Citrine snapped. She pulled a small Sleep Grenade from her pocket, no doubt ready to silence me.

"I did?" I asked, making my expression as blank as our pixie secretary's face normally was.

"Do not act innocent, *Princess*. We have the enforcers' bodycam feeds."

I widened my eyes and pulled a Tee.

"What's a bodycam? Oh, wait. Hold on. I'm trying…" I allowed my brows to furrow. "That's a human thing, right?"

I could clearly see that Citrine didn't believe me. But that didn't matter. I hadn't said it for *her* benefit. The other two fae in the elevator shared a look above my head. I wasn't sure if they thought I was crazy, or if they were starting to believe my crazy story.

I hoped it was the latter.

Seconds later, the elevator dinged, and we exited onto the fifth floor, heading toward the same room I'd originally met with the council in just weeks before—back when I'd still held the title Chief Enforcer.

One of the winter fae guards released my arm and strode ahead of us, opening the door for Citrine as she marched into the room.

I decided to aim one last parting shot at that bitch's plum-colored ass. "By the way, is the emergency notification system down? While I was being held captive, there was a massive fire near Skid Row. It destroyed *four* buildings. Not a single MP responded."

More silence. This time, it wasn't the accusatory kind. It was the guilty kind.

The two fae shared another look.

"It was a mage fire," I added. "Because the human police couldn't put it out."

Finally, the fae still holding me shoved me forward. "They've deluded you. They've wiped your memory."

"Go see for yourself," I told him.

But those were the last words I spoke, because seconds later I was inside the glowing, turquoise Movement Restriction Circle. Now, I was Citrine's bitch. But I wasn't about to roll over and show her my belly.

Citrine silently proceeded through the room toward the council table, which held five chairs behind it, and slid into the center seat.

My heart rate hit the gas, spun out, and crashed into the side of a building as four other Council members appeared in puffs of colored smoke. My father was no longer one of them.

Holy fucking kittens on crack, I thought to myself as a bead of sweat formed on my brow. *I hope I'm making the right move.*

Obadiah Jenson stepped out of his foggy cloud first. With his dark, deep set eyes, I felt like I was looking at a demon. His furious expression only reinforced that impression. His face was hard, but the smallest of curves at the edges of his lips showed that he was very much looking forward to this.

"Ahh," he said as he sat, his South African accent painting his words in vibrant colors. "Excellent work. We'll *braai* this one in no time."

"You can't barbecue a fireproof fae." Citrine rolled her eyes.

John Daggler appeared next, dusting swirling bits of smoke off his shoulder as he pulled out a seat next to Obadiah. He looked as prim and proper as ever in a three-piece gray suit. His weak chin wobbled as he said, "Perhaps not, but you can certainly give her frostbite."

Obadiah rolled his eyes. "I didn't mean literally."

The council snarked among themselves casually.

Did they only need to appear professional in front of those they expected to leave the room alive? I tried to smash that thought like a bug, but it was a cockroach. It skittered out from under my shoe, no worse for the wear, and taunted me, antennae twirling.

You're about to die, Aubry.

My inner turmoil was a contrast to the debate going on up at the table, as the councilors waited for everyone to arrive. Two seats were still left open.

"It's not as if anyone here actually believed we'd take that route," Obadiah argued.

I'd lost the thread of their topic during my panic, but Daggler was quick to make it blatantly obvious. "It's always bad form to hint at torture, chap. Decreases cooperation."

"I'd say the opposite," Obadiah replied. "It *increases* it."

Both men turned to me with amused expressions.

"Care to weigh in, former Chief Enforcer?" Daggler asked. "Give your professional opinion?"

"On the effectiveness of torture?" I asked with a bright, ditzy smile.

Those assholes. No, those hemorrhoids. Jeff Bridges, and whoever wrote that movie *Doorway* he was in, were right about that. There were people in the world far more irritating than assholes.

"Oh, I'd say it might get you some information," I added stupidly. "But, I'm pretty sure the information is going to be skewed by whatever it is the torturee thinks you want to hear. Remember the gnome, Jerome, two years back?"

Daggler gave me a crooked toothed smile. "Ah, yes. The rhyming one. Wanted more council seats or some such, correct?"

"That's what he said." I gave a casual shrug, "*After* you asked why he targeted the council."

I watched the snakes up at the table slither in their seats as they remembered how they'd squeezed the life out of that gnome, Jerome Bennett. He'd been pro-shifter, caught making explosives and sending them to council member's homes. His death hadn't been pretty.

"So, you're saying it's all in the wording?" Daggler steepled his fingers. "Let's test that theory, shall we?"

A gong rang between my ears. I tensed, glancing at the empty seats. Even through my panicked haze, I thought, *isn't Triton coming?*

Daggler saw my look and read my mind as if it were encased in crystal. He clasped his hands in front of him. "Triton spoke for you, you know." He shook his head almost sympathetically, as if he felt bad for the deranged mage. "He said you'd last been seen with a suspicious shifter. He thought you'd been taken."

My eyes widened and I tried to take a step forward, forgetting that I was locked in place by the Movement Restriction Spell. My feet refused to respond to my demands, and I had to shove down the trapped, panicked sensation that arose as I fought to keep my balance.

I took a deep breath before I stared at Daggler. "Triton was right."

Citrine scoffed. "The boy has always had a soft spot for you."

I knew that. But where was he? I needed him here. Without *him*, all was fucking lost and this entire plan was pointless.

A puff of smoke at the back of the room had my heart jumping, doing a giddy little heel tap.

But Trite didn't appear.

Lotus Mao came through the next puff of smoke and took the open seat at the right side, leaving a blank chair beside her—a chair that used to belong to my father. I was certain that was intentional.

Citrine laced her fingers. "Aubry Summerset, you stand accused of treason. Unlike most, you're being offered the opportunity to verbally defend yourself—"

I wanted so badly to snark, "You mean the opportunity to provide enough evidence that you can swoop in and destroy all the shifters at the college?"

But I didn't. I didn't want to make whatever was coming worse. Because I knew this council. I'd been there when we'd questioned and executed at least thirty different war criminals. I could only hope I'd last long enough for them to take a break and allow Triton to confront me.

But he had to show up in order for that to happen.

Alarm bells started going off in my head. What if he didn't show? What if this was all for nothing?

The overwhelming panic meant I hadn't heard Obadiah's opening question.

I blinked. "I'm sorry. Can you repeat that?"

Obadiah frowned, black eyes hard and unforgiving. "You expect us to believe that the night we stripped you of your title, you *just so happened* to be kidnapped by 'The Shadow'—the very fucking criminal we accused you of failing to retrieve during your op?"

When he put it like that, it did sound a little coincidental.

"Well, apparently 'The Shadow' isn't privy to these

hearings and didn't know about my demotion. So...
yeah." That was the truth.

Obadiah made a game show buzzer noise. The
incorrect "*bzzzzzz*" kind.

Citrine glanced at one of the winter fae and said,
"Martin, feel free to move wherever you please. Do
what you must to ensure Ms. Summerset speaks the
truth."

The fae MP in question—Martin, apparently—
stepped into the glowing turquoise circle with me. I
didn't look at him. I didn't need to. We both knew what
he was here to do.

He opened his hand above my back, and water
drenched my wings. I screeched in pain as he touched
the tip of my delicate wings, and the black veins on the
top ridge of my wing turned to ice.

Automatically, my body tried to flame in response.
But someone quickly threw a potion at my feet—a
Mage Fire Counter Potion worked its magic immedi-
ately and dulled my flames.

The ice stayed in place, burning my veins, sending
spirals of pain through my back and spine, making it
hard to think.

"Try again." Obadiah said calmly. "When did you
join forces with 'The Shadow?'"

"I hate that damned lizard!" I screamed.

That wasn't a lie. But it also wasn't the truth.
Because that damn lizard was brave and selfless to a
fault—the fault being that he allowed himself to be an

asshole in order to reach his goals. He'd killed my father. But he'd saved me. And he would do anything—

"Answer the question!" Lotus Mao stood and leaned forward, grabbing the far edge of the desk.

The winter fae behind me touched farther down my wing, freezing a new section. Pain rippled through me like an electric shock. My eyelids started to flutter. My brain started to scramble.

A little part of me started to whimper that I should just tell them everything.

But then I bucked the fuck up and crushed that inner voice with my heel, like I was stamping out the nasty butt of a cigarette. I was not fucking weak. I would not let them break me down.

The pain pulsed and I gritted my teeth, sawing them back and forth in the effort not to scream. *Fuck.* I hoped like hell that Larry's Movement Restriction Spell was working on the guys even half as well as this circle in here. I couldn't even fall to my knees in pain.

Their faces flashed briefly through my mind and inspired what I said next.

"I've been doing reconnaissance so I can take down 'The Shadow' like I promised! I used a spell to make his closest associates think we were mated."

Everyone in the room froze.

Citrine gave a snort. "Not possible. There's no such thing as a fake mate bond."

I grinned. "Haven't kept very good tabs on your boy, Triton, have you? Pretty sure he set that Skid Row fire without permission. He's gone a bit rogue lately. Did you know he's *very* into experimental spells?"

Obadiah shook his head. "Classic divide and conquer technique. She's lying."

But Citrine looked livid. Trite was her protege. She blinked rapidly before she reached into her suit jacket and pulled out her phone. Before tapping a single digit, she turned to the other fae—the one whose name wasn't 'Martin-the-Martian torturer extraordinaire'— and said, "Brendan, make sure our prisoner has enough to drink. I need to make a quick phone call."

My heart raced, but I did my best to control my breathing. Hyperventilation wasn't going to help me in the slightest—not when water was about to flood my system.

As Citrine made her call—to Triton, I presumed—I was met face-first with Brendan's palm.

Apparently, this guy's a torturer, too. Fucking lovely.

"Sorry," he whispered, just loud enough for me to hear.

Water instantly poured into my mouth and nose, burning as the harsh liquid infiltrated my lungs and caused me to cough and sputter. I choked until I gagged, gasped until I was sure I'd fucking drown, over and over again before Citrine ended her phone call and —in turn—my torture.

Brendan removed his hand and I immediately doubled over, choking, staring at the council room floor as I struggled for breath. Every inhale burned as if sandpaper scraped through my throat. Every exhale induced another fit of bone-rattling coughs.

By the time I could breathe again, and my brain kicked back into functioning order, I realized I needed to keep my prior story going. I needed to hold the other council members' interest before Citrine Pierce fucking killed me.

"Trite tried to extract me," I rasped. "On his own. After the fire. He knew exactly where I was."

Daggler shook his head. "No. That's a falsehood. Councilmen Vale had no such authority."

"Yeah?" I scratched the question out. "How many Portal Potions has he requested in the past month? I'm guessing he's used a few more than his quota for tracking down these shifters."

Everyone's gaze flickered over to Mao, who controlled the Portal Potions for the council. The Chinese councilwoman gave the smallest of nods.

The fury in the room became palpable. Even Daggler's fist clenched, and he could usually pull off his posh, rational, British bullshit even with bloodstains on his jacket.

More. I needed to keep pushing. I had to keep talking because the momentum in the room had changed. The power dynamic had shifted. I was in control for the moment and I had to keep it, just a bit longer.

"After that asshole dragon killed my father, I wanted to kill him myself. So badly. But, he's an elusive little fucker. That's why, even after I started to get my memory back, I waited to run... until I had enough info that you could bring him down."

Obadiah gave a deep chuckle. "Right. What information could you possibly have if you were truly their prisoner and not an accomplice?"

I swallowed back the retorts that naturally jumped up my throat. I didn't need those arrogant asses killing me yet.

"I was kept underground," I told them. "But they dragged me out on occasion. Every plan they make is kept in a filing cabinet. They don't use digital at all. *Ever*. You want to catch 'The Shadow?' Then you need that cabinet."

The council members leaned back in their chairs and exchanged narrow-eyed glances.

Finally, Lotus Mao asked, "And where is this filing cabinet?"

I swallowed a smile, because no matter what happened now, I'd just bought myself a few more minutes to live.

23

AUBRY

I GAVE THE COUNCIL MEMBERS DIRECTIONS TO THE building in Skid Row and it felt like I was laying down the winning hand in a round of poker—a royal flush.

I want to flush these fuckers—

I didn't let myself finish the thought, worried my disgust might show on my face. My wings still ached horribly, but my nerves had either died or grown used to the painful sensation. Or maybe it had just subsided to BDSM-level pain, a level I could tolerate.

Citrine tilted her head and stared down at me, her silver bun glinting in the small, overhead light. "I propose we recess while I send a few MPs to go investigate this claim. We'll reconvene in an hour?"

Daggler grumbled. "If you're off to go coddle that mentee of yours, don't bother." He stood. "I've been saying for months that boy has a personal agenda and he shouldn't have been trusted to take back that college."

I nodded. "I saw him lose four fae fighters without lifting a finger to help them."

I pretended to play along with Daggler's line of thinking but really, as my eyes slid along the table, I used my peripheral vision to see how the guard holding me had reacted. Brendan stiffened, his grip tightening slightly on my arm.

Citrine rolled her eyes at Daggler. "Don't we *all* have personal agendas? But so long as his personal agenda coincides with our—"

Daggler interrupted. "You mean coincides with *your* personal vendetta against dragons—"

Citrine stood sharply, eyes flickering toward the winter fae who flanked me. "Gentlemen, you have permission to move." She then addressed the fae on my right, the one who'd grown stiff. "Brendan, can you send someone else up here to watch our *esteemed*..."

I had to hold in a smile as Citrine tried to decide if she should call me a witness or a prisoner. Decisions decisions.

I lowered my eyes respectfully, pretending she was in charge. But I was pretty certain she'd seen how I'd directed things. I was topping from the bottom. I knew she was furious and was already planning out a way for me to pay for it later—painfully.

I didn't care.

So long as Triton *showed the fuck up*, I would be fine with nearly any damn outcome.

The door opened and shut behind me as the winter fae left to do Citrine's bidding without her having to make that awkward decision on what to call me.

I hardly noticed the scuffing sound of the door because I was worried about more important things. Like Trite, the acid-throwing ex best friend. Where *was* he? Hadn't Citrine called to summon him? I was almost certain she had. Who else would she have been dialing?

Fear chewed a hole in my stomach and crawled inside at the thought that maybe she hadn't called him to come here but warned him away.

No. Goddamn it, no!

I needed him here. I needed to look that sick, twisted fuck in the eyes...

But my hope faded to despair when the Mage Councilors stepped back from the table and started smashing Portal Potions against the ground. Colored smoke filled the room and crawled along the ceiling until I started to cough.

Next to me, Martin, who had stayed behind to guard me, started to cough too. He was allowed to move because of Citrine's orders, so he stepped away from me. I heard the hall door open as he got fresh air for himself.

I ended up closing my watering eyes and pounding on my chest. That's why I didn't notice when a new puff of smoke appeared. I only looked up when I heard a familiar, shocked voice.

"*Aubry?*" Triton's British lilt rang out.

He wore a collared black shirt and grey suit jacket today, not completely buttoned, like he'd gotten ready in a hurry—like he hadn't been expecting Citrine's summons. The necklace from his parents gleamed around his neck. I tried not to stare but I noticed that tiny glimmer of yellow again. Not from the chain… From a scratch on the stone.

"Trite!" My eyes popped open and the relief in my tone was completely genuine. I was so fucking relieved to see him. So goddamned fucking *relieved*.

He was the entire reason I was here.

His heart might've been full of hate, but he held the key to peace. Mayor Triton-fucking-Vale, with the key to the kingdom of Peace-ville draped around his neck.

I let the smoke-induced tears stream down my face as I stared at him, opening my arms like I wanted a hug.

"You stood with that dragon shit!" he shook his head, his tone scathing.

"If I hadn't distracted him, you really think you'd still be alive?" I taunted.

"I had him!" Trite's fury drove him around the table.

"You've been in *two* damn fights in your life! He was playing you!" I scoffed, furrowing my brows.

"Bollocks!"

"I fucking saved your ass even after you left mine on

the street. Admit it, Trite. You were never even there to rescue me!" I let all the fury and hatred and emotion drip into my tone and out my eyes. "You only found me in Skid Row because of that dragon. You left me then. You left me on that college rooftop. You don't give a shit about me!"

Trite shook his head as he walked toward me, avoiding the three-foot-wide glowing turquoise circle that surrounded me. "Please, Aubry. Your melodramatics are pathetic."

I shook my head. "Yeah. Yeah they are. But they were good enough to make Citrine and the council question whether or not they trust you."

That brought him right up to the edge of the circle at my side. Trite stood between me and the door. I couldn't even see Martin because my former best friend leaned in with a sneer on his handsome face. "They won't believe anything out of that whore mouth of yours."

"They already did."

"What did you tell them?"

I pulled a Drake move and turned away without answering.

That did it.

Trite, in his fury, stepped into the circle on my left side, slightly behind me and yanked my shoulder. "What the *fuck* did you tell them?"

I glanced up into his face. It was turning a putrid shade of red. He was shaking in anger.

I had to swallow down the victory I felt tap dancing in my chest. I wasn't done yet. And unlike I had when Trite had attacked Mag-Sorgin, I couldn't lose focus.

I stared up at him. "I just said you seemed to care more about Drake than any of the fae you brought with you. You didn't even lift a finger to help them. You used them as bait to lure the others away. You're willing to sacrifice other magicals for your personal vendetta without even trying to do what you promised the council."

Triton hit me. His hand smacked my face so hard I saw red. My eyes watered and my knees bent as I reeled from the impact, but I couldn't fall thanks to the damn restriction spell gluing my feet to the floor.

It was perfect. It gave me the chance to bend and cup my face.

My hand slid up to my ear and I undid an earring— one of the ones Easton had made me. I turned the back and carefully poured out the Growth Potion. The blade flashed in my hand and grew. I didn't even wait for it to reach full size before I stood and shoved it under Triton's ribs, up toward his heart.

I stabbed my best friend.

I struggled to shove down the ghosts that instantly sprung up to haunt me. Memories of biking on highway 101 along the coast with the ocean sighing in our ears. Memories of bad karaoke nights with him and other students. Memories of Trite tucking a drunken me into bed.

Those memories were *years* old. Outdated.

I shoved them back by pulling up Suzie's empty face. Mariana's mother—who needed a stranger to give her a moment to cry and mourn the son Triton had killed. The library and all those dazed shifters. That bottle of acid he'd thrown without giving a goddamn if it hit me.

I lifted my other hand to cover Trite's mouth and block his screams as I twisted the knife. I watched his eyes. They were wide in shock. His noises grew louder, more frantic, so I yelled to cover the sound in the hope that Martin wouldn't come rushing over.

"You hit a damn woman, you stupid bottle-throwing, baby-ass fuck! That's a goddamned coward's move! You just wait until I get outta here. It's called karma, Trite, and it's pronounced, 'fuck you!'"

The light started to fade from Trite's eyes. As his body slackened and started to slump, I moved my hand from his mouth to his neck, holding his full weight up with one arm.

From out of nowhere, I heard a loud *boom* near the doorway. My eyes went wide and my heart dropped out, like a beam tumbling from the grasp of a crane. Because that sound? It wasn't Martin slamming the door. No, what I'd heard... was a gunshot.

DRAKE

I WAS A GODDAMNED IDIOT WITH A DEATH WISH.

But then, so was Aubry.

Larry—the righteous old fuck—had apparently agreed to help her on her suicidal quest. But after the plan went into motion, he'd then waffled about the fact that she told him to go to our old hideout and leave some stuff—but not everything—behind.

"I don't feel comfortable going through your things without you knowing," Larry had mumbled, shaking that frizzled salt and pepper head of his. And the whole story had come tumbling out.

That was why I was currently breaking into the damned MP precinct, like a fucking shifter lemming, following this wasp off a cliff.

Ugh.

My dragon growled at me. He didn't like the wasp reference anymore. I told him to shove it where the sun didn't shine, but his slitted glare told me he didn't give a shit what I threatened him with. *Stupid overgrown lizard.*

God, now I even *sounded* like her.

My eyes scanned the roof one last time before I turned and used my fire to melt a top story window. With it, I liquified the alarm set to trigger upon break in. No alarm, no problem. So far, so good. I squelched my fire and climbed through.

The room I entered was an empty office. The silence ate at me, ringing maddeningly in my ears. My nerve endings felt like live wires hanging from a downed electric pole, just sizzling and sparking on the ground.

A fire formed in my hand unbidden. *Damn it.* Nerves hadn't gotten to me this badly since my first time as a dom.

I closed my eyes and tried to get rid of the stupid, conspicuous flame, but I couldn't. The little bastard was resilient. So I went over to a computer, found the electrical cord, and sent that fire sizzling into the wall. Hopefully it would reach a circuit somewhere below and start a little hot patch of fun for the MP. That might distract them for a minute or two, if the human grenade I'd just left in the parking lot didn't do the trick.

Boom.

I grinned as I heard the satisfying sound of some

MP's car exploding as I made my way through the office and over to the door.

I slid into the hallway, gun cocked. This top floor looked like it housed servers and old random shit. One room had a couple of broken desks. Another held an empty meeting room. But the nervous expectation and anticipation that filled me before I checked every single room, nearly gave me a heart attack.

Damn it to fucking hell. I was getting too old for this shit.

Why the fuck hadn't Aubry taken her mates as backup?

Even as I asked myself that question, I knew why. They'd never have let her leave. And just as I hadn't taken them as backup myself, I knew Aubry wouldn't want them getting hurt, or going down with her if this plan didn't work.

The goddamn MP had been there, waiting for her, ready to pounce the moment she stepped outside the university's restriction circle. Citrine *fucking* Pierce had been there, eyeing the campus. And then eyeing my Aubry.

I glared and let out a sigh, finally allowing the possessive tendencies I'd been fighting off to have free rein. She was mine. Just as much as the guys'. *Mine*. It was strange what a near-death experience and a suicide mission could do to a person. It forced all of my feelings to float to the surface, gasping for breath.

I had to stifle my dragon's possessive roar of approval.

Why was she doing it though? *I* could have done this fucking shit. I came at the MP and the stupid council all the damn time. Stupid woman and her martyr complex. Just like when she'd climbed that building during the Skid Row fire when she was in no fit state to save anyone.

She's an idiot. A goddamned perfect *idiot. Selfless. Beautiful. Fierce.*

And I was gonna fucking find her and get her the hell out of here.

Somehow.

I went down the emergency stairs, slowly descending to the sixth floor. I had barely cracked the door when I let it fall shut softly again. It sounded like a room full of secretaries or paralegals or clerks. Gossipy women. Probably not the floor the council was on, then.

I went down another flight, and as I reached the landing, I froze. I didn't even have to open the door and peer inside. I just knew. My chest thrummed. This was it. She was here. Her spirit was so huge it cast out this forcefield and drew me in whether I wanted to go or not.

I carefully pushed through the door. And instantly, I saw one of those winged snowflake fucks who'd flown off with Aubry.

He barely had time to look at me and reach for the

gun at his belt, before I put a bullet in his brain. I checked the hall to make sure it was clear—it was, but it probably wouldn't be for long—then I made my way over to where his body propped open a door.

Inside the room, I saw Aubry's beautiful wings marred by ice. And worse, in front of her stood the asshole who'd been trying to kill me all this time—Triton Vale. It looked like she was hugging him.

It felt like a semi-truck smashing through me.

No. Hell fucking no.

"Drake?" Aubry's tone was breathless, surprised.

I gave her a hard grin. "Have to admit, Dollface, this wasn't exactly what I expected to see. You, cozying up—"

She shoved Triton backward and his body bent at an unnatural angle as his feet stayed in place and the rest of him swung backward in a broken bridge pose. A huge silver knife with an engraved handle protruded from his chest.

Instantly, my heart shifted gears. It went from wanting to slam into reverse and peel out of the room, straight to flooring the gas, zero to sixty in less than a second.

My jaw dropped open. I couldn't fucking help it; I was too damn stunned. I looked up to see my sweet fae covered in that sick fuck's blood. "You killed him?"

She nodded, and I swore to fucking Christ that I heard choirs singing in my ears.

But then she glanced at the body at my feet. The

stupid MP fae. "Martin pressed his alarm button. We have a minute, at most, before guards and enforcers start flooding the place. You have to get out of here."

Less than a minute? In this mess? At the precinct? I'd been lucky enough to sneak in at all, let alone get this far without being caught. Getting out would be ten times harder. With any luck, some of the enforcers would still be dealing with the grenade and short circuit issues I'd caused. But even still, with an alarm going off? I had no doubt escape would now be... impossible.

I stared at Aubry. At her beautiful face. At her poor, broken, ice-covered wingtips. And sadness and longing swirled around in my gut. She couldn't fly. But she could escape. She knew this building better than me. She could make it.

If she had some help.

If *I* stayed behind and caused a distraction.

A boulder lodged in my throat as I stared at her. I memorized those gorgeous fucking eyes. I wanted them to be the last thing I thought about before I went down.

"Gimme a pout, Princess, then get the fuck outta here."

She stared at me, confused as she toyed with one of Easton's earrings. "What?"

"I'll stay. I'll keep them off you. I'll take the fall." *Damn.* That fucking boulder made it hard to talk. I shoved the words around it, anyway. "You basically just stole this kill from me, anyway."

I took a couple steps toward her, careful not to step inside the glowing turquoise circle.

She gave a bitter fucking laugh and ripped a necklace off Triton's neck. "No. *I'm* not going. *You* are."

"Not up for debate," I growled, but the gravelly sound didn't hold any weight or anger like it usually did, just sheer determination.

The thought of leaving her behind was intolerable. A buzzsaw ripped through my ribs at that thought. There was no fucking way I was going to do that. None.

"Oh really?" She dragged a nail across the black stone in her palm, the necklace chain dangling between her fingers. The blackness chipped and flecked off, revealing a glowing yellow stone beneath.

My mind shot straight into outer space. There was no fucking air. Hope, fear, joy, and terror swam around like sharks in the pit of my stomach at the sight. "A mage jewel?"

She gave a cocky little grin. "Didn't recognize it during our rooftop fight? Guess it must have been too cold for your lizard brain."

"Guess so," I said with a tiny half-smile.

I couldn't help it. Against my better judgement, I reached out to take the stone. I had to hold it, just once. It was hard to believe that something so tiny would solve our problems. I scratched a nail over the black enamel on the stone, revealing a tiny bit more of its yellow glow.

"How?"

Aubry smirked. "I was thinking about ghosts. Bodie kept saying Trite was a ghost. It didn't make sense. Why couldn't your best assassin, with a damn shifter nose, find a mere human?"

Her words sank in as realization dawned on me. *That's* why Bodie couldn't find him...

"Trite's worn that thing for the past year," she said, crossing her arms. "Told me it came from his parents. But that didn't really make sense, either. Considering he was never quite so sentimental in college."

I shook my head at the irony. Mage jewels had the power to hide things—entire communities, if need be—but also... people. Bodie couldn't track Triton because he'd been wearing this jewel nonstop. The very thing we needed had been concealing the one person hell-bent on stopping us from saving the shifters.

I held the glowing yellow jewel out to Aubry, shocked, grateful, just so damn glad she was a Nancy fucking Drew. "Take this and go," I ordered her.

But she was too busy shoving a tiny glass bulb into my hand.

"Larry switched out the Growth Potion on one of my earring backs with a Portal Potion—the first one he'd finished from the collection at Mag-Sorgin. Take it. Go."

She was so adorable when she tried to give orders.

I already knew all that—thanks to Larry spilling his guts—but when I'd asked the old mage if he had any for me, he'd shaken his head sadly. Said he'd only finished the one, then used a Shrinking Spell so it would fit into her earring.

But I didn't give a damn. The MP hadn't confiscated the potion from her like I'd feared. She could get away easy now. I pushed the bottle back towards her. "No. You go."

My alpha power blasted out without thought.

"That shit doesn't work on me," she glared.

"I know."

God, I'd grown to love that fucking glare. My heart jumped at the sight of it. And then... I just had to touch her. I reached into the circle and grabbed her hips, but her feet were stuck. So, I made a choice, and stepped inside the spell with her so that I could pull her body flush against mine.

Her eyes widened in panic. "You stupid reptile! You were supposed to fucking *leave*."

She tried to crush the Portal Potion she'd given me so that it splattered onto me, but I closed my fist around it and her tiny hands beat uselessly against mine. I used the hand not holding the potion to caress her furious face. And then I leaned forward and did the one thing I swore I'd never do. The thing I'd been both craving and fearing ever since I met the beautiful fae.

I gently ran my lips over hers.

Piles of gold and enchanting fires couldn't compare.

The thrill of shifting, the excitement of wind sweeping me up on an updraft and yanking me through the sky… faded to nothing.

This kiss was everything. The alpha and omega, the beginning and my end. My entire body tingled from head to my toe as magic coursed through me.

"Aubry," I breathed.

Was she as mesmerized as I was? Had her entire world just shifted on its axis? Did her soul long for mine like mine did for her?

Suddenly, footsteps echoed in the hallway.

The enforcers are here. We're out of time.

I pulled back to look at her beautiful chocolate eyes once more. Then I shoved the mage jewel into her hand and smashed the Portal Potion against her chest.

Colored smoke surrounded her, and she started to scream, "Asshole!" before she disappeared, leaving only her boots behind.

That mate bond yanked at me like a hook through my sternum. It sizzled under my skin. It screamed as it called to me, clawing and reaching out, but never quite touching me. And I couldn't help but smile at that vicious sensation.

Because it meant that Aubry was gone. *Safe.*

I'd never been afraid of death. I'd known it was coming for me for years. At least this way, I got an honorable one, which was far better than I'd ever hoped. I felt almost triumphant as I heard the MP whispering their orders in the hall.

I was dying in place of Aubry, the only woman who'd ever broken through my defenses. My... *mate*. And she was going to protect the shifters. Everything I'd ever wished for had come true. Who was I to be greedy and ask for more?

More time wasn't in the cards. Neither were more kisses. One would have to be enough. Because that one kiss held the truth. Our souls were bound together. We completed each other in a mystical way that I couldn't even begin to fucking understand. Nor did I try. I just felt grateful. So damn grateful that I could die with a smile on my lips.

But when the laser beam of a gun glided across the wall, I had to toss sentiment aside. Just because I'd die grateful, didn't mean I'd die without a fight.

I reached forward and grabbed Triton's body. The fucker might as well be useful. He'd make a decent shield—for a couple seconds, at least. But as I yanked on his lapels, I felt something in his inner jacket pocket.

Bullets ripped through the backside of the room, chewing up the wall and making their way over to me. One second, just one second more was all the time I had left. My heart hammered as I ripped the dead man's pocket open with a dragon claw.

And out fell a tiny, rainbow-colored vial.

I caught it in my unshifted hand. Hope, relief, and unadulterated joy ripped through me. The fucker had brought a Portal Potion with him so he could get home. *Oh my fucking god.*

Without another thought, I smashed it against my chest and wisps of red, orange, and blue smoke swirled up around me. I laughed as the MP burst into the room and faded from my sight.

A sensation of weightlessness overcame me as the potion's magic whisked me away, like riding a roller-coaster, looping through the hoops at zero-G. So fast and with so much pressure, I couldn't even breathe. Then gravity kicked in, and my vision cleared. With jarring clarity, I realized I was standing on a red rooftop somewhere else. The potion ride was over.

I glanced around, trying to regain my bearings. Apparently, I'd ended up on the Spanish Mission tiled roof where Bodie and I had stood and done our surveillance before we'd gone and taken Mag-Sorgin. I looked out over the campus until my gaze fell on Aubry.

I saw my mate sobbing as she walked along the grass, a hand over her heart like the damn thing was destroying her as it clawed at her chest.

My dragon roared. My beast didn't care that it wasn't dark yet or that we could be seen. He shifted, and a second later, I was in the air.

Beneath me, some little human boy pointed. "Mommy is that a kite? I want one."

I smirked and ignored them, keeping my eyes on my beautiful target.

The closer I got, the faster the magic of our mate bond flowed. I was captivated by the very sight of

Aubry. I was an asteroid, drawn to her gravity, to this invisible force that pulled us together. I crashed into her, *literally*, my claws wrapping around her to keep her from falling. My dragon gave a final contented screech before I shifted to human form and held her close.

She gasped, sobbed, laughed, and cried even harder as I squeezed her tightly, wrapping her in all the heat and love I'd never been willing or able to share before.

Then I spun her around in my arms and smiled into her tear-streaked face. "*Mate*."

She nodded, and I claimed her again, this time with a kiss. One that crushed all the excuses and burnt away all the fear and resentment from the past. One that left us with a bond that sparked and crackled with the heat of a thousand fires. One as beautiful and as mesmerizing as she was. My mate.

EPILOGUE

AUBRY

THE MAGE JEWEL DIDN'T SOLVE ALL OUR PROBLEMS.

But it sure as hell helped.

All shifters had temporarily relocated to Angeles National Park in order to hide, because making an entire section of L.A. disappear would *not* have gone unnoticed. While we waited, hunkered down between the trees and protected by the power of the jewel, my guys had snuck away and 'mysteriously' purchased a huge swath of land in Santa Paula. A whole little town nestled right next to some rolling green hills that claimed to be the citrus capital of the world.

Was it a coincidence that the guys thought I smelled like oranges and honey and we just so happened to move to the citrus capital of the world? I didn't think so.

Larry, Tony, and Decker—the ex-Mag-Sorgin student who'd agreed to become Larry's apprentice—

worked tirelessly on spells and potions that would surround our future sanctuary and enable it to remain as safe as possible. The jewel would always hide us, but their additions to the security—Compulsion Spells to keep people away, Confusion Spells for the very same reason, Movement Restriction Spells inside the border in case any bad guys miraculously made it that far, plus shit like Mage Fire Protection Spells, Lethal Protection Spells, and a plethora of others I didn't actually know the names of—were bound to be invaluable embellishments. We didn't just want this to be a temporary solution. It was going to be our forever home. We wanted it to be perfect.

We, however, remained far from perfect.

I continued to be a naughty badass who cussed like a sailor. That might have seemed like a good thing, until I accidentally taught Mariana, the little cheese hunter, the word 'fuck.'

Drake... still had asshole issues. I wasn't actually expecting that to change, nor did I want it to. It was part of who he was, part of his character, and I loved him in spite of his flaws, not because I intended to fix them.

Same with Bodie and Easton. Bodie was still a smartass assassin who thought of everything as a competition—one where he was determined to come in first. And Easton still remained my sweet honey bear, the guy who'd drop anything and everything in an instant if I needed him.

When the day finally arrived for us to move into our magically bedazzled town, everyone buzzed with joy, anticipation, and excitement. Including me. The suspense felt like walking down the white board of a high dive. It was thrilling and scary at once. This was the day we'd be *permanently* free of the war—at least the one raging in Los Angeles—and free of the Mage Council and their witch hunts—because, if there were no shifters left to target, then the hunts had no option but to cease.

Drake and Bodie—and a few other helpers—had gone ahead early to get things prepared for us. I'd wanted to go too, but Bodie had pulled me aside and insisted it would spoil the surprise if I did. So, I remained behind with Easton, wondering nonstop about what my wolf shifter might've planned.

I hoped his plans were naughty.

Finally, the big day arrived. A big, silver tour bus pulled up to the edge of the woods—the only thing besides a plane that would be big enough to fit us—and we all piled in. It cruised at a carefree-Cali pace up Highway 5 to Santa Paula. Bright chatter filled the bus as the shifters gossiped like morning birds chirping, singing back and forth. Some of them had literally shifted into birds. The excitement in the air was damn near palpable, and it had a constant smile tugging at my lips—lips Easton couldn't seem to stop kissing, which of course, made me smile even more.

When we finally pulled into the center of our new

town, the kids all but tumbled out the door. They giggled, squealed, and shifted, diving into a giant ornamental fountain in the middle of the town square. Fourteen different little animals squealed and growled and squawked as they splashed water at one another.

Of course, Mariana had to yell, "Fuck yeah!" before she joined them. I cringed, hoping her mother wasn't paying attention. *Way to go, Aubry.*

At the center of the fountain, there was a tall podium which held our tiny mage jewel, gleaming like a miniature sun inside a special crystal case Easton had designed for it.

It was a beacon of truth and remembrance. A promise of a brighter future.

I laughed when some of the spattered water droplets sprinkled down on me. "Part of me wants to jump right in!" I said, turning and smiling up at Easton.

He grinned and put an arm around my shoulder. "You can do whatever you want, sweetheart. But I think Bodie said he had a little surprise for you first."

Ooh, yes! The surprise.

I glanced across the square and spotted another of my mates. Drake looked up from the 'welcome' table he was manning—ironic, considering there was really nothing all that 'welcoming' about my black-haired, blue-eyed, brooding mate. He sat next to Lorena, the Hispanic grandmotherly wolf shifter who'd pulled a gun on me in her fabric shop. She stood with a warm smile, offering hellos, and distributing maps and gleaming house keys to the new arrivals.

Homes. So many of these shifters had been homeless or poor, scattered around Skid Row, bouncing from apartment to apartment as the rent was continuously raised too high for them to afford. Now, they had actual homes to call their own.

My heart filled up like a cup of water and spilled out over my eyes. "Damn it."

That shit was happening a lot lately. I'd never realized how much happy people cried. Probably because I'd never really been happy before. Not *truly* happy. Not like this.

I wrapped my arm around Easton's waist, and we walked down the street toward Drake, admiring the cute little Mission-style shops.

We passed many familiar faces as we went. Rocco, with a machine gun still slung over his shoulder—because apparently, old habits die hard. He was hanging around town until Tony was done helping Larry, then they'd be headed back to New York. He gave us a nod before he turned a corner.

Other couples strolled hand in hand, including Aaron and Tee. They'd decided that staying with us would be easier than trying to explain everything to their families. Plus, they already had jobs lined up. Larry's guilt over their can't-remember-jack-shit-anything-about-humans 'condition' had driven him to offer them positions at a magical supply store he wanted to set up in town.

Tee and Aaron had looked at one another and shrugged, both saying at the same time, "I'm game if you are."

Their easy change of heart wasn't mirrored by their cellmates. John and Tammy had chosen to go to the great beyond in the sky, instead, and Bodie had sent them there with mercy, as quickly and painlessly as he could.

The Mag-Sorgin students, on the other hand, had gotten another round of Sleep Grenade powder plus a heavy dose of Memory Wiping Potion. Since mages were human, and only gained their magic by learning spells and potions, it erased any memory of magic for them. When they woke, they couldn't remember the simplest of Shrinking Spells. The high-ranking mages of Los Angeles were going to have to get their potion makers elsewhere. They'd lost an entire generation of magical thinkers and laborers.

And I didn't regret that one bit. Those kids would be much happier as humans, without that mage bullshit twisting their thoughts. But, the other students—the fae, elves, pixies, sirens et cetera—I truly did feel bad about losing. We'd offered them the chance to come here and live among us since they wouldn't remember much about human life, but many of them refused. So, we'd let them go. We knew all too well what it was like to live in a city where you trembled in fear and always had to watch your back. Even though it was a risk, they were innocents. It was the right thing to do.

Larry hoped one day that gesture would help convince them to switch sides. It might have been a pipe dream, but then, so was all of this. Most shifters had thought getting a mage jewel was nothing more than a far-fetched fantasy.

Yet, here we were, living that dream.

When we reached Drake, I let go of Easton and leaned forward to give my dragon shifter a hug. But he grabbed my biceps and stopped me at the last moment, whispering softly so no one else could hear, "I missed you, Dollface. But right now, you don't get to touch me until I tell you to. And I'm not gonna tell you to until I've watched you come at least three times."

My hands froze. My eyes widened. My pussy screamed, '*yes!*' like the little hussy she was. I was so incredibly ready for Drake to dominate me again. The practicalities and necessities of the shifter situation hadn't left us tons of time for bedroom games.

A naughty smile slid across my face, but as I met his eyes, his look was reproving. I quickly lowered my gaze.

"Yes, Alpha," I said, knowing the effect those words would have.

Drake growled low and grabbed me by the wrist, marching me off down a side street with no explanations and zero fucks to give to our curious onlookers. I glanced over my shoulder and saw that Easton was following closely behind, a look of uncertainty turning his pale blue eyes a darker shade.

"Hey!" a voice rang out from behind East.

I stopped, Easton stopped, and for once, Drake stopped too, though he sighed impatiently. From around my honey bear's shoulder, I saw Bodie sprinting toward us.

He wore a wife beater and board shorts, and I'd never seen the assassin look so relaxed. Or young. Or hot. I decided he was never allowed to wear a shirt with sleeves again. Because *damn*! Those arms were delicious.

A grin spread onto my face as I realized all three of my mates were together with me. That hadn't happened in a *while*, since they'd been so busy planning this move.

When Bodie reached us, my green-eyed wolf swiped my free hand and tugged me away from Drake, who reluctantly let me go with yet another sigh. Bodie leaned in and gave me a quick peck on the lips, but then bounced on his toes, like he was excited or nervous or something.

I supposed we all were.

But when he dropped to one knee in front of me, I realized there was probably an entirely different reason for his nerves.

Panic flooded me. It felt like I'd been tossed over the edge of a waterfall with bloodthirsty piranhas lurking at the bottom.

My frantic gaze searched out Easton's as Bodie looked down and, with his free hand, dug around in his pocket. My gaze screamed at Easton, "*I told you we needed to discuss this first!*" But he looked just as shocked as I felt.

Fuck! I hadn't expected this to be my little surprise.

I turned back to Bodie and tried not to let my hand tremble in his grasp. I didn't want to hurt his feelings; I truly didn't. But how was I going to tell him that engagements were about as attractive to me as Ron Burgundy from *Anchorman*?

Damn it. How had we gone from impending sexy time to *this*?

Bodie finally grabbed what he'd been searching for and looked back up at me with the naughtiest grin imaginable.

Which, kinda made no sense.

"Aubry, will you accept my ring?" he asked, pulling his closed hand out of his pocket and opening it.

Easton and Drake both shouted, "No!" from behind me.

But I took one look at the ring looped over his finger and said, "Hell *fucking* yes!"

I practically pounced on him, ripping the keyring off his finger and checking out the key fob. A red flag and a black checkered flag made up the emblem on the fob.

"A corvette! You bought me a fucking *corvette*!" I squealed like a preteen girl at a boy band concert and started jumping up and down. I wasn't even a car person. But who could say no to a gift like that? *A fucking corvette*, my mind kept repeating.

Bodie leaned forward with a grin and pushed a button. Across the square, the headlights on my new, cherry red baby flashed at me.

I didn't sprint. I fucking *flew* toward that car, and while I did, emotions rushed through me. I was ecstatic, delighted, overwhelmed. I hadn't even gotten a car from my parents—driving was apparently beneath them; they believed that was what chauffeurs were for.

I reached the car and just stared for a minute. It was so beautiful. Then a thought came to me.

Shit. Was it an anniversary? Was I supposed to get Bodie something? Or was this a shifter thing that I didn't know about? Some kind of ritual?

I turned around, worry crinkling my forehead just as Bodie reached me. Drake and Easton weren't far behind. I could see the annoyance on Drake's features easily—the thin lips, the drawn-down brows, the ticking jaw. Easton was just watching me. As usual, he was always checking to see if I was happy.

"Bodie, why'd you get me this car?" I was actually too nervous to ask if I'd missed a damn anniversary. But even if I had, I was pretty sure two-month anniversaries didn't rate goddamned new cars.

My wolf shifter leaned forward and kissed my lips. "Because I wanna be your first for everything. I was your first mate. First to claim that luscious ass. First knotting. Now, I'm first at this."

"Fuck you," Drake growled.

"Yeah, man, that's not fair. This isn't a competition," Easton shook his head, his tone was the same one he used on the shifter kids whenever we babysat.

"Oh really?" Bodie asked smugly, yanking *yet another* key from his pocket. "Cause I just bought her a house, too."

Drake pulled his gun from his holster and pointed it at Bodie.

I might have laughed if I thought the fucker wouldn't *actually* shoot him. But as it stood, shock and fury smacked my cheeks and turned them red. I rushed in between them and glared up at Drake. He immediately holstered the gun as soon as I was in his way, but his eyes burned with a hard, blue flame and I was pretty certain they were about to turn gold. I decided to tread a bit softer.

"Alpha, you wouldn't deprive me of presents, would you?" I jutted out my lip and widened my big brown eyes.

The gold really *did* flash in Drake's eyes then. And I thought he'd been horny before...

He grabbed my wrist again and yanked me down the same side street as before, leaving my bright red shiny behind, while Easton and Bodie followed.

East called out, "Where are we going?"

While Bodie grumbled, "Stop fucking with my surprises."

Drake ignored both of them. *Of course.* Selective hearing at its finest.

I didn't bother to try and yank out of his hold, though. Because when Drake was dragging me places, it meant one thing: hot angry sex was our destination.

My entire body thrummed in anticipation. My wings fluttered, excited they were about to get stroked. My pussy set out a flashing neon 'vacancy' sign in the hopes that she'd attract some visitors. She didn't need to worry. I had three very eager shifters who would be more than willing to *bed down for the night* inside of her.

We approached a metallic industrial warehouse in a quieter, less crowded part of town. Drake grabbed onto a huge sliding door and pushed it open one-handed. That probably shouldn't have been hot, but I could see the way his back muscles bunched under his shirt when he did it. That door must have been heavy. My breasts were feeling just as heavy. I was so ready to see those muscles work as he used his hands on them too.

I licked my lips as Drake yanked me into the building, which was empty save for a few tables that were pushed along one wall. The floor was cement and the ceiling rose high overhead. The scent of earth and new plastic permeated the air. It must've been a new establishment.

"What the hell are we doing here?" Bodie complained.

But he had just started to speak when Drake formed a fireball in his hand and held it between my breasts. My clothes caught fire, and my breasts started to heat, but the flames were too far from my nipples for my liking. I looked up and met Drake's gaze, silently pleading for him to move the fireball to cover one.

He gave me a panty melting grin—literally, my panties melted off—before he suddenly magnified that fireball and forced it to grow until it encased us both. Seconds later, not a single remnant of our clothes remained; every stitch had burnt away. I barely even noticed the smell of the burnt fabric because that apple cider scent, Drake's alpha power, washed over me. That scent had become an aphrodisiac to me, because it typically meant naughty things were coming my way.

My dragon shifter reached down and used both of his fiery hands to caress my breasts and tease all around my nipples—never quite reaching my hardened peaks.

I tried to stay still and be a good sub, but he was driving me insane, and soon he had me moaning. I leaned forward, pressing my breasts into his palms.

That's when Drake reduced the fire on one side of us, forming a window of sorts so that the guys could see what was happening inside. *See*, but not *touch*.

"You're a fucking dick, Drake," Bodie growled.

But Easton merely chuckled and started shucking off his clothes, drawing my gaze as Drake twisted my nipples between his fingers and sent a bolt of lust down my spine. Easton's shirt came off first, revealing muscles that rivaled the burliest of athletes. His blond head dipped down as he grabbed his shoes and pulled them off. I watched with rapt attention as he lowered his pants…

Drake dropped my nipples and lifted a finger to my chin, turning my gaze back to him. "Eyes on me," he commanded.

"Yes, Alpha," I submitted, and my pussy grew even hotter than the flames.

Behind us, Bodie asked, "Dude. What the hell are you doing?"

I wanted to look at what he was talking about—*so freaking badly*—but I was determined to keep my gaze on Drake, as he'd ordered me to.

Seconds later, I felt another set of hands at my hips. I whirled around in shock to find Easton had walked right into the fire with us. My initial reaction was fear. But after a millisecond, I realized that Easton wasn't getting burnt.

I looked up at him, the unspoken question of *'how?'* absolutely gleaming in my eyes.

"Larry put the same Fireproof Spell on me that he'd used on El Fuego," Easton shrugged with a lopsided grin. "I figured it would come in handy."

I couldn't help but smirk as Drake growled, pulling me away from Easton.

"You want front door or back?" Easton asked pleasantly, the way waiters asked if you wanted shredded parmesan cheese on your salad.

"You *fuckers*!" Bodie shouted. His voice echoed off the metallic walls.

Hands caressed me from behind as Drake smacked the side of one of my breasts. The sting sent a delicious jolt through me as Easton's fingers teased my folds and spread my wetness over them.

"You disobeyed me," Drake said after another smack that made my breasts slam together and then bounce a little before they settled. "You didn't keep your eyes on mine. Now you'll have to be punished."

"Yes, Alpha," I lowered my head like a good little sub. But as his enormous erection suddenly came into view, the temptation to suck it overcame me. I'd never tasted Drake's cock. He'd never let me. And it was so big, and long, and perfect, that red tip was calling my name.

I dove down, encasing Drake's shaft with my mouth, my lips stretching wide. I licked it and then forced as much of it as I could down my throat until it triggered my gag reflex. Over the years, I'd come to find that sensation hot. I loved the dirty feeling of being used; I loved when a guy grabbed my hair and fucked my mouth for a couple seconds, because I knew that raw-throated sensation was going to lead to amazing and brutal g-spot stimulation later.

I pumped my head up and down slowly, taking Drake

as deep as I could each and every time, breathing carefully and trying not to gag. It was difficult to maintain that level of self-control with Easton's fingers circling my clit and dipping inside me, but I tried to stay focused.

To my surprise, Drake didn't spank me like I expected. Instead, he wrapped my hair around his hand a few times and gently guided me into a rhythm he liked.

As soon as I stopped worrying about the rhythm because Drake was keeping it for me, the sensations Easton was creating came to the forefront. Heat and desire built up like a campfire within me, as he slowly and steadily stoked it. I rode the edge of mindlessness, tiptoeing back and forth between awareness that two of my mates were fucking me inside a ball of flame and complete and utter animalism.

I wanted to jerk my hips against Easton's hand and come. Then turn around, and rinse and repeat with Drake. But I didn't. Because it wasn't perfect yet. I was still missing a mate.

Bodie paced outside our burning ring of fire, growls echoing above the crackling of the flames. But neither Drake nor Easton made any moves to include him.

I was going to have to top from the bottom.

I reached a hand out and started to caress Drake's balls. Then I slipped one finger around the rim of his ass. He jumped back and lost focus, his flames dying off.

Bodie rushed forward then, entering our midst just

as I popped off Drake's dick. I hadn't seen Bodie strip, but suddenly, there he was, naked, grabbing my hips and sliding into me without preamble. His dick was already slick with sticky precum, probably from the sexual frustration of watching me get played with by my other mates.

He started to rut me frantically, and Drake and Easton had already gotten me so worked up that it was only seconds before my pussy clamped down on his cock. As soon as the orgasm rocked through my body, I glanced up at Drake, who seethed as Bodie fucked me.

"Punish me, Alpha," I all but begged him. I hated seeing that angry look in his eye. I wanted to please him, to be the reason he smiled, and also the reason he came hard.

But his gaze remained stoic. The only hint of deviousness I could detect was the slight curve of his lips and the slow curling of his dragon horns as they appeared on his head. "No."

"No?" I whimpered. God, I hated hearing that word on his mouth.

He bent down and got right in my face as Bodie continued fucking me from behind. "I told you I wanted to see *three* orgasms, Dollface. That was only *one*."

His gaze flicked up to Bodie, who didn't slow his pace in the slightest.

"Make her come again, Fuzzball, then it's Papa

Bear's turn," Drake said, standing to pat Easton on the shoulder.

"You mean *baby* bear?" Bodie ground out as he pumped into me.

Drake's grin turned absolutely devilish then. "That's not what *she* said."

Bodie howled and I felt his claws dig into my hips as he half-shifted into a werewolf, rather than a full-fledged wolf. I could feel fur spring up along his torso and arms as he held me. His competitive nature spurred him on, driving him harder and deeper into me.

It was hard to think. I felt so damn good. The pain of his claws, the brutality of his thrusts, they were making me mindless.

"And *no* knotting," Drake warned, as if sensing that was exactly what Bodie was about to do. "It takes too long and she'll have too many orgasms."

"That's kind of the fucking point," Bodie growled through gritted teeth.

"*Two*," Drake growled. "No more, no less."

I wanted to pout. I liked the knot just as much as Bodie did. But I wanted Drake's approval more.

With a sigh, Bodie slowed, pumping in and out of me at a much softer pace. The change in tempo was maddening. My eyelids quickly fluttered shut as my breaths turned into pants. I couldn't get there if he stayed this gentle.

"East," Bodie said, before slipping out of me, shifting

back to human, and laying down on the concrete. "Let's show Drake what happens when we all connect."

Yessss. My pussy throbbed in anticipation. Just the thought of all three of them touching me at once made me approach the edge.

Easton smirked and moved closer to us.

But Drake said nothing, just watched in agitated curiosity as Bodie grabbed my hand and pulled me forward. He guided me and I lowered my pussy back onto his dick. He tipped me forward, and suddenly I was face to face with Easton's massive shaft, all thick and swollen and so fucking suck-able. I took him in my mouth and immediately the mate magic swirled to life, causing us all to moan at the same time.

"Come on, Drake," Bodie taunted. "Aubry's been a very naughty girl. And you know where bad girls get fucked."

Still, Drake didn't speak or make any move toward joining us.

"I'll give you a hint," Bodie rasped. "It's the last hole she has left. We saved it just for you."

I popped off Easton's dick to look over at my dragon shifter. Drake's gaze lowered to that forbidden fruit, his blue eyes darkening at my ass cheeks spread before him. He bit his lip and stroked his cock as he took a few determined steps our way.

I hid my smile by returning my mouth to my honey bear's swollen member.

But less than a minute later, Bodie lifted me up off

of him, incidentally jarring Easton's dick from my mouth.

"What the fuck?" Easton grumbled in a daze.

But Bodie merely glared at Drake. "If grandpa takes any longer to get his ass over here, I'm gonna come three times before his dick gets wet. He's like some fucked up product of a sloth-snail-turtle three-way gone wrong. Jesus."

Suddenly, Drake's hand was between my legs, his chin resting on my shoulder as he leaned in and planted hot kisses up my neck. With his fingers, he swirled my creamy goodness around before dragging it up and lubricating my ass.

"Is this what you want, Doll?" he asked, his hot breath on my ear giving me shivers.

I nodded. "Fuck yes."

Crack!

His hand came down hard on my butt cheek, and just as quickly, it rubbed out the shock and sting of my skin.

"What did you say?" he asked me, giving me a chance to amend my mistake.

I bit my bottom lip before replying. "Yes, Alpha."

He took his time, gliding into me slowly between rounds of spankings, and when he was finally sheathed to the hilt, he glared at my other two mates. "Well? Where's this magical connection you two were going on about?"

They quickly lurched into motion. Bodie pulled my

hips back down and impaled me with his cock, while Easton ran his fingers through my hair and slipped his massive shaft between my lips.

As soon as Easton's thickness slid across my tongue and all three of them entered me, a sensation shot through me like a rainbow, or a jet. I was streaked with this mindless magical beauty, like a prism spinning in the sunlight.

My eyes burst open and I moaned like... well, like a horny female fae getting gang-banged by three sexy shifter guys. *My mates.* The magic that coursed between us was incredible. If I thought it was powerful with Bodie and Easton, it was twice as powerful now. My limbs trembled from the intensity.

Drake groaned and thrust into me rubbing against that sensitive spot on my wings with his torso, shoving Easton's cock down my throat. As Drake pulled back, Bodie's cock rammed up in, making me see fucking stars. We only got a few more thrusts in like that before the magic totally fucking consumed us and spit out our bones.

All four of us cried out at once, the three of them filling me with hot jet streams of cum, while I clamped down and pulsed around the two shafts beneath me, and moaned around the one in my mouth, sending vibrations all the way up to East's balls.

My bear shifter had barely started coming down from that first orgasm when he shouted that he was coming again. Instantly, his admission started a domino effect, and soon we were all wrecked with another round of earth-shattering, mind-numbing ecstasy. Pleasure didn't even begin to describe what I experienced. It was euphoric. Ethereal. Unimaginable.

Before the magic could jolt through us a third time, and quite possibly kill me with the best orgasm of my life, I popped back off Easton's dick, leaned over Bodie's side, and slowly pulled away from him and Drake... and then I collapsed onto the floor. Easton and Drake did the same—Bodie was already laying down, panting as he gazed up at the ceiling with the most satisfied smirk.

"That was..." Bodie began.

"...Incredible," Easton finished.

Drake scooted in and grabbed me, rolling my body on top of his. Easton grabbed a thigh as I draped an arm across Bodie's chest.

"*This* is what I've been missing?" my dragon shifter asked incredulously, a tiny grin tugging at his lips.

I bent down and kissed him, sighing at the completeness I felt with all three of my mates surrounding me. "At least you won't be missing out on it ever again."

Drake smiled and curled a piece of long white hair behind my ear, his eyes glittering as they delved into mine. "Never again."

Because, we might've been living in some messed up version of a fairy tale, but I was gonna make sure we got our happily ever after, damn it.

ACKNOWLEDGMENTS

Special thanks to all of the people who helped us get these books together. A huge thanks to our husbands who not only watch our crazy kids but also help support us and turn our dreams into reality.

A huge round of applause goes to our beta readers for their feedback to make these books better than before. We're listing them in alphabetical order so we can't be accused of playing favorites. Allison, Brittany, Ivy, Jessica, Jessica, Lysanne, Raven, Thais.

Thanks to Sue for being our British phrasing consultant.

And thank you Lori Grundy for the beautiful covers.

ABOUT THE AUTHORS

Ann and Elle are both cool and amazing people. If you've read their books before, you'll know that one of them is sweet and the other is a demon with a human mask.

In their free time, they like to... wait, what free time? Both women are mothers. Elle has three wonderful children. Ann has two. Add husbands on top of that and you might as well nickname each of them Miss Hannigan (aka the witch that ran the out of control orphanage in the musical *Annie*). Oops. Ann's theater nerd popped out. It does that sometimes.

Unlike Ann, Elle is totally cool. One of her favorite things to do is play video games. Which is totally fun. But if you add wine or brownie batter, it's even better.

Both of them hope you enjoyed this book. Or at least don't want to use it to start a forest fire. Because forest fires are bad. So says Smokey the Bear. And Easton... also a bear.

And with that ramble, we'll let you peruse a few of our other books.

ALSO BY ANN DENTON

Magical Academy for Delinquents (Pinnacle Book 1)

Knightfall (Tangled Crowns Book 1)

Taken by Storm (Storms of Blackwood Book 1)

A Crown of Blood and Ashes (Enchanted Royals Book 1)